DESIRE'S CARESS

As he stood before her, she looked up at him with wonder. She had seen that look in his eyes only in dreams.

Without touching her, he bent his head and brushed her lips with his, lingering only a moment. He drew back slightly, his eyes claiming what they read in hers. As his arms folded about her she came into them. She pressed against him as he claimed her mouth again, now with an urgency matched by her own bursting emotions.

"Roanna. Oh God, Roanna," Giles murmured as his lips moved gently, teasing the corners of her mouth.

Nothing mattered, she wanted him, more than anything she had ever wanted in her life . . .

MARY PERSHALL

ROSES OF GLORY

BERKLEY BOOKS, NEW YORK

Mail to the author
may be addressed to:
Mary Pershall
P.O. Box 1453
Soledad, CA 93960

ROSES OF GLORY

A Berkley Book / published by arrangement with
the author

PRINTING HISTORY
Berkley edition / July 1987

ISBN: 0-425-10006-5

A BERKLEY BOOK ® TM 757,375
Berkley Books are published by The Berkley Publishing Group,
200 Madison Avenue, New York, New York 10016.
The name "BERKLEY" and the "B" logo
are trademarks belonging to Berkley Publishing Corporation.

PRINTED IN THE UNITED STATES OF AMERICA

10 9 8 7 6 5 4 3 2 1

To Barbara Lowenstein,
A lady who can do six impossible things
before breakfast.

Every man can tame a shrew
but he who has her.

—*John Heywood,*
16th century

THE DECLARES AND MARSHALS

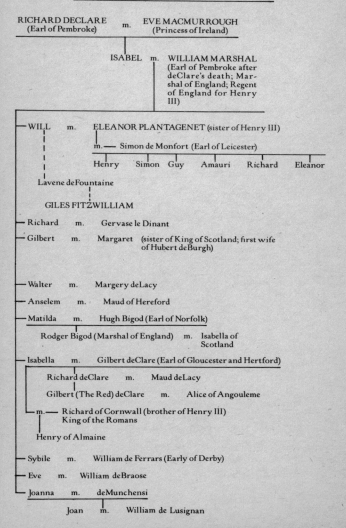

RICHARD DECLARE (Earl of Pembroke) m. EVE MACMURROUGH (Princess of Ireland)

ISABEL m. WILLIAM MARSHAL (Earl of Pembroke after deClare's death; Marshal of England; Regent of England for Henry III)

WILL m. ELEANOR PLANTAGENET (sister of Henry III)

m. Simon de Monfort (Earl of Leicester)

Henry   Simon   Guy   Amauri   Richard   Eleanor

Lavene deFountaine

GILES FITZWILLIAM

Richard   m.   Gervase le Dinant

Gilbert   m.   Margaret (sister of King of Scotland; first wife of Hubert deBurgh)

Walter   m.   Margery deLacy

Anselem   m.   Maud of Hereford

Matilda   m.   Hugh Bigod (Earl of Norfolk)

Rodger Bigod (Marshal of England)   m.   Isabella of Scotland

Isabella   m.   Gilbert deClare (Earl of Gloucester and Hertford)

Richard deClare   m.   Maud deLacy

Gilbert (The Red) deClare   m.   Alice of Angouleme

m. Richard of Cornwall (brother of Henry III) King of the Romans

Henry of Almaine

Sybile   m.   William de Ferrars (Early of Derby)

Eve   m.   William deBraose

Joanna   m.   deMunchensi

Joan   m.   William de Lusignan

PLANTAGENETS

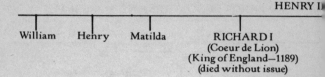

William	Henry	Matilda	RICHARD I
			(Coeur de Lion)
			(King of England—1189)
			(died without issue)

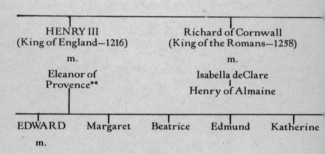

HENRY III
(King of England—1216)

m.

Eleanor of
Provence**

Richard of Cornwall
(King of the Romans—1258)

m.

Isabella deClare
|
Henry of Almaine

EDWARD	Margaret	Beatrice	Edmund	Katherine

m.

Dona Eleanora
of Castile

*THE KING'S MEN:
(Sons of Isabella of Angouleme's
second marriage to Hugh de Lusignan)

William de Lusignan
Guy de Lusignan
Aymer de Lusignan

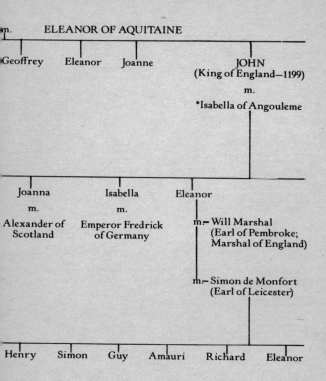

m. **ELEANOR OF AQUITAINE**

Geoffrey	Eleanor	Joanne	JOHN
			(King of England—1199)
			m.
			*Isabella of Angouleme

Joanna	Isabella	Eleanor
m.	m.	
Alexander of Scotland	Emperor Fredrick of Germany	m.— Will Marshal (Earl of Pembroke; Marshal of England)
		m.— Simon de Monfort (Earl of Leicester)

Henry	Simon	Guy	Amauri	Richard	Eleanor

**THE QUEEN'S MEN:
(The Queen's uncles; the Provençals and Savoyards)

William
Peter of Savoy
Amadeus

Part One

*Her only fault, and that is faults enough,
is that she is intolerable curst.*

—William Shakespeare,
The Taming of the Shrew
Act I, Scene ii

1

London
August, 1259

Roanna spooned the hot stew into her mouth, thinking that she had never tasted anything so good in her life. Her surroundings added to her feeling of contentment and she sighed, closing her eyes, allowing her senses to savor what she did not see. The heavy aroma of spices lifting from bubbling pots assailed her nose, mixing with the suggestion of roasting meat and baking bread and the tang of salt air that clung to her clothes. Her mind's eye could see the dark, weathered wood of the kitchen, layered with years of smoke from the cook fires. Heavy pots hung suspended from the low-beamed rafters in the company of herb clusters and strings of garlic and onions.

This is where I belong, Roanna thought; I should never have left. Here, with her aunt bustling about checking her pots, amid the sounds from the harbor without, interspersed with the lifted voices from the taproom. She had not felt so alive in weeks.

"La, child, 'aven't they been feedin' ye? Yer eatin' like yer 'alf-starved!"

"I 'aven't 'ad nothin' so good since I left," Roanna answered between mouthfuls. "None can cook good English fare as ye can."

3

"Well, better be careful, lass, or yer 'ips'll come to resemble me own," Matilda chortled, patting her own broad form as she returned to the sideboard to begin chopping vegetables for the midmeal. Smiling, Roanna watched her aunt attack the produce with a vengeance, wielding the large knife with as much dexterity as the most experienced knight.

As she worked, Matilda said, her voice lowered with purpose, "Are ye goin' ta tell me why ye've come 'ome? Lucky ye are that yer uncle's gone to West Wickham, or ye'd 'ave been sent back on a turnaround, that's sure."

A loud crash and a stream of profanity from the direction of the taproom saved Roanna from having to answer. With a mumbled curse, Matilda wiped her hands on her apron. "I'll be takin' care of it, lass; finish yer supper." She disappeared into the taproom.

Roanna sat back with a ragged sigh. The older woman was right—had her uncle been here when she returned, she would have been sent back. She pushed the bowl aside, having suddenly lost her appetite, and leaned her elbows on the table, resting her chin in her hands as she stared into the fireplace and the flames that licked hungrily at the dry wood.

She had tried, she thought; she hated failing at anything, and she really had tried. Her father had been the cause of it. He had done this to her—why couldn't he have left her alone! A man she had only seen twice in her life in brief, uncomfortable encounters, he had finally chosen to remember her on his deathbed. "Bleedin' sot," she muttered, then instantly crossed herself, regretting her ill thoughts of the dead.

Sixteen years before, Cecil Royston, to his horror, had found himself saddled with a motherless newborn babe —and a girl-babe at that. Within hours the child had been given into the care of his sister and her husband. God, the fates, or whatever forces controlled one's destiny, had certainly smiled on Roanna that day, for the childless couple had surrounded her with warmth, love, and security.

Then, two months ago, without warning, everything had changed. A burly knight accompanied by two men-at-arms appeared one day in the taproom of the Flying Sail Tavern. Sporting the colors of the earl of Leicester and bearing a summons from the Countess Eleanor, Lady de Monfort, they changed her life irrevocably. Cecil Royston, steward to the countess for her holdings at Odiham Castle, had died. With his last breath (wheezing, if Roanna's childhood memory served her) he requested that his "Dear Child" be placed in the countess's household, ". . . so that she might find the Grace of God in experiencing the rewarding life of service."

Had it been guilt that caused her father to change her life so unexpectedly, so unhappily? Or had he actually sought to improve her station? Not that it mattered. She had failed, miserably.

She had answered Lady Eleanor's summons, determined to make the best of it. She had entered Durham House, the manor where the countess took up residence when in London, determined to make her aunt and uncle proud of her.

Where had things begun to fall apart? The first few days had seemed easy enough. Lud, the effort demanded of her as a lady's maid seemed mere child's play compared to what she was accustomed to. Helping her uncle run an alehouse with the high reputation of the Flying Sail demanded hard work from before dawn until well after dark. Being a tirewoman for a lady seemed to entail what Roanna came to think of as pampering, scurrying, and flattery —and keeping one's mouth shut. It was the last part that Roanna found most difficult. In fact, it was that which led to a stern lecture from Lady Eleanor and a change in Roanna's duties, much to the obvious satisfaction of the lady she had apparently insulted.

She spent a brief interval in the kitchens assisting Durham House's head cook. Roanna felt at once at home —pish, she had helped her aunt for most of her life, and the Flying Sail was known for the succulent fare that emerged from Matilda's kitchen. Anyone knew that vegetables must be rinsed three times, not twice, to release them from the saltiness of the brine in which they were preserved. Any dolt knew that the best sugars came from Cyprus, and that one must check a hawker's nutmeg for wooden pellets and the peppercorns for juniper berries. But again Roanna stood silently and accepted Lady Eleanor's admonitions. If the countess wished to be cheated by her own head cook, then so be it.

Her next position was that of maid-at-large. The title

made Roanna smile; it conjured up a picture of a rotund wench rolling about her duties. But the responsibilities suited her well enough, as each day brought a bit of variety, her miscellaneous duties taking her wherever she was needed most that day. And the fact that the various heads of the household areas—the steward, the cook, the brewer, the butler, the laundress—all seemed reluctant to retain her services for long served to dispel the boredom. Hence, Roanna managed to keep out of trouble, moving from position to position, and except for missing her aunt and uncle, she had almost begun to feel content.

Then *he* came into her life. It was the beginning of the end. If she had even suspected, in those moments when she was wrestling with the goat, what was to come, she would have fled Durham House then and there. But nay, she had remained, day after day, until she had made a complete and total fool of herself.

Lord knew it wasn't her fault about the goat. She had merely been crossing the bailey from the chapel—where she had said mass, as a dutiful maid should—to the buttery, where she was to help Lavin, the butler, inventory the ale and wine. Perhaps she had been lost in her own thoughts, but was that a crime? How was she to know that there was a large billy goat running loose? And a rather disgruntled one, unhappy about the fact that two stockmen were in hot pursuit. How could she know that the goat had skittered into the bailey through the barrels stacked against the far wall, and that as she crossed the center of the courtyard it was charging through the rows of pikes lining the wall outside the weapons room, scattering both weapons and half a dozen chickens who clucked and shrieked in protest, feathers flying? It was only much later that others took the pleasure to recount those events, and more: how the stockmen had met the rolling pikes, how their feet had been swept out from under them as the ram lunged toward freedom.

Roanna only knew that, alerted by a shout from somewhere above her on the wall, she had spun about to see the goat charging toward her, its sharp horns lowered. She had acted purely out of instinct. She remembered that she had managed to step neatly aside while grabbing at the horns, instinctively judging the shift of the animal as it turned toward her. Flinging out a slippered foot, she tripped the animal's front legs and, her balance lost as well, tumbled onto the goat. When the stockmen reached her she was sitting on the struggling, prostrated goat, her temper in rags, railing at the goat, the stockmen, and the entire situation with a most unladylike stream of oaths. It was only then that she realized that laughter had erupted along the battlements, where the guard had seen the whole episode. That was bad enough, but then she saw *him,* her attention being drawn to him as he shouted curt orders to the men to return to their posts.

From his position on the parapet, she knew, he had seen everything. Nevertheless, she silently sent him her gratitude as the men obeyed and returned to their duties. Struggling to her feet, she had brushed off her kirtle with as much dignity as she could muster, then glanced back to see if he was still watching. He was, sporting a huge grin. Stiffening, she had thrown him a nasty glare, but he had merely laughed and tossed her a salute before he disappeared into the guard tower.

Oh, if only that had been the end of it, and not just the terrible, humiliating beginning. The horrible things that followed . . .

She jumped up from her chair, unable to bear thinking upon the raw humiliation any more. Grabbing an apron from the hook near the door, she tied it about her and went into the taproom, determined to rid her thoughts of Durham House and everything—and everyone—associated with it.

She paused just inside the door, her large brown eyes drinking thirstily of the familiar scene. Wall sconces and candles on the heavy plank tables cast the large rectangular room into wavering shadows. The oak walls, heavily beamed ceiling, and wide plank floors, scattered with rushes, were darkened by years of soot from the torches and trailing smoke from the huge fireplace that nearly covered the entire wall at the far end of the room. Along the wall to her left was the board—the ponderous oak trestle slab that constituted the focal point of the alehouse. Behind it were set huge barrels of ale and mead and shelves of tankards and pewter goblets flanked by ewers of wine.

Roanna hesitated, taking in the scene with a warm feeling of homecoming. The usual mix of customers crowded the popular tavern, where the forceful presence of the owner assured order and the absence of cutpurses and dishonest dice. Through the smoky haze she could hear the sounds of many languages, spoken by the mates of the ships lying in the harbor without. The captains of those ships would be settled in the grander rooms upstairs or in one of the back rooms allotted by Matilda for privacy. So would the merchants representing the powerful London guilds, who met often at the Flying Sail to discuss the matters of the realm. The makers of kings, they were often called.

The inn's reputation for relative comfort and safety, along with the excellent fare that emerged from Matilda's kitchen, brought a good crowd each day. Nobility, clerics traveling through London, farmers who came to the city to sell their year's produce, and the constant stream of regulars, all came here in search of a full belly and a round of cups. Roanna smiled, drawing a satisfied breath; the realization of the esteem and respect her uncle enjoyed never ceased to fill her with a feeling of immense pride.

She spied her aunt behind the heavy oak trestle bar and made her way across the room, pausing to greet old friends along the way. She slipped behind the bar and offered happily, "I'll take the board for ye."

"I could use the 'elp, that's sure," Matilda muttered. She maneuvered behind Roanna to leave, and added, referring to the barmaids, "Those girls are no earthly good, can't do a thing lessen they're watched. They be thinkin' of only one thing, to be sure, and it ain't servin' ale."

Roanna smiled as she watched her aunt return to her precious kitchen, with barely a pause to slap a wandering hand that sought out her ample bottom as she passed. Her feeling of homecoming returned, and she sighed contentedly as she turned to fill an order for a barmaid. The next hour passed easily as Roanna warmed to her duties and conversation with the customers, until a travel-worn customer entered and requested a room and a bath. The request triggered an unwanted memory of a certain tub and the unpleasant events associated with it. Suddenly out of sorts, Roanna snapped a tart order to a barmaid. The wide-eyed guest trailed after the maid toward the stairs, wondering what he had done to elicit such a response from the strawberry-blond beauty.

It wasn't her fault about the tub, Roanna thought irritably as she wiped off the top of the bar with angry strokes and glared at a barmaid who sauntered up to request a pitcher of ale and three tankards. Accustomed to Roanna's fits of moodiness, the young woman ignored her hostile reception and leaned against the bar to wait as Roanna filled the order.

How was she to know that those two imbeciles would try to carry a half-full tub through the upper halls of Durham House? thought Roanna. Any dolt knew that the tub should have been emptied first! But they had tried to remove it half-full, and they had made it as far as the hallway before it had slipped from their grasp. She had reached the top of the stairs at the fateful moment, her arms full of linens, and she had barely managed to step aside as the tub hurtled by—and then the deluge had struck and she had gone flying. But a governing rule of her life seemed to be that if a situation could possibly become worse, it would. It should have held no surprise for her, then, that as she tried to steady herself on the slippery floor, the soapy water swishing in little whitecaps about her knees and hands, and as she looked up through dripping strands of hair and opened her mouth to scream at the two culprits, who had managed to find a dry foothold and were prudently disappearing down the hall, she should have heard the inevitable sound of a male's grunt of surprise.

She wrenched her head about in time to see his feet slip out from under him as he turned the corner. They worked like a windmill over the watery planks. "Blood of God!" he roared, grasping at a heavy iron wall sconce. "What is going on here?"

Oh, Sweet Mother in Heaven, it was the blighter from the parapet. "What d'ye think be goin' on?" she snapped churlishly, spitting some strands of hair from her mouth. "Sodding buggers dropped a tub, just as I—"

"Tub?" he exclaimed, glancing about. "What tub?"

"Must be in the great 'all," she answered, jerking her head at the stairs that angled downward behind her.

"Good God. Was anyone on the stairs?"

"I was," she snapped. "Or nearly be."

"Wait. I'll try to help you up." Regaining his footing, he reached out to her. She took his proffered hand, noting at the same moment that he had let go of his hold on the sconce. Oh bugger, she thought.

He emitted another grunt of surprise as she was pulled

up, he went down, and she came down atop him. She raised her head to find his face inches from her own. Transfixed, she stared into deep blue eyes, crinkled at the corners with tiny laugh lines. Soft, wet, chestnut curls hung over a tanned forehead and a handsome face that left her breathless. His body was lean and hard beneath hers, his teeth white and healthy as he grinned at her. Lud, she thought, he's bloody gorgeous.

"Sorry," he murmured, then smiled a devastating smile that made her feel weak. "God, you're wet."

"Astute ye are, milord, I'll give ye that," she retorted, his flash of humor distracting her from more disquieting thoughts.

"You're a mess."

"I 'adn't planned on takin' a bath in the 'allway, milord," she gritted through her teeth. "Now, while ye may be enjoyin' this, I 'ave better things to do."

His soft laughter surprised her. "Hold on to me."

"Never considered anythin' else."

Slowly he pulled himself up, pausing to gain a footing on the slippery, worn wood. Easing himself along the wall as Roanna clung to him, he maneuvered around the corner, finally gaining dry floor. "Jesu!" he swore as she stepped away from him. He pulled at his tunic, lifting it away from his body. "I'm soaked!"

"Damp," she corrected.

He looked up at her and began to laugh. "You look like a drowned rat."

"Thanks fer yer assistance," she said huffily. Grasping at some measure of dignity, she turned and left him, squishing away down the hallway.

Oh, it was true that he had interceded for her when Eleanor had come across her, dripping wet, following reports that a copper tub had come bouncing into the great hall and nearly collided with old Lord Wolsey. But he could have tried to restrain his humor when recounting the events.

Enough! she thought. It was over, done with, finished! She forced a smile onto her face and tried to focus on the present and her duties in the tavern. She simply would not think about it again.

But as she lay in bed, hours later, she faced it once more. With an arm propped behind her head, she watched sleepily as the bright moon cast the irregular shadows of passing clouds about the walls and ceiling of her bedchamber. Then she groaned, reminded once again, tossing her head as if she could thus rid it of unwanted memories.

With a sinking sensation, she realized that those months in Lady Eleanor's household would not be so easily forgotten. They held memories she would live with for a long, long time. There were so many moments.

How could she possibly ever forget Lord Edward's banquet, the feast provided by the Plantagenet prince for his bachelor knights? It had begun well enough. In fact, she had been quite overwhelmed to be among those chosen to serve for the eldest son of their sovereign, King Henry. She had not dared to ask how it had happened, but she had learned by bits and pieces that Lord Edward's household at the Tower still was not completed, since he had only returned to London a few short weeks before. Lady Eleanor, as his aunt, had generously offered to lend some of her servants for the event. Oh, how Roanna rued that day!

She had never seen such grandeur. Upon entering the great hall of the White Tower she had been struck dumb and could only stare. Black trails of wavering smoke lifted from sputtering torches placed about the walls and into the deepening shadows of the high, heavily beamed ceiling, from which hung the brightly colored banners of the coats-of-arms of the great families of England. Great iron candelabra stood along a ponderous table reaching the length of the long, narrow room, and flickering lights from the squat candles cast the room in muted colors and played on the great murals depicting scenes of Antioch that ran the length of the plastered walls.

Even the sight of the majestic hall did not prepare her for the array of food that was to be served—twenty-seven courses in all. There were jellied lampreys, smoked halibut in pastry, salmon, turbot, and mussels in butter sauce—and a special presentation of sturgeon, the royal fish. That was to be followed by lark's tongue pie, venison with frumenty seasoned with saffron, mortrews of pork and beef, roast boar's head, roast goose, and large mazers of roasted capons, mallards, and quail, the latter served with tiny pickled eggs. Roanna was sent, with two of her fellow maidservants, to prepare an enormous salad of parsley, sage, garlic, mint, rosemary, rue, purslane, and fennel, dressed with oil, verjuice, and salt. Behind her, two male cooks were busy dressing a roasted peacock in full plumage, and at another table, desserts were being prepared: fathons, or tarts, of berries, and rapeye, a custard of almonds, milk, dates, apples, and spices, accompanied by bowls of dried raisins, dates, and figs.

Once the bowls of water perfumed with orange peel, marjoram, sage, and lavender had been set in their places on the table for hand washing, Roanna drew aside to the shadows with her workmates. There was nothing to do now but await the moment when the Prince made his appearance.

As her eyes traveled over the assembly, she tried to fix faces to the names she had heard for so long. Politics and other matters of the realm were standard topics in an alehouse such as the Flying Sail, and Roanna had been weaned on such talk. But while many a noble had frequented the tavern, this was the first time Roanna had been present at such a gathering; it was unquestionably a heady experience.

As Lord Edward joined his party, she drew in her breath sharply and her eyes widened with awe. The Plantagenet prince was everything—nay, more than everything—she had heard about him. He was the picture of elegant simplicity in a tabard of gold velvet banded in rich, deep brown. Imposingly tall—a full head taller than his companions —and athletic, he had earned the nickname of Longshanks. He was fair with sun-streaked hair, a ruggedly handsome face, and eyes that could only be called Plantagenet blue. His compelling presence, which was what had made her gasp, was moderated by the broad grin he offered to his companions in response to some comment that did not carry beyond the small group surrounding him.

"La, now I be understandin' of 'is reputation," murmured Maud, her salad-making companion, who stood next to her. "Lud, 'e's a beauty, ain't 'e? They say 'e's lifted 'alf the skirts in England."

"An' most like Normandy as well," chortled another girl.

"An' Castile," whispered another. "'ow old was Dona Eleanora when 'e married 'er? She can't be more'n twelve or thirteen now. Think 'e's been into that yet?"

"I 'eard that she be already wi' child."

"Agh!" Maud snorted. "Just rumor, that. All England would be knowin' if that be the case, 'im bein' the heir and all."

Roanna sniffed, disgusted by the habits of the nobility. Suddenly Edward did not seem so grand to her, for all of his glory. But she continued to watch as he moved from one small group of men to another, until she and the others were beckoned by the steward to begin carrying the repast to the table.

She had little time to think of Edward's bed habits or anything else in the hours that followed. She fetched and carried heavy mazers and mets, ewers of wine, and pitchers of ale to her section of the table below Edward's right hand. She and her companions had been carefully instructed by the supercilious steward, who had belabored the point to exhaustion, that they were to bear the food to the table but they were never, never to touch the table itself. All items were to be handed to the squires who stood behind their masters' chairs. All empty bowls, trenchers, mets, mazers, and drinking cups were to be taken from the hands of those selfsame squires or the pages who assisted them. Furthermore, and *most* importantly, they were never, but never, to approach within four feet of Lord Edward's chair. They were to stand outside the proscribed area and await the Prince's attendants, who would relieve them of their burdens.

The evening progressed so smoothly that as the meal began to show signs of ending, in spite of her fatigue Roanna felt almost lighthearted. Her thoughts turned to the moments when she would be with the other maidservants in their chamber at Durham House, and they could exchange tidbits of gossip about the evening past. And for once, she would not be the butt of their conversation.

It was at that moment, when she least expected it, that the atmosphere of the evening changed—abruptly. Roanna had taken a basketful of soaked trenchers from one of the squires, and as she stepped back to carry them away, she glanced toward Lord Edward and froze. He was leaning back in his chair, his elbow resting on the arm of his chair as he cupped his chin in his hand; he was looking directly at her. Having lived all her life in an alehouse, there was absolutely no way Roanna could have misinterpreted that look. Oh, balls, she thought. Oh, damn! Whirling, she fled the hall, even as an impending feeling of doom rushed with her.

She tried to hide in the kitchen, but was quickly found by the steward, who ordered her out in a strident voice that left her no choice. Shoulders slumped, she walked slowly along the corridor that led to the hall, barely hearing Maud as she passed.

"Lud, Roanna, ye won't believe it!"

Oh, she believed it, all right. The question was, what was she going to do about it? Preoccupied, she entered the darkened hall, not noticing at first that many of the candles on the table had been snuffed, or that lilting music was drifting from the gallery on the far end of the room. When she looked up, she blinked, her mouth dropping open. Young women, scantily clad, were dancing about the long table. They were dark-skinned with long black hair, wearing brief cloths about their breasts and hips, their legs covered only by thin veils of sarcenet.

"They're *Saracen* women!" Maud hissed, coming up behind her. "I 'eard a squire say that Lord Edward brought 'em 'ere just for this. They be captives, 'eld by some blighter earl in Normandy. Lud, Roanna," she said, giggling, "ain't it exciting?"

Aye, exciting, Roanna thought sardonically. Her eyes narrowed on the faces of the women. Captives, eh? Whores was whores, to her way of thinking. There was no way of misreading the intent on those faces. Well, at least they would distract Lord Edward. Roanna sighed and moved through the darkened room behind the dancers and approached the table to collect the last of the dishes. As she stood waiting in her place, wondering how long it would take the gawking squires to notice that she was there, she dared to shift her eyes in Edward's direction, then drew in her breath sharply. The sodding luck! Apparently Lord Edward's mind was not easily distracted.

She glanced about for a means of escape, knowing that she had to get out of the hall before the dancing ended. Without thinking further, she leapt forward, past the distracted squires, and grabbed for the empty bowls remaining on the table. As she reached across the table, vaguely aware of the sound of feminine giggles and male laughter as the dancers approached willing partners, she was grabbed roughly about the waist. Shocked, she found herself ensconced in the lap of a drunken knight with dark hair, a rather scruffy beard, and breath that reeked of stale ale and what had once been fine wines of Gascony.

Shrieking with rage, a sound barely heard above the knight's delighted guffaw and the rising bedlam in the hall, she fought to free herself from the grasping, seeking fingers. Years of experience in handling drunken sots—common and noble—came to her aid. With a quick gouge to the eyes with one hand, she twisted and jabbed her elbow sharply into the knight's vulnerable parts. Finding quick release, she jumped up and spun round on the gasping man. She would have landed a resounding clout on his ear, but her wrist was caught from behind by someone else. She was yanked against her second attacker's hard body as his strong arm snaked about her waist, pinning her other arm. To her complete horror, in spite of her protesting shrieks, she was half dragged, half carried toward Lord Edward, who was laughing uproariously. Apparently he found her encounter with the knight, and her present dilemma, exceedingly funny. Moreover, she was not just dragged toward Lord Edward, but well within the four-foot limit.

"Milord," a drunken voice drawled at her ear. "You said—if I needed anythin'—anythin' at all, I sh'ld merely ask."

"So I did," Edward said, chuckling. "I assume that the maid you hold would serve my offer?"

"Aye—milord," the voice hiccuped.

"If the maid is willing," the prince said, still grinning. "And I would note that well, if I were you. She appears to be well able to handle herself."

"She's—willing, mi-lord," the voice slurred happily.

As Roanna opened her mouth to protest, the arm about her waist tightened in a sharp jerk, squeezing the breath from her. Gasping painfully for air, she found herself half-carried across the end of the hall behind Edward's chair. As her feet managed to find contact with the floor, a hand gave her a shove between her shoulder blades, and she stumbled forward into a curtained alcove. Catching herself, she spun about as she drew in a sharp breath. "Let me go, ye stinkin', drunken sod!"

"Shhhh!" her captor hissed as he snapped the curtain closed behind them, plunging them into complete darkness.

"Would you rather go back in there? You would never make it through the hall."

"Some bloody choice!" she snarled.

"Undoubtedly so. But I assure you that you are quite safe with me," the voice said calmly, surprisingly with no evidence of the ravages of drink.

"Why should I believe that?" she hissed, poised to strike.

She startled at the sound of his soft laughter. "Because I would never harm my little goat girl. Nor one with whom I had bathed."

"You!" she gasped.

"None other. Sit down, Roanna. There is a padded bench behind you."

"I don't want to," she said tightly, feeling even more unsettled by this unexpected turn of events than what had happened in the hall. "If yer truly a friend ye'll take me back to the kitchens."

"Oh, come now, sweetling. I have just saved you from a fate worse than death, so it is said. I have my reputation to maintain—you could at least let them think that my attentions require more than a few moments."

She sat, stiffly. "Ye needn't 'ave done it, ye know. I can 'andle the likes of them."

"Oh?" he asked, sitting on the bench beside her. "And would you have used the same tactics against Lord Edward? Or could it be that you did not notice his interest in you? Could I have imagined an earlier moment when you fled from his rather intent perusal?"

"Ye saw that?"

"I noticed."

"Damn."

"So it would seem," he said, laughing softly. "But the danger is past as long as you remain in here with me."

"Who are ye?" she asked after a moment.

"You wound me, Roanna!" he said with feigned hurt. "After all that we have shared together, you have not even cared enough to learn my name."

"I've tried to forget all that," she muttered.

"Nonetheless, I am Giles fitzWilliam. At your service, my sweet, apparently whether I want to be or not."

"No one asked ye to 'elp me tonight," she snapped.

"True. But I'd offer one more bit of help, Roanna, some advice. You are a lovely young woman . . ." He wondered if she realized just how beautiful she was. The image of her rose before his eyes in the darkness. Large, expressive, heavily-lashed brown eyes that looked into her soul. High cheekbones, a creamy complexion, and a mouth that ached for a man's kiss. But most of all, what had first drawn his eyes to her from the battlements, her hair, a mass of gold silk burnished with rose. He cleared his throat. "I would advise you to cover that hair of yours. It is rather . . . memorable, not to mention distracting. But, be that as it may, my little goat girl—"

"Do not call me that!" she cried, flushing, undone by his mention of her hair.

"But why?" he countered. "It was handily done, Roanna. Most maids would have merely fainted and been seriously harmed by the creature. I shouted, and tried to warn you, but I knew it was too late—"

"You?" She was startled. "'Twas you that called out?"

"I fear so. And now I ask a boon for the deed."

"Oh?" she asked suspiciously. "And what would that be, milord?"

"Merely an answer to a question that has been plaguing me, nothing more serious." She winced at the humor she heard in his voice. "I learned from Lady Eleanor that you were brought to Durham House at the request of your father. However, I cannot fathom why he would choose to have you live your early years in a wharfside tavern, rather than under the protection of Lady Eleanor's service, as his position would have allowed. A wharf would not appear to be the most gentle of places to raise a maid."

She was silent for a moment. God, how protected these nobles were! Didn't it occur to the bloater that her father simply didn't want her? "So much ye know, milord. The docks may not be 'gentle,' as ye say, but there I be my own person. 'ere I cannot protest what be given me. Them out there, at the table, they be fops, all of 'em, intent on nothin' but their pleasures."

"Many are, I agree, but not all, Roanna. There are others who would have done what I did, had they been aware of the situation."

"Ye couldn't prove it by me," she snorted. Irritated by the conversation, by everything that had happened, suddenly she felt totally testy. "Now ye answer me a thought, fitzWilliam. Why be ye not out there, instead of in 'ere playin' the gentleman for someone ye barely be knowin' —don't ye like women?"

She smiled, satisfied, at the sound of his strangling cough. But he had the last word on the subject. "Aye, Roanna, I like women, very much," he said calmly, purposefully. "Shall I prove it to you?"

It took her a moment to rally. "Try it and ye'll 'ave to spend the rest of yer life dreamin' about it!"

"Roanna," he sighed wearily, "you cannot go about attempting to emasculate all of England."

"I kin try. Long as men go about thinkin' wi' their—"

"I get the point," he said quickly. "Roanna—be easy. We can only hope that age will temper that impulsive nature of yours."

She snorted, now really insulted. "I be ten an' six years, fitzWilliam! Fa, a noblewoman my age would 'ave been married an' borne 'er lord a child or two by now. And as fer yer precious fops, Lord Edward be no innocent; and I've 'eard that Lady Eleanor 'ad been married to 'er first husband when she were but nine years!" She shuddered at the prospect. "Bleedin' nobility likes 'em tender, that's for sure; they 'ardly give 'em a chance to finish mother's milk! The bloaters are bastards, every last one of 'em."

"You have been misinformed, Roanna," Giles answered quietly. "Lady Eleanor was betrothed at the age of nine, but the marriage was not consummated until she was eighteen."

She was puzzled by the sudden anger in his voice, but the undercurrent of disapproval only made her more indignant. "Believe what ye want, fitzWilliam, more the fool ye are for it. But there's no doubt in me that the blighter made the most of that tender flesh. You really expect me to believe that 'e left it alone for nine years? Pah, fitzWilliam, yer mad."

"Believe what you want," he interrupted sharply. He rose suddenly from the bench and lifted the curtain back to peer out, squinting into the light. Turning back, he held out a hand to her. "Our company seems to have left us for more private pursuits. Shall I see you back to Durham House?"

Rising, she countered haughtily, "Nay, milord, I'll return wi' the ones I came wi'. I'll only 'ave trouble if I don't."

"Are you certain?" he asked doubtfully. "You have been gone for some time, they may have returned without you."

She snorted at the comment. "My station does not find ease wi' the banquet's end, milord. There be hours of work ahead."

"I could see you released from that—"

"Ye've done enough, fitzWilliam. Believe me." Before he could argue, she swept by him and fled across the darkened hall.

Roanna leaned back against the hard wooden sides of the chariot carrying them to Durham House, the unaxled wagon jarring her thoughts as it lurched roughly over the cobbled streets of London. Vaguely, the weary chatter of the other women intruded and she struggled to hold her mind on the hours past. As she had worked into the late hours, her thoughts had drifted repeatedly to the alcove and the minutes she'd spent with him, although she had tried not to let her wandering thoughts become apparent to the others.

The kitchen had been abuzz when she returned, the thick silence that dropped when she appeared confirming that she had, once again, been the subject of conversation. Looks cast in her direction were mingled: pity or sympathy from those she counted as friends, disapproval tinged with jealousy from others. Ignoring all of it, she had quickly busied herself, grateful when the normal buzz of conversation rose again and she knew she had been forgotten, at least for the moment.

But Roanna could not forget the episode, neither during the following hours nor even as they now approached the last leg of their journey. Lud, had she imagined it? Oh, the reaction of the others confirmed that it had happened, but it did not seem real.

In spite of the confused anger she had felt when she was with him, she was grateful to him. She regretted that she had been so rude, but lud, what did he expect? In spite of his pretty words, there was no reason for one in her position to trust one in his.

He had saved her, though hardly from a fate worse than death—lud, only a man would say that—but certainly from a bloody 'orrible experience. But that wasn't what made her thoughts continually return to him. Oddly, it was the memory of his voice, and a feeling he had left her with. It was totally unreasonable, and totally compelling. Who was he, Giles fitzWilliam? Lud, why couldn't she get him out of her mind? Dorine, she thought suddenly. Dorine knew everyone and everything that went on at Durham House.

It seemed to take forever to complete their journey, and all too long before Roanna finished readying for bed in the long narrow room in the east wing she shared with the other unwed maids. The sound of light snores carried through the drafty chamber as Roanna approached the single candle burning at the end of the room, and the small group gathered about it. The young women sat on the few cots at the far end of the room, gossiping in whispers about events of the day past. Taking a place near a dark-haired wench whose voluptuous body nearly overflowed the thin chemise she wore, Roanna listened to Dorine, the undisputed leader of the maid's chamber, holding forth. Mostly, Roanna avoided these sessions—not that she disliked Dorine, but she simply found her uninteresting. Though she was unaware of it, Roanna's background had given her far more worldly knowledge, in spite of Dorine's superior attitude.

As Roanna sat wondering how she would approach the subject, Maud suddenly took the matter out of her hands. "Law, Roanna, are ye goin' ta tell us wot 'appened?"

It was a moment before Roanna realized that everyone's eyes had shifted speculatively to her. She stared vacantly at Maud and flushed. "Nothin' 'appened," she answered at last. "We—just talked." Her response was met with disbelieving laughter. "Really, nothin' 'appened!"

"Aw, come on, luv," Dorine smirked; judging by her manner, Roanna had been the object of discussion before she had joined them. "Ye expect us ta believe that? FitzWilliam dragged ye ta an alcove just ta talk? Do ye take us fer fools? Come now, share! There's not one 'ere who wouldn't 'ave traded places wi' ye tonight!"

"We talked," Roanna insisted, to continuing doubt. "'e was . . . kind. But, me bein' new 'ere . . . tell me, who is 'e?"

"Who is 'e?" Dorine laughed, her voice throaty. "What did ye talk about?"

"Me, mostly." Roanna shrugged.

"That be yer first mistake, my simple one," Dorine admonished. "Always, luv, *always* talk about 'im. *Never* yerself—unless ye really only want ta talk." She ignored the laughter of the other women, and ran her fingers through her thick, black tresses thoughtfully. "Who is 'e? Well, now. First of all, 'e be Lord Edward's cousin. If ye'd been quicker, ye'd 'ave bedded near the throne." Dorine smirked at the widening of Roanna's eyes. "Aye, little one. Now, what else? 'e's the grandson of William Marshal, the ol' regent of England, an' son of Will Marshal, that was King 'enry's closest friend—thus 'e be stepson to Lady Eleanor."

"Lady Eleanor's—stepson?" Roanna gasped in sudden apprehension.

"Aye. Ye knew that Lady Eleanor was married afore, surely. 'er first 'usband be Will, marshal of England. Lud, ye didn't even know that?"

Roanna wanted to die, to suddenly and simply disappear from the earth. Sweet Mother, it was *his* father who had taken Eleanor to wife when she was nine. No wonder he had been so angry!

"Nay, I didn't know," she stammered. "'e—'e must be a great earl, and I—"

"Pah, not so," Dorine interrupted, and sighed heavily with dramatic emphasis. "A waste, t'be sure, fer one so 'andsome—but alas, our 'andsome knight was born on the wrong side of the sheets. 'is mother be a mystery, one the family keeps guarded. Makes 'im all the more excitin', eh?"

"I suppose," Roanna said lamely, but her own thoughts were on a vastly different track. "'ow much pain 'e must 'ave known," she added quietly.

"Pain? Aye, when 'is family fell from favor," Dorine said. "Ye know—nay, I suppose ye don't—'tis rumored that 'is father, and 'is four uncles as well, powerful men all of 'em and each in 'is turn marshal of England, were all murdered."

The bed was all lumps. Groaning, Roanna turned on her side as the memories of that night, and all the days before, refused to let her rest. It was all too much. She had known that she could never, ever face him again, and she had fled. But even now, in the sanctuary of her bed, the conflicts she had felt then returned. She tossed off the covers and flung out her arms, then lay still staring at the ceiling. Lord, why did he haunt her so, even now when she was free of him and of all that Durham House had held for her? Here, in the life she knew and loved, she was safe. More than that, she was again her own person, not the butt of humor and gossip. But with these thoughts, she stirred uncomfortably. All the years spent in a wharfside tavern, the conversation, the politics, the grumblings of simple men, all formed to a strong feeling she could not yet define. Somehow, frighteningly, she knew that her life would never again be as it had been before. Most terrifying of all, though, was the impossible knowledge that Giles fitzWilliam would be the core of it.

2

Entering the knights' quarters, Giles found his squire, Geoffrey Wardell, bent over his hauberk with a polishing cloth, so intent upon his task that he did not hear the door opening. Giles repressed a smile at the sixteen-year-old's earnestness. The sandy-haired youth had his lower lip caught between his teeth as he industriously polished the chain-link mail to a dull gleam.

Crossing the room, Giles pulled his tunic over his head and tossed it on the warchest next to the boy. Geoffrey started up, barely managing to hold onto the hauberk as its weight threw him off balance. "Will you need to arm, Sir Giles?"

"Be easy, Geoffrey, it is early. Finish what you are doing."

Giles washed in a bucket of water as Geoffrey finished his task, and then the boy assisted him into his armor. First Giles slipped into a heavy wool tunic, then the heavy padded gambeson that would hold the mail away from his body, and then the jazerant-work hauberk. Over this he slipped the sleeveless surcoat of gold and green, his colors. The device on his chest had been designed by his grandmother, Isabel, before her death; its meaning was understood only by the two of them. The field was white, and bore the red lion rampant of his father. A bar sinister was there also, declaring a bastard, but instead of taking a normal position, superimposed over all, it was held firmly in the teeth of the lion, its lower corner caught in the talons of the left paw.

"Will you wear the coif?" Geoffrey asked.

"Nay, there is no need. Just bring my sword."

He buckled on the belt as the squire hooked the scabbard to Giles's side. Then, with a few words about what he wanted done that day, Giles left the room and made his way to the sheer, high walls that faced the river Thames. He paused there for a moment before he began his duties as captain of the guard. Eleanor had been horrified when he requested the post, protesting that such a gesture was not required, but he had insisted. Idleness was the one condition Giles could not abide, and he had no intention of spending his time in England with nothing to do but brood.

It was madness, all of it, he thought for the hundredth time. But then, life never made any particular sense; it was only to be dealt with as best as one could. His blue eyes, darkened with anger and doubt, shifted to the Thames and to the barges that moved slowly down the river's current. He leaned one shoulder against the crenellated wall of the high, turreted tower, momentarily distracted by the angry shouts of the bargemen as they cursed the operator of a smaller boat that had maneuvered into their path.

Madness, he thought again, to be here within the king's reach; insanity to bed with the enemy. But he stood his post, checking the lines of the heavily guarded fortress, as he had during each watch over the past month. Moving on, he found a guard dozing at his post and berated the man soundly, his own doubts momentarily suffocated beneath layers of duty.

Walking along the parapet of the lower wall, he paused and observed the activity below him in the courtyard. "Giles fitzWilliam," he mused silently, "why are you here?" But he grimaced at his own question, the answer ever the same: because Eleanor had asked him to be. How swiftly life changed, with twists and turns one could not even begin to imagine. He had once thought that the early years of his life had been spent in such turmoil that they could only lead to peace. He had found it, for six years, by withdrawing to his lands in Wales and Ireland and rejecting the conflicts of kings, bishops, princes—and most of all, of his own family.

Of the five sons and five daughters born to his grandparents, only four of the daughters now survived. Thank God Isabella was gone, he thought, thinking upon his favorite aunt with tenderness. She would grieve to see the way her eldest had turned out. None of Giles's cousins were of the mettle of those earlier Marshal men, he thought, but of them all, Richard deClare, earl of Gloucester, was the least to be trusted. Ironic that he who was named for the great-grandfather who had brought the family their great wealth and power, the lord marcher who had conquered lands from Normandy to Ireland, had proved to be the least like him. Moreover, deClare's son, Gilbert, showed evidence of the same fickle, irrational behavior. Yet because of his name and his power, Gloucester, along with Simon de Monfort, had been elected an undisputed leader of England's barons. It was given to them to protect the Great Charter and the Provisions of Oxford, the latter whereby King Henry had relinquished many of his powers to a baronial council—an act that had served to push England to the brink of a civil war.

England had suffered terribly under John, its most despotic king, but it had gained little with Henry, the son. Oh, he was not the lecher his father was; he revered his family, cherished his wife. But even that did not speak well for him. From the moment Queen Eleanor of Provence had set her dainty foot upon England's shores, she had become, with her extravagances and her contempt for her adopted home, the most hated of all of its queens, perhaps unto time.

Henry was arrogant, cowardly, ambitious, and impractical. He wanted to rule, yet was easily bent by those who advised him. And Henry had not had an adviser who cared for England since Will Marshal; since his father, Giles thought, there had been no one, for his uncles never had much influence with the king, for all of their wealth and power which he coveted. So many mistakes, leading to this day, with the promise of war as the outcome.

The king's half brothers, the de Lusignans, had drawn him into an expensive and ill-fated military venture in France. Outraged, the barons had begun to demand a voice in selecting the king's counselors, positions that had been handed over to the hated foreign influence—the royal relatives. The King's Men and the Queen's Men, they were called: the Lusignans on the one hand and the Provençals and Savoyards on the other, all of whom drained England's resources as they looked with contempt upon England and her people.

The king had repeatedly rejected the barons' proposals. Then, at last, Henry had made his worst mistake in judgment. He had concluded an agreement with Pope Innocent IV, promising to finance papal wars in Sicily in exchange for placing the Sicilian crown on the tiny head of his infant son, Edmund. Four years passed, and when Henry failed to meet his financial obligations to Rome, the new pope, Alexander IV, threatened to excommunicate him. When Henry appealed to the barons for funds, they had seen their opportunity and agreed to cooperate on the condition that he accept far-reaching reforms. He had reluctantly agreed, and the Provisions of Oxford were written. They provided for a council of fifteen, selected by the barons, that would advise the king and oversee the entire administration of the government. The royal relatives, of course, had resisted, frantically advising Henry to "ignore the traitors and take the reins of government." The struggle had led to a revolt, capture of the relatives, and their expulsion from England. Henry had followed them to the Continent, where he rushed, whining, to Louis of France for aid.

Giles rolled his shoulders against the uncomfortable warmth of the late summer sun. How many more days, he wondered, until all hell broke loose? There was a disgruntled king lolling in France—using the time to mount an army, Giles had no doubt—as the enemies of England whispered in his royal ear; apathetic barons comforted themselves with past laurels; the two most powerful barons argued bitterly with each other, while the better of the two was conjoining himself with a self-centered prince who was certain to turn on him when the opportunity presented itself.

Pushing his thoughts aside, Giles made his way to the weapons room, where he checked the tallies of the master-of-arms, then began another turn to recheck the posts of the standing guards. To his dismay, he found yet another man dozing at the far tower wall. After a stern reprimand that fully woke the man-at-arms, Giles left the wall, seeking the solitude of the room set aside for the office of the guard. He ducked under the low doorway and into the cool room set into the wall of the inner bailey, slamming the heavy oak door behind him. Damn, he thought furiously, how could he enforce discipline when he was just as confused about their mission as his men were? He poured a goblet of watered wine for a well-deserved, self-imposed break. Unhooking his scabbard, he dropped his sword on the desk with a clatter and slumped into a chair. His expression set moodily as he drew from the heavy pewter tankard; the door opened and he glanced up with irritation.

"Do not glare at me, fitzWilliam. Whatever has caused your mood, I am not at fault."

Giles's expression softened reluctantly. There was, perhaps, no one else in the world who could ease Giles's ill humor more quickly than Rodger Farnham. The third son of the earl of Bolton, the sandy-haired, hazel-eyed knight could draw Giles from the blackest mood with his unwavering loyalty. "Why are you here, Rodger?" Giles grumbled, and drew from his tankard. "Your post was not to end until vespers." He glanced at the calibrated candle burning nearby, confirming his judgment of the time. "Come to think of it, I do not recall seeing you at the east end of the wall. Where have you been?"

"Retraining a group of incompetents," the knight answered as he reached for the pitcher to pour himself a measure. "Damn English haven't the vaguest idea of how to hold a longbow."

"Oh?" Giles snorted with disbelief, hiding his amusement. "Damn English? When did you cease being English, Rodger?"

"When I became your man in Wales." Rodger grinned, leaning his hip against the desk.

Giles struggled against a smile, refusing to give the accolade his friend was so obviously seeking. His lands in Ireland were held for him by Sir Landon d'Leon, once squire to his father, then master-of-squires for Will Marshal, and thus Giles's mentor and oldest friend. But Rodger was his castellan in Wales, and as such had long since proven his loyalty and trust.

"So, then," Rodger asked with a grin, "what did you think of Lord Edward's banquet? And who was that delightful wench you disappeared with?"

"The banquet? Of that I smelled a trap."

"A trap? Oh, come now, Giles," Rodger said, grinning,

then added wryly, "But then, most likely you are correct—he certainly did plan for us to eat ourselves to death. As for the women . . ."

"Rodger, your wit overwhelms me," Giles said dryly.

"Give the devil his due, Giles. It was a very sober prince who entered London a fortnight ago—and thus he conducted himself at his own banquet as well. He has not shown any of his usual, ah, his usual—"

"Lasciviousness?" Giles finished for him. "I am unimpressed by the fact that he has apparently chosen to behave himself for a fortnight. Moreover, his morals do not concern me, but his politics do. Can you honestly believe that he has forgiven the barons, most particularly Simon, for stripping his father, and thus himself, of his powers?"

"Edward seems to have made peace with Simon," Rodger ventured, though he sounded less than convinced.

"So it would seem," Giles responded glumly. "That is what worries me."

"So, then, what of the wench?" Rodger grinned. "Tell me all of it."

It took Giles a moment to follow the shift in topic. "Who? Oh, she was nothing. That is, nothing happened."

Rodger laughed, rolling his eyes. "That good, eh? I understand why you don't wish to talk about it."

"I told you that nothing happened!" Giles snapped irritably.

"Smart lass."

"Dammit, Rodger. Drop it."

"This is getting better. She rejected you, right?"

"Nay, she didn't reject me, you fool."

"What was the matter with her?"

"Nothing was the matter with her!"

"Then why didn't you—"

"Dammit, Rodger, shut up," he growled.

"A bit touchy, aren't you? There's a good tale here, I can smell it."

"Don't you have something to do?"

"Absolutely nothing."

Sighing, Giles capitulated and related the events of the previous evening, as well as the events leading up to it.

As he finished the recounting, Rodger whistled softly. "So she's the one. All of Durham House has heard of her—ah, her exploits. Surprising, she's a beauty. That hair, the color of a bright dawn, and her skin is dewy and bright, and looks as soft as—"

"What a poet you are," Giles said with a grimace. "Get close to her, she'll remind you of a tempest. I don't begin to imagine why, but it would seem that I have been appointed by the gods as her protector. But then, the gods always did seem to have a rather twisted sense of humor."

Rodger shifted uncomfortably at Giles's reference to the deities. It was the only thing that he could not reconcile about his friend. He knew that Giles did not refer to plural gods in a literal sense, but Rodger fought the impulse to cross himself at such moments. For the thousandth time, Rodger wished that Giles had not been exposed in such depth to the philosophers, in particular to one called Aristotle. He often wondered who it was who had warped Giles's thinking: his father, his grandmother, his uncle— that damnable troubadour! But then, even Eleanor could be heard to comment with her stepson about such matters in the most serious manner, even when they knew themselves to be overheard. As always in such moments, Rodger rapidly changed the subject. "Gloucester is here."

Giles's head jerked up. "Richard? Here?"

"I saw him as I arrived."

"God. What does he want?" Giles muttered.

"How would I know? He is your cousin, not mine." Rodger ignored Giles's grunt of displeasure. "I have heard that he is insisting that what was gained at Oxford should apply only to those nobly born and is decrying Simon's stand—that all those dependent upon the peers of England should gain from the Provisions of Oxford. He claims that for the common people to be granted protection and rights under the law would create anarchy."

"I am aware of his opinion. And what are your feelings on it, Rodger?" Giles asked with an arch of a brow. "Now that you can look at it with the objectivity of the Welsh."

"You know us Welsh." Rodger grinned. "Anything to discomfit the English."

"Seriously."

Rodger's demeanor sobered. "'Tis an easy thing for a third son to understand how one feels who has nothing," he said quietly.

"Yet there was a time I would have envied you your place, Rodger."

"I know," Rodger said softly. Uncomfortable with the unusual strain in the room, he brightened. "Come now, Giles. Let us depart this place and find a hidey-hole where we can get drunk. Perhaps we can find a few delectable wenches to share our confusion."

"An excellent idea." Giles sighed. "It must be later, however, as Eleanor has requested that I attend her for supper. But then we might as well seek what pleasure we may—for as long as we can."

"Giles, I do not expect you to speak against your father's family. I know that you are loyal to them, whereas my loyalty was shattered years ago." Eleanor de Monfort smoothed a layer of honey-butter on to a slice of manchet and nibbled at the crust, ignoring the disapproving gleam in her stepson's eyes.

The evening hour was damp with the threat of a storm. The small chamber, located in the west wing of the manor, was cast in shadows, the chill kept at bay by a large fire crackling in the hearth nearby. Giles chewed absently at a piece of cheese, knowing that Eleanor had not asked him to join her only to rehash a subject they had long ago agreed not to discuss. While he waited for her to get to the point, his gaze traveled over her lazily. She was still breathtakingly beautiful, he mused, as beautiful to him as the day he first saw her, when he was a frightened, embittered child of ten and she . . . she had been Eleanor Plantagenet, Lady Marshal, his father's wife. But to him she had been light, warmth, the love he had never known, given unconditionally. The bond that had grown between them had deepened with his father's loss, even as the passing years, and the estrangement and conflicts between those he loved, had saddened him immeasurably.

His concern for the depth of Eleanor's grief at his father's loss had found little support among the Marshal women and their families, as the chasm widened over the question of Eleanor's inheritance. As one who viewed the conflict from without, Giles had understood the views of both camps: Eleanor's claim to her former husband's estate, and the Marshals' reluctance to part with what had been in their family for more than one hundred years—coupled with the concern that, if the dispute was not settled, the land would fall into the king's hands. Yet Giles had remained steadfast, delicately balancing his loyalties, and he had felt uncomplicated joy when Simon de Monfort had at last released Eleanor from the years of grief, if not the memories of his father. He had long since dealt with his father's loss, if not with the conviction that he had been murdered, a crime that had been avenged in any case. But to the loss itself, he had become reconciled, aware that they had been given many more years than most fathers and sons.

"Giles, are you listening to me?"

"Of course, Eleanor," he drawled. "But the antagonisms should be well healed. The matter was resolved when you were granted a yearly allowance against your dowry."

"Allowance? A payoff by my dear brother, the king, to keep the peace! I inherited one-fifth of your father's holdings, yet the Marshals refused to grant what was mine. Now it has all passed to Bigods, deClares, deWarennes, and deMunchensis!"

Giles fought a smile. "And to your own brother, Richard, through his marriage to my Aunt Isabella. Have you asked the duke to return what is yours?"

"Ask Richard?" She snorted. "He has the first coin he ever made."

Giles chuckled. "Be that as it may, you are hardly destitute, Eleanor." He glanced about at the sumptuous decor.

"There is never enough," she answered, distracted by her own thoughts. "Much more will be needed for what is to come."

His eyes returned to her and narrowed with interest. "Henry remains in France, sulking," he said quietly. "It will be some time before he forgives the barons for making him sign the charter at Oxford. Do you fear that war will accompany him when he returns?"

"Who knows my brother's mind?" She sighed, serving herself a portion of roast plover. "However, Henry is not one to brood overlong, particularly when another is whispering in his ear . . . Damn those Poitevin relatives! If only Henry had shown the wisdom of Louis of France when he married Marguerite and sent her uncles packing! Oh, but not Henry! When he married Eleanora, he loved her too well. Between the cow-eyed begging of his bride and the syrupy flattery of those parasites, he was lost."

"Do not overlook the King's Men, milady."

"I have never overlooked them, Giles. When your grand-father became regent, following my father's death, he should have locked my mother in the Tower instead of allowing her to return to France to breed that disreputable pack with Hugh de Lusignan. They are as contemptuous of England as are the queen's uncles, but they are the more dangerous, as they are dearer to the king."

Giles remained silent, reflecting on the royal cousins, the Lusignans. There was Guy, who had remained only a brief time in England after filling his pockets with Henry's generosity. Alice, who had been married in state to John deWarenne, the earl of Surrey. Aymer, for some unfathom-able reason a particular favorite of Henry's, who had been made bishop of Winchester; he had quickly proven his right to the office by locking his monks into their quarters for three days without food or water because they had dared to disagree with him.

But to Giles's mind, the worst of the lot was William de Lusignan, known as William of Valence. Effeminate, vi-cious, and covetous, he had gained great power when Henry had the poor judgment to marry him to Giles's gentle and beautiful cousin, Joan deMunchensi. As the youngest granddaughter of William Marshal, Joan had inherited one-fifth of the Marshal holdings, instantly making the greedy Lusignan a wealthy man. As the fief of Pembroke had been granted in Joan's holdings, William had the audacity to assert that he had deserved the title as well. Although the honor had been withheld, Lusignan had refused to accept that fact and proceeded to strut about England, declaring himself the earl of Pembroke.

This latter fact was the hardest for Giles to bear; to see the insufferable recreant declaring his rights, legally or not, to that which had once been borne by Giles's father, his grandfather, and his great-grandfather before him.

Realizing that Eleanor was speaking, he flushed. "I apolo-gize, milady. My thoughts were drifting."

"I noticed," she said wryly. "I was merely saying that it would have been preferable to keep his men in England, and the queen's as well, rather than exile them into his departing arms."

"The people would not have it," he reminded her. "Even in Ireland, we were aware of the outcry against the royal relatives. The rallying cry that reached us was that there were 'too many kings in England.'"

"Perhaps," she agreed thoughtfully. "But it does not serve to throw all our enemies into the same nest."

"It would appear that not all have been," he grumbled, reaching for his tankard. "There is one who seems to fly about freely, and into a rather strange roost, to my way of thinking."

"Prince Edward," she observed shrewdly. "Giles, do you not trust Simon?"

"With my life. But I would know why Edward is here."

"Simon is his godfather," she answered with a shrug. "Should they not spend time together?"

He arched a dark brow. "Eleanor. Do not mince with me. You asked me to come, and I did so, unhesitatingly. I came to offer my help, knowing that you may soon be at war with Henry, only to find you ensconced with Henry's heir!—and that one has no character."

"You are wrong, Giles. I believe that there is much good in my nephew."

Giles drew a breath. "Has he turned against his father?"

"Of course not," she answered, reaching for a damp towel to clean her fingers.

"Jesu, then I do not understand!" he grumbled.

"Giles, I do wish . . ." She hesitated, her gaze momentarily abstracted. "I wish that you had been granted more time to spend with your father."

"No more than do I," he countered. "What has that to do with this?"

She gifted him with a look of understanding, excusing his anger. "Giles, I am not a patient person. Indeed, I am cursed with a quick temper, a gift of my blood, so I am told. Your father had incredible patience, a depth of understanding lost to me. It often led to some rather—ah, heated arguments." She paused, smiling at the memory. "But he taught me one thing that has served me well, when I take the time to remember it: look beyond the obvious. Answers are found from within, beyond first reactions. What lasts is what comes later, from a deeper need that compels, ruling the best decision."

"In everyone except our king."

"Nay, even Henry," she said soberly. "But for him,

decisions are found in a different way. Will knew it; his son should know it as well. Henry blusters, reacting instinctively, but it is indeed what comes later, as others feed his thoughts, that lasts. Look to who is advising him, Giles. Know their thoughts, and you will know what Henry will do."

"And Edward?" he countered wryly. "Who is feeding his thoughts? Does Simon honestly feel he can change him?"

"Change him? Can one truly change another? It would seem that such must occur within one's self. Giles, you must try to trust Simon on this matter. He needs allies, now, men he can trust. If you had been in England the past few years you would understand what he faces."

"I understand well enough, Eleanor. Henry's extravagances, and those of the queen, might have been tolerated by the barons, but the line, as ever, is drawn against foreign influence. What amazes me is that Henry never seems to learn from his errors. My father helped to rid England of that damnable Poitevin bishop Peter desRoches, though not before the barons nearly revolted because of his influence with Henry, and his son, Peter desReveaux, who proved too free with England's resources. But now, Henry has again allowed foreign influence to rule him in the form of his blasted relatives!"

"Your own family did not do so well by their get," she observed wryly with narrowed eyes. "Richard of Gloucester is no prize. And Rodger Bigod, while a courageous soldier, has no guile, a necessary quality for shrewd planning. If he hadn't backed down at the Hocktide Parliament, the matter might have been well settled."

Upon his return to England, Giles had apprised himself of the events leading to the parliament, where Bigod, as marshal of England, had been spokesman for the barons. Henry had demanded a tallage of one-third of all wealth in the kingdom to finance his new adventures at home and abroad. Bigod had countered with the barons' insistence that all important offices, including those of treasurer, chancellor, and justiciar, be held by those chosen by the baronage. In order to force their demands, on the last day of parliament the barons had attended in full armor—a message Henry could not ignore. He cried out to them, asking if he was their prisoner. Instead of pressing his advantage, Bigod had backed off, assuring Henry that no violence was intended. The king yielded, but with no force behind their threat, the barons knew he would not hold to his promises.

"And that weakness of the barons led to the Provisions of Oxford," Giles observed.

"More or less. The details were to be worked out at Oxford. When Henry arrived, the city looked like an armed camp—"

"Allow me to finish," he interrupted, guessing what had happened. "Henry capitulated. The barons forced their council upon him, stripping him of many of his powers. Now he is in France licking his wounds, and building an army for retaliation. If, however, they had solicited him with firm diplomacy, yet played upon his vanity, he would have accepted the council of fifteen without a struggle."

"Exactly."

"I learned more at my father's knee than you give me credit for, Eleanor. Henry, more than anything else, wants to feel loved."

Eleanor's eyes widened. "You do understand," she said softly. Then she added grimly, "Unfortunately, so do those who are now close to him, and they use their knowledge without any true feeling for him. They have closed off his mind to any who truly care."

"You—and Simon."

"Aye." She sighed. "Not long after Oxford, a great storm occurred, on a day when Henry was traveling from Westminster to London. Henry is terrified of thunder and lightning, so the bargemen made for the first water stair within sight, which, as fate would have it, was here. Simon met him at the stairs, and brought him in. Later, as they dried themselves by the fire, Simon tried to reassure him of his loyalty. Henry spun on him and cried, 'By the hand of God, I fear thee more than all the thunder in the world!' Simon answered him calmly, and tried again to reassure him. He told him that Henry had no reason to fear him, that Simon was his true friend and that his sole desire was to preserve England from ruin, and to protect Henry from the destruction that his false counselors were preparing for him. I watched Henry's eyes as Simon spoke. He believed none of it."

"Is that why Simon has closeted himself with the son?" Giles asked softly. "To achieve what he cannot achieve with the father?"

Eleanor stared at him for a moment. "It was Edward who sought out Simon, Giles. As for the reasons, you will have to ask Simon."

He opened his mouth to question further, but she stayed him with a gesture of her hand and a look. Frustrated, he could only concede, knowing that she was firm and would not discuss the subject further. The tension eased, however, as the conversation moved on to other matters, touching on the passing years and his lands in Wales and Ireland. Servants came into the room to remove the remains of their supper. As they left, Eleanor glanced at Giles, who was gazing after them, in particular after one winsome lass who had turned away with a promising smile, which fact the countess had not missed.

Stifling a smile, she chose a sweetmeat from the tray before her and studied him. "Giles fitzWilliam, have you given thought to the matter that it is time you were wed?"

He glanced at her vacantly, then took in what she had said. "Me? Wed?"

"You are twenty and eight years, Giles. A man needs a wife."

"Do you have someone in mind?" He grinned. This was not the first time Eleanor had tried to settle his life.

"Nay, but it would not take much effort," she parried, picking up her goblet to sip from it. "There are not a few eligible maids who look upon you with great favor. I would see you well settled, Giles, as well as your interest withdrawn from the maids within my care."

He grinned, but his response was forestalled as the door opened, and he looked relieved.

"We shall finish this discussion later, Giles," she assured him. Her face softened into a smile as she caught sight of her husband, and she lifted her cheek for his kiss. "Simon, I thought you were seeing Edward at the Tower."

"Not this morning," the earl of Leicester answered, nodding in response to Giles's offer of ale. "Did I disturb something of importance?"

Eleanor smiled warmly at her husband as he took a chair at her side, noting as ever the cut of his tabard over the broadness of his shoulders, the handsome features, the compelling dark flash of his eyes as they fixed upon her. "We were merely discussing Giles's need of a wife."

The earl laughed deeply and exchanged a look of sympathy with Giles. "Giles, you are in serious jeopardy; you may as well count yourself wedded. Who is the fortunate lady to be?"

"No one as yet," Giles grumbled, the humor in his eyes belying his growl. "But I am certain that we shall both be advised momentarily who my life-mate shall be."

"Cease and let be!" Eleanor threw up her hands in mock defeat. "Would I attempt to throw reason between the two of you? Would I force my will upon either of you?"

"Without question," they answered in unison.

"Go rot," she snapped, as her eyes began to twinkle.

The men chuckled, exchanging amused glances. "I cannot aid you here, Giles," Simon drawled, leaning back comfortably in his chair. "I admit, only this once, to agreeing with my lady. If you are to protect your lands, it can only be done with an heir, and for that you must have a wife."

"One that *I* shall choose, as my right," Giles countered easily. "My position does not draw the interest of the Crown, as my lands were granted beyond its writ and there is no title to be considered."

"You are the king's nephew," Eleanor said. "If not through me, then by Isabella's marriage to my brother, Richard."

"Nay, Henry has much more important matters to dwell upon than the bastard son of his former favorite. I am safe enough, and glad for it."

Noting Eleanor's look of determination, Simon came to Giles's aid and changed the subject. "I understand that Edward offered some rather unusual entertainment last evening," he said, grinning. "It recalls my days as a bachelor knight—days happily gone," he added hastily, glancing at his wife, who smiled sweetly but with a dangerous flare in her eyes.

"Unusual? Aye, it was that," Giles agreed. "Our prince endeavors to make a good impression—one way or another. I cannot but wonder why."

"Perhaps he has begun to realize the importance of his position," Simon said smoothly. "I think that, perhaps, Oxford began it for him. Being held with the King's Men under siege at Winchester Castle proved a rather sobering experience."

"He should have divorced himself from the Lusignans

then and there, instead of aligning himself with them," Giles grumbled. "He is fortunate that the barons did not exile him along with the rest."

"I insisted that he be allowed to remain," Simon countered. "Edward is England's future—I would not have him exiled with that nest of vipers."

"Why is he here, Simon?" Giles asked bluntly.

"According to the Provisions, parliament is to be held three times a year, no longer only when the king calls it. It is for that Edward has come."

"Parliament is not to be held for months. Besides, I did not ask why he was in London, but why he has been here—at Durham House. Simon, as the leader of the barons, you are responsible for curbing the king's powers; yet you closet yourself with the son—"

"Closet myself?" Simon laughed. "Giles, our visits have hardly been clandestine. Edward sought me out for advice —most particularly on matters of warfare, points I began instructing him on in his earlier years—"

"And other subjects dear to a future sovereign, on points of ruling a kingdom?"

"That, too," Simon conceded.

"Are you certain he is not merely attempting to discover the finer points of your thinking? You may find your own subtleties coming back at you later, my earl of Leicester."

"Perhaps, but I will take that risk, Giles. I believe Edward to be worth it."

"I fear that there are few who share your confidence."

". . . and you are not among them."

"I am not. I see too much in my cousin that resembles his grandfather. The wounds that John Plantagenet inflicted upon this country have yet to heal; it is a sore time for another like him." Giles tossed off the remains of his tankard and rose from his chair. "You have my loyalty, milord, now as ever, but I cannot agree with you on this point. I can only pray that your decision does not lead you to the end of all that you are trying to do for England."

As the door closed behind him, Eleanor reached across the table and laid her hand over Simon's where it rested on the handle of his tankard. She smiled sadly at the grim look her husband wore as he stared at the closed door. "The rigidity of the young," she said softly. "He will come to understand, Simon. Give him time."

"Will he?" He turned his head and smiled at his wife, patting the hand that covered his. "Perhaps—or maybe he is correct. If God would grant me a wish at this moment, it would be to know once again a portion of that youthful assuredness. Life was so much simpler when one lived without doubts."

"Oh, Simon!" she exclaimed, laughing. "When was that, when we were toddling? Personally, that time is beyond my recall! Ever there were doubts, questions!"

"Not about the matters dear to men," he countered, shaking his head wearily. "Nay, in my youth I can remember only one question that would plague me."

"And that was?"

"Women," he said, grabbing her wrist to pull her around the table and into his lap. "And it plagues me still, though it has proved to be the one question that age has made enjoyable."

"Oh, and why is that, milord?" she asked, chuckling deep in her throat as he nuzzled the nape of her neck.

"Because, my love, long ago I capitulated and resigned myself to being the willing slave to your superior designs. Lead me, Eleanor, I surrender."

Giles paused after he closed the door behind him, taking several moments to contain the anger he had not wanted to show to Simon. With every fiber of his being he believed that Simon was walking into a trap of Edward Plantagenet's making. He shuddered, aflame with a desperate feeling of helplessness. He believed Simon to be the salvation of England; and if Giles was right about this trap and Simon should fall, there would be no one, *no one,* to take his place.

He walked slowly down the hall, his mind searching for a solution. Finally, he sighed heavily. For the moment there was only one thing to be done: find Rodger and, as his friend had suggested, seek a hidey-hole. For a few blessed hours he'd put the subject aside—bloody all of it.

The following morning found Giles grasping the edge of a table as he tried to focus on what was being said. His head pounded relentlessly like a hammer marking Eleanor's words, and his mouth felt as if something had sucked all the moisture from it.

"You want me to do what?" he gasped, wishing his

stomach would cease its relentless churning. Distantly he reflected on the pleasures of the past night, recalling what a humorous fellow he had been, the giggles he had brought forth from his buxom companion—those he vividly remembered. Could that have been the same man?

"Find her," Eleanor repeated, ignoring the desperate rolling of his eyes.

"Why me?" Giles said hoarsely.

"Because I can trust you." Eleanor shook her head, puzzled. "It is amazing—but no one told me of her disappearance for two entire days. In any case, I promised her father that she would be cared for. I am depending upon you, Giles."

Damnation. Giles left the solar, pulling the door gently closed behind him. He swore again as he leaned against the wall for a moment, willing the pounding in his head to stop. Where had the chit gotten to? And by the blood of Saint George, why him? Pushing himself away from the wall, he made his way to his chambers, where he doused his head with cold water and changed into fresh clothes, trying to give thought to his quest. Find her. Oh, he would find her—and then, God help her. What was he, her keeper? Roanna Royston, you are more trouble than you are worth, he mused, and I rue the day I first spied you with that damn goat.

3

Biting her lower lip, Roanna managed a calm smile as she looked up through her lashes at the immense form before her. Her gaze rested momentarily on his beefy hands where they gripped the edge of the table, then moved up to his face, wincing at the anger she saw there.

"Good morning, Uncle! Was yer trip successful?" she blurted out, ignoring her aunt's incredulous grunt.

"None of that!" he growled. "Does Lady Eleanor know that ye've gone?"

"Nay," Roanna answered without hesitation, unable to lie to this man who had been a father to her. "I told no one when I left."

"By the Blood, lass!" His voice became strained and the skin around his heavy black brows turned red. "Ye just left? But why? 'ow'll I explain it?"

"You'll not 'ave to," Roanna said soothingly, knowing how the silent, soft appeal of her eyes would affect this gentle giant. "Uncle Roscoe, there be no 'ope for me there. This is where I belong!"

"Well, now." The burly man shifted his weight uncomfortably and pondered her appeal. "Ye can stay the night," he grumbled finally. "I understand as 'ow ye may be 'omesick. But in the mornin' ye'll go back. Do ye 'ear me now?"

"Aye, Uncle. If that's all I'm to 'ave," she answered

demurely, hiding her pleasure. One day at a time, she mused.

The large man plopped into a chair across the table from her as the hired kitchen girl, Jolyn, scurried from where she was turning the roasting meat over the fire to dish up her employer's meal. As Roscoe attacked his stew, Roanna leaned her elbows on the table, resting her chin in her hands and affecting a look of innocent curiosity.

"Uncle, tell me of Eleanor de Monfort."

Roscoe's beefy face gathered into a frown at his niece's question. His tongue flicked out to catch a dribble of gravy that threatened his chin. "I told ye afore ye went there, lass. She be the countess of Leicester, yer father's lady, to whom 'e owed allegiance as 'er steward."

"Nay, not that. I want to know more about 'er." Roanna's eyes glinted. "No one knows more about the peers of England than the owner of the Flying Sail Tavern, where merchants meet to talk in their cups of England's affairs."

Roscoe's eyes narrowed at this obvious flattery, and he paused between mouthfuls. Then his dark eyes took on a decided twinkle. "And why would ye be wantin' to know, a mere slip of a lass like yerself?"

"Because ye raised me, Roscoe Dorking. Behind that gruff front ye do not miss a word that's said in London. Tell me about Eleanor de Monfort."

"Tell 'er, Roscoe," Matilda said, laughing softly. She dropped a basket of manchet bread, fresh from the oven, on the table before she turned back to her tasks.

The man was at a loss, glancing at his wife, whom he loved to distraction, and then at the girl who had been his only child. He shrugged, slouching over his bowl in a gesture of resignation that disguised the feeling of pleasure that welled up in him. He was the most blessed of men, he mused, to be loved so by two such women. "What would ye know?"

"Tell me about the time afore she married Simon de Monfort."

"Ah, well, now. The poor lass. For thirteen years she lived in those great 'alls of Windsor after 'er first 'usband died, not knowin' the love of a man, until Earl Simon came into 'er life. And come 'e did, fresh from the Continent, demanding 'is rights as lord of Leicester from King 'enry."

"I thought ye despised foreigners," Roanna asked with a doubtful arch to her fine brow.

"I do, I do, lass," Roscoe said, frowning. "But Simon is different. 'e cares for the common man, though where 'e comes by it I can't say. A good sort. But yer distractin' me from yer question. Lady Eleanor lived like a nun, declarin' openly that she 'ad taken vows of chastity, she grieved so for the loss of Marshal—"

"Will Marshal," Roanna interrupted. "'er first 'usband. Aye, tell me about 'im."

"Will Marshal?" Roscoe frowned, glancing at his niece as his thoughts shifted. "Ah, there was a good one! England's loss. The make of 'is father, the Good Knight—and I could fill ye wi' stories about *that* one," Roscoe added with reverence. "Men fer England were the Marshals. 'Twas Will Marshal who 'eld King 'enry at bay, no doubt of it. The only one who could bring 'enry to reason."

"Is it true 'e was murdered?"

Roscoe's brows lifted at the question, and his brown eyes darkened. "I believe it, lass, though it cannot be proved. There's been no family more powerful than the Marshals— a dire threat to their enemies, to be sure. Between them and their relations, they controlled most 'alf of England's 'oldings. Uncrowned kings, lass."

"Then . . . the king would not 'ave been displeased by their loss of power," Roanna said thoughtfully. "I mean, friendship aside, such power must 'ave been a threat to the throne."

"Ah, there ye 'ave it." Roscoe nodded, pleased at the girl's shrewdness. "Oh, King 'enry's affection for Will Marshal would not allow treachery, be assured of it. But if others deemed the earl of Pembroke's power too great, and once the favorite's presence be no longer an issue, the remainin' brothers be a matter the throne could well turn its back to. Understand?"

"Aye," she said, nodding solemnly.

"And more the worse for England," Roscoe said tightly. "When they passed, there was none other to contest for England. Until Simon de Monfort."

"Eleanor seems a good judge of men," Roanna mused.

"What—oh, I suppose so," Roscoe conceded.

"And what of Giles fitzWilliam?" Roanna asked innocently.

"Who?" Roscoe frowned, then pondered her question. "Will Marshal's bastard son, I 'ave 'eard of 'im. It be rumored that 'is mother was of the nobility. God knows that the earl went to great effort to keep the lad at 'is side. Moreover, Lady Eleanor seemed to accept 'im, a mark of the lad's promise, I suppose. Perhaps the only mismark of the curse."

"The curse?" Roanna blinked, then bent forward, peering at her uncle impatiently as he drew deeply from his tankard of ale. "Ye cannot leave the story there!" she protested, laying a hand on his arm. "What curse?"

"Lud, child, 'ave ye never 'eard of it? The curse—the curse upon the Good Knight. Everyone in London knows of it, perhaps all of England."

"Well, I don't," Roanna protested. "Tell me, please!"

"Roanna wasn't even born when it 'appened, Roscoe," Matilda said, dropping into a chair across from him and pouring a tankard of ale for a well-deserved break. "'Twas laid upon 'im by the bishop of Ferns, lass. Those blasted Irish—trouble looks fer 'em, and finds 'em right enough. Anyway, there were some dispute in Ireland over land the Good Knight 'eld there fer 'is wife, Isabel deClare."

"The ol' bishop was a right choleric man," Roscoe picked up, glaring at his wife for taking over his story. "'e laid claim to the same lands as William Marshal felt to be 'is. William 'ad no doubt that the lands be 'is, as 'e'd won 'em during Ireland's civil wars. The bishop fought every legal claim, even to King 'enry, who supported the Good Knight. Finally, the churchman damned William wi' excommunication. Well, Marshal wouldn't give in. When 'e died, King 'enry began to worry about 'is own soul, what wi' the ol' bishop still pressin' 'is claim and all, an' swearin' to excommunicate all involved. So the king asks Will, the son, to give over the lands. Will refused, and 'twas then that the ol' miser laid 'is curse."

Roanna squirmed impatiently as Roscoe paused to take a long pull from his tankard. Drawing the back of his hand over his mouth, he said, "Let's see now, 'ow did it go? I disremember all of it, somethin' about 'is church bein' despoiled an' all, but the gist of 'twas that in one generation the Marshal name would be destroyed—that their sons would be wi'out increase and their in'eritance would be scattered."

"And were they—was it?"

"That they were, lass, all died wi'out legal issue. Odd fer them too, it was. An 'ardy family, they was. Old William and 'is lady had a flock of children, and not one of 'em died as babes. Will and 'is brothers be strong men, yet each of 'em died sudden-like, after they be made Marshal of England. Moreover, while they 'ad bastards about, not one of 'em 'ad a babe by 'is lady, though all the women were proved fertile with other 'usbands, afore or after. Yep, they was cursed, all right."

"Or murdered," Roanna said reflectively.

"A curse still, to my way of thinkin'. As fer that, enough stories fer now. This inn'll be cursed, by those in the taproom, if I don't see to business."

Roanna watched the door close behind her uncle, thinking upon what he had told her. Fascinating, but it still didn't answer her questions about Eleanor or the manner of the man who had taken her to wife at such a tender age. Lud, she didn't even know why she wanted to know. She never wanted to see any of them again, so why should she care, after all? One thing was certain: she was *not* going back there! Her cheeks grew hot as she remembered the fool she had made of herself, guessing at the stories that must be flying about the halls of Durham House. Nay, she definitely was not going back.

Determined, she rose from her chair and grabbed an apron from a hook by the door. Tying it about her waist, she left the kitchen and her aunt's bemused look, eager for her duties in the taproom.

She moved among the tables toward the long trestle bar, pausing to greet old friends with an exchange of friendly barbs, turning their rude suggestions back with a few of her own. Reaching the board, she took up the two tankards her uncle had just shoved across the polished wood toward a barmaid.

His dark brows fell into a scowl. "And what d'ye think ye be doin', lass?" he growled.

"Earnin' my supper, Uncle," she said, smiling. "Ye did give me till tomorrow, remember?"

"Till tomorrow," he grumbled after a moment, then jerked his head toward the other side of the dark room. "Them tankards be fer the two ship's mates, next to the draper." His frown deepened to hide a glint of amusement as she gave him a delighted smile and turned toward the dry-mouthed sailors. With a swish of her skirts, she sauntered toward the tables.

The afternoon passed all too quickly to suit her, and the supper pots had been scrubbed before Roanna began to get the germ of an idea of how to convince her uncle to allow her to stay. It came with the evening round of customers, and a brief encounter with a burly tradesman who had judged Roanna as a delectable piece he thought would be better served in his lap. A sharp elbow to the ribs and boot to the instep settled the immediate issue quickly enough, but as she returned to the board and noticed that her uncle had witnessed the exchange, an idea began to kindle.

"I see that a fortnight or two among the gentle set didn't slow ye down any," Roscoe chuckled as she leaned against the board.

Oh, sweet justice! He had played right into her hands. "Oh, that," she scoffed, glancing back at the tradesman, who was glaring painfully at his laughing companions. "'Twas nothin'. I could 'andle the likes of 'im when I was ten, as ye well know. I wish I could say the same . . ." She let her voice trail off and shrugged one slender shoulder, as if to dismiss what she had been about to say.

"Eh, what's that?" Roscoe frowned and stared at his niece.

"Oh—'tis nothin'."

"Tell me, luv. What's botherin' ye?"

"'Tis just that—oh, Uncle Roscoe, I don't want to upset ye. After all's said, what can ye do about it?"

"About what? I can't do anythin' if ye don't tell me! Out wi' it!"

"The irony is . . ." She sighed raggedly. "My father wanted me at Durham 'ouse to improve my station. Yet—there be little chance that I'll be more than bedmate fer some bleedin' lord."

"What's that?" Roscoe choked out, his beefy face flushing. "'as someone—"

"Oh, not yet!" she assured him quickly. "But 'tis only a matter of time. There be"—she swallowed heavily—"one already, who 'as suggested that 'twill soon be my fate—and what can I do about it?"

"Ye tell Lady Eleanor, that's what! She'll see there be none who'll bother ye!"

"Lady Eleanor cannot watch out fer me all the time, Uncle. The truth of it is, I'm not one of 'er well-born ladies; I'm not respected, like 'ere. And there's one most of all—'e frightens me!"

"Well, now, we'll see about that," Roscoe growled, the angry sound rolling up from his massive chest. "Do not worry, luv, I'll not be sendin' ye back there till yer safely put, my word on it."

"Aye, Uncle, whatever ye think best," she demurred, and turned away before he could see her mouth twitch with a satisfied smile she could not contain.

Life was really quite grand—when you could control it, Roanna thought happily as she worked through the evening. However, one thought did keep pressing on her, darting through her mind at odd moments: she would never see Giles fitzWilliam again. Not that she should care, she told herself as she served a bowl of steaming stew to one of the few remaining customers who was not falling into his cups. The other barmaids had gone home—or were involved in business of their own abovestairs with overnight guests— and Roscoe had joined Matilda in the kitchen for their evening cup of warm, spiced wine, so Roanna worked alone.

In the quiet, she faced the thoughts that had been plaguing her, determined to come to grips with them. Her every encounter with him had been a burning agony of humiliation. But it was natural that she should remember him, she assured herself. Why shouldn't she remember the broadness of his shoulders beneath the fine cut of his chanise and surcoat, the gentle curling of his rich chestnut hair, the startling blue of his eyes and the way the corners crinkled when he smiled? Of course she would remember him, as any lass would recall moments spent with a handsome knight. In fact, now that she knew she would never see him again, she could almost look back on what had happened with some measure of humor. Almost.

Humming, she hitched the top of her slipping skirt back into her belt, raising the hem to her ankles so that she would not trip when she removed the trays of empty tankards and bowls and the remains of the succulent meat pies favored by the customers of the Flying Sail. Her hips swaying pleasantly with her mood, she approached a booth on the far wall to take the order of a cloaked latecomer, whom she had seen enter from the corner of her eye. Setting her hand on her hip, she smiled at the man, whose head and shoulders were shadowed by the high booth wall.

"Lud, sir, yer candle is out," she observed, and turned to the table behind her to pick up the squat candle burning there. She bent over to relight the extinguished candle in the booth and glanced up, smiling. "That should be better — You!" she gasped, jerking upright.

His hand shot out too late to grab the candle she was holding. The hot wax had dripped onto her wrist, and she dropped the candle into the rushes at her feet. He was out of the booth in an instant, crushing the small flames catching in the straw and swearing under his breath.

"What're ye doin' 'ere?" she snapped furiously, oblivious to the harm she had almost done. "I don't want ye—!" The rest of her words came out in a squeak as she was abruptly lifted off her feet and thrown flat on her back on the table. "What're ye doin'!" she shrieked. He threw his cloak over her, and then sat on her and thwacked her! The bloody sot was beating her!

She screamed, the sound muffled in the full mantle, and began to struggle frantically. Images of suffocation flashed through her mind when she was suddenly lifted up, twisted about, and plopped roughly down on the bench in the corner of the booth.

"Be still, Roanna!" he warned blackly as he tossed the mantle onto the opposite bench, then slid in next to her. "Damnation! That was a new cloak!"

"Ye're bleedin' mad!" she hissed, trying to scoot farther away from him, only to find the wall at her back.

"Me?" he asked, rolling his eyes. "Roanna Royston, you have been nothing but trouble for me since the first time I set eyes on you!"

"Ye throw me down, sit on me, hit me, and then ye say that *I'm* trouble?" she exclaimed indignantly.

Reaching under the table, he grabbed her skirt. Good God, what was the madman doing now? Her hands flew to stop him—and then suddenly she felt sick all over. He was holding the hem of her skirt before her face, his eyes glittering angrily at her over the scorched fabric.

"Oh," she said softly.

"Oh," he repeated with a snort, dropping her skirt.

She smoothed it down with badly damaged dignity. "My thanks, Sir Giles," she said stiffly.

"Please, do not thank me, Roanna," he groaned. "Just get your things so we can go."

"Go?" She blinked, her back stiffening. "I'm not goin' anywhere wi' ye!"

"Aye, you are. Now. I am taking you back to Durham House."

She swallowed heavily. "'ow did ye find me?"

"That was easy—a varmint always returns to its lair. I would have been here sooner, but I had other demands upon my time, all more pressing than spending the day tracking you down."

"No one asked ye to!" she said huffily.

"If that was true, I would not be here," he said, grimacing. "Lady Eleanor is worried about you."

"Well, now that ye've found me and ye can see I be quite safe, ye can tell 'er that she no longer need be concerned."

"Oh, nay. I have been ordered to bring you back, and that is exactly what I am going to do."

She stared at him for a moment, seeing the determination written in his face. Her heart sank. He meant what he said. There was only one alternative, she reasoned, plotting her escape path. Appearing to capitulate, she looked up at him and sighed. She moved her hand toward the candle and flicked at the flame. "Well, then. I imagine there be no way I can convince ye to tell Lady Eleanor ye couldn't find me."

"None."

"That's what I thought." She pinched the wick, plunging the booth into sudden darkness; bunching her skirt, she leapt up, intent upon scrambling across the table to the bench on the other side and freedom. She found herself flat on her back again, with Giles bent over her, his face inches from her own.

"Going somewhere? Not without me, Roanna," he said softly. Suddenly the entire room above them seemed to go black. From his position above Roanna, Giles wrenched his head up, and stared at the mountain that had blocked out the light.

"Well, now, lad," a deep, rumbling voice said. "That's my niece ye've got there beneath ye."

Giles straightened up. Sinking back down on the bench,

he stared up at the massive form, wondering how this animal could possibly be related to the slender, unassuming steward he had known to be Roanna's father. "I've been sent by the Countess Leicester to return Roanna to Durham House," he said reasonably.

"Oh, I do not think so," Roscoe answered quietly. "Not as things be." He glanced at his niece, who was slithering off the table.

Giles stood up, measuring himself against the larger man. Though he knew himself to be above average height, having attained the stature of his father and grandfather, the other man towered over him by a full hand—at least. And he was twice as broad, and all muscle, if Giles was any judge. Damn, he thought, here was another mess she had gotten him into! "As I said, I am here by Lady Eleanor's order, to see Roanna safely back to Durham House."

"Ye 'ave an odd way of carryin' out yer order," the other man drawled.

"What you saw—it's not what it appears. I assure you that I mean your niece no harm."

"As I said, she'll not be goin' back till matters that be weighin' on me be well settled." He glanced back at Roanna, who was peeking out from behind him. It was not lost on him that she was sporting a most satisfied smile. "Go fetch us some ale, lass. We've some talkin' to do."

Sending the reluctant Roanna on her way with a stern look, Roscoe gestured for Giles to sit and then took the bench across from him. "I be Roscoe Dorking, Roanna's uncle. My wife was sister to the lass's father, may 'e be wi' God. And who might ye be, lad?"

"Giles fitzWilliam, knight in service to the countess of Leicester," Giles answered smoothly, his tense muscles easing. He ventured a smile, but it faded as he noted the surprised look that came over the other man's face and the puzzled glance he threw in Roanna's direction. His alarm rekindled when the large man's questioning gaze shifted back to him and the dark eyes flickered, then gleamed with anger.

Roanna set the tankards on the table and began to sit down, but Roscoe caught her arm and pushed her up to her feet. "Go to the kitchen and wait wi' Matilda. Now!" he snapped, seeing her reluctance. "Do not come back till I call ye." When he heard the door slam behind her he turned

back to Giles. "Now, then, lad. I want some plain speakin'
—*not now!*" he roared at one of the remaining customers
who had dared to ask for more ale. *"Be gone!* The Flying
Sail be closed!" Ignoring the sudden scurrying toward the
door, Roscoe's eyes were grimly pinpointed on Giles, who
suddenly wished he had brought some of his men. "Ye say
yer Giles fitzWilliam. Will Marshal's bastard?"

"I am."

"Yer father was a good man, as was yer grandfather. I
revered 'em both, as did all good men in England." He
paused and sighed. "It's only fer that, mind, I'll not be
feedin' ye yer liver. A sorry day, lad, a sorry day." Roscoe
shook his head sadly.

Giles stared at him, bewildered. "What—" He cleared
his throat and began again. "Just what is it that I am
supposed to have done?" Somehow, he knew, Roanna was
behind this.

"Well, now. 'Tis an awkward thing fer a man to speak of
wi' another. But ye gotta know that girl's like me own.
When 'er father decided 'e wanted a better life fer 'er, I tried
to tell 'im she wasn't right fer service. But, nay, 'e 'ad to 'ave
'is way. Wanted to give 'er what he never gave 'er in
life—'ad no way, not 'avin' a wife and all. Insisted she
become a lady. I tried, traded goods wi' those who could
teach 'er to speak right, and sew and such. Then sent 'er to
Durham 'ouse when Lady Eleanor said it was time. For
what, I ask? For what?"

Giles tried to keep pace with Roscoe's reasoning, losing it
about halfway along. His mind sought a solution, but there
was little he could say. "Indeed," he agreed with a sympa-
thetic nod. "For what?"

"Ye ask that!"

Giles's stomach flipped as Roscoe's face turned an ominous red.

"God's Teeth, lad! Lud, I know she's a delightful bit of
fluff, a temptation fer any man! But she's nothin' to trifle
wi', do ye understand?"

Trifle?

"Oh, she didn't say it was ye, but I'm no fool. The
questions she asked me today about ye—well, I can set a log
upon another, be sure of that!"

"I'm certain you can."

"So, now. What are ye goin' to do about it?"

Do about what? Giles wanted to ask, but he restrained himself. "I assure you, Dorking, whatever ill befell Roanna at Durham House, it was not of my doing. On the souls of my father and grandfather," he added as an inspired afterthought, "my interest in her has been only in the most—the most protective sort of way. Like a brother."

Roscoe studied him for a long moment, and Giles was gratified to see the easing of the muscles in his face. Then the giant sighed. "I'm glad 'twas not ye, lad. 'Twould sorrow me deeply to 'arm the son of the Marshal, believe me. But ye see my problem. She's not safe at Durham 'ouse, the way things are. She's a tender lass, ignorant in the ways of the world. Soft and pliable, she is, open for the smooth words of some young buck. I fear for 'er, such as things be, do ye see my meanin'?"

Giles wondered if they were speaking of the same girl. "Of course. I promise you, Dorking, I shall see to her welfare."

"Will ye personally guarantee it?" Roscoe pressed, leaning toward Giles.

"I will," Giles assured him, wishing he had remained in Ireland.

"Good," the larger man grunted. "Ye see, fitzWilliam, 'tis a matter most dear to me heart. I take what ye say as a matter of personal honor, 'tween ye and me." The handle of Roscoe's pewter tankard crinkled slightly in his hand with his last words, a fact which Giles noted.

"You have the word of a knight, Roscoe Dorking. Your niece shall come to no harm in my keeping."

"Well, now!" Roscoe exclaimed happily. "'Tis all I wanted! Roanna!" he bellowed. Roanna appeared so quickly that one would have thought she had been listening at the door. "Get yer things, yer goin' back to Durham 'ouse." He beamed at her.

"Nay!" she cried.

"Now!" Roscoe roared, sending her scurrying. Leaning toward Giles, he grinned broadly. "Oftentimes ye 'ave to let 'em know ye mean business, lad."

"I'll try to remember that," Giles answered dryly.

A few minutes later, Roscoe opened the door to the bedchamber where Roanna was stuffing the last of her things into her bag. From her angry gestures, it was not difficult to judge her mood. "Lass, 'tis for the best," he said lamely.

"If ye say so."

"'Tis what yer father wanted," he pressed, his own heart silently breaking.

"Oh, and we know 'ow important that be!" she said grimly as she tied the strings of the sack. "My father—a man who found no place for me in 'is life until 'e lay dying. Only then 'e thinks of me, decidin' my future, and off I go to a life caterin' to the needs of others who think themselves beyond me. Oh, I shall be a lady, or as much of one as my dear, departed father could see for me. I wonder, Uncle, what lies ahead of me?"

"Roanna . . ."

The gruff voice, softened with pain, brought her into his arms. "I'm sorry," she gasped between sobs, clinging to this man who loved her so. "I did not mean to hurt ye. 'Tis not yer fault!" She drew away to look into his rough, beloved face. Smiling through her tears, she wiped them away with the back of her hand. "They're really not such bad sorts —some are good, after all. I'll find the best, I promise ye I will. I'll be all right." Pulling away, she sniffed, closing her sack.

"I know ye will be, lass. I know ye will. FitzWilliam promised 'e'd see ye well cared fer." He saw the defeated slump of her shoulders as she gazed at the bundle on the bed. "Come now, 'tis time to go. 'e be waitin' for ye," he said gruffly, picking up the sack.

With one thick arm about her shoulders, he walked with her down the hallway to the stairs. Suddenly a thought struck him, and he stopped, turning to regard her strangely. "Tell me somethin', lass. 'Twas an odd situation I found ye in wi' fitzWilliam. Why did ye not shout out fer me, when 'e 'ad ye there beneath 'im on the table?" In fact, how had she come to be there at all? he wondered.

She shrugged. "It 'appened so fast—I didn't think of it."

"I see." Roscoe nodded solemnly. "'e just, er, took ye by surprise and overpowered ye."

"That was it."

"I see," Roscoe repeated thoughtfully.

As they entered the taproom, Giles came forward and took Roanna's bag from him. "Are you ready, Roanna?"

"Ready?" Her head jerked up and rage flared in her eyes.

"I'll never be ready for this, ye bleedin' sot! Why can't ye let me be? Yer always interferin'—"

"Do not make this harder than it is, you little chit! If you don't behave, I swear that—" Suddenly remembering Roscoe, Giles stifled the rest of his words and turned to stride toward the door, where he paused to wait for her.

Roscoe watched this exchange with interest, his bushy brows rising slightly. "Go on, now, lass," he said after a moment, pushing her gently toward Giles. "'Tis time ye got on wi' yer life."

As the door closed behind them, he stared at it for a long moment. Then he chuckled, the deep sound rolling around the timbered room. "On wi' yer life, Roanna, and all it 'olds for ye." Hearing a pot clattering in the kitchen, his dark eyes fired with a new light. "And I shall be on wi' mine. Never did finish that mulled wine." He leaned over to blow out the remaining candle.

4

Giles stared as the room about him became unfocused. He could feel blood surging through his heart, which seemed to have skipped a beat. He was aware that his palms had become clammy, and that he had been rendered totally mute. He could only stare, silently, into two large pools of violet, his senses assaulted by a lingering scent of roses. Then lilies came to his mind, soft white petals kissed with the lingering dew of morning.

". . . Lisette d'Quincey, daughter of Rie d'Quincey, count of Vachel," Eleanor said smoothly, completing the introduction. Then, miraculously, the vision spoke to him and he found his voice.

"Milady," Giles murmured, bending over a hand whose touch made him light-headed.

"Lisette's father was our most gracious host during our recent stay in Gascony," Simon said lightly, his dark eyes dancing with amusement as he observed Giles's reaction. "I am pleased to say that we have been allowed to return the favor. Lady Lisette has gifted us with her presence for an extended stay."

"The pleasure is completely mine, Lord Simon," the vision protested, the heavy Gascon accent of her lilting voice ringing in Giles's ears. Then she turned back to him and he was again lost in those incredible violet eyes. "You did not accompany Lord Simon to the Continent, Sir

Giles," she said with a soft smile. "I am certain that I would have remembered meeting you."

"My lands are in Wales and Ireland, milady. I have not been away from them in the past few years—now to my sincere regret." Glancing about, Giles was gratified to note that Lady d'Quincey's arrival had coincided with a quiet moment at Durham House. But he knew that soon the household would gather for the midmeal, and the bachelors would begin to swarm about this bit of nectar like the proverbial bees around honey. He fully planned to use the advantage of being the first to meet her.

Eleanor, always in tune with the heart of the matter, glanced at her husband, who was grinning at the young couple. She laid a hand on his arm. "I find myself in the mood for a game of chess, milord? Will you humor me?"

As the lord and lady of the house drew away to a game table near the massive hearth of the great hall, Giles considered his next move.

"Ale?"

Giles turned to find Roanna standing near him, a tray in her hands. "I think not, Roanna. Some light wine perhaps?" he suggested gently to the slender form at his side.

Lisette answered his suggestion with a sweet smile. "Aye, some wine would be refreshing, Sir Giles—well-watered, of course."

"Ale be better on a 'ot day than sweet wine," Roanna countered, staring at the other woman.

"Roanna," Giles said firmly, his voice touched with annoyance. "The lady would like some wine."

"Whatever ye say, luv." Roanna shrugged. "Sweet wine, it is."

Giles's eyes darkened with anger as Roanna swished past them. Damn, he thought, now what had gotten into her? In the past fortnight since he had brought her back to Durham House, he had thought she was beginning to behave herself. At least she had not caused any more trouble. She had even taken his advice and started wearing her hair up under a linen cap. He had begun noticing the interest of other men when she had passed by—not that he could blame them; that red-gold mass of silk was what had first caught his eye, after all. But when he'd overheard some bawdy conversation in the knights' quarters regarding a certain succulent, golden-haired wench, he had become determined to take action.

His gaze passed over her departing form with approval. The shapeless kirtle she wore should help to keep the bucks at bay, now that she was wearing a cap—though he noticed that she continually tugged at the latter, and he had a suspicion that it would not last long.

But thoughts of Roanna were quickly dismissed as his attention was again drawn to the slender form dressed in a gown of light blue silk, the color accentuating lavender eyes fringed in heavy black lashes. Her creamy skin was touched with the sun of Gascony, and her raven hair hung in soft curls beneath the sheer veil of sarcenet. Her lovely, lilting voice bewitched him.

He drew her to a bench along the wall beneath the high glazed windows. There, light conversation soon gave way to Giles's determination to woo Lady Lisette d'Quincey in a manner that would withstand the impending assault by his cohorts. Taking up a lyre, he began to tune the instrument, knowing that she would beg him for a song, and only too happy to comply.

His pleasing voice drifted out into the hall as he recounted a selection of love songs designed to melt the most recalcitrant heart. Roanna returned with the wine, placing it on a table near them, and then paused to listen. He began a new lyric of tragic lovers, star-crossed in their eternal need of each other. She listened for a moment, then snorted, rolling her eyes in disbelief as she turned and left.

As he finished the last lines, Lisette clapped her hands and laughed delightedly, a sound that caught at Giles's heart. "Sir Giles!" she exclaimed. "You have the gift of a bard! I have not heard such a pleasing recounting since my last moments at Louis's court! Be truthful—you are no mere courtier, you have been trained as a troubadour!"

"Nay, milady, not I. But I do confess that my uncle was a goliard. 'Twas from him that I learned to play."

"A goliard!" she gasped. "How perfectly scandalous! You are teasing me!"

"I fear not. He was a defrocked Franciscan who made his way through life offering blasphemous and treasonous song, decrying Crown and Church—but he had the true gift of the troubadours."

"And was he a murderer, a seducer of maids?" she asked breathlessly, leaning forward, her eyes wide with expectation.

"I would be cautious, were I ye," Roanna interrupted, appearing again to set a plate of sweetmeats with the wine. "I 'ear that such things run in the blood."

Giles looked up, his eyes flaring with anger, but Roanna had swished away again before he could react. He smiled apologetically at Lisette, whose fair brow was drawn as she stared after the departing maid. "An impudent girl," she said with wonder. "Perhaps I should speak to Lady Eleanor about her."

"Ignore her," Giles said, shrugging, even as he made a mental note of due punishment for Roanna. "Another song, milady?"

"Oh, aye, please!" She smiled, forgetting the awkward moment.

The morning hours wore gently on until the bell for midmeal brought with it the deep sounds of male laughter and the lighter merriment of ladies. Soon the large, narrow hall was filled with brightly colored gowns and the buzz of conversation, and, as Giles had anticipated, the bees immediately swarmed about the honey. Giles stood back, leaning against a support of the screen that hid the passage to the kitchens, watching the flirtations with an easy smile. His fellows had played into his hands, as he'd known they would, clustering about and fussing over her, each vying for attention while none stood out. He had reserved that honor for himself. Indeed, it was time to retreat, to be remembered as an island of gentle flattery and attentive amusement, apart from the exhaustive demands of the other bachelor knights.

"Oops."

He heard a soft gasp and the swish of skirts behind him. Twisting about, he caught Roanna's arm as she turned to flee back toward the kitchens. "Oh, no, you don't," he said grimly, pulling her behind the privacy of the screen.

"Let me go!" she hissed, trying to twist from his grasp.

"What in the hell were you trying to do in there?" he hissed back, tightening his grip.

"What are ye blatherin' about?"

"Blathering, am I? You know what I'm talking about. Why were you so rude to Lady Lisette?"

"Ye mean that simpleton ye were gogglin' over? Oh, Sir Giles!" she mimicked, fluttering her eyelashes.

"Dammit, Roanna, what is the matter with you?" He glared at her, reaching up to yank her cap straight.

"Me? Nothin's the matter wi' me. Which is more than I can say for ye! Never 'eard such prattle." She tugged at her cap, and more red-gold curls escaped. Then her expression changed, and she looked at him keenly. "Yer uncle was truly a goliard?"

"My mother's half-brother," he grunted, frowning blackly. "Don't try to change the subject. Roanna, I swear that if you ever—"

"Ahem."

Their heads turned simultaneously to find Ackerley, the Durham House steward, standing in the passage, frowning at the tableau before him. "Is there a problem, Sir Giles?" the steward asked stiffly, regarding Roanna with suspicious displeasure.

"No problem—now," Giles assured him. Feeling a good measure of satisfaction, he turned and left abruptly, leaving Roanna to the annoyed steward.

As he stepped around the corner of the buttery screen, he stopped short, thoughts of Roanna swept from his mind. There, speaking with Simon, was his cousin Richard de-Clare, earl of Gloucester. As always, it was difficult for Giles to disguise his dislike for the eldest of the Marshal clan, and he paused, attempting to quell his emotions.

Richard had been eight years old when his father died, and he had been made a ward of Hubert deBurgh, chancellor of England. A few years later, by then the most eligible bachelor in England, he had fallen madly in love with Margotta, deBurgh's lovely daughter, and had secretly married the maid. King Henry's hatred of deBurgh, a feeling that reached back many years before Richard's birth, had been further inflamed by the illegal marriage. Separated by force, the youthful Margotta died, broken-hearted, and Richard was swiftly married off to Maud de Lacy, the daughter of the earl of Lincoln.

Giles often wondered how much that youthful bitterness had formed his cousin's character. Giles wanted to love his family and ever tried to excuse their weaknesses, even as he despised them. But try as he had over the years, he could not see his cousin for anything but what he was.

He paused in the shadow of the buttery screen and observed the tall, red-haired earl, trying yet again to see him objectively, to see in him some sign of his ancestors. He was broad-shouldered, a man who wore his expensively cut clothes with unmistakable grace, but there was a strength missing that Giles remembered in their forebears. His jaw seemed weak. His blue eyes darted, not quite expressing the determination that should be there. His voice faltered; instead of conviction, Giles heard only pompous lecturing.

Forcing himself from his musings, Giles reluctantly joined the group. Their words suddenly focused for him as he approached.

"Richard, I cannot agree with you," Simon was saying with strained control, his eyes sparking angrily. "England has seen enough of days where her wealth is wasted on the foreign favorites of the king and queen. We have seen too much of our lands and power given into the hands of royal relatives."

"You overstate the problem, Simon," Gloucester snorted. He held out his goblet, which was quickly refilled by his squire. "The baronage of England is what is at issue. Our rights must be protected at all costs. Your suggestion that the Crown is the servant of the people is preposterous! With each degree of power that the throne loses, so it is also for the nobility. My God, man, you would reduce us to the level of our villeins!"

Simon swallowed heavily, attempting to remain calm as he faced the rigidity of this man whose views were so diametrically opposed to his own. Yet, with him he shared the reins of England's leadership, including the heavy new responsibilities gained from the greatly reduced powers of the Crown.

"We shall see, milord," Simon said quietly. "When the barons meet at parliament, the matter shall be decided, once and for all."

"So it shall, Simon, so it shall. But you shall find that the barons vote with me—on that matter as well as on your intolerable suggestion regarding the composition of our parliament! Every reasonable man knows that the common man is well suited as he is; he cannot see more, as it is beyond his reasoning powers. Good Lord, what would they do with such a vote? They would look to their lords for guidance, as they have always done!"

"Lud, what dribble," a voice muttered.

Giles looked down to find Roanna at his side, carrying a fresh pitcher of ale. "Hush," he warned her.

She glanced up at him. "'e's a soddin' twit!" she hissed. "'ow can ye listen to that?"

"Roanna, be silent!" he repeated through clenched teeth.

"Bugger that."

He groaned and stepped in front of her just as Richard looked in their direction. "Go away, Roanna," he murmured.

"I was told to serve the ale," her voice said from behind him.

"Then serve it and go away!" he gritted, and nodded to his cousin, who was regarding him oddly. "Dammit, Roanna, this is not the Flying Sail!"

"That be truth," she said, stepping around him. "There, men speak reason."

He watched, guardedly, as she moved to set the tray on a table. Glancing about, he caught Ackerley's eye, and jerked his head in Roanna's direction. Understanding, the steward frowned and crossed the room to her quickly, bending to utter a few brief words. She turned to follow him back across the hall, pausing only to throw Giles a nasty glare. His brows rose slightly at the foul epithet she mouthed, and he chuckled softly as he turned back to the others. Refocusing on the conversation, he realized that Henry, Simon's eldest son, was speaking.

". . . it can only be decided, once and for all, by war —not by a meeting of parliament with King Henry at the head."

"Let us hope you are wrong, Henry," Simon said gravely. "We must believe in the law, never in anarchy or war. Parliament will convene soon, and there we may press for the enforcement of the Magna Carta and the Provisions." His eyes lightened as he paused for a moment and his smile became genuine. "This is as good a time as any to tell you—Lord Edward has joined us in our cause. He has pledged to support the rights of all Englishmen, in the council as well as in parliament. It is a turning point for us, gentlemen, for all of England."

Giles stared hard at Simon. "Edward supports this? He will stand against his father?"

"Nay, Giles, never that. But he will speak for us, for our

cause. He is certain that he can convince Henry to see reason."

"You believe that?"

"I believe in his word, Giles. He will attend parliament in support of the Provisions and the Great Charter."

Giles exchanged a long look with Simon, then turned away, unable to face the trust he saw there, while himself not believing a moment of it. He left the hall quickly, and went searching for his squire, suddenly feeling the need for the open English countryside.

The night was clear and dark, the slivered moon giving a ghostly light to the courtyard, woven with thin, wavering shadows. Giles moved silently to avoid disturbing the sleeping inhabitants of the thatched hovels attached to the walls of the bailey, as he walked on his nightly journey. Making his way to the parapet overlooking the Thames, he nodded as he passed the tower guard and sought out his accustomed spot. Settling himself comfortably against the merlon of the crenellated wall, he leaned back against the cold stone, gathering his cloak about him, and stared out at the slowly moving river beneath him.

Loneliness attacked him as it often did at such moments, striking relentlessly. So it had been for him since the day he had left Chepstow, the great castle in Wales that was once the seat of his father's power. He had not known then that he would never see his father again, nor that he would never return there. Oh, he had been asked again and again by his aunt Matilda to come. She was the Countess Bigod, whose husband, Hugh, had inherited the lands and the title of count of Striguil upon Will Marshal's death, to add to his own title of earl of Norfolk. Giles loved Matilda dearly, but he would never go back. He could not bear it.

These were the most painful moments, these hours when the rest of the world had succumbed to its dreams and he found himself wandering alone like a specter seeking its place on earth. Other men rose and retired with the sun, marking its coming and going to form their day. But not Giles. In this he was more Marshal than any other of his generation who could legally claim descent. This habit marked his loneliness, and his memory was sharp of the hours spent with those he loved. While the world had slept, he had shared the hopes and dreams of the day with his father, his grandmother, his aunts and uncles, before the warmth of a low fire—soft voices speaking, sharing. Now all were gone, and he was left with a treasured memory of a unique Marshal tradition, remembered and missed by him alone.

Sighing, he leaned his head back against the stone. Then he caught a glimpse of another form in the shadowy moonlight. Rising quietly from his place, he moved through the shadows of the wall, his hand falling to the hilt of his sword, only to drop away. She had turned when she heard him sigh, and she waited as he drew near. "Contemplating escape?" he asked, surprised to find her here at this hour.

"If I decide to leave again, I'll not need to contemplate it first."

"Perhaps it is your conscience that keeps you awake at this hour."

"Why should it?" she countered, then frowned. "Oh —thanks *ever* so much for turning Ackerley on me. The blighter threatened to 'ave me 'orsewhipped."

"He was wrong," Giles said tightly. "It is your uncle who should be horsewhipped."

"Promise I can see ye try it?"

"He should have taught you how to behave in polite company."

"Polite company? Ye mean that mindless sot who spoke tonight? Do ye believe that men must ask their lords 'ow to think?"

He saw no purpose in pointing out that the "mindless sot" was his cousin. "I think that you have been raised with too much freedom and not enough understanding. Whether you like it or not, Roanna, conditions exist that you do not understand. Unless you learn to keep silent, you will find yourself in a good deal of trouble. But you are changing the subject—as usual. Why are you out at this hour?"

"None of yer bloody business."

"Ah, but it is. Would you prefer that I call the guard and have you forcibly escorted back to your quarters?"

"Ye wouldn't!"

"Try me."

"I couldn't sleep," she answered sulkily. "I'm not used to beddin' so early—'tis 'ard not 'avin' someone to talk to.

When the tavern be shut for the night, we—Uncle Roscoe, Aunt Matilda, and me—we'd sit over a cup of mulled wine and talk. I miss that most of all, I think."

The shadows hid his surprise. The similarity between her words and his own recent thoughts struck him uncomfortably. Strangely, he felt invaded to find her thoughts and needs so closely paralleling his own. "What did you talk about?" he asked with a heavy edge of sarcasm. "The price of peppercorns and fish?" He felt a moment's satisfaction, hearing her sharp intake of breath. There was a long silence.

"Sometimes," she said at last, and he could hear the anger in her voice. "But mostly we talked of politics —matters of the realm—*milord.*"

He laughed shortly. "Come now, Roanna. Matters of the realm?"

She bristled, hearing the amusement in his voice. "'Tis the main topic of conversation in an alehouse, milord," she retorted. "At least, it is in one like the Flying Sail. Ye'd be surprised what is said in the back rooms where the guild merchants meet to share their cups."

"I can imagine."

"Don't 'umor me!"

"I would not dream of it."

"Ye really are insufferable, ye know, all of ye bloody sods. Ye prance about in yer fine linens pontificatin', runnin' other blokes' lives, and ye 'aven't any idea of what ye're talkin' about."

"Pontificating?" He laughed, beginning to enjoy the exchange. "What, in particular, comes to that wonderfully complex mind of yours?"

"I could tell ye—but ye don't really want to know. Fine manners is what ye want, and ye think that's all it takes to make 'polite company.' Well," she added primly, "I can speak nearly as well as ye—you, if I've a mind to. Aye, Uncle Roscoe saw to it that I was taught in speech and manners, for my future, he said. Frankly," she added, lapsing into her normal speech, "it never seemed bloody important—and now I'm bleedin' certain of it, from what I've seen of them what knows."

Giles was silent for a moment; then he chuckled softly. "My, my, Roanna. You are a constant source of amazement. Please, without any further pontificating from me, tell me what I don't know."

"Go rot in bloody 'ell."

"Come now, Roanna. If you wish to prove me wrong, you will have to be specific. Since you cannot, I have won the argument. The point is mine."

"Oh? Well, then, milord, try this point: Lord Simon will never 'ave the opportunity to present 'is position afore the barons."

"What do you mean?"

"Simply that there'll be no parliament."

"Roanna, you do not understand," he drawled with a patience that made her bristle. "New laws have been established in England. Parliament is no longer to be called only when the king wishes it—it will be held three times a year, the first to be at Candlemas. It is then that Simon will present his case."

"There'll be no parliament," she repeated. "If ye don't believe it, tell me why the king dallies in France."

"Partly because he is angry over the Provisions he was forced to sign at Oxford. Also because of the treaty he is making with Louis of France, declaring peace between our countries."

"Oh—the treaty," she said, dismissing it summarily. "That matter was settled months ago. So much fer that. But 'e's angry all right; that's why there'll be no parliament."

"I told you, 'tis not a matter for him to decide."

"Ah, but 'tis necessary for 'im to attend. Soon there'll be a letter on its way to the chief justiciar sayin' that 'e cannot possibly be back in time—more matters concernin' the treaty, so it says—and that the parliament will 'ave to be postponed."

Giles swore softly into the silence that followed. "How can you possibly know this?"

"I told ye." She shrugged. "Lud, milord, in just the few days I was at the docks I 'eard as much. The merchants know it, why don't ye?"

"Impossible! How could such information be known by the guilds? 'Tis rumor, nothing more—it must be!"

"Really, now?" She smiled. "'Tis said that King 'enry's developed a new system for carryin' messages from the Continent to London in only six days. The merchants can do it in four."

"Corp an Chriost!" Giles swore, leaping up. Grabbing her wrist and pulling her to her feet, he began to stride down the

parapet, dragging her after him. He added unnecessarily, as she stumbled to keep up, "You're coming with me!"

Roanna shifted uncomfortably from one foot to the other, faced with a sleepy lord and lady of Leicester still in their bedclothes. Under Giles's prodding, she repeated her story, her words abruptly bringing the earl and countess to wakefulness.

"You believe her, then?" Giles asked as Simon began pacing about the bedchamber.

"Of course I believe her!" Simon said grimly, glancing back at the maid. "I can believe you, can I not?"

"Aye, milord," she answered firmly, lifting her chin under his stern appraisal.

"Damn Henry!" Simon muttered, resuming his pacing. "He could not have thought of this on his own. It is far too subtle, too easy. Nay, Henry would push for war to prove his position. Since my return to England, he has been frantically writing letters to every peer of power, even the leaders of London! His letters and his panic increased when I began to spend time with Edward. Indeed, he even appealed to Louis for aid—for war."

"The Lusignans—or the Queen's Men, perhaps . . ." Giles suggested.

"Nay." Eleanor shook her head. "He has ceased listening to them since their ill-given advice in Oxford. Moreover, when we exiled them, it proved out their weakness. Simon, I believe it could only be one: John Mansel. I warned you about him. He has been acting as Henry's chief adviser on the treaty, and—"

"The man is of no consequence," Simon interrupted, waving the suggestion away. "Lud, we cannot even determine the man's parentage."

"Simon." Eleanor sighed softly, and tried again. "Few men have managed to keep Henry's ear for long." As she spoke, she rose from her chair and crossed to a small table, where she poured wine into a cluster of pewter goblets. "Henry wants to be king in fact, not just title." She handed a goblet to her husband and another to Roanna, who started with amazement at the attention. Giving one to Giles, Eleanor smiled, reaching up to touch his face lightly. "Your father, Giles, was the only man who knew how to handle Henry with real effect. Will dealt with my brother successfully by allowing him to feel the power of a sovereign. Subtly, he brought Henry to think that his decisions were his own, leading him to where he wanted him to go. Others who surround the throne wheedle and bring pressure to bear, not realizing that Henry will suffer it for only so long until he rebels. Until John Mansel. I warned you about him, Simon, because I recognized Will's talent in him, though without his purpose—a dangerous situation."

Simon paused in his pacing and smiled at his wife. "You are correct, with one exception. There was one other who could rule Henry."

"Nay," she sighed. "I did not rule him, not in the same way. Oh, there was a time when I could induce him to do what I wanted, when there was great love between us. That died when he betrayed us, my husband. My loyalty now is only to you; thus I no longer have any power over Henry."

Giles's gaze strayed to Roanna, who was watching the scene intently. Clearing his throat, he set his goblet on the table. "I will see Roanna back to her chambers."

"Good," Simon grunted, offering a gentle smile to the girl. "I thank you for what you have told us tonight, Mistress Roanna. The information is vital. Sleep well."

Giles stepped forward, but Eleanor laid a hand on his arm. "Roanna, please wait for Giles in the hall. He will only be a moment." When she had left, Eleanor turned to him, her blue eyes glittering. "Now, Giles fitzWilliam, you might tell me how you came to be in the girl's company at this hour."

Giles's mouth dropped open, and he glanced at Simon who seemed to be equally interested in the answer, though a glint of amusement tempered his expectation. "We were talking—on the parapet," Giles answered lamely.

"Talking?" Eleanor repeated, one delicate eyebrow arching. "On the parapet?"

"You know that I often linger there before I retire," he protested.

"Oh, aye, that infernal Marshal custom." Eleanor grimaced. "I never could adjust to it. And what was Roanna doing there, walking in her sleep?"

"It appears that she also finds it difficult to bed early." He shrugged. "Tavern hours are not those of a keep."

"I see," Eleanor answered quietly, and glanced at her husband, who merely shrugged. "Giles, I must point out that the request of a man on his deathbed, particularly a dear and trusted retainer, is not to be taken lightly. My soul would be in jeopardy should I neglect to carry out his wishes—a matter *I* do not take lightly. I placed the girl under your protection because I trust you. It is a matter of honor, Giles, between you and me."

Giles suffered an uncomfortable feeling of déjà vu. "You have my faith and trust, milady. Now, as always."

"That is all that I ask, Giles." Eleanor smiled. "Now, please see the girl safely to her bed." Giles thankfully made his escape.

"Giles?" Roanna asked, trying to keep up with his long strides as they made their way through the darkened halls of Durham House. She took his grunt as acknowledgment. "What did King 'enry do to loose faith wi' Lord Simon and Lady Eleanor?"

"Don't you know?" He glanced at her with a sardonic grin. "I thought you knew everything."

"Don't be a sod," she panted. "Tell me."

"Not tonight," he grumbled. "I've far too many things on my mind. Including seeing you safely to your bed." He stopped suddenly and gestured to a point behind her.

Glancing about she realized that they had reached the door to the women's quarters. "Won't ye tell me?" she whispered.

"Sometime, perhaps, not tonight. Good night, Roanna."

"Good sleep," she responded, feeling defeated, yet not knowing why. As she turned to open the door he laid a hand on her arm and she looked back with surprise.

"Thank you, Roanna," he said softly. His eyes, in the light cast by a nearby wall sconce, were surprisingly tender. "What you did tonight was vitally important."

"'Twas nothin'." She shrugged, suddenly tongue-tied. What was the matter with her, why could she suddenly not find anything to say to him? she wondered.

"Nevertheless, my thanks." He reached up to touch her face gently.

Leaning past her, he opened the door and waited until she was safely inside. She closed the door behind herself and leaned against it, still feeling where his hand had touched her as her heart pounded strangely in her chest. She stood there for a long moment, staring vacantly into the large room as the dim moonlight cast soft shadows over the sleeping forms. Lud, she wondered, what *was* the matter with her?

She pushed herself away from the door and made her way along the rows of sleeping forms to her cot. Quickly undressing in the chill of the room, she slipped beneath the covers, shivering until her body heat warmed the narrow bed. Exhausted, she tried to make her mind go blank, to allow the release of sleep to come, but the events of the past hours kept replaying in darts of consciousness. Thoughts kept pressing on her, demanding attention, until she finally sighed and gave in to them, allowing them to focus.

There was no use denying it. She had known, that moment in the Flying Sail when she looked up over the candle and saw the angles and shadows of his face, that she had been waiting for him to come for her. It made no sense, they were a world apart; yet why did she feel so drawn to him? She was so fulfilled and complete in some undefined way, each time he came into her life. It was madness, it had to be. He was insufferable. Such thoughts were totally impossible.

A soft voice deep within her cried the truth, and she closed her eyes tightly, defying what the voice was telling her. But in her mind's eye she saw his blue eyes with the crinkles at the corners, the wayward lock of chestnut hair that fell recklessly over his forehead, and she felt herself falling in a spiral toward him to certain disaster. Never, never in the whole of her life had she felt so afraid.

5

"I do believe that this very morning I saw a bud breaking on the apple tree just beyond the kitchen yard!" Lisette's voice lifted happily and she wrapped her arm more tightly about Giles's as they walked in the winter-bare garden. "Giles fitzWilliam, you are not listening to me!"

"Of course I am." He smiled. "You saw a bud on the apple tree just beyond the kitchen yard this very morning."

"Ah, then you were listening!" she said, laughing, and pulled away to spin about in front of him.

"I listen to everything you say," he assured her, pausing to study the fetching picture she made. Her long black hair hung in gentle waves, restrained only by a slender fillet of gold. The soft green silk of her bliaut curved tantalizingly over her slender form and, as ever, the vibrant violet of her incredible eyes impaled him, leaving him slightly breathless.

God, the girl was bewitching, he mused. She was everything he had ever wanted in a woman, beautiful, gentle, in every way pleasing to a man. And she made him feel as if he were the only male on earth, at least the only one with any value for her. The past months had been—enchanting.

"Come, sit with me," she said, sitting down on a stone bench beside the garden path and patting the place next to her. "Now, tell me what has distracted you so these past few days. Nay, do not deny it. You have been distracted."

He hesitated, not even knowing why he did so, and found himself searching for the words to explain his thoughts to her. "I am guilty, I admit it. Soon parliament will be called, yet King Henry absents himself. Simon and Lord Edward will convene the session without the king."

"Has it been decided?"

"Aye. It is to be held in a fortnight."

"Then why are you so disturbed, dear heart? What will be, shall be. Life has a way of taking care of itself."

"It is not that simple, Lisette."

"Then explain it to me."

Words flew through his mind, concerns about Henry's reaction, about the depth of Edward's commitment to Simon, yet he could not express them. "It is nothing. You must not concern yourself with it," he said finally.

"Men," she scoffed sweetly. "You do wind yourselves into the most curious dilemmas, all of which seem to work themselves out. Now, kiss me, Giles fitzWilliam. That seems far more important at this moment."

Obediently, he drew her into his arms, bringing his lips down upon her willing ones, drinking of her warmth. With the greatest effort, he finally drew away. "You see?" she whispered breathlessly. "We do have far greater matters at hand—matters that supersede all else." Her hand slipped about his neck, drawing him down to her once again.

As they kissed, Lisette's thoughts raced onward, beyond what Giles imposed upon her willing lips, eyes, and the nape of her neck. She had known it the moment she laid eyes upon him—she wanted him, and she fully intended to have him.

He was a bastard, but that would only be a concern if his father and uncle had not been so generous, gifting him with more than adequate estates of his own. And she knew that, with her help, his associations with the throne would bring them all that they could want. Moreover, he was incredibly handsome and virile—in short, everything she could desire in a husband. And she had fallen in love with him, making the prospect of pursuit even more pleasurable.

Few obstacles remained. There was her father—she knew that his plans for her exceeded wedding her to the bastard of an English noble. But that stumbling block was a matter easily rectified. Once Giles had bedded her, her father would quickly see the advantages of having her wed to the man of her choice, instead of one of the stuffy, overfed bores he had presented to her in the past.

She moaned, pressing against him, her arms clinging about his neck. "Oh, Giles," she breathed, "Giles."

He drank of her eager mouth as his hands slid, as if driven by their own force, to her waist and then up to one breast, cupping it tenderly as his thumb stroked the nipple through the thin fabric. His usual restraint was numbed by her response, and his hand went to the laces of her bliaut, pulling them apart and slipping beneath, searching, finally finding the object of its quest in the warm, eager flesh.

Moaning, she encouraged the play, never wanting him to stop, even as her thoughts turned calculating. She knew that the culmination of his attentions must be played out on a much more private stage. She pulled back, barely resisting at first, then with more determination. "Oh, Giles, my dearest love," she cried softly. "Someone is certain to come upon us!"

He drew away, pausing to plant a light kiss on the tip of her well-turned nose. Pulling her bliaut closed, he drew her up to her feet. "Do not be frightened, Lisette, I would never hurt you," he murmured.

"Oh, my dearest!" she cried softly. "How could you doubt my trust in you? For I wish to have what you want to give to me, with equal measure, my dearest love." She nestled into his arms, laying her head against his chest. "But not here, where anyone might come upon us. A private bower. A place where I might show you the depth of my feelings."

A feeling of tenderness welled up in him that he had never known before. "I promise you," he whispered, holding her close.

"Soon?" she asked timidly.

"Soon." He bent to kiss her damp brow, even as his mind began to calculate how it could be done.

Durham House granted meager facilities for lovers, quartering the bachelor knights together in shared quarters, and the women in theirs, segregated only by rank. There were a few spare private rooms, but the guard was vigilant —ironically, by Giles's own orders. Assignations were not impossible, but privacy was. The difficulty of Giles's plans was keeping them private so that the encounter was not the source of common gossip by the time the sun rose over the parapet.

His plans were soon set, and he moved through the following days impatiently, measuring each moment as Lisette's constant presence continued to strain his emotions. Her company was enough to set him off, until he had to spend hours jousting to rid him of his turmoil.

He was grateful for the absorbing hours spent with Simon, planning for the coming parliament. Simon had sent messages to the far reaches of England, calling the session and assuring the barons that Lord Edward would be in attendance to represent the throne. More detailed plans centered on the appeal to the barons and countering their objections, certain to be led by the earl of Gloucester as he protested against Simon's plea for an expansion of England's laws.

In the past months, since the first night he had found her there, Giles had spent more and more time on the parapets in Roanna's company. He found himself increasingly delighted by her outspokenness, recognizing that she had a ready wit and was quick to use it, particularly as she grew more and more at ease with him. He found himself reminded, in brief, startling flashes, of his lovely, fiery aunts and beautiful cousins in his childhood, and the memories plucked at him with warmth and pain. Odd that this girl, whose background differed so drastically from theirs, should remind him of them.

Full of sass and independence spiced with impudence, she appeared to face life without apology. Beneath the shapeless kirtles she wore, he suspected that a woman was growing; she was blooming before his very eyes. Certainly, she now appeared to be absorbing the benefits of her new surroundings with a quickness he found amazing. Her earlier resentment seemed to have dissipated, and she now approached her life at Durham House as a new challenge she fully intended to conquer. Giles began to suspect that the world would prove an easy conquest before her determination.

Each night she brought him a new anecdote, dissolving him into laughter as she related her observations of members of the household, bringing to life the stiff-necked panderings of staff and noble alike.

She constantly asked questions, and he offered what answers and solutions he could. To his continuing amazement, she listened seriously and more often than not offered comments of surprising depth. At times, he was struck by a twinge of discomfort, sensing that she was, perhaps, hanging too much on his words. But the warm moments they shared quickly disarmed him, and he found himself opening up, gradually sharing thoughts and memories that he was startled to hear himself voice.

On this particular night, half his thoughts were fixed upon the fact that in a short time he would be with Lisette. The other half delighted in Roanna's company. He leaned against a merlon, smiling at her laughter as she appreciated his story. "I swear it," he said, grinning. "I tried to leap out the window. I was ten years old at the time. One of my father's squires and a yeoman were closing in on me, and she was waving the bedgown in front of me like an enemy's banner. There was no way that I was going to wear that bloody thing—it had lace on it."

"All that because ye didn't want to wear a bedgown?" she gasped, catching her breath painfully against her laughter. "Ye were raised to wear frills, why should it upset ye?"

"Raised to wear lace and frills? Hardly." He snorted, and his manner became more serious. "Roanna, you truly believe that I was born into comfort and wealth, don't you?"

"Weren't ye?" she asked, wrapping her arms about her knees as she tried to make herself more comfortable on the hard stone of the wall. "Ye were the son of the earl of Pembroke."

"A bastard son," he corrected. "I . . ." He paused as a shout below announced the change of guards. It was time. Swinging his legs down from the wall, he stood up. "I must go, Roanna," he said abruptly. "Come, let me see you to your chamber."

She rose, confused. "Now? Will ye not finish yer story?"

"Not now," he answered, wondering why he felt so uncomfortable. "Another time."

He accompanied her to the end of the wall, where she turned to stop him. "See to yer duties, Giles. I can find me own bed."

She turned and left him struggling with a momentary guilt at having changed their routine. He watched her for a moment, then shrugged. As he turned away, he glanced about in the shadows, then slipped up the steps at the end of the wall and into the tower room, closing the door quickly behind him.

Roanna made her way along the battlements to the narrow steps that led down to the upper floor of the keep. Though she went cautiously for fear of slipping on the smooth steps, her feet felt light, her mood swimming pleasantly from the camaraderie of the past hour. She had never spent such moments with another person. Oh, there were the times with Uncle Roscoe and Aunt Matilda, but this was so deliciously different. Giles was—had become, her best friend.

Then she paused in the shadows, leaning against the wall as she chuckled softly. Who was she fooling? There was more than just a warm friendship growing between them. He cared about her, in a way that left her breathless. Their time together had made the moments at Durham House almost bearable. She could not even remember why she had been so terrified in those first moments when she had faced her feelings about him. Her fear seemed so distant now, as if she had always felt this way.

She had found peace at last, treasuring the moments when she would come upon him unexpectedly, warming to the easy smile that spread over his face when he saw her, thrilling to his delight as she endeavored to improve herself. She was trying so hard to please him, to make him proud of her! To make him want her.

Wallowing in a deep feeling of contentment, she took several moments to realize that someone was approaching —not the expected footsteps of a guard, but the soft, muted sound of a woman's slippers and the rustle of a skirt along the parapet. She watched the shadowed form pause and glance about before it moved on. There was only one reason for a woman to be out alone at this hour of the night, Roanna mused. Except for herself, of course, but then everyone had assumed that she was meeting someone. But then she was, wasn't she? She smiled warmly at the thought. As to its purpose, let them believe what they would; she cared not a whit what others thought. But as for this one who passed so surreptitiously, there was no doubt about it. The woman was meeting a lover. In her newfound contentment, the realization brought a smile as she silently wished them well. Then, as the heavily cloaked figure passed near her, something uncomfortably familiar about the woman touched her.

Now curious, Roanna watched as the form crossed the parapet to the door of the guard tower. Knocking softly on the door, the woman turned her head to glance behind her. As the moon emerged from behind a cloud, the woman's identity was revealed. So, Roanna thought with a satisfied smirk, the Lady Lisette was not the demure innocent she pretended to be. Not that Roanna was surprised—she had suspected that the Gascon maid's delicate exterior hid a calculating, strong will.

The door of the tower room opened, the light from within illuminating the drama as the tall male figure in the doorway reached out to gather Lisette to him, pulling her into the bower as he closed the door behind them. Roanna stood paralyzed, and her heart lurched painfully. She felt as if the breath had been punched out of her.

Giles was Lisette's lover. Only moments ago she had been sitting with him, not far from that room, talking and laughing, and all the while he had been marking the moments until he could be with *her*. That was why he had brought their visit so abruptly to an end—he wanted her out of the way before the lovely Lisette came!

She burned with humiliation and pain, realizing now that the hours that had been so precious to her had meant nothing to him! Gulping back a sob, she leaned against the cold stone wall, biting her lower lip to keep from crying. And then she became angry, more at herself than at him. What had she expected? She was nothing more than a bloody, sodding twit! How could she have been such a fool as to think that he could ever really care about her? To him she would never be anything more than a doxy from the London docks.

That was fine—fine! In fact, they deserved each other: the insufferable Sir Giles and the insipid Lady d'Quincey. As for herself, what she had seen tonight only confirmed what she had always known, but for a momentary lapse of sanity. There was no place for her here, there never had been, there never would be. Even someone she had thought of as a friend, trusting him with thoughts she had never shared with another, had used her. Oh, it was clear enough now, he had marked time with her, pretending to enjoy her company when he was only using her as an excuse to be near the tower at the appointed hour, watching over her shoulder for the appearance of his companion, looking forward to their love nest.

She almost laughed out loud at the irony, realizing bitterly that he had not even been at fault. She had tricked herself—a victim of her own foolish dreams. In doing so, she had lost her sense of herself, of who and what she was. Never again would she allow these lace-trimmed fops to use her, to look through her as if she weren't there, as if she were a mere fixture for their convenience. Never, ever again.

Lisette drew her eyes from Giles's face, wondering at the grin he wore, and turned, exclaiming with delight. There at the center of the small round room was a table set with a light supper. "Oh, Giles," she gasped, clapping her hands, "how perfectly thoughtful!"

"I noticed that you ate little at supper." He smiled, pleased by her reaction.

"I—I found that I was too nervous to eat today—after you whispered in my ear about tonight," she answered softly. She glanced about the small room, from the table to the warchest set against the wall to her right, and then to the bed, half hidden in the shadows thrown by flickering candles set in the iron holders on the wall. She dropped her gaze suddenly and flushed.

"Would you like me to return you to your chambers?" he murmured as he drew her cloak from her shoulders, noting her embarrassment. "I will understand if you wish it."

"Oh, nay," she said breathlessly. Spying a lyre leaning against the wall, she spun back to him. "Sing for me, Giles, the song of star-crossed lovers you sang on the day we met."

He laughed, handing her into a chair at the table. "In the event that you might ask, I came prepared." Taking the chair across from her, he picked up the lyre and strummed it softly.

A shout along the battlements announced the change of guard, the sound striking oddly against the gentler night sounds: an occasional hound baying the moon, the bleat of a sheep protesting a shifting nudge in his byre, the shrill chirrup of the cicadas calling for companionship in the meadows beyond the walls.

Within the small tower room, the silence had become palpable. Giles leaned back in his chair and drank lazily of his wine, his hooded eyes watching Lisette over the goblet's rim. She continued to pick at the food on the pewter plate before her, though he knew she had already eaten more than she was accustomed to. But what made him study her, and wonder what was going on in that lovely head, was the pensive, almost thoughtful look she wore. She showed no fear, no sign of nervous anticipation, rather an air of concern.

Lisette was, indeed, concerned. She had fully enjoyed the past hours. In fact, the entire past week had been thrilling, as she reveled in anticipation of the culmination of her plans. Moreover, she was not a little curious about what it would be like to be made love to by this man. If she had her way—and she always had—by the time the sun rose over the battlements, her commitment to Giles, and more importantly, his to her, would indeed be a fait accompli, their future secured. Unless she had totally misjudged his intentions. She considered herself a good judge of people—particularly men—but she had suddenly, and horrifyingly, realized halfway through their romantic supper that he had never actually declared his feelings for her *before others.* As much as she cared about him and wanted him, she had no intention of surrendering the prize of her maidenhead unless he was fully committed to her. Love was one thing, but her virginity was another entirely. Without it, she would have no value for marriage; a husband would repudiate her, ruining her, if he found her unpure.

The problem that faced her now and set furrows into her lovely brow was how to make absolutely certain that the coming night left him with no choice about their future. She realized that she had made a terrible mistake in keeping their tryst so private.

Deep in thought, she jumped when he laid his hand over hers. "Lisette, what is troubling you?"

She forced a shy smile, looking somewhat flustered. "Why, nothing, whatever could be troubling me, Giles? This has been perfectly lovely, everything a maid in love could possibly ask for."

"Tell me," he pressed gently. "This is not a time for us to hold anything from each other."

She forced her gaze up to his, focusing on the tender seriousness of his eyes. Indeed, Giles fitzWilliam, she thought, this is not the moment for doubts. "I am troubled, Giles," she admitted softly, dropping her gaze. "I realized —that is, it occurred to me, you . . ." She raised her eyes to his, their corners filling with tears. "While the evening has been perfect in every way—" She paused, drawing in her breath painfully. "Oh, I cannot! 'Tis unseemly!"

"Lisette!" he said with concern. Rising, he came around the table and pulled her into his arms, cradling her gently. "Tell me," he murmured softly.

She pressed her cheek against his chest, sniffling as she wrapped her arms about him. "You—you have never declared your intentions to me, Giles fitzWilliam," she cried softly. "My love for you has brought me to you this night—but what of the morning? Do—do you love me?"

"Is that it then?" He smiled, relieved, holding her more closely to him. "Lisette, I will ask you a question, sweetling. Will you steal my heart tonight and abandon me in the morning, or will you share tonight as a pledge to our future? Is this to be only one night of pleasure for you, or will you always be mine?"

As he spoke, her mind turned over his words with deliberation. Private declarations were all very well, she mused, but they did not give the assurances she needed. She bit her lip in frustration, realizing that she would have to call a halt to her plans—at least momentarily. But she was loath to do so—she wanted him.

Just then, her thoughts were interrupted by a shout from the battlements as one guard called to another. Slowly, a secret smile spread over her face as she realized that the answer had just been given to her.

"Oh, Giles!" she giggled, her face lightening as she pulled back to look up at him. "You are terrible! To suggest that I only mean to love you this night and abandon you at the dawn, to meet the loss of your heart! I could never do thus, milord." She smiled up at him through her thick lashes. "Indeed, if I have you tonight, you are mine forever!"

"Thank God," he sighed dramatically, rolling his eyes. "I feared you only meant to have your way with me."

She laughed delightedly, her eyes dancing with pleasure

and relief. "Kiss me, Giles fitzWilliam. Dawn is rapidly approaching."

In moments their clothes were discarded, thrown carelessly over chairs and draped on the table in a path to the bed. Giles's eyes moved over her body in the moonlight coming through the high window beyond their bed. He drew one hand slowly down over the curves of her lovely, slender form, taking pleasure at the sound of her soft gasps as he stroked her back and hips. He stroked upward again to one small, perfectly formed breast that quivered at his touch. Bending his head, he teased the nipple, drawing his tongue about the tightening tip before he claimed it with his mouth.

She cried out suddenly at his touch, her hands moving frantically over his back. "Shhh," he said softly, laughing and pulling away to kiss her tenderly. "You'll draw the guards, sweet." But as he began to reapply his attentions, she groaned and cried out once again, and then a third time. He began to suspect that, if he were going to keep the guards stationed along the wall from pounding on the door, he was going to have to gag her.

Instead, he kissed her once again, drawing her moans into him as his hand swept gently down over her hips and thighs. Suddenly, she lay still beneath him. He drew his head back, wondering if he had frightened her, but a smile touched his mouth as he read her look of ecstasy; her face was a study in anticipation. Gently, he slid his hand between her legs, and his fingers searched the tender, moist depths.

She cried out, loudly declaring her pleasure—declaring it, he was certain, to everyone on the battlements. His mouth claimed her cry, but it was too late; his belated gesture coincided with a pounding at the door. Swearing, he rolled away from her.

"Giles! What is it?" she cried.

"Quiet!" he hissed. "Sit back—into the shadows!"

Swearing under his breath, he slipped on his chausses and crossed to the door. He opened it halfway, prepared to order the guard back to his post, only to gape with surprise. "Rodger! Damnation, what are you doing here?"

His friend grinned sheepishly. "Eleanor told me to find you." At Giles's furious glare, he shrugged helplessly. "Ah, perhaps you had better dress and come out here."

Moments later Giles closed the door behind him and

confronted Rodger with barely controlled anger. "This better be good."

"Eleanor told me to find you."

"So you said. How did you know I was here?"

"It's a matter of wager in the guardroom."

"Wager?"

"Whether or not you would succeed tonight. I placed a quid on you."

"Generous of you," Giles growled.

"Your good fortune has always been mine," Rodger quipped.

"Get on with it, before I plant my fist in the middle of that stupid grin."

"Ah, well. No one is sorrier than I am, Giles—after all, I guess I've lost a quid. I did, didn't I?"

"Dammit, Rodger—"

"All right. Eleanor sent me to find you because Roanna has disappeared again."

Giles stared at him. "What?"

Rodger repeated his news. "She wants you to find her and bring her back."

Giles swore violently.

"Now—she wants her back before morning. You haven't much time," he added, glancing at the sky, which had begun to lighten. "Eleanor said you would know where to find her."

Assorted early morning customers had gathered quietly in the taproom and were nursing warm tankards of ale as they slowly awoke to a new day. Conversation was muted. For some this silence was due to a riotous night, while others were simply contemplating the coming day's business.

The heavy iron-banded door flew back and crashed against the wall, shocking the taproom of the Flying Sail to total silence. All eyes turned to the tall, cloaked knight who stood in the doorway, then shifted in unison to the owner of the tavern, who stood behind the bar.

"Top of the stairs, last door to the left," Roscoe drawled, jerking his head in the direction of the staircase as he continued to polish the oak board.

Giles strode across the room, ignoring the speculative looks that followed him, and took the stairs two at a time. He found the door, and shoved it open with a vengeance.

She was bent over by the bed, tucking in fresh linen. She jerked upright in surprise as he stepped into the room, slamming the door behind him.

"By all that is holy, give me one good reason why I shouldn't beat you black and blue!" he roared.

"Beat me!" she cried. "Try it, just try it! There be a dozen men below, not to mention Uncle Roscoe, who would throttle ye if ye lay a 'and on me!"

"Oh? Roscoe told me where you were!"

"'e wouldn't!"

"He did! Probably couldn't wait to be rid of you! Just been waiting for me to come! It's certainly easy to understand why!"

"Yer not takin' me back!"

"Want to bet a quid on it?"

"I wouldn't give ye the back end of an 'orse, much less a quid!"

"Get your things, you little chit! I'm fed up with you and all the trouble you've caused!"

A thought suddenly struck her, and she began to laugh, momentarily forgetting her own predicament. "Oh, Sir Giles!" she said mockingly. "Did ye abandon the lovely Lisette in 'er bower, poor thing? But don't worry, I 'ave every confidence in 'er—she'll find a way to arrange fer another time!"

That did it. He strode across the room, and in one sweep, he hefted her across his shoulder. Squealing and kicking, calling him every name she had learned in a lifetime of working in a tavern, she was bound down the stairs into the taproom. The silence that met them confirmed that the company had been eagerly awaiting their entrance. Striding across the room toward the door, Giles braced himself for Roscoe's objection to the rude departure of his niece; in his present mood he was almost looking forward to it. But he was not prepared for the bland expression that met him. Barely pausing in his tasks, Roscoe threw him a cloak, which Giles caught with his free hand.

"Better 'ave this," Roscoe drawled. "'Tis a cold mornin'."

Roanna shrieked, realizing that her last defense had crumbled.

The shock of cold air hit her, stifling her protests for an instant, just before the wind was knocked from her as he virtually threw her up on his horse. Gaining her breath, she tried to throw herself free, but he was already in the saddle behind her. He wrapped an arm tightly about her waist and settled her in his lap. "Do not try it, Roanna," he warned. "You won't get far."

He tucked the cloak about her shoulders, then urged his mount forward through the narrow, fog-drenched streets of London.

It took a long moment for Roanna to collect her wits. She wouldn't go back, she couldn't! "God, I 'ate you!" she spat.

"At this moment, the feeling is mutual."

"Why did ye 'ave to come?" she asked as a choked sob escaped.

"Because Eleanor ordered it."

"Ye do everythin' she says?" she gasped furiously. "Ye told me ye were yer own man—that ye 'eld no allegiance to an English baron."

"I told you that my allegiance was freely given, as it is to Eleanor. What you will not understand, Roanna, is what it means to give your word."

"I 'aven't given my word to anyone!" she cried, struggling against him.

"Be still!" he growled, holding her against him. "Do you want to fall? Dammit, Roanna, grow up! Are you going to spend your life thinking that you are responsible only to yourself? You first, beyond everything and everyone!"

"What's wrong wi' that? My life is mine! If I do not consider myself first, then I 'ave no value!"

"If you consider yourself before all else, then indeed, you don't have any value."

Even as they argued, and as Giles struggled to keep Roanna fixed securely in his lap while trying to control the horse, he was struck by a feeling that something was amiss. As they rode through the narrow streets, he grew more ill at ease. He stopped arguing and only half-listened to her ravings as his eyes strained to see through the thick, shrouding fog. He braced himself for the unexpected. Finally, as they approached the last street before the gate to the walled city, he suddenly knew what had been plucking at him. He hissed for Roanna to be silent.

Hearing the urgency in his voice, she broke off abruptly, her eyes widening with alarm. "What is it?" she whispered.

"Listen."

She turned her head and strained to hear. "I don't 'ear anythin'."

"Exactly," he said grimly. "Damn, 'tis too quiet."

Then he heard a shout, followed by another, and he tensed, recognizing the military precision of the sounds. He slowed his mount, rounding the turn in the street that led to the gate. He drew back on the reins sharply, bringing the horse to a halt. "Jesu," he swore softly.

"What's 'appenin'?" She gaped. The street was filled with lighted torches and the movement of soldiers and men-at-arms. The gates were closed and heavily guarded.

"Be silent. Roanna, for once in your life, say nothing."

He urged the destrier slowly forward, approaching the gates, as soldiers stepped out to block his path. "We are bound for Cheringe Village. Allow us to pass."

A sergeant stepped forward, shaking his head. "The gates are sealed, milord. No one is permitted to enter or leave London."

Giles grinned at the other man and winked. "Ah, but you see, I must have the lass home—before anyone awakes."

The soldier's gaze passed over Roanna with interest, and he smiled appreciatively. "I see your problem, milord, and I wish I could help, but it would be my neck for sure."

"On whose order were the gates closed?" Giles asked.

"Richard, duke of Cornwall," the man said in clipped tones.

"Impossible," Giles answered. "The duke is on the Continent."

"Nay, milord, he is within London," the sergeant insisted, "and has ordered that we allow no one to enter or leave the city."

Giles swore softly under his breath. "So be it." He turned his mount and they rode away from the gate, turning down a side street.

"Giles, what is it?" Roanna asked at last, her fear growing at the tenseness she could feel in him.

"Disaster, if what I suspect is true," he said quietly.

"Where are we goin'?" she pressed, not recognizing the streets through which he was taking her.

"To see Richard of Cornwall."

"What!" she twisted about, trying to see his face. "Ye cannot! 'e's the king's brother! Ye cannot just drop a visit on the duke of Cornwall!"

"Be quiet, Roanna, I'm thinking."

"Well, while yer thinkin', try to figure out 'ow we're goin' to keep our 'eads from the bloody noose!" she snapped.

"Do not worry, you are safe enough," he said distractedly.

"Safe enough? We're goin' to prance into Richard of Cornwall's presence, demandin' audience, and land in a bleedin' dungeon! Giles fitzWilliam, ye're soddin' mad!"

"Dammit, Roanna, I told you that I was trying to think! Stop worrying about Richard, he won't harm us. He's my uncle."

She was struck dumb for a moment. "Sweet Mother Mary and Joseph. Giles fitzWilliam, is there a peer in England who's not yer uncle?"

"A few." He grinned. "Some are merely cousins."

6

They rode to the duke of Cornwall's London manor, which he used when he preferred privacy to the spectacle at court. Giles's suspicion that he would choose the house in lieu of Winchester proved right when they approached the gate and found it guarded by men-at-arms wearing Richard's colors. Giles identified himself and requested audience with the duke. They were soon admitted to the courtyard where a groomsman ran to take Giles's mount, and then were led into the manor to a small room off the main hall, and left alone.

Giles settled Roanna into a large chair near the hearth where a fire burned. They were both damp from the heavy fog and, seeing her shiver, he glanced around for a ewer of wine or a pitcher of ale. Crossing back to the door, he opened it and stepped out into the hall, stopping a passing servant to request some warmed wine. Then, as Giles began to turn back to the room, he stopped short, staring with disbelief. There, entering a chamber at the other end of the long hall, was Richard of Gloucester.

Giles returned to the small room, setting his face so as not to show the concern he felt. "There will soon be something warm for you to drink," he said distractedly as he crossed to stand before the fire.

As he stared into the fire, Roanna watched him, frowning. "Giles? What is wrong?"

"You know what is wrong, Roanna," he said quietly, not raising his gaze from the flames. "The city has been closed."

"Nay, there's somethin' else botherin' ye. What is it?"

"So, now you imagine that you can read my mind?" He smiled at her, but she sensed that it was forced. "There is nothing wrong, beyond not being able to leave London."

"A necessary order, Giles," said a deep voice from behind them.

Giles spun toward the door and Roanna twisted around in her chair. She watched Giles cross the room to exchange a grasp of wrists with the man who had entered. He was middle-aged, tall and broad-shouldered, with blond hair intermixed with grey. His middle tended to paunch slightly, but he was, to any English eye, a Plantagenet. His grey eyes were warm as they fixed on Giles, the skin at the corners wrinkling as he smiled with obvious pleasure. Feeling slightly overwhelmed, Roanna leaned back into the depths of her chair, trying to be unobtrusive as she watched and listened.

"It has been a long time, Giles."

"Aye, milord. Too long."

"Milord?" Richard, duke of Cornwall, king of the Romans, laughed heartily. "Evidently it *has* been long. Whatever happened to 'Uncle Richard'?"

Giles grinned in response. Any comment he might have made was lost as the servant entered with the requested spiced wine and a tray of goblets. Giles presented Roanna to the duke as they were being served; the latter's brows rose slightly upon the introduction, but his smile remained warm. Turning back to Giles, his look became wistful. "You look like her," he said quietly.

Giles knew he referred to Isabella, his own father's sister, who had been Richard's first, much-cherished wife. "You know that all Marshals look the same." Giles grinned. "I believe the king is said to have remarked once that my grandfather and grandmother had little imagination; that once they had settled on the mold they were loath to change it."

"Indeed he did," Richard said, chuckling. "But you are the only one of the grandchildren to take the look. It is even more evident now that you are older."

Sipping his wine, Giles sought a way to shift the conversation to the purpose of his visit. "Are matters so well settled in the German states that you have found time to honor England with your presence?"

"So, we come to it." Richard sighed. "I am here, Giles, by Henry's request. I cannot not allow parliament to be held."

"And to that end you have sealed London," Giles said quietly, his fears confirmed.

"Aye, that and more. The justiciar has been ordered to summon the barons loyal to Henry to be in readiness for armed action. An inner council is being established to guard the king's interests."

"A council including Gloucester?" Giles asked evenly, noting that Richard's eyes flickered at the question. "Is it your intention to replace the barons' council established at Oxford?"

"It is."

Giles stared at him for a long moment. When he spoke again, his voice was strained. "Milord, what is being done here will certainly lead to war."

"Perhaps." Richard shrugged, turning to the fire. "If it must. But the authority of the Crown must be reestablished."

"I assume you are aware that Edward called the parliament jointly with Simon."

"I know of it. But Edward will not go against his father. Henry's decision in this will bring the prince back to his father's side where he belongs." He turned back to regard his nephew with a steady gaze, but his voice was filled with genuine concern. "Giles, you know that I cannot allow you to leave the city. I wish you no harm—not just in memory of Isabella and your father, who was a close friend, but also because I cannot forget a young boy who became most dear to me. So I give you some advice. Lose yourself in the city. Disappear. No one will learn of your visit here, but beyond that I cannot help you." He paused, choosing his words carefully. "There are those who will not forgive your loyalty to Simon, and will consider it a real and present threat. There are others who regard you as dangerous merely because of the man who was your sire. They would not be held accountable for actions against you. My brother . . ." He sighed deeply. "Henry is not above forgetting loyalties and affection when he has been convinced that a threat has been removed."

"I understand," Giles said quietly.

"Good. Now, finish your wine and warm yourselves, but then you must go." He placed his goblet on a nearby table and turned to leave, then paused to look back with regret. "I wish it could be different, Giles. It saddens me deeply to see what has come to pass, family fighting against family, friends mistrusting those they have known a lifetime."

Giles exchanged a long look with Richard, and then he smiled grimly. "Nothing ever really changes, does it? For all the turnings of years, we continue to fight the same battles."

Richard nodded silently, then turned to go, pausing once more at the door before he closed it behind him. "God grant you peace, Giles fitzWilliam, and keep you safe. I pray that we shall meet again in a better time."

By midmorning London had returned almost to normal, the city having become accustomed to its drifting changes. Commerce returned, merchants went about their business, people moved about the streets in silent resumption of their lives.

Giles urged his destrier through the crowded streets, he and Roanna both falling silent as they rode away from the oppressive moments with Richard of Cornwall. Giles pondered what he had learned, including the knowledge that his cousin, Gloucester, had turned against Simon. His action would split the baronial forces and make war almost a certainty.

Roanna's thoughts were more jumbled, flitting from the recent news to excitement over having been in the presence of Cornwall to the fact that she would not be returning to Durham House. The latter thought won out and she twisted in Giles's lap to look at him.

"Where are we goin'?"

It took a moment for Giles to fix on her question. "I am returning you to your uncle's care."

"And after that—where are ye goin'?"

"I'm thinking on it."

She turned around again and leaned against him, considering that statement. Then her mouth drew into a small smile. Uncle Roscoe would know what to do, and would very likely confirm her own ideas on the matter.

* * *

Giles expected moments of amazement and confusion when he returned Roanna to the Flying Sail. However, Roscoe showed no surprise when they appeared, merely pointing them toward the kitchen as he turned to a barmaid and ordered her to take his place at the board.

Once they were settled by the warmth of the kitchen hearth, he leaned his massive form forward on his elbows, listening intently as Giles recounted the morning's events, occasionally punctuating the recital with a grunt of understanding.

"I learned of it soon after ye left, lad," he said finally. "'oped ye'd made it through the gates afore they closed. Cornwall is right—ye need to disappear, and quickly."

"I was thinkin'," Roanna interjected. "'e could stay 'ere. No one would suspect—"

"Nay, lass. 'Tis too late fer that." Roscoe shook his head. "'e was seen comin' in with ye, and too many know 'e's 'ere. Moreover, yer in danger yerself, lass—bein' at Durham 'ouse, and in 'is company. Nay, ye both 'ave to leave, and quickly."

"Both leave?" Roanna's voice rose.

"I said so," Roscoe snapped. "Giles, 'tis a 'ard thing I'm askin', but do ye think ye could manage to pass fer a villein, just fer a time?"

Giles regarded him silently for a long moment. Then he smiled, his eyes blank. "I think I could manage it."

"Nay, I mean really look, act, even feel like a villein," Roscoe pressed, looking doubtful.

"I said I could," Giles answered.

"Well, then," Roscoe grunted. "There's a place I know, ye'll be safe there."

"What are ye talkin' about?" Roanna broke in, her voice shrill.

"Be quiet, Roanna," Giles said, still staring at Roscoe. "How will you manage to get us there safely?"

"I 'ave me ways, lad, do not worry about that. Yer concern is 'ow well ye can play the role."

"Do not concern yourself about me, Roscoe. The role of a villein will not come hard to me. Moreover, I am not the one we need worry about."

Both men's gazes turned simultaneously to Roanna.

She glanced from one to the other, her eyes widening.

"Oh, nay," she gasped. "I'm not goin' anywhere! And that be absolutely final!"

"I won't do it." Roanna grimaced, rebelling.

"You'll do it," Giles said firmly.

"I won't!"

"You'll put it on or I shall do it for you."

Roanna stared at the grungy garment lying on the narrow cot and shuddered. The past day held no reality, the present even less, and this was the final straw, proof that she was losing her sanity.

She had always known that on the docks Uncle Roscoe was a force to be reckoned with. But not until the past few hours had she begun to understand the power he wielded.

Richard of Cornwall had been correct in his warning, just as Roscoe had been right on the mark. Within hours of their visit to Richard, they had been forced to flee, whisked out from under the very noses of those searching for them. Roscoe had been prepared. As soldiers came through the front door of the Flying Sail, they were being slipped out the back. They had been passed from one hand to another throughout the night, among men and women Roanna had previously considered too insignificant to perform such feats. Yet, their saviors had shown no fear, no hesitation in the face of the dangers involved, acting with calm deliberation.

It was well after dark when they had found themselves in a tiny village on the fringes of the city. They were led to a haphazard structure and informed by their guide, just before he disappeared into the darkness, that it would serve as their lodgings. Inside, Roanna had collapsed onto a sagging cot and fallen immediately into a deep, exhausted sleep, not even pausing to wonder where Giles would find his rest. The answer to that unasked question presented itself when she awoke to the sound of a rooster crowing outside and found Giles curled up on the earthen floor under a single blanket.

She sat up on the cot and yawned. Glancing about the hovel, she cringed. Lud, it was too small and poor even for a fire pit! There were two shuttered windows and a hide-covered door. The floor was bare, except for her cot, a stool, a cloth-covered bucket in the corner, and Giles. She glanced down at him as he began to stir. "Wake up, Giles," she said, yawning again. "It must be time to leave."

He rolled over on his back and looked up at her sleepily. "Leave? Roanna, we're here."

She stared at him. "'ere? This is it?" Her eyes grew wider. "Not bloody likely!"

"Roanna," he groaned, stretching. "You wear that word to death."

"I won't stay 'ere."

"Aye, you will. Neither of us has a choice at the moment."

If she had any lingering feelings of guilt about where he had slept, they were dispelled by his words and the offending garment he withdrew from his knapsack moments later. The color of the rough woolen kirtle was obscured by layers of soil.

Glancing at Giles, she winced, realizing that he meant his words—one way or another she was going to put it on. Shuddering, she picked it up, holding it away from her with two fingers. Her lip curled with distaste. "All right, I'll wear it if I must." She paused, waiting. "Well?"

"Well, what?"

"Aren't ye goin' to leave?"

"Don't be ridiculous, Roanna, we are supposed to be man and wife." His mouth twisted into a grin. "You needn't worry, I'm not interested in watching you dress." As she stiffened indignantly, he laughed. "Besides, I too must change. I won't peek if you don't." Then he turned and she was left to glare at his back.

Turning away from him, she slipped quickly out of her linen kirtle, dropping it on the cot. She pulled the rough garment over her head, wincing as the scratchy wool dropped down over her. As she laced up the bodice to the neck with trembling fingers, she gave in to a moment of self-pity, wondering how she had ever gotten into this situation. Finishing, she waited to turn around.

"All right," he said finally.

She turned and stared, and then burst out laughing. The mighty Giles fitzWilliam, knight of the realm, had been transformed into a grubby, shabby villein. His wool tunic was as soiled as her kirtle. The leggings beneath were ill-fitting and badly patched, and a rope served as his girdle. His hair was ruffled and, if she was not mistaken, he had rubbed it with dirt from the floor, as he had done also about his neck and ears.

"Milord," she gasped through her giggles, dropping him a deep curtsy.

"M'lady," he responded in a heavy North Country drawl as he swept her a courtly bow.

"We certainly are a pair," she said, still chuckling. "No one would take us for anythin' other than what we seem."

"Almost."

"Almost?" she repeated, her smile fading. His grin gave her a swift feeling of dread.

He bent, scooping up a handful of dirt from the earthen floor, and stepped toward her, a silly grin on his face. She backed away and her eyes widened with horror.

"Ye wouldn't!" she gasped.

"As easily as breathing."

"Don't ye touch me!"

"Be reasonable, Roanna. You must do it." The laughter in his voice belied the reason in his words. He grasped her arm and pulled her to him as his hand went up and he began to rub the dirt into her hair. Ignoring her squeals and the run of profanity, he thoroughly treated her hair, face, ears, and neck to the earthy scrubbing. Finally he released her and stepped back. "There, that's better," he said, studying his work.

She was panting, trying unsuccessfully to find new words to express how she felt about him. "We'll never get away with it! It's all been for nothin'! We'll be discovered afore a day 'as passed!"

"Sit down, Roanna," he said calmly, nodding toward the cot. She glared defiantly, and he repeated, "Sit. We must talk." Finally she sat, and he took the squat stool near the bed and leaned forward with his elbows on his knees, his manner suddenly serious. "Roanna, we must be believed, everything depends upon it. These villages on the edge of the city are seldom visited, but we are not so isolated that we cannot be discovered. If you do not care for yourself— or for me—so be it. But think upon your uncle and aunt. If we are found, it will not take much reasoning to determine how we came to be here, and all of those who helped us will be in danger. Their only protection is that we have, indeed, disappeared. Vanished."

"Villeins do not look like this," she said, glancing down

at herself and then at him. "I think ye've overplayed it, to 'ave us so poor."

"On the contrary. We will represent that portion of humanity that is anathema. We will not be seen, because others will choose not to see. It would prove uncomfortable to notice us, thus we shall truly vanish—the only way that a man can disappear while he still exists."

"How?"

"The crippled, the ugly, the grotesque."

"How will ye do that?" She forgot her anger, suddenly intrigued.

"Me?" He smiled. "I shall be without wit, feeble-minded."

"A well-cast role," she said, smirking, although she doubted that he could carry off the role of a villein, much less what he now proposed. "And me?"

A grin spread over his face. "Roscoe and I discussed that at length, though the answer was obvious. You have a role that will serve quite well in protecting all concerned. You, sweetling, are to be quite mute."

"What!"

"You cannot utter a word. Moreover, when one cannot speak, people assume they cannot reason, as well. That, of course, should come quite naturally to you."

"Bastard!"

"The wrong choice of word for offense, kitten."

"I cannot do it."

"Roanna, you can and you must. All you have to do is keep your mouth closed. Keep in mind that if you open it, you may speak the destruction of those you love." Her shoulders slumped as his words sank in. "You will merely go about the duties given to you—"

"What duties?" she asked as her head came up.

"The village is harvesting. You will be cooking for them, along with whatever else is asked of you."

"And what will ye be doin' while I am scrubbin' their pots?"

"I'll be helping with the harvest."

"You?" She snorted with disbelief.

"You might be surprised at what I am capable of," he muttered.

"They do not know who we are?"

"Nay, we will be safer that way, Roanna, as will they. Any more questions?"

"Too many to answer now," she said exhaustedly.

He stood up and offered a hand. "Then let us see to it." When she remained seated, he frowned. "What is it now?"

"I . . ." She glanced up at him and flushed. "I don't know about ye, Sir Giles," she snapped irritably, "but I—'ave certain needs when I wake up."

"Oh." He grinned. "I'm sorry, Roanna, I should have thought of it. I'll step outside—join me when you're ready."

"But where—"

He paused at the door and gestured toward the filthy bucket in the corner. Following his gaze, her puzzled look turned to one of repulsed horror.

"Bugger!" she muttered to his departing chuckle.

A few minutes later she ducked under the oil-soaked hide that served as a door to the thatched mud-and-wattle hut, and stepped into the sunlight, blinking against the sudden brightness. She paused at Giles's side as her gaze traveled dismally over the scene that greeted her in the bright light of morning.

"Oh, lud," she breathed. "What is it?"

"It's a village."

"It is not."

He glanced down at her. "You've never been away from the heart of London, have you, Roanna?" His gaze traveled back to what she was seeing. "Well, I assure you that it is a village. They have a plow, plus the required nine structures to make it so."

"Says who?"

"The king's writ," he answered grimly. "By law they are a hamlet, and thus owe tallages to their lord."

"What do they gain by it?"

"His protection—when he remembers them."

"Bet the blighter remembers 'em quick enough if they don't pay 'im," she muttered, missing the sharp look her words earned her as she looked about her.

The largest building lay directly ahead of them, across the road. It was a ramshackle structure consisting of a hodge-podge of hasty additions covered over by a heavy thatched roof that sagged at its center from time and weather.

Roanna was surprised to recognize what had once, to her practiced eye, been an inn. At the right of the building was the roof of a root cellar, and at the left, meager excuses for stables and a corral. The rest of the village lay east of the road. The hut behind her, which was to be hers and Giles's home for whatever length of time they were condemned to remain there, was set well back from the others—due possibly to whatever demon spirits might accompany those of their ilk, she grimly surmised. A cluster of mud-and-wattle huts, slightly better and larger than their own, lay to her left. The nearest structure, identifiable by the forge set beneath a thatched, open-sided canopy, was the smithy. To their right, a crumbling wall of stone about four feet tall at its highest point enclosed a chicken coop, a byre for cows, and a low-roofed structure that she guessed, by its lack of windows, to be some sort of storehouse.

She stepped away from Giles as her eyes swept over the hamlet with dismay. "Sweet Mother," she muttered. Giles's sudden hiss reminded her of her "condition." She clenched her teeth, wondering how she was ever going to remember her role. Then she saw the reason for his warning. A man had appeared in the doorway of the "inn." He paused for a moment, shading his eyes against the sun, before he stepped from the doorway and began to cross the road toward them. At the same moment, a woman appeared at the gate to the livestock yard, carrying a basket. Good Lord, Roanna thought, they're comin' in from both sides.

The man was of medium height with wide, sloping shoulders that accentuated his rangy body. His narrow, angular arms extended from sleeves that were too short and his thin legs emerged from the bottoms of ill-fitting chausses. His brown hair was flecked with grey, reaching to the shoulders in a thick ruff that was matched by his wide brows. The thought occurred to her, as she watched him approach, that she was observing a scarecrow moving along on strings operated by an unseen force; she wouldn't have been surprised to see crows flying above, uttering mocking screeches as they pulled the strings right and left, left and right.

"We let ye sleep late, this one time only, seein' as 'ow ye've traveled far. But don't think ye kin do it again!"

Roanna jumped and spun about, to find the woman at her side. She opened her mouth to speak, then clenched it shut, swallowing against the realization that she had almost given them away before they had even begun. Instead, she stared at the woman with what she hoped was an uncomprehending look of wonder. The woman matched the scarecrow, though her hair was hidden beneath a coif tied behind her head; she wore a shapeless woolen kirtle that, unlike Roanna's, at least was clean. The woman's shallow cheeks seemed to suck with displeasure as her hazel eyes gleamed with anticipation. Then the scarecrow reached them.

"'ave ye forgot that Roscoe said she were dumb, Gilda?" the man exclaimed. "Won't do no good ta wait fer 'er to answer ye."

"She's filthy," the woman spat, her eyes surveying Roanna with disgust.

"She'll clean up," he countered. "Don't know no better, but we'll teach 'er."

Roanna glanced from the woman to the man, whose dark eyes studied her over a long nose that tended to hook at the end. Too dirty, was she? she thought, her eyes straying to the dilapidated structure across the road. Sweet Mother! And then she remembered Giles. Why in the devil hadn't he said something? But before she could turn to find out where he had gone, a voice came from behind her, deep and guttural, so heavy with the accent of Northumbria that she could only make out a few words—and she wasn't certain of those.

". . . awd . . . wot 'twere . . . eat."

The last word came through clearly enough, and all three turned to the speaker, their reactions varied. The woman bristled. The scarecrow firmly but slowly explained that they would eat once their jobs had been clearly understood, and when they had proven to himself and his good wife that they could earn their keep. Roanna simply stared, now truly bereft of the power of speech. This . . . person . . . standing behind her bore no resemblance to the powerful, self-assured, handsome knight she had known only a few moments before. In his place slumped a pitiful fragment of humanity. Shoulders stooped, Giles had assumed the attitude of one crushed, his body cringing from the expected blow, his eyes darting with confusion and fear. Even his skin seemed to have assumed a nondescript color.

Still staring, she became aware that the woman had

grasped her arm. "Come on, I'll be showin' ye what needs ta be done." Dumbfounded, she allowed the woman to lead her away in the direction of the inn. She could hear the man behind them, speaking to Giles in a firm, clear voice, and paused to look. The woman pulled at her arm. "Don't be worryin' 'bout 'im. 'e'll be all right. Come now, we've lots ta do afore midmeal."

Midmeal, Roanna wondered, for whom? And how had Giles managed to transform himself like that? As the woman pulled her around the side of the building and through the kitchen door, she began to think that she would much have preferred to remain with Richard of Cornwall and face whatever would have come. Or even to have returned to Durham House and Lady Eleanor.

7

Roanna sat on a low stool before the hearth with her legs spread apart. Her elbows rested on her knees as she tapped the ash shovel idly on the stone, and the half-full bucket of ashes next to her was forgotten as she gave in to her thoughts in the deep silence of the empty inn.

She had never realized that life was so difficult. Not just hard work, she had never known a time without that; but seemingly endless, draining work, with so little hope.

Her initial anger over her situation had ebbed, partly from exhaustion, and partly because of Giles's coaxing. But then a new anger had bloomed. By the end of the first week she had come to know many of the inhabitants of the village, and she had found herself both drawn to them and repelled. She liked their earthy, easygoing nature, yet increasingly grew impatient with their apparent acceptance of their lot. They had so little: meager huts of mud and wattle, a few forged implements for cooking, rough garments of wool, and the barest of food—the best being sent to their lord, who lived a distance to the east. Yet there was no fight, no resistance in them for their unjust lot. Without being moderated by logic, her anger had begun deep within her, smoldered, and grown beyond the heat of the dung fires they burned upon their hearths.

The inn itself proved perhaps the sharpest contrast to what she had known. By Gilda's recounting, the inn had once been a thriving concern, known by the auspicious name of Running Stag Leaping. When the original owners had died without issue, Gilda and her husband, Tomas, who had worked as servants in the inn, had simply stayed on, having nowhere else to go. This had happened during the time of King John's reign, as he cut a bloody, burning swath across England in revenge against those who had forced him to sign the Magna Carta.

Others had come, a few of the thousands of villeins left homeless by the civil war that followed and by the invasion of the French. As in other places, they had banded together in a small group in an attempt to avoid starvation. Eventually, when England again found a moment of peace, the lords had turned their attention back to their lands. Gilda had told her this a few days ago as they pared roots for a stew. She spoke of the day when the lord's men rode into the hamlet, making them once again serfs under the rule of a master. Being supposedly mute, Roanna could only stare at her, amazed at the relief she heard in the woman's voice, as if the moment had been her salvation.

Roanna's eyes wandered over the large room with its weathered beams, worn floors, and grey, dingy walls, its sparse furnishings consisting of a few tables and benches, left, no doubt, from that time when the inn had been more than just a cookhouse for the occupants of the village. Each day at noon, they gathered for a meal provided from the meager supplies the villagers were allowed to keep, or forage: turnips, coarse wheaten bread made from oats or barley, beans, oatcakes, and an occasional bit of meat consisting of a stringy rabbit or a bird unlucky enough to venture within the fields allotted to the villeins.

In her frustration, Giles became the object of her anger. Every time she looked at him she felt her irritation grow. After all, it was his fault she was here, his fault that she had been cast in the role of a villein. She could have lived happily the whole of her life without knowing what these people suffered. What could she do about it, after all? And what had he done about it? He had become one of them, doing so with an ease that had both shocked and disgusted her. He was the great knight, born into ease and comfort, yet he fell into his new role as if it were a game—nay, more than a game—and it confounded her.

If that wasn't bad enough, Rodger Farnham had appeared, without warning, making it all so much worse. Alone in their hut, she and Giles had been hissing at each other, the nearest they were allowed to a screaming match, as they fought over who was going to sleep on the floor. "Roanna," he had begun, a warning lift to his dark brow, "the cot is big enough for both of us. I simply cannot continue to sleep on the floor and put in a full day's work!"

She had regarded him with horror. "If ye think ye're goin' to sleep wi' me, you better think again, ye bloody bugger!"

"Dammit, Roanna! Why is it that every time you get mad you start talking like a damned London doxy? You heard me, I said *sleep!* Don't flatter yourself that I am suggesting anything more," he snarled, eyeing the bed.

"If ye want a bed, build one."

"How would we explain that? We're supposed to be married, Roanna, perish the thought. Your uncle trusted me, why can't you?"

Her eyes narrowed suspiciously. "'ow do I know that we're supposed to be married?"

He sighed impatiently. "Roanna, would you be living with a man not your husband?"

"Ye could 'ave been my brother!" she argued.

"And you would have been open to any advances you met, without the protection of the Church."

"I 'ave the protection of an addle-brained nitwit!"

"A strong, jealous nitwit," he countered. "I mean it, Roanna, it's the bed or the floor."

"Take the floor."

"I don't mean me."

She stared at him. "Ye don't mean me?" she said incredulously. He broke into an easy grin, answering her question. "Ye, sir, are no gentleman!"

"I never claimed to be," he pointed out. "As I see it, since you are averse to my suggestion, the only answer is to take turns. Tonight is mine."

"Ye can't be serious!"

"Deadly."

He meant it. Well, taking turns was certainly preferable to the alternative he offered. Fair enough—the slime—after all, how bad could the floor be? It was then that she saw his head come up as his eyes darted to the door. Motioning her to be quiet with a finger to his lips, he moved to the hide in the doorway, pulling it back slightly.

To Roanna's amazement, which only slightly exceeded Giles's own, Rodger Farnham slipped through the narrow opening, his face brightening as he stepped into the meager light from the solitary candle. "Rodger!" Giles gasped. "God's mercy, what are you doing here—how did you find me?"

The knight's hazel eyes flickered over the mean hovel to Roanna where she sat wide-eyed on the cot. As his eyes flashed with amusement, he offered her a warm smile. "Pah, Giles, that was easy. Last seen you were pursuing Mistress Roanna—I see that you've found her." Noting Giles's black look, he shrugged. "Roscoe Dorking told me where to find you. But do not worry, no one saw me. Eleanor gave me ample coin to bribe one of the guards at the northern gate, then I waited until dark to come in." He patted the small leather sack at his waist with satisfaction. "I have enough here to see us both out of here; just give the word."

Giles's face grew grave at Rodger's last words. "Just tell me what has happened."

"I am for Wales," Rodger answered solemnly, then glanced about. "Lord, Giles, have you some wine or ale? I'm dry as old straw."

"We have only water," Roanna answered apologetically, slipping from the cot to draw him a ladleful from a bucket she had hung on the wall.

"My thanks, mistress," the knight said, drinking deeply from the dripping ladle. As Roanna resettled on the cot, Giles sat next to her, gesturing Rodger to the stool. "I could not leave England without seeing you," he said, sighing, as he sat down, slipping back the wool hood of his tunic.

Noting Rodger's garments, Giles smiled grimly. The heavy wool of the plain tunic did little to conceal the evidence of a hauberk beneath. "Who is after you?"

"No one—yet," Rodger said with a grimace. "Giles, the king has gone mad. When he returned, he gathered those barons closest to him, and others are flocking to him following Gloucester's betrayal of our cause. They hope to be rewarded with the lands of those Henry deems traitors. The king is determined to take the reins again, and to punish those who dared to defy him. He has renounced the Magna Carta and sent John Mansel to Rome to intercede with the pope to repudiate that which was gained at Oxford."

Giles appeared to take the news calmly, but Roanna saw a muscle twitch in his cheek as his eyes grew cold. "What of Eleanor and Simon?" he asked quietly.

"They bide their time. Henry does not dare confront Simon openly. He knows that could be the catalyst that spurs the remaining barons into action. As for me, the countess advised me to return to Wales. Word reached her"—he paused, exchanging a hard look of understanding with Giles; they were both fully aware of the vast network of spies in Eleanor's employ—"that your lands in both Wales and Ireland are in jeopardy."

Roanna heard the sharp intake of Giles's breath. "Tell me, all of it!" he snapped.

"You have become somewhat of a celebrity, Giles. You were seen entering London, and Richard of Cornwall's residence. Rumor has it—depending upon which rumor you choose to believe—that you are either a traitor or a secret supporter of the Crown. The king, of course, in his usual amazing manner, has chosen to believe both, depending upon who has his ear at the moment. And, as usual, he is covering his bets. He has praised you openly in court, reminding those nearby that you are the son of his 'Dear Will,' the best friend a man ever had. Meanwhile, he has issued orders to take your lands. He has sent men beyond his writ to take what is yours, to keep it in security against your good faith." He paused as Giles swore violently under his breath. "I swear to you, Giles, no one shall take Trahern while I live. And as for Ireland, I have already taken the liberty of sending missives to Sir Landon, advising him of the situation." He chuckled, a sound that seemed out of place in the hut. "I would like to see anyone try to take Castle Kinnell with Landon on the wall."

"You have done well, Rodger," Giles said quietly. The tension in his voice caused Roanna to turn and look at him. Suddenly she began to realize, for the first time, the burden of responsibility, the conflict of loyalties that he carried. Her awareness of him had been only of a personal nature: a handsome knight, too often the bane of her existence, one apparently sent to test her fortitude. It seemed strange to consider his life apart from her experiences with him, odd to think that he had a life beyond that moment of their first meeting. A flash of something elusive, and acutely uncomfortable, touched her sharply. She was jealous of his life beyond her, of the experiences, joys, sorrows, fears, and sense of living he had known before her. Watching him, she suddenly sensed what he was about to say, and she felt a strange mixture of sadness and joy.

"I cannot go with you, Rodger. There are things I must do here."

Rodger was silent for a moment. Then, rising, he held out his arm, which Giles rose to grasp. "I did not really expect that you would do otherwise," Rodger said quietly. "But I swear to you, Giles, your lands will be held safe or I will not face you again in this life." Turning a sudden grin on Roanna, the familiar twinkle reappearing in his hazel eyes, he bowed over her hand. "Mistress Roanna, I pray for your good keeping, and that we shall meet again in a better time." Then, in a lowered voice meant only for her hearing, "Take care of him." And he was gone.

They were silent for a long moment, in the sudden emptiness of Rodger's departure. Touched and oddly stirred by the knight's last words to her, Roanna stole a glance at Giles. He was lost in his own troubled thoughts, as evidenced by the deep creases in his brow, and she marveled at the charge given to her by the knight. She thought that Giles must be daft. "Why did ye stay?" she asked. "Ye could 'ave gone with 'im."

He turned his head and looked at her. "Could I?"

Now, as she sat in the dilapidated inn before the cold hearth, she recalled the look he had given her and shivered suddenly. When Rodger had left they had not spoken beyond those final words. Silently, she had taken a blanket from the bed and curled up on the grass pallet he had made by the far wall, accepting without further argument her turn upon the floor. It was a long time before she slept, because of the unaccustomed hard-packed earth beneath her and the disturbing thoughts that ran relentlessly through her mind. She knew, from the tossing she heard upon the cot, that he was finding it impossible to sleep as well. When Giles had shaken her awake the following morning, she had struggled to rise, every muscle and bone in her body screaming in silent protest. She was aware of muscles she had not even known existed. Each hour of the day had seemed to stretch into three, her only comfort gained from the fact that she was too tired and sore to think. Gratefully exhausted, she had slept well that night. Throwing Giles a satisfied smirk as he rose stiffly this morning from the hardpacked floor, she'd gamboled out of the hut to her daily duties.

Now, as the day waned, she was again facing disturbing thoughts that had flashed through her mind throughout the past few days. She had been granted no exhausted release this day—she had not even had Gilda to distract her. The woman had left to take supper to the men in the fields, and Roanna had been left quite alone with thoughts she would sooner have ignored.

Roanna didn't like being confused. Oh, she accepted problems; they were part of life, after all. Face a problem, think about it, solve it. At least, that was the way it had been before Giles fitzWilliam had entered her life. Since then, she had wrestled with a goat, bathed in a hallway, come close to sharing a bed with the heir to England's throne, nearly set herself on fire, drunk wine with a duke, fled the king's soldiers, and become a cindermaid in a run-down inn outside of London. And she was living with a man she knew nothing about, except that he loved another, while she—

That last thought brought her up short, and she blinked into the empty hearth. While she what? An illusive feeling passed through her, a feeling she had had before, one she had fought ever since the night she had seen the insipid Lisette slip into her lover's bower. As had happened then, she suddenly was seized by a terrifying awareness of vulnerability. Confusion returned, filling her with a vision of Giles, and the awareness of his increasing presence in her life.

Then she heard a door slam, and Gilda's voice. Rising wearily from the stool, she picked up the bucket of ashes to dump it outside on her way back to the hut she shared with him. Damn, she thought grumpily as she crossed the road; with everything else, it was her turn to sleep on the floor.

She could have strangled Giles for his cheerfulness when he returned. Pouting, she curled up on the cot with her back to the wall, and silently defied him to remove her. He splashed his face with water, drying it with a rag Gilda had given them for bathing. "Well, Roanna, 'ow was yer day, lass?" His eyes crinkled at her over the cloth.

"Fine," she answered sulkily, smoothing out a wrinkle in her skirt.

"Good as all that, eh?"

"What d'ye want from me?" she snapped.

He regarded her for an instant, then tossed the rag on the stool. "What is wrong, Roanna?" he asked quietly.

"What is wrong?" she sputtered. "Bugger! I think ye're enjoyin' this!"

"Don't be simple," he retorted. "I am merely determined to make the best of it. It would seem to make little sense to do anything else."

"Instead of acceptin' it, why don't ye try to find us a way out of this mess?" she said accusingly. "I—I cannot stand any more! I want to go 'ome! I can't sleep on that floor, live in this filth, work fer a woman who's too addlepated to realize that she's a slave to some blighter who doesn't care if she lives or dies!"

Giles struggled to control his temper. He would have liked nothing better than to have it out with her, to allow her to vent her emotions and the tension they were both feeling, but sounds carried in the night hours and they could not afford that luxury. But he realized that the passage of time had finally allowed her to recover from the numbness that had followed their departure from the Flying Sail, and he sensed that she was about to break. He had to deal with her now, when he was there to control her outburst. He grabbed their cloaks and then reached for her wrist, pulling her from the cot.

"What are ye doing?" she exclaimed.

"You're coming with me," he answered grimly, pulling her out of the hut. "And for God's sake, be quiet!"

He led her around the hut, lifted her over the low stone wall surrounding the hamlet, and began to lead her over the harvested field. The stubble caught at her skirt as she tried to keep up with his long strides, and she swore at him under her breath. "Giles fitzWilliam, where in damnation are ye takin' me!"

"Where no one will hear us," he growled, yanking her abreast of him.

He led her, half stumbling, across the pasture to the far

hedge of white thorn. "This should do it. Now, sit down! We're going to have a talk."

"About what?" she gasped, trying to catch her breath. "Giles, ye're bloomin' mad!"

"So you keep telling me. But before you say anything else, I have a few things to say, and you are going to listen. Sit down."

She obeyed him, and he hunkered down next to her, his elbows resting on his legs. "You know, it amazes me that one who was raised as you were should be such a spoiled brat. Do not say a word!" he warned at the sound of her gasp. "I know that you are an intelligent, feeling young woman, and moreover, you've not been reared in luxury— but dammit, Roanna! You continuously refuse to apply the advantages you've had!"

"Advantages?" She blinked. "What advantages?"

"God," he breathed. "Don't you know? I remember moments on the battlements at Durham House when you showed promise, an understanding of people, of conditions, that few are privileged to see. You gained that understanding from the life you've led, and from your uncle, who treated you as a person, not just a body to warm some man's bed! But then, when I begin to expect real reason, some depth of thought from you, you throw a half-witted tantrum!"

Her mouth was open in shock. Swallowing, she could find no response other than a petulant shrug. "I don't like it here," she said sulkily.

"Sweet Mother, and you think I do?" he exploded. "Evidently I need to remind you who brought us to this! You, Roanna, in your bratty self-indulgence! If you had remained at Durham House, we would not be here now!"

"Oh, so that's it?" She bristled, her own anger flaring. "We both know what ye'd be doin' if ye 'adn't been ordered to bring me back! Seducin' the fair Lady Lisette!"

"Oh, Christ!" he roared. He leapt up and flung away from her, fearing what he might do if he did not remove himself from her presence. Gathering his wits about him, he finally turned back to her, his anger carefully controlled. "Roanna, what I do with my life is of no concern to you. What is of concern to us both is what we must do now—here. You will not mention Lisette again—do you understand? Beyond that, I brought you here so that we might speak freely. Say what is on your mind—let us settle it, once and for all."

"I don't care what ye bloody want!" she cried, hating him. Oh, why had he mentioned those nights on the parapet, when she had tried so hard to forget them!

"Roanna, if you say 'bloody' to me, one more time, I'll—"

"Ye'll what?" she screamed. "Try it and I'll—" Suddenly she stopped short, with her own words ringing in her ears. She felt totally drained, and her mouth tasted bitter and sour. Oh, Lord, what was the matter with her? When had she become such a shrew? He was right. Did she hate him so much that she was blaming him even for this? It had been her fault, all of it. Yet, until now, though she had deserved it, he had never blamed her, not once. And she knew now, since Rodger's visit, how much he had to blame her for, how much he had lost because of her impulsiveness.

One thing was certain: she could not discuss her reasons for leaving Durham House, not with him, of all people. Before today she had thought she had buried those feelings, only to find that again she felt raw, vulnerable, etched with pain. Yet new thoughts and feelings had been added to the old ones as she had listened to him talk with Rodger. She was suddenly aware of the depth of his life—there was so much about him she did not understand. How childlike she felt, with a man she wanted, as never before, to look upon her as a woman.

Feeling tongue-tied, she said the first thing that came to her mind. "I don't like it 'ere," she repeated softly. "I don't like them."

"Why, Roanna?" he asked. His voice was suddenly gentle as he sat down beside her. "Have they been unkind to you?"

"Nay." She shook her head. "They're never unkind, exactly, but—they're so distant."

"As you have been to them. They are not people who will open their hearts easily; it is too easy to be hurt, Roanna. But they will return whatever you offer."

She had the grace to blush at the truth of his words. "Their life is so 'ard," she said with feeling. "But they do nothin' to improve their situation—they just accept it!"

"What would you have them do?"

"I—I don't know, but somethin'!"

"Ah, that is a solution, certainly."

"Don't make fun of me, Giles!" she said sulkily.

"I'm not, I only want you to think. What would you have them do?"

"Fight back!"

"Fight who? Their lord, the earl of Waltham, and his knights, his men-at-arms, his pikemen?" He reached out and lifted a heavy red-gold plait from her shoulder, fingering its silkiness. "Your ancestors were Saxon, Roanna; mine conquered them. Why did they not fight?"

"They did!" she protested.

"Yet the Normans conquered them. They continued to fight, and they were subjugated."

"If ye believe that 'tis 'opeless, why are ye 'ere?" she asked, frustrated. "Why don't ye go back to Wales? Just give up, if that be what you expect others to do!"

"No, Roanna, it is not what I expect. Not for me, and not for them. But one cannot fight against overwhelming odds. Success is for those who see it at the proper moment, and grasp it when the signs are right."

"Pah," she snorted. "They could starve waitin'."

"Some will, many have."

"And ye, what are ye waitin' for, Giles? A sign from 'eaven?"

"That would be convenient," he said, laughing softly. "Nay, I am waiting for an earthly sign—I have been waiting for it all my life. I do not claim to be patient, Roanna. Many times I have been sorely tempted to claim that I have received it, and only in hindsight do I realize that the results would have been disastrous—and worse, ineffectual. Patience, I think, is the hardest virtue of all."

She held her breath, sensing that if she played the moment right, she might find answers to some questions that had long plagued her. "Ye—ye really do care about these people, don't ye?"

"I care."

"But why? Ye were born into position and wealth."

"Born into wealth?" He laughed, but the sound, while it held no bitterness, was empty. "Sweetling, I was born a stableboy, and thus I spent the first ten years of my life."

She gaped at him. "A stableboy?" Then she snorted with disbelief. "Ye think I'm a twit, if ye think I believe that!"

"Believe what you will. It is true."

"Lud!" she gasped. "Truly? Oh, Giles, tell me!"

"Do you really want to hear this?"

"Oh—aye! I want to know."

"All right, then." He shrugged. "I was born in a convent, where my mother had been sequestered to hide her shame of bearing me unwed. She died birthing me. Although her tirewoman had been instructed to take me to my father, should anything happen to her, the woman carried me instead to Northumberland, to my grandfather."

"Why would she do that?"

"She had been paid to do so by my grandfather, who was a northern lord."

"And yer father? What did 'e do?"

"Nothing. The sisters in the convent had been well paid to swear that I had died with my mother. My father did not learn of my existence until I was ten."

"But why? I mean, why did yer grandfather do such a thing?"

He hesitated, unwilling to reveal the answers, even after all these years. How could he tell her of a man who was so depraved, so perverted, as to seek the child of the daughter who had fled his advances before her very soul had been destroyed? How could he tell her that he had been saved from the evils of his grandfather only by the old man's death? "He died before I grew to know him. The answer resides with him."

"But ye said ye were raised as a stableboy. 'ow could that be, if yer grandfather were noble?"

"Roanna, are you going to let me tell this story?"

"Sorry," she said meekly, earning a doubtful look from him.

"I was raised by a nursemaid and, in those very early years, by my uncle, Darcy, a former Franciscan monk turned goliard. But he was a truly great man—"

"The goliard!" she exclaimed, fascinated. "'e raised ye?"

"Only for a brief time, to my regret. My grandfather died and the lands passed to a cousin. Then, in rapid course he too died, and the demesne passed to an even more distant relative. 'Twas then that I found myself relegated to the stables—a quick resolution of an unwanted problem."

"What of Darcy?"

"Long before, he had been refused visits to me. I lost track of him for many years—although I learned years later that it was he who told my father about me, of my existence."

"What 'appened?"

"I am trying to tell you," he said, sighing. "When I was ten, my father suddenly appeared. I remember that I was in the stable mending a harness, and I heard a voice calling to me, so I put it down and went toward the voice. He was there, with the light of the courtyard at his back. I'll never forget that moment. He stood in the doorway—I didn't know who he was, or why he was there. I asked him if he desired a mount to be saddled. He merely said my name. He was so tall, gazing down at me . . . That was the first time I saw the red lion—emblazoned on his surcoat." He smiled, his eyes distant. "I didn't know that I looked just like him. But somehow I knew that, at that moment, my life had changed. He took me with him, and from that day on, no man could have asked for a better, more loving father."

"Then—that is why ye can meld yerself so easily into this life," she mused.

"Easily? Hardly, Roanna. This life is never easy—but I understand it. More importantly, I understand the desperation of a villein, perhaps even more than those here. They, by virtue of distance from their lord, are left largely to themselves. I know what it is to live under the will of another who sees you as less than an animal, who gives more care to his favorite horse, to the swine who will give meat."

"What 'appened to 'im?" she asked after a moment. "The lord who treated ye so."

"My father saw my dear, distant cousin ruined, though he used the law to accomplish it. As marshal of England, he brought Saebroc up on charges of crenellating his walls for defense without license from the king to do so. Eleanor saw to it that his lands were given to me, but I could not bear to hold them. I petitioned Henry to trade for lands in Wales, adding to those my father and uncles had given to me."

Roanna was silent as she considered all that he had said. A deep feeling of shame overwhelmed her. Sweet Mother, she thought, what he must have suffered; yet he lived through it without bitterness. She had heard no cynicism in his voice, and she could not help but wonder at its absence as he had recounted his story. Lud, she realized that she had not even been able to live a few days in far better conditions than he had spent the whole of his early years without acting like a termagant. She felt deeply ashamed, and moreover, embarrassed as she realized the things she had said to him, her spiteful anger. She swallowed heavily. "And so ye came to be Sir Giles fitzWilliam, knight of the realm, and then again the villein—because of me. I 'ave much to apologize for, Giles."

"Roanna, we make mistakes, that is the human condition. It is how we deal with them that makes the difference. Try with me to make the best of it here. That's all we can do."

She could not look at him. The soft understanding in his voice touched her in a way that pierced her remaining defenses. She trembled, glad that it was dark and he could not see how his words had affected her. Nothing had been as she had thought it was. He was not the uncaring, selfish nobleman, the hardened, callous courtier; he was everything her heart had known—and feared—he would be from the first moment she had seen him upon the parapet at Durham House, smiling down at her as he saluted her from the battlements. He had taken her heart at that moment, and she had swiftly thrown up a wall, knowing that to face her feelings would lead to terrible pain. Her fears had been confirmed since the moment after he had first touched her, when he had left her at her chamber door, his mind and thoughts already on other matters. It would ever be this way—his duty, his world, his Lisette would allow nothing else.

So be it, Roanna, she thought. So it shall be. But, oh, God, I will love him as no other will love him. And I will take what I am given and hold it to my heart, not daring to ask for more.

When she spoke, though it cost great effort, her voice was light. "On the morrow I'll try to do better, I do promise, Giles."

"Tomorrow will prove easier. It's hard to be unhappy at a celebration." Seeing her confused look, he laughed softly. "Did Gilda not tell you?"

"Tell me?"

"We are going to a wedding. It shall be a holiday for us all."

"A wedding?" she gasped.

"'Tis a very special time for a village, Roanna. Beyond the bonding of the lovers, it is a promise that the village will endure."

"Will ye explain it all to me?"

"Of course." He grinned. "On two conditions. One, that you will remember that you cannot speak. And secondly, that you will save a dance for me."

8

Giles shook Roanna awake before dawn. She opened her eyes sleepily to find him grinning down at her. Moaning, she rolled away to face the wall.

"You'll have to get up now if you want time to bathe."

It took a moment before his words registered. Bathe? She rolled back and gaped at him, and he gestured behind him. Glancing where he indicated, her eyes widened. It was a tub—a rather small wooden tub, but a tub nonetheless. She sat up. "Oh, Giles! Where did you get it!"

"From Gilda, with some gesturing and grunting," he said, grinning. "The water is hot, you'd better hurry."

"Oh, Giles!" she exclaimed, leaping from the bed.

"You don't think I'd let you go to a wedding without a bath, do you?" he said, pleased by her obvious pleasure. "I have to feed the stock, so be ready when I get back."

"May I wash my hair?" she asked hesitatingly, staring hungrily at the steaming water.

"Aye," he said over his shoulder as he left. "But bind it in a coif."

It took her only moments to strip herself of the soiled garments, and she sank into the precious, steaming water. Her knees bent up at sharp angles in the narrow space and her elbows stuck out over the sides, but it did not matter—it was a bath, a real bath. Giles had set a pitcher of warm water on the stool next to the tub along with a bar of lye soap and a clean cloth for a towel. She immediately lathered her hair, relishing the tingling sensation of the soap as it foamed against her scalp. Oh, Lord, she thought, how wonderful it will be to feel clean once again!

She scrubbed her hair, and then her body until it was flushed a rosy hue. Then she settled as comfortably as she could in the small tub, determined not to leave the unexpected luxury until the water had turned impossibly cold. Her mind drifted back over the past night, the things Giles had told her—and the moments that passed when they had returned to the hut. She felt a warm flush run the length of her body.

At first she had thought Giles was being wonderfully noble when he told her to take the cot—until he told her to move over. She had simply stared at him. On the one hand, she wanted him—oh, how she wanted him—and she knew that if he so much as touched her, she would be lost. On the other hand, she knew he did not love her, that his feelings were engaged by another at Durham House; she was repelled by the idea of giving herself to a man who loved someone else. She had stared, speechlessly, but he took her silence as agreement and she had found him on the cot beside her. Then she had continued to stare in the darkness at his back; but before she could recover, his breathing had deepened to even, light snores. Soon, she too had slept.

It had been wonderfully comforting, to sleep beside him, sharing the warmth of his body. Thinking on it now, she smiled softly. At least neither of them would have to spend another night on the hard-packed floor. Besides, considering the fact that he obviously did not feel for her in that way, she was quite safe—both from his attentions and from her own confused emotions.

"Damn!"

Startled by the oath, she looked around and found him standing in the doorway, staring at her. He turned his head away, but not before she saw that his face had suffused with color. "Roanna, get dressed, there is not much time," he said in a strained voice, then snapped the hide door back into place.

She stared at the oiled hide, and slowly her mouth drew up into a smile. The blighter was a fraud! Chuckling, she stepped from the tub and hurried to dry herself. So, she thought happily, perhaps he was not so oblivious to her charms, after all. Not that he could have seen much, the way she was folded up to fit in the tub. Then her smile faded as she realized that she was going to have to put on the gamy kirtle again, and she shuddered, repelled by the prospect. Sighing, she reached toward the hook where she had hung it, then paused, her eyes widening as she stared at the hook next to it. In her eagerness to take a bath she had not noticed that he had hung another garment on the peg he usually used for his own clothing. It was a coarsely made but clean kirtle of blue wool, with a chemise of soft muslin and a yard of linen to use as a coif for her hair. She could not stay the tears of gratitude that welled up in her eyes as she took down the garments, realizing everything he had done for her.

She slipped into the chemise and kirtle, then called toward the door, "You can come in now." As she suspected, he was waiting just outside, and he ducked through the low doorway. As the morning light through the open doorway fell on her, he paused. "You look rather pleased with yourself," he commented gruffly.

"I am pleased—with ye. 'ow did ye manage it?" she asked, stroking her hands over the wonderfully clean wool.

"More grunting." He shrugged.

Then she noticed that he had changed as well, wearing patched but clean leggings and a linen chanise covered by a sleeveless tunic of brown wool. "Won't we appear different to them, now that we're clean and better dressed?"

"Not in their own clothes," he said. "Besides, their opinions have been quite formed. If we do nothing drastic to sway them, we're safe enough. They are convinced we've improved due to their encouragement and help." His eyes passed over her slowly; then he suddenly frowned. "You'd better cover your hair."

"Oh, could I not just braid it?"

"Cover it."

Obediently she twisted it into a knot and bound her head with the length of linen, tying the ends at the back of her neck. Nodding approval, Giles held back the door flap. She stepped into the sunlight, then stopped abruptly, leaning back against him as he stepped out behind her. "Oh," she exclaimed softly. "What is happening?"

The villagers had gathered in a cluster, their number increased by friends and guests from nearby hamlets. A path had been cleared through their midst for the advance of an angry-looking man of middle age, who was striding purposefully toward one of the cottages.

"Oh, Giles!" Roanna gasped. "Is there going to be a fight?"

"Not in the sense that you mean," Giles said, chuckling softly near her ear. "The father of the bridegroom must seek approval from his lord for the marriage. This has already been done, and he has paid the demanded coin. Then the two fathers argue the details: the dower the bride will bring to the father of the groom, the settlement of land the lad's father will grant to the couple, what gifts shall be made to the Church. This has also been done. What you are seeing is symbolic. The irate man is the bride's father. He is calling upon the father of the groom to demand a secure place for his daughter. He will enter the house of his future in-laws in anger, acting out what has gone before."

"Then it is just a play!" she whispered.

"More or less. Just a play, though as old as England itself. What you will see today represents a vital part of their lives. Watch."

The man shouted angrily at the door to the cottage, then disappeared within. The gathered company waited quietly, the silence broken occasionally by the sound of a restless child and the hushed reprimand of a parent. Eventually the man reappeared with the father of the bride. The latter made a brief, emotional speech saying that an agreement had been reached, much to the riotous approval of the crowd.

The gathering quieted suddenly as the bride appeared, flanked by her mother, aunts, and maiden cousins. Bedecked in her finest kirtle of green-dyed wool, her hair bound in a coif of white linen held about her forehead by a circlet of wild flowers, the bride stood among her women, her eyes modestly downcast. Roanna gasped softly, her eyes widening as they fixed on the bride and her flowering form.

"Giles," she whispered, "she is with child!"

Her announcement met with silence. She finally glanced up at him and found her watching him with an odd look of speculation. "Come," he said softly, taking her arm. "'Tis a long way to the church. As we walk, I will try to explain a few matters to you."

The morning fog had burned off, leaving the rolling green hills basking in the warmth of morning. Giles and Roanna walked behind the others, remaining apart so that they might talk, but he found himself uncertain what to say to her. Breath of God, he thought, how could one mere slip of a girl so change one's life? He did not recall asking for the opportunity; she just seemed suddenly to have been there, and his life had not been the same since. Now he found himself walking to a wedding in the company of a maid who was dismayed by the discovery that a bride came to the church door carrying the proof of her love. How did he explain this to a girl whom he suspected to be a virgin? How much *did* she understand?

"Roanna . . ." he began, clearing his throat. "A villein's life is measured by the amount of land he can farm to support his family. This land is granted to him by his lord. When he has a son, he can look forward to the time when there shall be grandchildren to increase his holdings. As there are more hands to work the land, his lord will increase his acreage. Thus, it is vital that children be brought from marriage. Do you understand?"

"Of course," Roanna assured him, watching the gaiety of the wedding party ahead of them.

"Good," he grunted. "Well, then." He hesitated, clearing his throat again—an uncharacteristic sound that finally gained her attention. "If a woman proved to be barren, you understand how unfortunate it would be. No children, no additional lands . . ."

She listened intently, wondering where his conversation was leading.

"Well, then," he repeated. "The betrothal of a villein is called hand-fasting. Once the pledge is given, the couple can choose to—to live together. It is important that the bride prove her ability to bear children before the final vows of marriage are taken. Can you understand this?"

Her expression softened from curiosity to affectionate disbelief as she realized the source of his discomfort. Lud, she thought, she might not understand the traditions of a rural villein, but how could she be raised amid the comings and goings of a tavern and not understand the basic facts of begetting a child? How could he think her so naive? His caution made her feel wonderful, in a warming, happy rush. He actually had thought of her as a delicately reared maiden who would have fairly swooned at such information! Why else would he suddenly be so tongue-tied? It made her feel quite special.

So it suddenly became imperative that he not be made to realize the foolishness of his feelings. "Oh, Giles!" she exclaimed softly, trying to flush becomingly. "Ye mean that—dear me, I see!" Her eyes were dancing and she fixed them upon the road ahead of her to avoid letting him see, but his silence finally made her venture a glance at him.

"'Dear me'?" he repeated mockingly, his eyes narrowing with suspicion. "Aren't you overdoing it, Roanna? Do not play me for the fool, sweetling," he added grimly, his eyes touched with anger.

She began to affect an innocent look, denying that she understood his meaning, but she gave it up, unable to deceive him. "Pish, Giles, I know where babies come from. 'ow could I not, considerin' where I was raised? But—'twas rather nice for a bit, to be treated as ye would a gently bred lady."

She wondered at the strange look he gave her. She finally had to look away, growing uncomfortable under his piercing regard.

"Have I treated you so badly, Roanna?" he asked softly.

"Treated me badly? When?" She frowned.

"Since we first met."

"Nay! I mean—" Oh, Lord, what could she say to that? "Whatever 'as 'appened 'as not been yer doin', Giles. I know that now."

He frowned and fell silent. Stealing a sideward glance at her, he noted the pink flush to her complexion as she fixed her gaze on the villagers ahead of them. He knew she was unsettled, in spite of her easy words.

Had he treated her badly? It had never been his intention to do so. Of course he had not behaved toward her in the same manner that he would a lady nobly born—as he would, say, toward Lisette. They were different women. Lisette had been isolated, gently reared. Roanna had been raised in the sometimes brutal reality of a dockside tavern. Lisette was naive, cocooned from the harsher side of life. Roanna saw life as it was, and even beyond to the deeper twists of man's condition. Lisette held the security of her world tightly about her, as a woman bred for the comfort of her husband should. Roanna, on the other hand, brought her innocence to life head-on. What she did not know was only from lack of experience, which she would eventually gain as she met each day with enthusiasm, making a wealth of mistakes along the way. Lisette would give a man a life of comfort, an easy harbor to sail into following each voyage. Roanna—he drew a shallow breath—Roanna would be the bane of a man's existence, a storm that would make a tempest at sea appear as a gentle swell. Lord, even he, who only sought to give her the protection of a friend, a brother, found himself rowing against an exhausting current.

Lost in thought, he started as she tugged at his sleeve. "Giles?"

"What is it, Roanna?"

"Uncle Roscoe told me that the barons once made a law sayin' that if a child began out of wedlock, even if the parents later wed, it could never inherit. 'ow then can this babe 'elp the village?"

He blinked at the question, so totally in contrast to the idle wandering of his own thoughts. "The purpose of the Council of Merton, to which you refer, was to strengthen the rule of primogeniture, Roanna, protecting legal heirs to title and land. If followed to the letter, it would indeed affect this child, but the villeins are not bound by the law. For them, the customs of the individual manors are observed."

"Then—'tis only those like yerself who are 'eld to the law," she observed.

His eyes shot to her, but the open look she wore, without a trace of guile, disarmed whatever anger her words had brought. "Aye. Like me," he answered. "Even if my parents had later married, I would not have been able to inherit."

The road ahead of them absorbed her attention as her face became a study in thought. He watched her brow wrinkle in concentration and gave in to a smile, oddly pleased by her questions. The thought struck him, as he watched her pensive, ever-changing expression, that she was really quite lovely, and he wondered how it was that he so seldom noticed her beauty. Then he was distracted by laughter ahead of them, and he realized that the church lay just ahead and the wedding party had gathered before its doors.

"Enough, Roanna," he whispered. "Say nothing more."

She nodded slightly, and directed her eyes eagerly to the scene before her.

After they had been greeted by the bridal couple and their families, Giles drew Roanna apart where they could stand unobserved by the others. Silence fell over the festive gathering as the doors of the small stone church opened and the priest appeared. The bridesmen and bridesmaids gathered about the couple, urging them forward to the steps of the church where the cleric waited. His voice rose over the gathering to ask if there were any present who objected to the binding of the couple in marriage.

After a respectful pause, the groom stepped forward. His voice cracked nervously, to the amusement of his kinfolk and guests. "I—I bring ta me bride me dower of land as given by me father, a pledge that she'll be cared fer, even beyond me own life." The girl went down on her knees, took his hands in hers, and placed a kiss upon them. Helping her to rise again, the groom brought out a small packet from his tunic and handed it to the priest.

Giles bent and murmured in Roanna's ear, "She knelt before him in gratitude for the pledge he made to her, the assurance that she will be cared for if he should die. The packet contains a ring, meant as a pledge, or wed, to fulfill the marriage contract."

Everyone was now looking at the bride, who flushed becomingly; her voice could barely be heard. "I give to me 'usband tha' which 'as been given me by me father as dower: three bolts o' wool, a kettle of iron fer me 'earth, two geese fer our flock, an' a sucklin' pig."

The priest smiled and nodded with approval. "Do you, Almer Stedman, consent to this marriage?"

The groom nodded, then turned to take the bride's hand in his. "I take thee, Maida, as mine."

"And I take thee, Almer, as mine," the bride responded softly.

The priest unwrapped the packet, blessed it, then held out the contents to Almer. The young man took the ring and slid the band onto the bride's middle finger. "Wi' this ring, I wed thee," he said thickly. Then he took the three coins from the priest's hands and pressed them into his bride's palm. "And wi' this gold, I honor thee."

Softly Giles explained that the coins were a pledge of his

lands, and meant that if he died before her, his lands would be hers until her death, that she could not be turned out by his family to starve. "She is a lucky lass," he murmured. "The giving of the coins is not often done. He must love her very much. She'll guard those coins with her life. Mass will be said, but it is this part of the marriage, what is pledged at the church door, that carries the most importance for the villein."

They moved into the church for the nuptial mass. As the service began, the bridal couple knelt at the altar and a length of white linen was placed over their shoulders as the priest blessed them. Roanna glanced up questioningly at Giles as they stood in the shadows by the open door.

"'Tis the care-cloth," he whispered. "Any children conceived before marriage are placed beneath the cloth and legitimized as mass is said."

When the mass ended, the couple rose and the groom received the kiss of peace from the priest. He then turned and kissed his bride, sealing the pledges made that day.

The festivities began as soon as the party arrived back in the village. Trestle tables were quickly set up and were soon laden with the villagers' contributions in celebration of the young couple, a promise of the future that would benefit them all. Musicians had been hired from London by the absent lord of Waltham, who had also sent along a few coins for the bridal supper. The quality of the players left little doubt that the earl's purse had not been sorely strained, but even the poorly played lute and lyre, overbalanced by a rather enthusiastic drummer, began to sound acceptable as the bride-ale flowed and the company was caught up in the joy of the day.

Roanna held back, watching the revelry of the villagers with a half-smile as she leaned against the wall of the byre. Her gaze strayed to Giles as he carried a heavy platter of roasted woodcocks and curlews to the table. Her heart constricted as his mouth broke into a grin over some remark by Ferris, the village smithy. Even in his villein's clothing he was the handsomest man she had ever known, not only in face and form, but also in character.

He quaffed a cup of bride-ale in a contest with another man as a small group about the pair boisterously cheered them on. Giles had been right about the villagers' acceptance of the change in them, but how he had managed it she couldn't fathom. He no longer bent his body; his speech had improved, though it still held the heavy accent of Northumbria; his apparent comprehension and intelligence had improved considerably. And he had been totally accepted by the villagers, as she had been. The gradual change had not been regarded with suspicion, but simply accepted. Loyalty had replaced distrust, as the improvement was gained under their growing affection. She shook her head, still amazed as she recalled Gilda's words of but a few days past, as the woman remarked with almost personal pride on Giles's remarkable improvement: "Love an' carin' is strong, lass. It drives the demons out."

But who would drive her demons out, she wondered, those demons that would haunt her until the end of her life? Only one man's love could do so, and it would never be hers.

She had never suspected that there could exist a man of so many contrasts. Self-assured, his own man among men of greatness, Giles bore his trials without apology, without bitterness or hatred for what he had been dealt. Another man would have railed against what could not be his, watching men of inferior ability rise to greatness by a trick of birth, but he seemed to be as much at home among the people of a poor village as in the great halls of the nobility. He had not lost his love for the people of his childhood, had not rejected them along with the bitter memories he certainly must have. Where did his strength come from? How had he managed to become the man he was?

Roanna sighed raggedly, swallowing the lump that formed in her throat. The past hours in his company as they shared in the ceremonies and the celebration had only served to remind her of what she could never have. She loved him. Silently, wrenchingly, she admitted it. Yet she also knew that she had fallen in love with someone who would never, could never, truly be part of her life.

Each time she thought of him with Lisette, she felt a small death, knowing that his liaison with the Gascon maid was inevitable. Lisette was everything Giles's wife should be: nobly born, wealthy, a lady of gracious stature. She was a good match, one who would bring him much honor, which he deserved.

Roanna noticed that Giles had stepped away from the group and was looking around, as if searching for someone.

Unable to face him at that moment, she turned and slipped into the inn by the kitchen door. The room was dark and cool, and it soothed the heat of her feelings as she began to stack the pots and wooden bowls for washing. She needed something to do, anything to do, to keep away her troubling thoughts.

Gilda found her there a short time later. Roanna realized in a moment that the woman had imbibed more than a little of the heady bride-ale. "Lawd, girl, wa' ye be doin'? There be time fer that later!" Gilda grabbed her arm, ignoring the suds that flew from Roanna's arms as she spun her about and pushed her toward the doorway. "Go on wi' ye an' dance! Yer man's lookin' fer ye!"

Roanna turned back to protest with a wave of her hands, but Gilda spun her about again. As she was pushed through the doorway, Roanna thudded against a hard body. She felt arms go about her and looked up into blue eyes that were filled with amusement. Gasping, she tried to pull away from him, but she was swept up into his arms and carried outside.

"See that ye found 'er, lad!" Ferris called, laughing, his bellow followed by rowdy cheers and good-natured comments that brought a flush to Roanna's cheeks.

"Giles, put me down!" she whispered sharply.

He looked down at her and grinned. "You promised me a dance, as I recall," he murmured.

As they neared the others she had to bite her lip to prevent herself from speaking and could only throw him a glare. They reached the edge of the meadow where boards had been laid for the dancing and he set her down, his arm lingering firmly about her waist as he drew her into the circle that had formed for the next dance. The lyre struck an out-of-tune chord with the lute, and she glared at him as he turned her about, but he merely grinned in answer. Then she began to be caught up in the music, the feel of the dance, the touch of his hand as he led her through the steps. Her feelings tumbled in a mixture of happiness and despair as she realized that he had been searching for her, to claim her for their dance. In full view of everyone he had carried her across the village. The look he was now giving her was warm and affectionate. The thought struck her that here, among these people, she was his wife. They were playing a game, admittedly, acting out roles. It was all that she would ever have of him, but she would have it—this moment.

Suddenly her happiness shone from her eyes, and to her delight he laughed, spinning her about into the arms of another dancer as they moved about the circle. Then, in a warming rush she remembered the conclusion to the steps of this dance. She felt light-headed, her body tingling with anticipation as she realized that the final strains of the music would be accompanied by a kiss. The music suddenly seemed intoxicating, and her body burned where Giles touched it as she was spun back into his arms. Hardly breathing, she turned her face up to his, closing her eyes because she was afraid to look into his blue ones and see only indifference there. It seemed an eternity that she waited, imagining that her heart had stopped. Then she felt the warmth of his lips lightly touching hers. Gently, his mouth formed to hers, his arms tightening about her, and tears began to draw to the corners of her eyes as the kiss deepened, lingering.

They drew apart slowly and Roanna turned her face away, not wanting Giles to see her tears, nor the love she could not conceal from him at that moment. She felt his fingers under her chin as he turned her face up to his.

"Roanna?"

She could hear the soft wonder in his voice and it gripped her heart, squeezing the breath from her. Opening her eyes, she smiled at him, thankful for once that she could not speak. She pretended not to notice the question in his gaze as he studied her face, and she spun away, flipping her skirt saucily. She turned such a dimpling smile upon Ferris that the large man's mouth dropped open, and he fairly tripped over his feet in his hurry to reach her for the next dance. It took all of her effort not to glance in Giles's direction as he stood at the edge of the platform. She could feel his eyes upon her as she turned in the smithy's arms. *Oh, Giles,* she thought as she dipped a curtsy in the movement of the dance, *I do love you so. But I will not burden you with my love, forcing you to confront what cannot be. Your friendship is too dear to me for that. I will cling to it, cherishing it as the one bond between us that can ever be allowed.*

9

A light, cooling breeze lifted above the heat radiating from the dry earth. The breeze turned, sweeping in relieving gusts, lifting branches of white thorn enclosing the field, sweeping beyond to bend blades of the grasses rolling over endless, undulating hills. White cow parsley bent before its approach and pink blossoms of dogrose released their heady scent to its pull; it wafted the fragrance on its tide to swirl with the reaches of oak and birch of the forest beyond.

A solitary hare paused, lifting its foreleg as its ears perked forward, its shortsighted brown eyes straining as its nose wiggled, catching the scent of man on the breeze as it passed. Pausing another instant, the powerful legs bunched, carrying the buck away into the grasses, moments before the man placed his foot where the animal had been.

Giles paused, watching the hare in its flight, before he bent again to his task, the jagged edge of his hoe coming down to bite into the earth, releasing the roots of the heavy grasses in preparation for those who followed him to turn the heavy, rich soil. The sun burned against his naked back, already a deep golden brown, and he welcomed the cooling touch of the breeze.

The uncommon warmth of the season had encouraged the elders of the village to attempt a late planting. They hoped to set the seed before it became bound by frost, granting an early harvest in the spring. Much discussion had been given to the weather. Village councils had met and respectful attention was paid to the older members of the hamlet, who could recall such warmth so late in the year only twice before. The vote had been taken and the precious seed had been committed in the hopes of additional income for the village.

Giles worked with scarcely a moment's pause, aware of what was being risked by the people who had befriended them. Muscles corded in his back as he brought the hoe to bear upon the stubborn soil, forcing it to release the freshness beneath as he struck row after row. But while he worked, his thoughts were his own, far removed from the actions of his arms and the muscles of his shoulders and legs.

He envied the hare its freedom, in spite of the dangers of its narrow world. It had no options. It fought to survive within its capabilities; beyond that it had no choices to make, no doubts to resolve. But then, he realized, the hare went into shock when cornered, ceasing to fight in its final struggle. Perhaps there was no difference. Like the hare, he had become torpid, benumbed.

This isolation had consumed him. He had not felt such hopelessness since childhood, felt so totally given over to the whims of others. It was akin to the wretchedness of poverty, and he had sworn never to know that desperation again. Yet it had come again, claiming him, and he knew that if he could not change it he would break.

Choices would be simple but for Roanna. Dear Lord, whatever was he to do about her? What did he want to do? Nothing was clear anymore. His thoughts turned to those moments, three days before, when he had held her in his arms as he had danced with her. He hadn't been able to chase her from his thoughts: the tears in her eyes as he turned her face up to him, the soft surrender of her mouth beneath his kiss. He remembered the shock he had felt, still tingling from that kiss as he watched her dance with Ferris. Then she danced with another, and yet another, while he had merely watched. How could everything change so quickly? Again he struggled with his emotions, as he had done then, and he struck the earth with a vehemence that sprang from his suddenly surly mood. God help him, he wanted her.

It was beyond reason—it could never work between them. But was it so unreasonable? She was beautiful; she had a fire that would stir any man's blood. His tempest —his! But he had no right. His future was uncertain; with what was facing him, there was no place for her in his life. Sweet Mother, he did not want to hurt her, but if he took what he wanted from her now, he could not help but to give her pain.

Roanna surveyed the room with a practiced eye. She could do so much with it, if only she had the coin and a free hand to change it. New shutters, a feather bed laid with a down counterpane, whitewashed walls, a rag rug on the floor. A stand by the window, holding a pitcher and bowl, and on the far wall, a wardrobe. It could be done so easily; there were such possibilities. . . . Sighing, she shook off her imaginings and set to changing the worn flannel sheets on the lumpy straw mattress, feeling again the unstated desperation of Gilda and her husband, the weight of their thwarted dreams.

She was quite alone, the objects of her thoughts having traveled to Waltham to attend the birthing of a niece. They had been gone for two days and would not return until the end of the week, and their absence had left Roanna in a dreamy mood.

As she pulled the dusty sheet from the bed she paused, thinking she heard a noise belowstairs. Cocking her head, she listened, frowning as she wondered if she had imagined it. Hearing nothing more, she shrugged at her own foolishness and took up a new sheet, shaking it from its folds. She flung it over the bed and bent over the mattress to smooth it out. At that moment the door opened suddenly, and she jumped, backing against the wall with a soft cry.

"Roanna, it's only me." Giles stood in the doorway, spreading his hands in apology. "I am sorry if I startled you."

"What're ye doin' 'ere? 'Tis the middle of the day!" she stammered.

"We finished the field. Roanna, I am sorry. I should have whistled, or something."

"Aye, ye should 'ave," she admonished breathlessly, her hand fluttering against her chest as if to stay the wild beating of her heart.

"I said I was sorry," he repeated, stepping into the room, though now there was humor in his voice, which did not escape her. "Well, the least I could do, under the circumstances, is to help you finish your chores."

"Fine," she snorted. "Ye can do the wash, then cook supper."

"You don't think I could, do you?" he countered as he leaned a shoulder against the wall near the bed. "Fact is, I make a fine stew—the result of necessary skills learned in my youth."

"Is that a fact?" She smiled, tucking in the corners of the sheet.

"It is. Oh, I'll admit that, while it fed me well enough, no one ever wanted to share it with me. A stable cat bit me once when I tried to feed it to him."

She glanced up at him to see if he was serious. Her brow arched at the glint of amusement in his eyes, belying the gravity of his expression. "Giles fitzWilliam, ye are a great soddin' liar."

"Me?" His eyes widened innocently. "I've never lied in my life. 'Tis the gospel truth."

"And ye blaspheme as well," she added. She pushed back the tendrils of hair escaping from her coif and regarded him with fond exasperation. They stood looking at each other across the room. Slowly, Roanna became aware of a change in the atmosphere, and she swallowed heavily. The air seemed to gain weight, and she found it difficult to draw an even breath. Her eyes locked with his, and what she saw in those clear, blue depths made her tremble with recognition.

"Could—ye really—cook supper?" she asked, aware of the stammer in her voice. The silence around them in the room became palpable.

"If you promise not to bite," he answered, with a soft huskiness that made her skin tingle.

A distant voice within her urged her to leave—to run —but she was transfixed as he stepped nearer. Deep feelings compelled her, filling her with a trembling anticipation. As he stood before her, she looked up at him with wonder. Only in dreams had she seen that look in his eyes.

Without touching her, he bent his head and brushed her lips with his, lingering only a moment. He drew back slightly, his eyes claiming what they read in hers. Then his arms folded about her as she came into them. She pressed against him as he claimed her mouth again, now with an urgency matched by her own bursting emotions. They clung to each other, and Roanna's mind reeled with the realization that his need, his desire, was as great as her own. She marveled at the taste of him, the power in his hands as they moved over her back and hips. Yet he caressed her with an infinite gentleness that bespoke a tenderness that left her breathless.

"Roanna. Oh, God, Roanna," Giles murmured as his lips moved gently, teasing the corners of her mouth.

Nothing mattered. She wanted him, more than anything she had ever wanted in her life. Her mind went blank to the realities—that he loved another, that only pain was in store for her. She simply did not care. This once, just this one time, he would be hers. Her arms slid about his neck.

She felt herself lifted into his arms. He carried her to the bed and they sank together into the depths of the mattress. She pulled boldly at his tunic as his hands found the laces of her bodice, pulling them apart with a gentle deliberation that made her ache with love and longing. He drew in his breath sharply as his hand met the soft, warm flesh within the opened bodice. His mind spinning, he heard her cry out softly as his fingers touched her breast and he claimed her mouth with his, drawing her kiss into him. Then his lips trailed downward, pausing at the tender spot at the base of her neck, to the softness of her shoulders, and traveled in light, butterfly kisses to the trembling flesh of her breast.

God, oh God, she thought confusedly, this is what passion is about. Not the groping, the loud moans she had heard all her life from behind the closed doors of the Flying Sail, but the looks that passed between Uncle Roscoe and Aunt Matilda when they thought themselves unseen. She caught her breath as he touched her, caressing her breast, teasing it with his mouth and tongue, and she writhed beneath him with pleasure and anticipation.

He was nearly beyond reason. Then a sound pierced his fevered brain: footsteps. Footsteps that caused his entire body to tense. Instinctively his body twisted away from his position on top of Roanna and he found himself standing by the bed. With rapid movements, he grabbed his chausses together with one hand and jerked her skirts down with the other, just as the door swung open.

Roscoe Dorking's smile died on his face as he stared dumbly at the prone figure of his niece on the rumpled bed, her skirt ruffled up about her legs and her bodice gaping, and at Giles fitzWilliam standing by the bed, a stunned expression on his face as he gripped the front of his chausses in his hand.

Roscoe's dark, bushy brows flew up to his hairline, then plummeted to form an ominous bar above his eyes—eyes that had suddenly grown stormy. His head jerked to a point behind him. "I'll be in the room across the 'all, fitz-William," he said evenly. "Join me there." And the door closed behind him.

Giles stared at the closed door for a long moment, then expelled a painful breath. Glancing down at Roanna, he saw that she had become exceedingly pale. He came to life. Retying his chausses, he reached down and pushed aside her trembling fingers to relace her bodice. When he had finished, he drew her upright. "Roanna, go down to the kitchens and wait for me," he said firmly.

"But—"

"Do as I say!"

"Nay!" she protested, at last regaining her wits. "We are both at fault, I'll not allow ye to face 'im alone! I can 'andle 'im, Giles, ye must let me—"

"No, Roanna. It is for me to do. Now, do what I tell you!" Turning her, he propelled her out of the room and, encouraging her with a tight smile, nodded toward the stairs. She began to protest, but swallowed her words, seeing the grim determination in his eyes. As she started down the stairs, she paused to look back, unwilling to allow him to face Roscoe on his own. "Roanna . . ." he warned. Biting her lower lip, she turned to do as he bid, though she trembled to think of the confrontation between the two men she loved more than any in the world.

He waited until she had disappeared into the kitchens, then turned to face the closed door behind which Roscoe waited. He drew a steady breath, preparing to face whatever would come. Then, without warning, the tension that had been building steadily in him over the past weeks suddenly snapped. Furiously angry, he strode to the door and flung it open. His eyes swept over the room, finding a scowling Roscoe seated in a chair before the window, his beefy arms folded over his stomach, waiting.

"Don't say a word!" Giles roared, striding into the room. "By God, the first word is mine!" He slammed the door behind him and confronted the other man. "You are well

within your rights to challenge me for what I have done!"
He glared at Roscoe, whose eyes had widened at the
outburst; then he turned away to pace, his hands flailing
with the emphasis of his words. "Damnation, I could not
explain it to you if I tried! Never in my life have I taken
advantage of a maid! Moreover, Roanna was given to me in
trust—oh, not just by you, but by Eleanor, damn her! I
never asked for it! I don't even know how I came to be here!
God's Breath, I was minding my own business, and suddenly I found myself chasing after an insufferable chit whose
only purpose in life seems to be to drive me completely
mad!"

He saw Roscoe's mouth open, and lost whatever control
he had left. "Dammit, Dorking! Before we have it out, I *will*
have my say! Don't ask me how it happened, I couldn't tell
you—the question would drive Solomon mad! But this is
how it is, whether you like it or not: she is the most
infuriating, demanding, confusing, intolerable excuse for a
woman I have ever met! Since I met her, there has not been
one moment of my life that I have remotely considered
normal! The man who weds her can resign himself to
spending the remainder of his life in total chaos!—and I'm
not saying that is me, in spite of what you saw. Point is, I
don't know what I feel for her. Lust? Certainly—she's
beautiful. Love? How could any man love someone who
is certain to see him to an early grave? Though I must
admit that he will probably die with a smile on his face.
But the fact is, I don't know what I feel for her! And
you are just going to have to accept that. Until I figure it
out!"

Out of breath, he spun around and faced Roscoe with his
hands clenched, tensing for the onslaught. Roscoe stared at
him through narrowed eyes. Giles braced himself as the
other man pursed his lips and continued to regard him
coldly. Suddenly Roscoe slapped his thighs with both hands
and stood up. "Dammit, fitzWilliam," he muttered, "all
this talk 'as made me thirsty. Let's get some ale." He strode
past Giles to the door and threw it open, leaving Giles to
stare bemusedly at the empty doorway.

Roscoe was sitting at the table filling two tankards when
Giles entered the kitchen. Roanna stood aside. Her hand
nervously wrenched the folds of her skirt as she looked up;
her face fell into unmasked relief when she saw him.

"Thank God," she mouthed silently. He merely shrugged, and gave Roscoe a puzzled glance. He sat down across from the huge Londoner as a tankard was slid across to him and he took a long, needed draught.

"Don't just stand there wringin' yer 'ands, lass," Roscoe grumbled at Roanna. "Sit down." As she dropped into a chair, his eyes shifted back to Giles. "I do 'ave a reason for comin'. 'enry is within London. 'e's found safety at St. Paul's, and 'e 'as three 'undred knights at 'is back."

Giles paled. Everything else was pushed from his thoughts as he stared hard at Roscoe. "What of Simon?" he asked quietly.

"The king 'as drawn up a list of charges against 'im," Roscoe answered grimly. "Even complained that the earl did not bid 'im a proper farewell when 'e left Paris."

Giles took the news badly, swearing under his breath.

"There's more. It looks as if John Mansel will be successful in his plea to the pope. 'Tis said that the Provisions of Oxford should be done away with."

"What of Edward?" Giles asked on an indrawn breath. "How has he reacted to all of this?"

"'e resisted. But 'e would not deny the Crown."

"I expected as much," Giles said bitterly. "Where is Simon now?"

Roscoe sighed, shifting uncomfortably. "'Tis said that Louis of France is alarmed that one 'e thinks to be a great peer should be treated so poorly by 'enry. Lord Simon is sailin' fer the Continent to seek support from France. 'e also 'opes to maneuver against Mansel's plea to Rome."

Giles's expression became grimmer at Roscoe's words. "I must go."

"Nay!" Roanna cried softly, but her protest was cut off by a glower of warning from her uncle. As she sunk back in her chair, he turned back to Giles.

"'Tis why I've come. With the king's return, the gates 'ave been opened. Moreover, once ye've gone with de Monfort, the lass'll be safe enough, I'll see to that. I've 'orses without; there be one to see ye to Dover, where ye may meet up with 'im."

Giles turned to regard him strangely. "You did this? Why?"

Roscoe shrugged. "England be in trouble. There be need fer a Marshal to aid 'er."

"I am not a Marshal, Dorking," Giles responded grimly. "Those men are gone."

"Are they?" Roscoe's brow arched.

"Aye, and with them the power and resources that will be needed."

Roscoe shook his head slowly. "FitzWilliam, yer grandfather, the Good Knight, 'e who was regent of England and brought us the Great Charter—'e was born without title or power. 'e was what 'e made 'imself." Seeing Giles's doubt, he smiled. "A man can only do 'is best."

Roscoe drew Roanna to his side, clasping an arm about her shoulders as they watched Giles ride away. He felt her tremble, knew her pain, and he held her close. "There be great times comin', lass. 'e will be part of it."

"'e's gone, that is the only reality for me!" She swallowed, holding back her tears.

"Did ye really expect to 'ave 'im?" he asked quietly.

She could not answer for a long moment. "Nay. But I did want this. Why did ye 'ave to come now? What would it 'ave meant to wait? Nothing to ye—but everything to me," she whispered.

"Then what? What if 'e'd missed this—could ye 'ave lived with it?"

"Aye! In a moment! What great times can there be for 'im, in spite of your words? I could 'ave given 'im so much more than what 'e'll find out there!"

"Nay, Roanna, ye're wrong. What 'e'll find out there is the meanin' to 'is existence. The lad is a Marshal, Roanna, 'e just does not know it yet. With you 'e would remain only Giles fitzWilliam, 'olding an emptiness 'e would not even discover till 'e reached an age when solutions would be beyond 'im; 'is future would be bitter." He smiled sadly at her silence, and squeezed her gently. "Come, Roanna. 'Tis time fer us to go 'ome."

Part Two

He that knows better how to tame a shrew,
Now let him speak.

—William Shakespeare,
The Taming of the Shrew
Act IV, Scene i

10

False summer gave way abruptly to winter. The hope of warmth was shattered by arctic winds that swept through England. Cattle and sheep huddled together beneath bending hedges of white thorn, turned out and left for the strong to survive. Pigs rooted in the forests, turning half-wild, as men withdrew into shelters to wait. The sweet season gone, hearth fires were kindled as hearts grew dormant with winter, awaiting the warmth of spring.

Roanna often thought of those in a small village at the edge of London, wondering how they fared. She knew their gamble with late seed had been lost beneath the sudden onslaught of sleet from the north. Barges had ceased to move upon the Thames; ships were frozen in port as the river's surface was bound by a layer of ice. Normal topics of conversation were ignored, lost to the unusually brutal winter. Then at last the ice began to melt under the sun's warmth, dropping bit by bit, and the sweet season returned.

Like an alert, winter-hungry animal, Roanna listened. Paying special attention to what was said in the back rooms of the Flying Sail, she waited, feasting on the smallest scrap of news. Understanding her need, Roscoe and Matilda more frequently assigned her duties in those rooms, even as they cautioned her against unfounded dreams. Later, each piece of news was repeated and discussed in the darkened kitchen. A single lamp of oiled hide protecting a squat candle cast wavering shadows about the room as Roanna digested the rumors with her aunt and uncle.

John Mansel had been successful in his plea to Rome. A bull of absolution had been granted, dissolving the provisions given at Oxford, to which the king had announced, "I have resumed royal powers." The people were incensed. Their small, tenuous hold upon freedom had been whisked away so quickly, as to leave them wondering if they had imagined it. In its wake, Henry, to the rage of the London guilds, began replacing officeholders with men of his own choosing, a firm rebuff meant to show his royal displeasure.

"Only the barons can say nay to 'im! Why don't they respond?" Roanna asked angrily, swirling her pewter goblet and staring at the glimmers of light moving in the mulled wine.

"Who is to lead them?" Roscoe said, shrugging. "Even men of power must 'ave direction, Roanna. Richard of Gloucester be dead this winter past, and 'is son be a youth of no experience."

"England is better off without that traitor!" she snapped. "If 'e'd stood by Simon . . . and Simon remains on the Continent," she added quietly. "Why did he not return with the king?"

Roscoe exchanged a look with his wife. Both knew that her question was not for Simon but for one who remained with him. "The king went back to France only because Louis pressed fer it. When the attempt to reconcile 'im wi' Simon failed, 'enry would 'ave returned even sooner, but that 'e became so ill that 'e could not travel. 'is return 'ad nothin' to do wi' Simon. They still be at odds."

Roanna knew it well, as did all of England. The king had been so ill that upon his return he could travel no farther than Canterbury, where the court spent Christmas. When word reached him that hostilities had broken out with the Welsh, he had been forced to send for Prince Edward, who had been jousting with his bachelor knights on the Continent. But Edward had not proven successful against the Welsh, as he could not enlist the support of the barons to aid him. The English peerage had apathetically turned their faces from the Crown, silently waiting for a turn in events.

Thus the king had taken power. The Lusignans returned from the Continent, as did the uncles of the Queen, and

England again felt the oppression of those who cared little for her, and of those who cared not at all.

Until, in the spring, Simon de Monfort landed at Dover. His unheralded arrival awoke the barons from their apathy. Simon de Monfort had returned, and he had come to make war.

At first Roanna thought it a trick of her mind, to suddenly hear words that echoed her dreams. Simon had returned! She refilled the tankard with a trembling hand, focusing upon what Abram, the goldsmith, was saying. Her eyes flew to her uncle, who was seated across the table. His steady gaze met hers, calming her enough to finish her task. Then she fled the room, suddenly unable to deal with the reality.

Roscoe found her in the courtyard behind the tavern. He noted the tension in her expression as she clucked to the chickens rushing about her feet and tossed dried corn from her apron. Roscoe led her to the bench beyond the kitchen door, and they sat in the shadows of a heavy trailing vine that covered the roof of the small porch.

"Do ye understand what 'e was sayin', Roanna?" he asked quietly, watching the antics of the chickens as they fought over the remaining kernels.

"Simon 'as returned," she said softly.

"Simon 'as returned to make war," Roscoe pressed. "There will be war, Roanna."

"Did ye ever doubt that there would be?" she asked.

"Nay." A moment of silence followed. "'e too has returned fer war, Roanna."

"I know."

"Do ye still love 'im?"

"With all of my 'eart," she whispered.

Watching her, Roscoe's eyes narrowed, and he seemed to come to a decision. "Then there be only one thing to be done fer it. Go to 'im."

His words seemed to hang in the air. She stared at him with disbelief. "What are ye sayin'?"

"I believe I said it. Go to 'im."

"But—'ow can ye say such a thing to me?" she gasped. "Ye—ye're my uncle!"

"Roanna," he said, shaking his dark head, "there be nothin' in this life I want more than to see ye happy. If you can only find that wi' Giles fitzWilliam, then so be it. Do ye think I would prefer to see ye properly wed to a man who'd make ye miserable? Ye are nearly ten and seven years, yet ye've never looked upon another the way ye looked upon 'im."

"But—" She caught her breath, letting it out slowly. "'e—'e does not feel fer me as I do for 'im. Moreover, ye know it would never be allowed. Would ye 'ave me go to 'im, and be thought a fool?"

"No one can make a fool of us, lass; we can only do that fer ourselves. I do not fear that ye will ever do so. Would ye prefer to remain 'ere, always wonderin' if it could 'ave been? Take chances, Roanna, experience life, grab on to it. Ye might be surprised at what ye find."

"And if I fail?" She swallowed hard, not daring to look at him.

"Ye cannot fail, not in my eyes. But if—if ye should not find what ye are seekin', ye'll always 'ave an 'ome 'ere. There'll never be a time when ye cannot come back."

"A safe 'arbor?" She smiled tremulously.

"Never an escape, Roanna," he said seriously. "Life's to be faced, not run from. But an 'ome—always."

With coins sewn into the hem of her skirt, Roanna departed amid her luggage in a cart loaded with goods bound for Northumbria. Roscoe had hired four men-at-arms who were returning north as her escort. They were to take her as far as Kenilworth, the seat of the earl of Leicester, where he had taken up residence upon returning to England. The weather held during their journey, but for fits and starts of rain, and they encountered only two storms along the way that required them to take shelter for more than a day. As usual, Roscoe had chosen well, and her companions were protective, if not born conversationalists. Having completed business in London for their Northumbrian lord, they were anxious to return home as the rumblings of war grew louder.

At the end of their second week, they rode across lands belonging to Kenilworth. Roanna marveled at the sight of the rich, rolling hills and valleys bordering the river Avon. She quickly realized, however, that her appreciation of the earl and countess's lands was not shared by her companions. Their expressions became increasingly grim with each mile they traveled.

"Out wi' it, Guy—what is it that concerns ye?" she asked at last, pressing the question on the leader of the small party as they paused to rest the horses. The lean-muscled soldier frowned, his expression dropping into a glower as his brown eyes passed over the valley below the small knoll where they stood.

"It has begun," he growled. "De Monfort has begun his war."

Her eyes widened with surprise, and she glanced out over the peaceful valley. "'ow do ye know? There's no sign of war 'ere."

"Ah, but there is, lass, if you know what to look for." He grimaced, reaching up to scratch his unshaven cheeks. "We've passed through two hamlets since we've entered de Monfort's lands. Have you seen so much as a pig or a chicken?"

"Ohhh, ye are right!" she whispered as her eyes widened. "Where is everyone?"

"I'd bet my wages that they're within the walls of Kenilworth. But we'll know soon enough."

They knew as soon as they reached the last rise before the castle. Before them lay a large valley, spreading beyond into the distance. "Sweet Mother!" she gasped, never having seen anything so magnificent as the castle that stood at the center of the valley. "'Tis built in a lake!"

Guy had reined in his mount next to her, and he shook his head. "One of his making, lass," he said grimly. "He's flooded the meadows."

As they moved down into the valley, Roanna could not take her eyes from the structure. Lud, she thought, it must cover ten or fifteen acres! The towers of the keep were visible from their vantage, as were the crenellated walls of the inner ward. The outer wall, which seemed to run for miles, was broken by five large, strategically set towers, and was surrounded by a vast body of water that itself seemed to cover more than a hundred acres. The only entrance to Kenilworth was across an earthen causeway that stretched south from a formidable two-storied gatehouse.

"Gawd," one of her companions was heard to mutter as they approached the causeway. "I hope they know we're friendly."

They were admitted with some effort, including a shouting match between Guy and a guard who leaned out a narrow, second-story window of the gate-house, and did not seem to think them worth the effort of raising the portcullis. Finally, he shrugged and let them pass. Once inside the outer ward, Guy's suspicions were confirmed. Kenilworth Castle had become a small city of makeshift shelters and swiftly constructed stockyards.

Roanna was rendered speechless as they moved through the bedlam. Narrow streets had been formed by temporary structures built from pole frames and covered with thatch or hides. Bleating and bawling livestock protested from makeshift bowers and poultry squawked, flying out from beneath the horses and cart as they passed. Hawkers shouted their wares; children laughed or cried as they played, their voices intermingling with the deeper ones of their elders. Smells assaulted Roanna—the rancid odor of unwashed bodies wafting with the odor of meat turning over open fires, and the throat-catching pungence of animal excrement.

Upon reaching the gate to the inner ward, Roanna barely had time to say farewell to her companions before they were ushered away to quarters in the south end of the wall. She was led through the calmer atmosphere of the inner ward by a rather brisk soldier whose method of speaking consisted of short and long grunts. Though quieter and more organized, the bustle within the inner bailey reminded Roanna of what she had heard about the court itself. It was said, in fact, that the countess's household rivaled that of her brother the king; Roanna could well believe it, as she hurried to keep pace with her escort.

Soldiers were everywhere, the colorful badges on their shoulders declaring not only for de Monfort but for many of the greatest barons in England. A group of knights came down the stairs of the towering keep set in the corner of the bailey, and disappeared into a room in the wall of the ward. Beautifully gowned ladies loitered in the shade of the wall, taking the air in gossipy groups. There were servants rushing about everywhere, on errands for their mistresses and masters.

Roanna had expected to be taken to the steward, but instead her escort left her in a small chamber on the north side of the ward, set in the wall near the keep. She glanced about the small windowless room; the only natural light came from the open doorway. Sighing, she sat down on a chair near the door and waited. She should be grateful, she thought wryly, that he hadn't shut her in and left her in the dark. The room was bare but for a small bed with an overstuffed mattress—of straw, Roanna's experienced eye noted—a small table with two solid-backed chairs, one of which she was sitting on, and another table by the far wall that held a pitcher and bowl and had a cupboard beneath it.

"Well, Roanna, I see that you have chosen to return to us."

She leapt from the chair with a start, and spun about. There in the doorway, with the sun at her back, was the unmistakable form of Lady Eleanor. "Milady—" Roanna stammered, gathering enough wits to drop a quick curtsy.

Eleanor turned to hand the basket she was carrying to someone behind her, saying, "Take these. I will join you in a moment." Then she stepped into the room, her eyes sweeping over it critically before they returned to Roanna. Her lips pursed momentarily and her fingers jingled the keys at her girdle, while she regarded Roanna with interest. "Will this chamber suit you?"

"This?" Roanna blinked with surprise. She had expected to be quartered with the other unmarried women, not to be given a room of her own! She was even more stunned to be asked her opinion on the matter. "Aye, milady, of course, if ye wish it."

"My chambers are in this north wall. The keep was built long ago, with few windows; I find it dreary," she said; the statement apparently was meant to be an explanation. "You will need candles, linens. . . . Did you bring ample clothing with you? We may be here for quite a long time." Seeing Roanna's confusion, she smiled. "I knew of your coming, Roanna; a letter from your uncle preceded you by a week. My dear, it is clear to us both that you are not meant for service—an error on your father's part, I think. But now, apparently, you are choosing it of your own will. So, then, we shall try again.

"I have decided to place you in my own service. Your uncle told me that you can read, is that true?"

Roanna was surprised by the question. "I was taught to cipher—in order to 'elp my uncle with 'is accounts. The priest also taught me to read a little."

"What would your response be, if I told you that I wished for you to become accomplished at reading, and to learn to write as well? Do not be afraid to tell me the truth."

Roanna was dumbfounded for several moments. "Me? You want me to learn to read and write? Oh, milady, that would be the grandest gift!"

"Gift?" Eleanor's stern expression softened and her eyes widened in mild surprise. "An odd choice of words, Roanna. Many women—particularly a young, unwed woman—would view the prospect with horror. Do you not feel that such a—gift—would make you unwomanly? Most men would not find such an accomplishment desirable in a wife."

"Pah, such a man be not worth 'avin'," Roanna said scornfully, then sucked in her breath with horror as she realized how boldly she had spoken.

Eleanor's mouth twitched. "You are probably correct, Roanna. Be that as it may, along with your other duties, I will expect you to study with my chaplain. For now, find the steward and request the items you will need for your chamber. You may have the day to rest from your journey. Report to me at first light, and I will describe your duties." She turned to leave, then paused and looked back, one dark brow arching above eyes that were suddenly hard. "There are difficult times ahead of us, Roanna. More than ever, I expect total loyalty from those who serve me." Then she was gone.

The next morning at dawn, Roanna had barely risen when she was fetched by a young woman of around her own age. There the similarity between them ended. The woman curtly introduced herself as Lady Margot. As Roanna accompanied her across the inner ward, she stole a glance at the woman, wondering at the stern look she wore. She was still stunned by the events of the previous day and she speculated upon the possibility that she might find some answers here. Well, she mused, one can but try.

"Are all of Lady Eleanor's women quartered as I am?" she asked.

"Of course not," Lady Margot said stiffly. Disapproval lay heavily in her voice, and Roanna suspected that it went deeper than the question itself. "Only those the countess requires to be near enough to her own chambers to come at a moment's notice. If she sends for you, you are to go to her immediately! Do you understand?" Lady Margot trained a steely look on her. It was obvious that Lady Margot, who Roanna later learned was a ward of the countess, did not approve of her guardian's selection of handmaidens.

"She certainly does things differently," Roanna observed, unfortunately out loud.

"Lady Eleanor does things her own way," Margot snapped. "Her decisions are *never* to be questioned!" It was clear to Roanna, however, that her companion most definitely questioned this one concerning herself.

Persisting with her questions, she quickly learned, by way of curt, clipped sentences from Lady Margot, that the twenty-foot-wide walls of the inner ward held the living quarters of the household, the great hall, the armory, and the chapel. The turreted towers of the keep housed the knights' quarters. The main floors of the eighty-seven-foot-high structure were used only in time of siege. The mention of siege turned Roanna's thoughts to the reason she had come to Kenilworth, and she glanced at her companion, wondering how she could turn the conversation to elicit answers to some pressing questions of her own. But the opportunity was lost as Lady Margot swept through a doorway, and Roanna quickened her steps to keep up.

Rushing through, she stopped short. The room was empty of furniture, but for tables set together in a long row, their surfaces stacked with books.

"Bugger!" Roanna exclaimed. She had never seen so many books.

Lady Eleanor stood by the table with a book in her hand. Her conversation with an elderly Franciscan brother had been cut short by Roanna's entrance. A gesture silenced Lady Margot's shocked reprimand.

"Impressive, isn't it?" Eleanor said, smiling and glancing about with pride. "I am gratified that you are impressed, Roanna. Simon and I are endeavoring to compile a great library; this is just the beginning. Are you aware that when a great bishop left for the last Crusade, he bequeathed his greatest prize, his library, to the king for safekeeping? His library consisted of eighteen books, Roanna—only eighteen. But this is not surprising, when you consider that, until recently, the Church looked upon books as unnecessary—all truth and knowledge being found in the Bible." Turning to her companion, she smiled again, and there was laughter in her voice when she said, "This is the one you're to teach to read and write. Roanna, this is Brother Vincent. You will be studying with him each afternoon. I warn you, he is a hard taskmaster."

The gentleness of her voice and the tender regard with which she looked upon him belied her words. Roanna caught an amused glint in the Franciscan's eyes, and she recognized the true affection between the two.

"Come with me, Roanna," Eleanor ordered, brushing past her toward the door. "You shall begin your duties."

By the time Roanna dropped, exhausted, onto her bed that night, she had learned that her duties consisted of following Eleanor de Monfort about during the morning hours, studying with the good brother in the afternoon, and then attending the countess again until bedtime.

Brother Vincent was indeed a hard taskmaster, but he was kind and gentle, and she found herself working hard to please him. Lady Eleanor was another matter. Roanna's experience at Durham House, a temporary household, had not prepared her for what she found at Kenilworth. If she had ever had the idea that noble ladies merely lolled about, waiting to be waited upon hand and foot, that idea was dispelled by the end of the first day and continually during the following weeks as she learned what it meant to rule a feudal state.

During the course of the first week, she scurried after the countess, running such errands as were needed, as Eleanor oversaw each operation that contributed to the running of the small city. In one day alone Eleanor personally ordered from the brewess 190 gallons of ale, at a halfpenny a gallon, and 80 skins of Gascony wine. From the tenants, who had drawn within Kenilworth's walls, she bought apples, pears, cherries, geese, chickens, and 300 eggs. She oversaw all purchases, daily checking her household rolls to the last halfpence spent on rice. Her shrewd eye did not stop there, but ranged over all activity within her city. No servant, steward, wafer maker, smith, or groom escaped her notice.

Eleanor held her own courts of justice, settling matters ranging from price disputes to felonies. She spent time each day checking the defenses and conferring with her captains. From the conversation, Roanna quickly began to suspect that the countess was fully capable of mounting Kenilworth's defense, should the need arise. However, judging from the countess's passion for beautiful clothes and personal adornment, Roanna doubted that she would, in the manner of other great ladies including her own grandmother, Eleanor of Aquitaine, don armor and lead her own army.

The attire of the ladies at Kenilworth was indeed extravagant, particularly that of Eleanor herself and of her beautiful young daughter, affectionately known as Demoiselle. The finest silks, satins, and velvets were imported from the East, and a breathtaking new fabric, baudekin, came from Syria; interwoven of silk and gold threads, in sunlight it seemed to glow with a light of its own. Furs of miniver, vair, and ermine were used for trim; girdles were encrusted with precious stones. There was one vanity, however, that the Church decried. Trains of an extravagant length suddenly became a favorite design to enhance a woman's grace of movement. Roanna's eyes had widened in amazement when she first saw the innovation; shaking her head, she had wondered yet again about the idiocy of the nobility. Lud, she thought, what frippery. But then, the trains did help to clean the floors.

She was present when a visiting priest flew into a rage over the fashion, particularly in the case of trains so long that it took a page to carry them. The ladies' very souls were in jeopardy, he cried, for surely such decadence prepared the way for evil; demons would ride upon the trailing skirts! Eleanor took the news calmly. After the red-faced priest had stormed from the room, she had turned to her unsettled ladies and waved away the cleric's admonitions. They had no reason for concern, she assured them. They merely had to pause occasionally and shake out their skirts. It was the final word said on the matter.

Roanna hungered for news about Giles. Although messengers came and went from Kenilworth on a regular basis, they were ushered into private audience with Eleanor, and proved to be as closemouthed about the news they carried as was the countess herself. It was always possible—even probable—that a household as large as Kenilworth harbored a spy, and it was obvious that Eleanor was taking no chances that a careless word would cause harm to her husband and his forces.

A month passed in a welter of contradictions for Roanna. The days were long, but so filled with new experiences that she barely had time to think of anything but the present moment. She quickly began to look forward to the hours spent with the kindly and wise Brother Vincent; they were the brightest moments in her day. He never questioned Lady Eleanor's decision to teach Roanna to read, although the ladies of Kenilworth, led by Lady Margot, continued to offer disapproving looks and sharp comments when the countess was not about.

Aside from her letters, Roanna and Brother Vincent worked on her manner of speech, an added discipline that came about in their first hour together. She had stared at the work before her, and suddenly blurted out, "Oh, sot! 'ow am I bloody ever goin' to do this?" One glance at the surprised arch to his bushy brows, and she knew she was doomed. At the end of the first hour, as he looked over her efforts, he casually remarked on the absence of h's. She merely shrugged, commenting that it seemed silly to write what she didn't say. He agreed wholeheartedly. As he saw it, he said, for effective communication she had two choices. First, that the people of England drop their *h*'s; he would pen a note to Canterbury within the week. The other option, of course, was that she could pick up hers. She began to work on them that very day.

Over the weeks, he seemed genuinely pleased at her rapid progress. Occasionally he caught her gaze traveling from her work to the shelves of books that had begun to grow along the walls, each carefully catalogued and recorded. When time allowed, he would rise, remove a book from the shelf, and lay it on the table before her. Putting her work aside, they would talk about the book and the thoughts it contained. Thus Roanna began to be exposed to the teachings of Aristotle, Ptolemy, Thomas Aquinas, and Roger Bacon.

The first such experience had made her visibly uncomfortable, a fact Brother Vincent had quickly noted. "Why are you troubled, Roanna? It is only a book, not an instrument of evil as was once believed."

"Oh, I know that!" she exclaimed. "Men came from all over the world to me—my—uncle's inn: Arabs, Greeks, Spaniards. I often listened to them talk, not just of things they 'ad seen, but of matters they 'ad learned from books. They were not evil—they were just men. But they knew so many things, wonderful things. Yet, in mass the priests spoke against reading secular works. But it seemed to me that if one read only what was written by the Church, then the Church would 'ave control over thought."

Brother Vincent smiled and his blue eyes began to twinkle. "So it would—in its effort to keep man from committing heresy. The Church saw its duty in keeping men's souls safe for our Lord."

"Pah," she snorted with disgust. "The Church once warned against the evils of bathing, insisting that water would endanger the soul. All it served to do was to make one great stinkin' country."

Brother Vincent roared with laughter. "You are most correct, Roanna. For our acceptance of bathing, as well as for the rebirth of knowledge, we can give thanks to those whom our Crusaders met in the Holy Land. Moreover, in order to reach Acre, our men first had to rid the seas of the Barbary pirates, thus opening England's trade routes for the first time in centuries, which brought us new riches and new standards of living. So, then, if that is not what concerns you, wherein lies the problem?"

She did not know how to answer him. Thoughts she had struggled with since the first day she had begun working with the Franciscan returned. "Why are men so against a woman learning to read and write?"

His eyes flickered at the question. "Not all men are, Roanna. Those who are feel threatened, as one always is by what one does not understand. Through his Code of Chivalry, a knight sees himself as the protector of woman, thus her superior; it would not do to have her accomplished in something he is not. Moreover, reading and writing have been accomplishments usually left to the priests. All knights once looked upon such things as unnecessary, even as something that would rob them of their masculinity. Fortunately, those ideas are rapidly changing, perhaps because of those selfsame Crusaders who found themselves at a disadvantage when facing their Saracen counterparts. Though it has taken many years for the average man to accept the change."

"Then—do you think that—if a man were well read, 'e would not object to a woman being accomplished, too?"

"That, again, would depend upon the man. There have always been exceptions, Roanna, even back to the first King Henry, who was an accomplished scholar. There have been many men who have understood the advantages of being able to read and write—if for no other reason than to have their messages in battle kept private, and not entrusted to a scribe. But a man who sees women only as subservient creatures, and wishes for them to remain so—well, I rather imagine he would object."

"But most everyone does!" she protested.

"Most, but again, not all." He studied her as she stared absently at the book in front of her, her mobile expression mirroring her uneasiness. "I do not know why Lady Eleanor has instructed me to teach you, Roanna, beyond the fact that she recognized that you were capable of learning. Be assured that she has a reason for everything she does, beyond a kind heart. But it is your life, Roanna, and she has given you the choice. Only you can make it."

She contemplated his words, her eyes troubled. Then, suddenly, she pulled the parchments back toward her and grimaced at the scratchings she had made upon them. "Oh, fuss and bother," she muttered. "What does it matter anyway? This, at least, I can 'ave for myself."

Smiling, Brother Vincent leaned forward and handed her the quill. "Then we best be to it, lass. We've lost a good bit of time today."

Her thoughts had returned to the same subject one evening a couple weeks later. She was alone with Lady Eleanor in the countess's chamber, as had become their habit. For reasons Roanna could not fathom, Lady Eleanor had soon begun dismissing her other ladies after vespers, keeping only Roanna for the evening hours. Not that Roanna objected; as the stiff-necked ladies departed, she could only feel relief. She had never expected to count friends among them—her station would never allow it, even if she desired it—but it was difficult to be an outsider, nevertheless. Led by the supercilious Lady Margot, the women's disapproval of Roanna grew as the countess's deference toward her increased. But she was lonely and often longed for the servants' quarters, to be among friendly women of her own age and station.

She carefully folded a rich bliaut of sky-blue silk and laid it in the wardrobe chest, smoothing out the wrinkles before she shut the lid. In the silence, as Eleanor sat at her writing table with her journals, Roanna's mind wandered to her studies, then to her private worry. What *would* Giles think of her newfound talents? she wondered. How would he react when he found her here? Lud, would he even care? And what of Lisette? Roanna had managed to learn that the Gascon maid had remained in France when the de Monforts returned to England. She had also learned, with prodding she had hoped was subtle, that Giles had not married. But that, in itself, meant little. Of course Giles would not bring a bride with him when war was certain. But did his heart remain on the Continent? Remembering the fair Lisette—and that lady's determination—Roanna had little doubt of the outcome of that liaison. Well, Uncle Roscoe, she mused, you were right about one thing: we can only make fools out of ourselves. And, without doubt, that is exactly what I am doing. Sighing, she picked up a chemise and crossed to the small sewing basket on the hearth.

Hearing her sigh, Eleanor looked up from her journal, pausing over the entry. She noted the dejected slump to the younger woman's shoulders, and her eyebrows rose slightly in question. "Roanna, that work is not pressing. Go to the buttery and fetch us two goblets of spiced wine. I believe that we both could use a respite."

Two weeks ago, Roanna would have been surprised by the offer, but she had long since ceased being startled by the countess's bursts of familiarity. She also knew better than to consider taking advantage of them. Eleanor usually approached those about her with a studied casualness, according to her mood. But there were lines drawn that one did not cross, unless one cared to suffer a Plantagenet rage—an experience Roanna had never felt personally, though she had heard enough about it to tread warily.

She left the large chamber and smiled at the ever-present guards as she crossed the inner ward, humming to herself. She would go to the kitchens as well, she thought, and ask Cook for some sweetmeats to go with the wine; Eleanor loved them. A commotion at the gate tower of the inner ward drew her attention. She glanced briefly in the direction of the gate, then stopped suddenly. Staring, she felt the blood drain from her face. Her heart began to beat wildly, thumping erratically in her chest. Dust-grimed and travel-weary, Giles came striding across the bailey toward her.

11

She could not move, her legs would not obey her. She could only stand, as if frozen, and wait. Then he saw her. His expression was puzzled for a moment, as if his mind was pulling away from disturbing thoughts. Then his face lightened and he stopped, gaping. "Roanna! Good Lord! Is it really you?"

She smiled awkwardly, with mingled relief and self-consciousness. "Aye, Giles, 'tis really me."

He laughed, grasping her hands in his. "What are you doing here?"

"I . . ." Words lumped in her throat. How could she answer that? she wondered frantically, Lawd, luv, I came to see ye? "What are *you* doing here?" she asked instead, flushing. "What has happened?"

Fatigue and strain appeared in his face. "Ah, for that I must see Eleanor," he said softly. Then suddenly his expression changed to one of bewilderment. He looked back at her. "Roanna, say that again."

"Say what?"

"What you said."

Her brow furrowed with confusion. "What has happened?"

"That's it!" He laughed delightedly. "Roanna, you've discovered your *h*'s! Where did they come from?"

Bugger, she thought, and changed the subject. "Lady

Eleanor is in her chambers. Do you want me to take you to her?"

Eleanor looked up as they entered, and her face paled when she saw Giles. Recovering quickly, she rose from her desk and crossed the room to him, turning a cheek for his welcoming kiss. "Welcome," she murmured. "Nay, Roanna, do not leave. I wish you to remain."

Roanna regarded her with surprise. "There," the countess added, gesturing to the parchment and ink on her writing desk. "I want you to make note of what is said."

Unsettled by this astounding request, Roanna crossed to the desk. She was aware of Giles's puzzled glance, but she sat down and took up a quill, quickly checking its point. When her gaze strayed back to him, she found that he had moved away to drop wearily into a chair near the hearth.

Eleanor stood near him; the only evidence of her tension was in the way she clasped her hands tightly in front of her. "Is my husband well?" she asked quietly.

"Simon is well, and sends you greetings," he answered with a fatigued smile. "I have ridden directly from London—"

"London!" Eleanor exclaimed, losing her composure. "Simon is within London?"

"Aye. 'Tis ours."

Eleanor lowered herself shakily to a chair. "Tell me— Nay, first tell me who has joined you," she said, her voice growing stronger.

Giles snorted unhappily. "Eleanor, you ask me to recount the most difficult part of it."

She smiled wryly. "That is what I would hear first."

"Then you shall have it." His eyes shifted with interest to Roanna and he gave her a weary smile. "Roanna, I trust that you will be discerning in what you write."

"Lead on, Sir Giles. I shall try not to compromise you," she said lightly. Lud, she thought, no one would be able to read it anyway. How could the countess ask her to do this? She wasn't nearly ready! For an instant, she considered suggesting that Brother Vincent be summoned, but she held back. Calling him would mean that she would be dismissed, and she could not bear that. To be so near to Giles after the long, long months . . . Nay, she would do her best, committing the words to memory if she must, and struggle with the writing later.

"Well, then," he said, his attention returning to Eleanor. "We couldn't know, of course, who would answer our summons to Oxford Castle, but in our wildest imaginings we would not have guessed who did come. Henry of Almaine was the first to arrive—"

"Henry?" Eleanor exclaimed. Then, calming herself, she glanced at Roanna. "Henry of Almaine, the duke of Cornwall's son." She turned back to Giles. "I cannot believe that my nephew has turned to our cause."

Giles shrugged. "I judge that he was drawn to the gathering by Gilbert—you know how close is his friendship with our new earl of Gloucester. But I must credit Henry with enthusiasm. He gave great energy to the others."

"You do not trust him," Eleanor observed.

"He is likable, and a brave soldier," Giles answered. "Moreover, he has Isabella's character; it speaks well for him. I am only concerned because of the pressure his father will bring to bear upon him. However, it worked well for us. The appearance of his baronial cross lent great comfort and enthusiasm to our cause."

"Advise my husband to make the most of it, Giles, for I agree with you. Henry is certain to bend to the will of his father, for they have great regard for one another, in spite of Henry's present leanings. It is only a matter of time. Who else attended you?"

"John deWarenne, earl of Surrey, and Roger de Leyburn, who brought with him his companions."

"Humph," Eleanor snorted. "De Leyburn is a libertine, a thief, and an opportunist. I am hard put to grant the queen, my dear sister by marriage, any claim to wisdom, but I must give her credit for correctly judging the man. I have no doubt that the charges brought against him were true, that his accounts as Edward's steward were indeed lacking. The only reason he sought our cause was to avoid more pressing legal claims at court."

"I'm certain that you are correct, Eleanor," Giles sighed. "However, thus far the man has comported himself well, even though he may not be acquitted before the king. Be as it may, I feel the best of all those who fight with us is John de Vescy—from Alnwick Castle in Northumberland—" he added for Roanna, pausing as she struggled to keep up. "—He appears to be of the mettle of his grandfather, he who was a leader at Running-Mead. That one, if no other, I believe we can trust."

"To those we already count loyal to us, there are only these to add," Eleanor mused, and sighed. "I agree, only de Vescy would I trust to remain. As for Gloucester, beware. He is the image of his father."

"I share your opinion," Giles said with a grimace. "But for now, they are loyal. We have London." Seeing her look brighten with interest, he smiled. "It was almost too simple. From Oxford, we struck westward to the Severn River. As those in the west oppose the king, we were well received, and communications to the west are now withheld from the king. Simon was brilliant!" Giles's eyes began to shine, alight with his belief in the man he had chosen to follow. "While others wished to use the moment of victory to rest, he pressed for a rapid sweep to London. He knew that only with a command of the Cinque Ports would we be able to control the sea. So we began a forced march to London. We learned later that Cornwall had tried to stop us at Wallingford, but Simon's speed served us well and we were gone before he could counter." Pausing, Giles laughed and shook his head. "At the last moment, Simon bypassed the city, pushing us into the very heart of Kent. There was great protest, and the leaders almost rebelled at this point, arguing that we were plunging to the very heart of enemy territory, and would be destroyed. But Simon held firm. And he was proven out—we reached Romney to find that the people of Kent welcomed us with open arms. Thus, we now hold an area from the western reaches to the ports, and are firmly established. London—and the command of the sea—are ours."

To Roanna's relief, Eleanor broke off the conversation to order that a light supper of celebration be brought for them. As talk turned to lighter matters, Roanna looked at her efforts with dismay. Gathering the parchments, she excused herself, mumbling something about copying them, and hurried from the room.

In her chamber, she lit a candle against the deepening sunset and readied the quills and parchment Brother Vincent had given her for practice—a task she set herself each night before bed. Sitting before them, she stared dismally at the vellums with her notes, tears gathering at the corners of her eyes as she saw what a mess she had made of them. Lud, she groaned, she could barely read the words herself! If only they hadn't talked so fast!

Sighing raggedly, she leaned back in her chair. He was here, he was really here, though in the past hour she had hardly had time to think about his return. All the months and months of waiting, dreaming . . . Well, Roanna, she mused, nothing in your life is ever quite like your dreams. Grab for life, Uncle Roscoe had said. Oh, she had grabbed for it all right, and caught it squarely by the horns. The unwelcome image of a goat passed through her mind.

He was home. Now what? Life would continue the same as ever, she reasoned. She would have whatever part of him allowed her. She would be his friend and help him, if she could. She would share a small part of his life. Her eyes strayed to the wrinkled vellums on the table before her, their curled corners and the black splotches of ink accusing her. She would be thought of as a twit, she thought, grimacing.

Moving the spoiled sheets to her left, she spread out a new page, chalking it carefully as Brother Vincent had shown her. Taking a deep breath, she dipped the pared quill point into her inkwell and paused over the vellum, sending a silent prayer to whichever lingering saints were not too busy with more pressing matters at that particular moment. She became absorbed in her work.

A soft knock at the door made her gasp and jump. She swore violently as a darkened spot began to spread on the paper, and glared at the door with fury. Jumping up, she crossed to the door, pulling it open as her mouth formed words that would convey her feelings, only to suck in her breath sharply. "Giles!"

"Really, Roanna, such language." He grinned.

Realizing that he had heard her through the closed door, she flushed. "I—it was nothing," she said lamely.

"Obviously I disturbed something," he observed, glancing behind her. "I can come back later—"

"Nay! I mean, you are not disturbing me."

They stood looking at each other for a long moment; then his brows arched with question and he grinned again. "Well? May I come in—or are you hiding someone in there?"

"Come in?" she parroted, shocked. "But—it would not be proper!"

"Roanna, you once lived with me, remember?" he said, chuckling. Before she could stop him, he stepped past her into the room. She closed the door and scurried around him, blocking the way to the table as she gestured to the only other chair in the room, by the bed. "Sit there," she blurted out. "Would you like some wine, or ale?"

"Be easy, Roanna," he said, taking the chair. "Nay, no wine, no ale. Just tell me how you've been."

"Me? I am fine. I'm just fine."

"Roanna, why are you so nervous?"

"I'm not nervous."

"Aye, you are. What is the matter?"

"Nothing."

He peered at her for a moment, and then his face relaxed into an easy smile. "I've changed my mind; I would like some wine, if you have it."

She drew a breath and crossed to the small table by the door, where she kept a pitcher of watered wine, goblets, and a plate of cheese and bread covered by a damp cloth. She poured the wine, but as she turned back she gasped softly with alarm. He was standing by the table, reading one of the parchments. He looked up at her with puzzlement. "Why were you trying to hide them?"

"I wasn't," she stammered, flushing furiously with embarrassment.

"Aye, you were. Why?"

She stared at him blankly for a moment, unable to think of what to say, and then crumpled. "Is it not obvious?" she cried. "They are terrible!"

He glanced back at the one in his hand. "Aye, they are." He looked up at her again, and smiled with understanding. "Is that why you've been so nervous? You didn't want me to see these?" She merely shrugged. "You were copying them." She nodded. He glanced at the fresh parchments on the table, and saw the splotch. "That is when I knocked." She nodded again, biting her lower lip. "Roanna, come over here," he said, stepping away from the table. Timidly, she took her place at the table, setting the goblet down across from her as he pulled the other chair over beside her and sat down. "Now, take a fresh sheet and I'll help you."

"Nay, Giles—you needn't, really," she protested. Oh, Lord, she thought, his eyes are so blue.

"Of course I shall. Now, be quiet for once, and trim your quill."

She did as he ordered while he studied one of the vellums. "Well, it seems perfectly clear to me," he observed. " 'Wer lef ocfod am rod fot the wet.' "

She blinked and leaned over to look, then glared at him. "It says, 'We left Oxford and rode for the west.' "

"That's what I said." He grinned. "We merely have to change a few letters to make it clearer."

"But I don't remember all of it!" she lamented.

"I do. Don't worry, we'll have it done in no time."

"Why, Giles?" she asked softly, staring at him.

"Because you're my little goat girl. Now, stop asking questions and let's get it done."

They worked slowly, Giles guiding her hand and helping her to form letters when they escaped her. She marveled at his patience, the gentle encouragement in his voice, his easy praise when she accomplished a line. At moments she had to force herself to concentrate. Aware of his nearness, the touch of his hand upon hers, his breath upon her cheek as he bent to show her a stroke, she had to hold her breath and force her mind to focus upon the task. Finally, it was done.

"Now," he said, sitting back with a smile. "Sign your name, there—at the bottom."

"My name?"

"Of course! A chronicler always signs his name to his work—or hers. Do it," he ordered.

She smiled with pleasure, scratching her name across the bottom in her best letters, then laid down the quill and leaned back, totally exhausted. "Lud, I'm glad that's done!" Then she looked at him, perplexed. "What I do not understand is why Lady Eleanor asked me to do it in the first place. Why didn't she call for Brother Vincent?"

"Never attempt to understand Eleanor's mind," he answered, shaking his head. "But be assured, she has her reasons."

"Were you not the least bit surprised when she told me to stay?" she asked.

"Very. And that is why I came—I saw you struggling with it, and near to tears when you left."

"You—you knew?"

"Eleanor told me what you've been doing. I am very proud of you, sweetling."

His little goat girl. Sweetling. She warmed at the easily given terms of affection—even in her distaste at being reminded of the goat. "You must be very tired," she said softly.

"I am," he agreed, rising from the chair. "And so I am for bed. Geoffrey has settled me somewhere within Kenilworth's walls. I'd best find him."

"The knights' quarters are in the keep," she said, accompanying him to the door. "Oh—but you would know that."

"Aye, but 'tis possible there was no room there to lay my pallet."

As he opened the door, Roanna laid a hand on his arm. "Giles—my thanks—for what you did tonight."

"My pleasure, sweet." Leaning down, he brushed her forehead with a kiss. "Sleep well."

She stared at the door after it closed behind him. It was a long moment before her heart ceased its thumping and settled to a normal rhythm.

Throughout the days that followed, Roanna was afforded only brief moments with Giles. When he was not closeted with Eleanor, he was conferring with her captains or riding out with his men beyond Kenilworth's walls. She learned, through normal castle gossip, that he had been charged by Simon to see to Kenilworth's security before he departed to rejoin the earl; he took the responsibility very seriously, which left him little time for anything else.

As she readied for bed one night a week after his return, she pondered the problem. She'd spent all of these weeks here, only for that all-too-brief moment with him? Soon he would be gone again, and then what—more and more months of waiting? There were so many things she wanted to ask him, so much she had to know. She needed to know something of what he was telling Eleanor. What of London —were those she loved in danger? Moreover, it was time to face what she was doing with her life. She had come to Kenilworth to be near him, but what did that mean? He had not referred in any way to his last moments with her —when he had begun to make love to her. The fact that he had made no reference to it confirmed the truth she had tried desperately to avoid: that for him, it had been a moment's passion, a whirlwind stilled as quickly as it had begun. Was friendship enough for her? If it was not, then what were her alternatives?

Suddenly she brightened, remembering the days at Durham House—in particular, the late hours when most others were sleeping. She dressed and left her chamber, making her way across the darkened ward to the towering form of the keep. Keeping to the shadows, she skirted the south tower and found the door to the pentice, the enclosed staircase that ran along the outside of the massive structure. Opening the door quietly, she slipped inside, and paused. She smiled with satisfaction; a torch was still burning in its holder on the wall by the door. It didn't surprise her—the porters were probably still engaged in their nightly game of dicing. Pulling it from the heavy iron bracket, she gathered up her skirts with her free hand and began to make her way up the staircase, pausing to listen at each turn for any sound of someone approaching. Lud, she thought, if Eleanor found out that she had come to the keep at this hour . . . she pushed the thought aside and climbed the stairs. She paused at the top, slipping her torch into a holder on the wall. Bracing herself, she pushed open the door and stepped out onto the parapet.

A three-quarter moon hung above the tower walls, illuminating the sawtoothed crenellations and the wide parapet that ringed the keep. As her eyes adjusted to the darkness, she saw him. He was sitting on the wall with his back against the merlon, deeply lost in thought as he stared out at the countryside beyond. Startled, he turned his head sharply as she approached.

"Roanna." He laughed softly, shaking his head. "I should be surprised, but I'm not. Dare I ask if you came through the knights' quarters?"

"Of course not!" she answered primly, though inwardly she felt weak. It had not occurred to her until now that he might have been furious with her. "I came up the pentice."

"In the dark?"

"Nay, there was a torch by the outer door."

He grunted. "The luck of fools."

"I wanted to speak with you," she said, ignoring the comment. He made room for her, and she sat down, wriggling as the cold of the stone bit uncomfortably through the thin wool of her kirtle.

"What is so important it has brought you here at this hour?"

"Everything."

"That could take some time. Could you be more specific?"

How to approach it? she thought. She couldn't just come right out with her deepest thoughts. Ask a lighter question first, she reasoned, something impersonal. Then she remembered something she had overheard in the kitchens that morning. "Is it true that the people of London attacked the queen and called her a bitch?"

"A witch, Roanna, a witch," he corrected, chuckling.

"Oh. Lud, that seems bad enough. What 'appened —happened?"

"The citizens' retribution for her blatant contempt for English people," he answered grimly. "As we approached London, the king took refuge in the Tower. La Belle Eleanora, however, tried to escape to Windsor. Her barge was recognized as soon as it left the Tower—typical of the queen not to take another craft. She got as far as London Bridge, whence the citizenry began to pelt her with rotten vegetables and eggs, screaming, 'Drown the witch!' She returned, posthaste, to the Tower."

"Served her well," Roanna said with a smirk. "And the king?"

"He was safe enough." He paused. In the moonlight, she could see his expression change as if a painful memory had crossed his thoughts. "Angry mobs rushed the Tower. When they realized the futility of their action, they turned their anger on the Jews, blaming them for financing the king's follies. Hundreds died that night, Roanna. When we entered the city, flames still engulfed their homes."

They sat in heavy silence, and Roanna fought back tears. She had counted many Jewish merchants among her friends at the tavern. "Was—was the wharf endangered?" she managed to choke out.

"The Flying Sail is safe, Roanna, and all of those within. Moreover, I understand that your uncle sheltered and protected many people that night. I'm told that he stood at the door with a battle-axe, daring any to enter."

"That sounds like Uncle Roscoe," she said with a rather watery smile. Then she turned a puzzled glance to him. "How did you learn this?"

"I sent Geoffrey to inquire. Roanna, do you think that I would not assure myself that my friends were safe? My only regret is that I was unable to go myself. Perhaps, in that event, I would have learned that you were at Kenilworth. However, I was busy with deClare, pursuing Lord Edward."

"Why?"

"Before we entered the city, Edward went to the New Temple, demanding entrance of the Knights Templars in order to remove his mother's jewels, which were being held there for safety. These he took, along with thousands of pounds that belonged to the merchants of London. Unfortunately, he escaped the city with his Welsh guard."

Roanna studied his profile as he spoke. She barely heard his answer; his nearness had brought her last moments with him in the village rushing back, filling her senses. His voice affected her physically, touching off sensations in her body that left her breathless.

The moon had risen to its apex, casting its shimmering light onto the lake beyond the outer ward, and their eyes were drawn to its wavering reflection as they both fell silent. She tried to clear her mind, to re-form the questions that had brought her here to find him. But before she could speak, he rose and held out a hand to her. "It is growing late, we both should be in bed. Eleanor has requested that we attend her together, after mass."

She looked up at him with surprise. "But I always attend her in the morning."

"Ah, but this time we are to do so together." Taking her arm, he led her to the tower door and pushed it open. The light from the torch inside the passage fell across his face as he turned back to her; she wondered why he had suddenly become so serious. "Roanna, I would caution you. I do not know why Eleanor wants to meet with us, but remember this: whatever she has on her mind, whatever she requests of you, be honest with her. She may be angered by your response if it does not agree with her purpose; you may even see evidence of that Plantagenet rage—and it can be unsettling, particularly if you have never witnessed it before. But do not back down. Be honest, remembering that I am with you."

"Lud, Giles," she said, laughing nervously, "if you meant to frighten me, you have done it."

"Good," he grunted. He took the torch from the wall and

led the way downstairs. "Think well upon it, Roanna. Eleanor expects absolute loyalty. Once you have given your word to her, you must never fail. So if you do not agree with her, if you doubt your feelings, then never, never pledge yourself to her. No one loves her more than I do, no one knows better than I her generosity, her ability to love, her devotion to those she loves. But never, never underestimate her, Roanna. She is first, and always, a Plantagenet."

Roanna had the long hours of the remaining night to think about what Giles had said. By the time she entered the countess's chambers the following morning, she was prepared for anything. Or so she thought.

Giles was already there when she arrived, having escorted Eleanor to mass, and they were sitting before a crackling fire finishing their breakfast. Noting that none of the other ladies were about, Roanna began to clear away the remnants of their meal.

"Leave it," Eleanor said, rising from her chair. She took a few steps toward the fire and turned about, gesturing toward the vacated chair. "Sit down. I wish to speak with both of you." Roanna took her seat, clasping her hands before her as she sought to affect an appropriate demeanor.

Eleanor glanced at Giles, slumped comfortably in his chair with his long legs stretched out before him, then at Roanna, her eyes narrowing as she seemed to measure them. "In the weeks that you were hiding in that village near London, did you get along well?"

Giles sat up quickly, frowning. "Milady, I assured you that nothing happened—"

"So you did, Giles." She cut him off with an impatient gesture of her hand. "My question was, did you meet well? Do you care for one another?"

"I—of course I care for her," Giles blurted, not giving Roanna a chance to answer—a fact she was grateful for. "But I swear—"

"You need not swear, Giles, I believe you." She paused, turning her gaze upon Roanna. "But then, you have not answered me, Roanna. Can you abide this rake?"

"'e—he is not a rake!" Roanna protested, then flushed, embarrassed by the quick passion of her defense.

"I know him better than you do, my dear," Eleanor remarked with the hint of a smile. "But your quick defense speaks well of him—and it answers my question. Well, then . . ." She paused, studying one and then the other. "I want you to become lovers."

Roanna's stunned expression was matched by that of Giles, her gasp countered by a strangled sound that came from his direction. They both goggled at Eleanor.

He recovered first. "What?" he roared, leaping out of his chair.

"Oh, sit down, Giles," Eleanor said, waving him back. "If you can manage to compose yourself, I shall explain." She waited until he dropped back into the chair, ignoring the fury in his face. "Roanna, my dear, now you may begin to understand why I wished for you to learn to write. By the way, I have not told you how pleased I was over the notes you recorded the night Giles arrived. I am delighted with your progress. Now, then, you must understand how unsettled these times are—and they are likely to become more so. There are spies everywhere, even within Kenilworth —we would be foolish to doubt it. It is imperative that there be an effective channel of communication established between our forces, one that will not be suspect. Messengers are waylaid, secrets discovered. It has been the cause for many a battle to fail."

"But messages sent between lovers may not be suspected," Giles said quietly.

"Exactly so." She turned to pace. "If my plan is to be successful, you must be believed. All you must do is act to the world as though you are lovers. However, you must convince the traitors among us that you are sincere."

"A play so perfectly acted that those watching are at first distracted, then convinced. The traitors will then turn away to more pressing matters," Giles observed.

"You have it. And there will be a parting so painful that it can only be relieved by a constant stream of love notes, their lines coded with their real intent."

"How long have you planned this?" Giles asked, his eyes narrowing on Eleanor as she paced.

"Since I received the letter from Roanna's uncle that she was returning to us. It was no coincidence that you were selected to bring news to me, Giles."

In the silence that followed, Roanna, who had been staring at her hands tightly clutched in her lap, looked up to find them both watching her, waiting for her response. She withdrew her eyes quickly, closing them for a moment. Oh, God, she thought miserably, how could they ask this of her? Anything else—anything! It was obvious, by Giles's silence, that he had already agreed to the plan. Now they were waiting for her. . . . How could she give them the answer they wanted? She loved Giles so very much, yet she had come to accept that the feeling would never be returned. She had accepted his friendship, cherishing it in lieu of deeper, desired emotions. Now they were asking her to play a role that she lived in her dreams. And not a role merely accepted unquestioningly by others, as it had been in the village, but played openly, convincingly, for all to see. She was to pretend that she loved him as he showered her with false words, words she so longed to hear from his heart. She would feel his loving touch, knowing that for him it was only a role he was playing. The moments in the village when she had danced with him, loving him so, had been almost unbearable. And now it was to be the role that would fill her days. Ever a game, never real.

They were waiting for her answer. She remembered what he had told her the previous night on the parapet: be honest, even in the face of Eleanor's anger. Once committed, she would have to go through with it, at whatever cost. . . . She had no childish delusions about why she was the one being asked to do this. Her innocence slowly sloughed away as she faced the truth. Eleanor's kindness to a wench from the docks of London—her generosity—had all been to this purpose. Roanna had been groomed for this act; her reputation, her feelings, simply did not matter.

She knew, though she could not yet give her answer, that she would do it. Not for England—that was beyond her. Not for the politics that men—and Eleanor—played. That was ever the same, and would ever be, acted only by different players. De Monfort professed noble reasons for what he did; perhaps they were, but power was the usual motivation for those of his ilk. For Roanna, there was only one consideration: people. She thought of a small village that would continue to suffer under Henry's rule. Jews who were still in hiding for doing nothing more than giving the funds demanded by a king for his twisted dreams. The friends who had risked themselves to protect Giles and herself on a terrifying night when they had fled the king's men. And her uncle, as she imagined him on a torchlit night, defending others from a maddened mob. Oh, she would do it for all those reasons, helping de Monfort's cause, whatever his true motivations, because he was fighting the man who had caused such misery.

Her heart twisted painfully, her dreams slipping away as she made ready to answer. Oh, Giles, she thought miserably, what will this do to us? Above all, she was terrified that what they were about to do would destroy the innocence of their friendship, the only thing she had with him that was hers. That too, gone.

"Aye," she said softly into the silence. Looking up, she forced herself to smile, then passed off the moment with a shrug. "Why not? Seems simple enough."

"Are you certain, Roanna?" Giles asked doubtfully. His eyes touched hers, filled with concern. "You do not have to do this."

"I know," she assured him, forcing herself to regard him evenly. "We did it before, Giles, rather well, I think. Now it should prove as simple as breathing. No effort at all." Turning to Eleanor, she forced a note of lightness into her voice. "Providing, of course, that this time I'll be allowed to speak. Lud, I thought I'd strangle." In the laughter that followed, Roanna smiled, thinking her heart would break.

12

Roanna tried to look directly at the sun. She was forced to glance away immediately, its brightness dancing before her eyes in bursting lights. A foolish desire, she thought, but she'd only wanted to feel its warmth upon her face, to look upon it fully for a moment to feel its total effect. But it cannot be done, any fool knows that—any fool but me, she thought.

"Roanna. Are you all right?" Giles asked with concern as she rubbed her eyes.

"I'm fine." She smiled up at him and stepped away into the shadows of the wall. "The sun is too hot. Linger with me here in the shade—just for a moment."

He joined her, leaning against the wall in the cool shadows. A moment later he turned his head, puzzled, as she laughed softly. "What is it?" he asked, smiling.

"Nothing, really. I was just thinking—our whole world has gone mad, yet we are pledged to enjoy ourselves. We are players in the greatest of masques, and the outcome will be a kingdom."

"Roanna." His voice was low and had lost its humor. "I know that this is not easy for you—but do not discount its importance."

"Oh, I do not," she said softly. "But I must not lose my sense of humor, Giles, or I think I shall go mad."

"Is it so difficult?" he asked quietly.

Oh, God, she thought, difficult? It would be easier not to

breathe. "Of course not," she answered. "I only meant that—it is different."

Different, she mused, indeed it was different. Even during those weeks in the village, those long weeks, their time together had been private, but for those few moments when they danced at the wedding. Now, every waking hour, when they were not at their duties—and Eleanor had arranged for them to be free as often as possible without drawing undue suspicion—they were together. Together, openly flaunting their budding "relationship." Oh, word had spread rapidly. Reactions were mixed, as could be expected: approval from those eager for a new, budding love to gossip about or savor, disapproval from those who could not condone a man of Giles's position cavorting with a woman of Roanna's. Cavorting—a word she'd overheard from Lady Margot.

"Roanna, what is it?"

She realized that she had been frowning. "I told you, nothing," she assured him.

He spun to face her, placing his hands on either side of her against the wall. "Roanna, in spite of what you say, I know that this is difficult for you," he murmured. "I am proud of you; you have played it well."

"I am trying." She wished he wouldn't stand so close.

"I know. Perhaps . . ." He paused, turning his head slightly as the sound of footsteps came from around the corner. Then, before she knew what he was going to do, he bent down and kissed her.

She stiffened, shocked by the kiss. Then she felt herself drifting into it, drawn by the feel of his lips against her own. Her lips parted under his, and for a moment she was unaware of anything but his mouth as it moved softly over hers. Oh, Lord, she thought confusedly. Then she gradually became aware of someone clearing her throat. She blinked dizzily at Giles as he pulled away, turning his head toward the sound.

"Really! Giles fitzWilliam, I am surprised at you! Such a display, where anyone might see you!"

Roanna focused on that biting voice. Miserably, she now understood the reason for his kiss. She turned her head, noting with irritation that Giles was smiling. "Lady Margot," she acknowledged tightly. It occurred to her that the young noblewoman had not mentioned that she was surprised at Roanna. The woman was a puzzle. Roanna had never expected friendship from Margot, but she was baffled by her hostility—not just toward Roanna, but toward everyone. There were even moments when she had caught Margot glaring at the countess's back with a smoky expression.

Suddenly, Roanna was fed up with everything, especially the petulant Margot and her irritating barbs. "I do apologize," she heard herself purring. "Must be right shockin' to a lady like yerself—'specially seein' as 'ow ye must be wonderin' what it feels like. It be good, Margot." She smiled, leaning forward with a sultry expression. "Bleedin' good."

The young woman gasped, then fled, her dark skirts swishing as she passed them.

"Roanna!" Giles gaped down at her, his eyes glinting with amused disapproval. "That was unkind. Even if she did deserve it."

"Oh, fuss and bother. Let me go, Giles. I 'ave things to do," she answered tightly, slipping beneath his arm.

"Roanna—"

She ignored him and fled across the ward to the safety of Lady Eleanor's chamber. To her relief, it was empty. She took up a chemise that needed mending, and sat in the window embrasure of the large room to finish the task she had commenced the day before. She had just begun when the door opened and the countess came in. Roanna answered the warm smile Eleanor gave her, then bent her head to her sewing, hoping that she might be ignored. Then her worries pressed in, and she sighed softly, laying the needlework in her lap. Eleanor's disapproval was bound to be faced eventually, and she might as well face it now. "Milady?" she began, clearing her throat.

"What is it, Roanna?" Eleanor murmured, her dark head already bent to her journals.

Roanna stood up and crossed to stand before Eleanor's desk. "Milady—I fear I have—done something terrible. Actually, I do not feel that it was terrible—but you likely will. I would rather have you hear of it from me."

Eleanor sat back in her chair and regarded Roanna with a question in her eyes. Roanna took a deep breath, then proceeded to recount what had occurred with Lady Margot. When she finished, she stood stiffly, waiting for Eleanor's reprimand.

Eleanor's mouth worked for a moment; then, to Roanna's surprise, she chuckled. "Sweet Mother, you do have a way about you, Roanna. I am gratified that you warned me. But please, in the future, attempt to restrain yourself." Relieved, Roanna began to turn away, but Eleanor stayed her. "Sit down a moment," she said, gesturing to the chair across from her. "Many comments are reaching me about the love affair that has sprung up between you and Giles. You play the game well."

"I am trying," Roanna murmured.

"As you must be aware, there are those, such as Lady Margot, who do not favor such a liaison. Hurtful things will be said, Roanna, but you must not count the words for more than they are: jealousy on the part of those who can only wish for such a love. You are a most attractive young couple."

"Aye, milady," Roanna answered listlessly. Who was she fooling? she wondered. It was apparent to everyone that Giles was merely—cavorting with her. Poor Roanna, to reach so far above her. Little tart. She was in for a fall—a fall from grace that would forever lie upon her soul.

A moment of anger made her bold. "I am certain that we will be forgotten when they have other things to dwell upon," she said, shrugging. "One day I shall be home again, and forgotten. I should be more concerned with Giles and what the Lady Lisette will think when word reaches her. But then, perhaps it will not. After all, I'm only a dalliance for one of Giles's station." She dropped her eyes on her last words, missing the narrowing of Eleanor's eyes.

Eleanor picked up a small dagger that she used to carve her meat, and played with the handle as she studied Roanna. "The Lady Lisette was married to the Compte d'Masson soon after her return to France," she said quietly. Her rising suspicions were confirmed as she noted the slight intake of Roanna's breath, the stiffening of her back, the unmistakable look of joy that showed in her eyes for an instant before it again faded into resignation. "Indeed," Eleanor drawled, pursing her lips to avoid a smile, "the wedding was one of great pomp and ceremony. The bride was most lovely, and quite enthralled with her bridegroom, a handsome and enormously wealthy young man her father had found for her. It was a good match."

Oh, poor Giles! Roanna thought. What had happened? Dare she be so familiar as to ask? "I—imagine that 'twas difficult for Giles," she said, bracing herself. "I only mention it, as I would not want to say anything to him without meaning to, of course, that would cause him pain."

"Of course," Eleanor said wryly. "But have no fear on that account. Soon after arriving in France, those budding relations were well nipped, as it were. The lady made untoward comments on more than one occasion regarding the barbarians of Wales and Ireland. You know that Giles's lands are there, and his heart resides in those places, Roanna. Any woman who would catch his heart and hold it must look with great favor upon what is his."

"Of course," Roanna agreed. "But then, I am certain that—somewhere—there is a beautiful and kind lady, one he deserves, who will look kindly upon both him and his lands."

"Indeed, I have no doubt of it," Eleanor said, smiling. "He deserves one who will love him for the man he is." She sighed, sitting up straight as she dropped the dagger and again picked up her quill. "Fortunately, due to his position, Giles is free to choose for himself. I have no doubt that he will choose the right young woman."

"Aye, milady," Roanna answered, swallowing hard. Seeing that she was dismissed as the countess bent her head to her journals, she rose and returned to her window seat. She picked up the mending, but was soon staring out the window, lost in thoughts she dare not consider, unaware that Eleanor had paused in her writing to glance at her daydreaming maid with a brief but satisfied smile.

Roanna left the chamber for her supper soon after the remarkable exchange with the countess. Her head was spinning with possibilities; yet reason fought relentlessly with dreams. A woman of his choosing—wonderful for him, but for her? It made no difference, she was what she was, a tavern maid from the docks of London, while he was a landed knight. But then, she remembered, William the Bastard, he who had been known as the Conqueror, had been mothered by a dairymaid, and he had become king of England. But the other voice in her head told her that Giles would not become king of England, or even a baron. He would need, and deserve, the wealth and position that the proper marriage could bring him. What could she bring to him? She could cook. She could handle rowdy men. Well, those talents could help in an emergency, she thought wryly. She knew the words that, roundly used, could send subordinates scurrying. The thought of using them during an event such as Lord Edward's dinner made her smile. "By the balls, ye bloody bugger, move yer friggin' arse!" That ought to liven up a banquet, though Giles would probably expire.

Nay, she was no lady. But, damnation! She could understand the ways of men—and the politics that confounded them—far better than most of the addle-brained doormats she observed among the ladies of the noble class! But then, what man truly wanted to know what his wife was thinking? Nay, a woman was merely a sounding board for his own thoughts. She was to give a slight nod as he expounded, affirming that she agreed, of course, with his brilliant intellect—even though, with almost any man that Roanna had observed, if you put his brain in a fish it would sink.

Oh, not all men treated their wives that way. Lord Simon did not, but Roanna was no Eleanor Plantagenet. Nay, Giles wanted—needed—a lady. A gracious, soft, submissive lady who would never bring shame upon him. Besides, she thought, what made her think for a moment that she had a chance with him? They were playing a game, nothing more. For God and England.

Weary of the whole situation, she walked through the shadows along the wall toward her chamber. She had no appetite left; she wanted no supper, only the solitude of her own room, a candle lit, a warm cup of wine, and her notes to copy for her dear Franciscan teacher.

As she passed the turn in the wall by the passage leading to the kitchens, an arm suddenly reached out, snaking about her waist, and she was yanked into the darkness. Instinctively, she fought. Her feet, which were swinging above the ground, lashed back, seeking solid flesh while she clawed and shrieked against the attack.

"Not this time," a voice grunted near her ear. "You are my prisoner, totally at my mercy. And, by God, I will have my way with you!"

Released, she spun about. "Dammit, Giles fitzWilliam!

You're completely and for all time a madman! What do you mean, scaring me like that!"

"Thank the gods that I do not ravish you, here and now," he grinned, his eyes flaring.

"Thank the gods that you did not lose those gems most precious to you! I have the ability—as you once told me—to strike at the heart of the matter."

"I was ready for you." He kept grinning, and in spite of herself, she had to struggle not to smile.

"Why don't you leave me be? All I want is a moment to myself. Besides, no one is looking, so there is no point to it."

"No point?" He affected a look of great injury. "Oh, Roanna. I thought you would be pleased." He bent and picked up a woven basket, holding it out in front of him like a peace offering. "My way of apologizing," he explained. "I offended you this morning."

"What is it?" she said, laughing, unable to remain angry at the foolish, pleading look on his face.

"Our supper!" His grin grew even more sheepish. "Come on." He grabbed her hand and pulled her across the ward. She gasped with surprise, trying to keep up with his long strides. When they reached the gate to the outer ward, Geoffrey was waiting, holding the reins of Giles's palfrey and, to her horror, of another mount as well. Dread washed over her as she realized that she was expected to ride! It did not help matters that Geoffrey was wearing the same foolish grin as Giles. Before she could respond, she found herself lifted up to the saddle, her skirt tucked in about her knees. Looking down from her perch, she had to laugh, in spite of her shock. How could anyone so completely virile, so totally masculine, look so like a little boy caught with a guilty secret?

As she held on for dear life, he led her through the gate tower and across the causeway to the open countryside, where the sun was lowering above the horizon. They stopped near a small copse of oak and maple trees not far from the castle. Giles reined in his mount, slipping from the saddle, and came to her, reaching up to help her down. "It is not safe for us to go farther," he said, setting her on the ground. "But this should be private enough."

"Private enough for what?" she asked, one eyebrow arched speculatively.

"To talk," he answered, turning back to take the basket from behind his saddle. He spread a blanket beneath the trees, setting the basket on it, and then turned, holding out a hand to her. "Come here," he said quietly.

She hesitated for a moment, caution pressing its insistent voice, but he compelled her, and she went to him. They sat side by side on the blanket, looking out over the country-side from their vantage point on the slightly raised knoll. Kenilworth lay in the near distance, and on either side of them were the undulating green hills of West Anglia. Dusk painted shadows against the bright pink glory of the ap-proaching sunset.

She couldn't speak. She didn't want him to say a word, not yet, or to make a move toward her. If he did, she would probably throw herself on him. Please, Giles, please don't touch me, she thought. I don't want to make a fool of myself, and I'm not certain I can handle this.

He handed her a chicken leg. "Hungry?"

Not for chicken, she thought. "Famished," she said, taking the food.

"I thought you weren't hungry—looked to me like you were about to skip supper."

"Riding always makes me hungry."

"Have you ridden a lot?" he asked casually. From what he had glimpsed, as she bounced beside him on their short ride, the answer was no.

"I was born to the saddle," she said airily, munching on the chicken.

He stifled a grin, and chose a thick breast from the basket. "What about hawking?"

She turned a quizzical eye on him. "What about it?"

"Do you enjoy hunting with a falcon?"

"Not particularly," she said, ignoring the fact, which they both knew, that she had rarely even seen a hawk. "Birds belong in the sky, flying about—or in a pot."

"Well, it is one way to get them into the pot," he observed dryly.

"Inefficient."

"Perhaps. But a good sport, nonetheless."

"I'll take your word for it."

He lay back, propping one arm beneath his head as he stared up at the clouds. "Roanna, what is it that you want out of life?"

She turned her head to look at him. Lord, why were people always asking her questions she couldn't answer? "What do you want, Giles?"

He turned his eyes toward her. "You are avoiding my question."

"That I am, Sir Giles," she answered huffily. "I did not ask to be brought here, or to be asked impertinent questions."

"Impertinent questions?" He laughed. "Well, have it your way. I'll begin with me, if that is what you want." He glanced at her wryly. "Or even if you don't. What do I want out of life?" He paused, staring at the sky. "To find peace, and to be left to enjoy it. To return to Wales, where my only concern would be how to divide my time with Ireland."

"Doesn't the court draw you?" she interrupted, amazed. "If Earl Simon is successful, you could become a most powerful man."

"Powerful? Roanna, have you thought of what it means to be in favor at court? I have seen many men, normally reasonable souls, who spend their lives currying the king's favor by assisting with the royal undergarments."

"Oh, Giles, be serious. I meant, to have the power of your father, or your grandfather, or his father before him. Great men of England—"

"I thought you had nothing to say," he reminded her. "Aye, my forefathers had power—great power. Perhaps no individual man shall have such influence again beyond the throne. But it cost them dearly. I do not think that one of them ever had peace of mind. I will fight for England, for I love her; that was instilled in me, and will ever be part of what I am. But I will not compromise myself the way they did, the way they had to. I am lucky in that, Roanna—I can adhere to my principles, as no one will ever challenge them."

"If that is so, how can you be sure of what they are? It is easy to say 'I believe in this,' or 'I believe in that,' unless you have to prove it."

He turned his head to stare at her and his blue eyes filled with amusement. "You are a little chit, you know that?"

"I know. But you have not answered me. You sound bitter, Giles. I have never heard that from you before."

"Bitter?" He snorted, but the humor left his eyes. Turning again to the sky, he stared at the drifting clouds and his expression changed to bemusement. "I thought I had gotten over that. Perhaps I haven't, completely. If I still feel that way, it is not bitterness toward the men who rule the lives of others; that will always be the condition of man. Stupidity angers me, when I see men of power and position ruling others ineptly, led by greed. I watched my family decline. I see the greatness my cousins were given, the opportunities they were born with, yet not one of them—not one—has the capability to lead. What happened to them? How can a family change so, in one passing?"

It has not, she thought. Oh, Giles, it has not. But she kept silent.

"I look upon my cousins, and I despair. And it is the same, throughout England. Who shall lead? Since the time of the Conqueror, there have been great peers of England, those who have aided her. Where have they gone? It ended with my father."

That, she reasoned privately, is why he was murdered. "Yet you serve Simon. 'ave—have you no faith in him?"

He sat up abruptly, bending one knee and wrapping his arm around it. "I serve Eleanor, and through her, Simon. And, aye, I have faith in him—he may be the one exception in our time. What he believes is pure and good, and will lead him to greatness. But there is still a vital element missing, that quality that causes men to follow, even into hell. I think—and I have thought long on the subject—that it is an unwavering strength of purpose, which draws men because they must be near to it. Simon—Simon's hatred keeps him from finding it."

"Hatred? For whom?"

He hesitated, glancing at her. "Henry Plantagenet the Third of England. His brother by marriage." He smiled at her surprised look. "Could you not know, kitten? How have you missed this juicy piece of gossip? Our king and sovereign publicly accused Simon of seducing his royal sister. It was nothing less than an accusation of treason. This, from the brother who had himself arranged the marriage, and was the only party to it. Our Henry thought a secret marriage between his sister and the man she loved to be irresistibly romantic—until the feathers flew. When an outcry was raised that a princess had married a mere commoner, and the council called him to account, he retreated quickly enough. He condemned them publicly—

accusing his sister of adultery, and Simon of treason. They have never forgiven him. Indeed, he has never offered an apology."

"I'd spit in 'is eye," Roanna exclaimed, outraged.

"You probably would." He laughed. "In front of the entire court."

"What did Eleanor do?" she asked, intrigued.

"What a Plantagenet does when enraged, particularly at another Plantagenet: the ground shook. It took the king of France to placate the two of them; however, the truce is only on the surface. They will never be appeased, or reconciled."

"Is that why Eleanor has gone to war with him?"

"Sweetling, it is Simon who is at war with Henry."

"Of course," she said with a smirk. "Is that why Simon is at war with him?"

He shook his head. "Roanna, Simon is not a whipped man. His war is his own, and he truly believes in his cause: to bring freedom to England's people. He believes in the Great Charter, and the provisions gained at Oxford."

"Then what is it that leads you to believe that he will fail?"

He sighed wearily. "I did not say that he would fail."

"You hope he won't, but you have doubts."

"Everyone has doubts."

She drew up her knees, wrapping her arms about them as she studied him and thought about what he had said. So much had happened in the months that she had been at Kenilworth. It was odd, but she didn't feel like the same person she had been. The hours spent with Brother Vincent, the things he had taught her, had given her more than just knowledge about places and about people who had lived before. She had begun to think for herself, and the strangest thoughts sometimes entered her mind, their depth surprising her.

"Aye, everyone has doubts," she said softly, "but yours are eating at you. I listened to what you have said about what brings men to follow another—even into hell, you said. From what I have been told of your father and grandfather, their greatest strength was their unwavering loyalty. Not blind loyalty, but a loyalty of conviction, a determination to bring about a dream, to shape the muck of man's mistakes to a better purpose, to build. You fear that in spite of the nobility of Simon's purpose, his hatred will blind him, causing him to miss the essence of what will be needed."

The silence sharpened with the shrill chirping of the cicadas in the meadow below them. "Go on, Roanna."

Her eyes touched on him with gentle sadness. "Oh, Giles. Do you know how many men I've seen who make a complete muddle of their lives? You forget where I've stood, watching life. But I've seen them make good work of it too, against all odds. I've seen silent hopelessness, and great cries covering desperation. Most people live that way, Giles—laughter covering pain, courage hiding fear. What wins out is what is important. Simon's hatred is not of concern, but only if he cannot conquer it. He may yet."

He gazed fixedly at her for a long moment, and slowly his eyes began to twinkle. Suddenly, with a great burst of laughter, he threw her to the ground and, ignoring her squeal, pinned her to the blanket and grinned down at her. "Roanna Royston, you are the most complicated and surprising woman I have ever known. Did a mystical sprite drop you into my lap? Where did you come from? The wind? The sea?"

"The dredges of the Thames," she said, grimacing. "Giles fitzWilliam, let me up, you fool."

He began to tickle her, sending her into peals of laughter as she gasped and kicked, trying to push him off her. As she heaved for breath, they finally lay still. "Roanna, you are the best friend I have ever known," he murmured breathlessly in her ear.

Her voice was muffled against his shoulder. "Then let me up, you great oaf."

He pulled away, leaping to his feet and then pulling her up. "I am sorry, Roanna. A moment's passion—will you forgive me?" He grinned. "I have never wrestled with a girl before."

I seriously doubt that, she thought silently, as she bent to retrieve the remains of their supper. But a best friend? He had said it, and she warmed with a pleasant flush at the remembered words. It was something. Aye, it was that, and more.

13

They rode into Kenilworth as the last vestiges of day faded to wavering shadows cast by torchlights set along the stone walls. By some mysterious cue, Geoffrey appeared and took the reins of their mounts. Lud, Roanna thought, had he been waiting all this time? Or had some instinct, sharpened by years of training, told him when he would be required?

She slipped away as Giles spoke to Geoffrey, suddenly needing the solitude of her chamber. She needed time to think about the hours just spent with him, the things he had said. Oh, sweet angels and saints, she thought as she rubbed her arms against the chill, there was so much to consider, to reason through . . . Shivering in the cold night air, she hurried through the shadows along the bailey wall. But as she passed the north side of the keep, she stopped short. Before her, stumbling from the darkened passage leading to the buttery, a small group of knights appeared, blocking her way.

"Well, nowww," one of them slurred, obviously in his cups. "Roanna, eh? What're ya doin' about, lass?"

"Seems Giles lost 'er," another drawled.

"Or mayhap he's n-not man 'nough ta keep 'er," said the third.

"Ya may be right, Thomas," remarked the first man, belching. "Pr'aps we'd best show her what a real man kin do."

"I don't see a real man among you!" she snapped, drawing back as she braced herself against the wall.

"Come here, lass, I'll show ye!" he snickered, staggering toward her.

"Take another step and I'll break yer friggin' balls!" she cried, furious.

The men broke into laughter. One reached out and grasped her arm as another grabbed her about the waist. Shrieking, she wrenched her arm free, landing it across the face of the third man, who yelped in pain and fell back with a bloody nose. Her knee came up sharply, ramming one of her abductors in the promised spot. He bellowed in pain and rage, doubling over; but the remaining man redoubled his assault, and she found herself dragged into the shadows, a large hand clamped over her mouth as two arms pinned her against a hard body. She began to panic against the smell of stale ale and the groping hands. Oh, God, she thought, not like this!

Then she heard a soft, sickening thud. Twisting her head about, she saw that the second knight was staring at her with a look of surprise. Still holding his private parts, he keeled over with a thud. The third knight, who had managed to recover from the blow to his nose, turned and fled back down the darkened passage to the buttery. The man holding her pushed her away as he spun upon the intruder. Roanna cried out as her shoulder struck the stone wall and pain radiated down her arm and through her body. She slumped against the wall, willing herself not to be sick, then twisted about to confront her attackers. Her eyes flared with surprise and relief, even as she struggled against a heavy wave of nausea.

Giles was holding a length of wood, his legs spread in a ready stance as he confronted her remaining assailant. "Come on, Rolf," he said coldly, gesturing the other man forward with his free hand. "Or are you afraid to take on someone your own size?"

"Drop it, fitzWilliam, and I'll see you to a fair fight," the man snarled.

"What would you know of a fair fight, Rolf?" Giles said grimly. "You're only interested in defenseless women, and you need two others to help you do it." With that, he swung the board, connecting with the side of the knight's head and landing him in a heap near his friend. Dropping the board,

Giles gazed down at the duo with disgust. Then he looked up at Roanna. Grabbing her by the arm, he jerked her around and pulled her in the direction of her quarters, mumbling furiously under his breath as she stumbled after him. Reaching her chamber, he threw back the door and pushed her inside. She tripped into the room, catching herself as she heard the door slam behind her.

"Of all the stupid, inane things I've known you to do, that was the worst!" he bellowed. "Why did you leave me? Don't you know better than to wander about a castle the size of Kenilworth at night? You might as well wander about the streets of London, for God's sake!"

"I've never had trouble before!" she said defensively, shaken.

"God protects fools!" he roared. "But even fools find their time!"

"Ooooh! How right you are, milord!" she cried, fighting back tears of rage. "Though fools are overlooked for their follies, but not whores! Certainly not the whore of Giles fitzWilliam!"

He flinched as if her words were a physical blow, and froze. He stared at her. "What are you saying?" he said, very quietly.

"What else?" she snapped through her tears. "I am your whore, Giles, and a whore is there for the taking!" She shook her head and was filled with a deep, painful sadness at the dumbfounded look on his face. "What did you expect? We have played the game well, and we have succeeded. Oh, aye, it was successful: the looks you gave me, before your fellows, declaring your feelings; the moments taken when you blatantly drew me into the shadows of the hall—out of their sight, but not out of their understanding. Would you treat a lady thus? Who would you treat in such a way, Sir Giles, but your harlot?"

He stared at her. The expression on his face caused her to turn away, unable to face the confusion she read there. Oh, God, she thought, could he truly not know? What had he expected?

"Roanna," he said pleadingly, his voice filled with anguish. "What have we done to you?"

"Giles," she whispered painfully, "go away. Please. It is done. I do not blame you, I knew it would be so. There is nothing to be done for it." She braced herself against the silence that followed, the rending emptiness. Please, she cried silently, please, Giles, go now. Listening for the sound of the door closing behind him, she gasped as his hands closed over her shoulders. "Oh, Giles, 'ave pity, if you care for me at all," she cried out softly.

"Roanna," he whispered, his breath against her ear, the softness of his voice reaching into her heart. He turned her to him, his hands slipping up to cup her face. "Roanna, I would die before I hurt you. Don't you know that?"

"I—I know that you would never mean to hurt me," she choked out, dropping her gaze from the painful intensity of his eyes. "You are my dearest friend. Neither of us wanted this to happen."

"Friend?" he asked huskily. "Oh, Roanna, you are that and more, so much more to me. You have become every woman in my life. My mother, whom I never knew, but dreamed about. My grandmother, who first gave me love. Eleanor, who held me close and was mother to me. My impossible aunts, those women of strength, who left me in awe. My beautiful cousins, who fill me with such tenderness. And more, so much more that I want to discover. Oh, God, Roanna, don't you know that I love you?" As she looked up at him in wonder, he lowered his lips to close upon her cry, taking it into him.

His mouth moved over hers with a tenderness that overwhelmed her, bringing tears to her eyes. He kissed them away, tasting the saltiness upon his lips, softly touching upon one fluttering lid, then the other. His arms folded about her, drawing her close.

"Giles," she cried softly, but his mouth returned to still her cry, and she slumped against him, her own lips opening in sweet surrender. His tongue slipped into the velvety recesses of her mouth in a play that left her breathless. She realized that his hand was unlacing the neck of her kirtle, and pleasure purred in her throat as she took his words into her heart, trusting him.

She gave herself up to him, reveling in the exquisite sensation that anticipation brought her. Leaning back, she closed her eyes as she felt his fingers continue their steady progress as they unlaced her gown. He pushed aside the bodice and she gasped softly as he touched her breast, laying his hand gently where no one but he, in those all too brief moments so long past, had touched her before.

Ohhh, she thought dizzily, such sweetness he gave. His hand cupped the fullness of her breast as his thumb reached gently to touch the tip, playing in slow, teasing circles that nearly drove her mad. She arched against him, holding her breath against the heat that was spreading over her body, the delicious ache that had begun to consume her from his touch and the anticipation of what he might do next.

He slid the gown from her shoulders and let it drop to her feet. It was quickly followed by her chemise. She couldn't open her eyes. She wanted to imagine what he was seeing, even as she hoped, prayed, that he was pleased. She felt his eyes on her in a heat that traveled slowly over her. Her skin tingled, each part of her body taking on new meaning as it flamed with a bittersweet ache. She heard his voice whispering words that seemed to have no meaning except in feeling, but they touched her and she was ready as he drew her against him.

His body was hard, and she realized, dizzily, that he had discarded his clothing. His skin felt hot, and she was amazed at how soft she was against him. She had never imagined that her body could feel so different from his.

He lifted her in his arms and laid her on the bed. She felt him beside her, and as he touched her she drew in her breath painfully, her body alive with feeling. She felt the hot, moist sensations of his mouth as it claimed her breast and his tongue began its play, crying out softly at the unexpected waves of pleasure that shot through her.

She called his name as his tongue circled the nipple, touching lightly, and moaned with pleasure when he began to pull gently, suckling. Arching her back against the intense sensations he was causing, she felt sudden heat flame through the length of her body, igniting a need in her belly. Her hips moved against him and he answered, slipping a hand between her thighs, spreading them as he began a new play that left her gasping for breath and moaning as she moved with his hand and begged for a release she couldn't understand.

But it soon came. He slipped into her. Distantly, she marveled that there was no pain, only tight, delicious sensations that intensified with each gentle stroke as he moved within her. He slid one hand under her hips, drawing them up to him, and plunged more deeply, steadily drawing her with him up the heights of pleasure to that place where he wanted her. And it came, in a tightening, a tension, a drawing together that suddenly exploded, radiating out in wave after wave.

She lay in his arms, nestled against him. His hand rested against her breast, and his measured breathing told her that he was asleep. The total darkness of the small chamber heightened her other senses, and she focused on the warmth of his hand against her bare flesh. A strong hand, fingers that offered protection—or pleasure. Such pleasure, she thought, curling into his arms. It was done, she was his. She would never regret it, no matter what happened. He had taken her in love. The words he had spoken, the way he had loved her with such tenderness—no one could ever take that from her. You were right, Uncle Roscoe, she mused. Life was for the taking. The day would come, she knew, when he would leave her. But she would have this, a moment when she had been truly and completely loved. Her mind drifted.

She awakened as he stirred against her, and nestled into his arms, moaning softly at the realization that it was morning. Opening her eyes, she found that he had lit a candle, and she stared into the bright blue eyes that watched her, filled with question. A large hand covered her mouth gently as his eyes filled with tender amusement.

"Nay," he said softly. "I'll have no denial of what we had. For once, be silent, Roanna."

She moaned, stifled by the hand, then lay quiet, her eyes wide as she looked up at him.

"Not a word," he cautioned, his brows arching. "You have beautiful eyes," he mused, "but beware, my love, they look into your soul. They tell what you are thinking. And they are about to tell me that we must forget what passed between us last night. Sweetling, I am not about to forget, nor shall you. You are mine, do you understand? Forever."

Aye, she thought, in my heart, truly forever. Seeing the softness in her eyes, he released her and claimed her mouth with his own. His hands slipped beneath the covers and soon they forgot everything but each other.

Much later, he roused her from her lethargy, shaking her lightly. "Come on, sleepyhead. It is time to get up."

Pouting, she kept her eyes closed and feigned sleep.

A hand slipped between her thighs, and her eyes flew open.

"Ah, you're awake," he said, grinning.

"Bastard," she murmured into the pillow.

"Bastard?" He laughed. "That was not what you said only a short while ago. Was that not you who moaned: 'Oh, Giles . . . ooooh, Giles' "? he mimicked.

"You are vile," she groaned, fighting a smile as she rolled to the edge of the bed.

"I know," he said wickedly. "Without doubt, sweetling, you shall again know the baseness of my behavior, but not now. 'Tis morning, and we will be missed." He rolled from the bed, reaching for his chausses. Finishing with them, he pulled his chanise and tunic over his head. Then he reached across the bed and flipped the covers from her. "Get up!" he said, emphasizing the order with a slap on her bottom.

Protesting crankily, she dragged herself up and picked up her chemise. She pulled it over her head and turned to find him watching her with interest.

"A lovely view," he remarked with a grin.

Tossing him a scathing look, she turned to the washstand, then stiffened. Straightening abruptly, she felt an uncomfortable stickiness between her thighs, and a soreness that squarely brought into focus the cold light of morning. "Oooh," she whispered, closing her eyes.

He was suddenly there, the warmth of his body pressing against her back as he dipped a cloth into the washbowl. He bent his head to the nape of her neck, kissing her tenderly. "Here," he said softly, pressing the cloth into her hand. "I love you, Roanna. Never doubt it, sweetling. Would you like me to help you?"

"Go away," she said affectionately, loving him.

"Are you certain?"

"Go away."

"As you will, love. We both have duties that must be seen to—but then . . ." He kissed her and, with a gentle pat to her rump, left, quietly shutting the door behind him.

Humming contentedly, she bathed and dressed in a fresh linen chemise and a bliaut of fine rust wool. The gown had been a gift from Eleanor, one Roanna had felt was too fine for normal duties. The long-sleeved gown curved against her body in soft folds, accentuating her breasts and hips.

She gathered it about the waist with another of Eleanor's gifts, a copper-linked girdle with a trail of ribbons that hung to the hem. Picking up the linen cloth she used as a coif, she stared at it, fingering the fabric, hating the thought of binding her hair. Suddenly she was filled with a strange restlessness.

Odd that she had not thought about it before, but it was her hair, the strawberry-blond of the Saxon, that had first drawn Giles's eye, as he had told her in the quiet hours of the past night. Yet long ago, he had cautioned her to bind it, so as not to draw attention to its unusual color. Unusual for whom? For Normans, she thought wryly, though it is said that we are all simply English now. So it was said. Saxon blood is what runs through me, she thought, as pure as the Norman blood of Kenilworth's ladies.

On the docks of the Thames she was a free woman; when she left them, she became something less. She had come willingly, drawn in search of—what? Giles's love, she silently answered, and she had miraculously found it. Why did she feel so strange now, so incomplete? Was it guilt? She considered the thought, then pushed it away. Nay, she felt no guilt for what they had shared, nor did she feel fear. She would ask nothing of him beyond what he could give. Should she quicken with child, there would be no care-cloth for them. She would treasure any moments they were granted, and when it was time she would go. That fact too she had faced when she left London, and nothing had happened to change it, nor would it ever.

She fingered the cloth, pulling it through her hands as she thought back over her life—the easy, joyous freedom she had taken for granted until Durham House, the changes in her life since that time, the person who had grown inside her over the past year, with all that she had learned and experienced. And then she understood.

She loved Giles with all of her heart, but she did not like herself very much, or what she had become: a simpering, submissive lump, obedient to the demands of others. Even in moments when she had shown some spine, she had done so hatefully. She had begun to think of herself as a victim, and had become one.

Standing up, she tossed the coif onto the bed and swiftly braided her hair into two gloriously thick plaits that hung down her back in the old Saxon style. Then she bound her forehead with a fillet of copper. No more servants' caps, no more coifs, she thought, no more apologies for who or what I am.

She left her chamber, noting by the position of the sun that she was late. She hurried across the ward to the keep, making her way through the crowd that had gathered before the broad stairs leading to the raised first floor. It was midweek, the day Eleanor held her court of justice, and those milling about the keep were awaiting an audience with the countess. The crowd parted for her as she made her way through, and she smiled at the occasional appreciative male comments thrown her way. "Ah, go on. Ye an' who else?" she remarked to one fellow, bringing laughter from the crowd.

Happily, she passed through the doorway, drawing a startled look from one of the guards as she winked at him. Still grinning, she spotted Eleanor with her ladies at the opposite end of the room near the dais. With some effort, she affected a serious demeanor and approached the small group, bracing herself.

Heads turned toward her, drawing Eleanor's attention to her. The countess's eyes widened slightly, sweeping over her in a glance.

"Roanna!" Lady Margot exclaimed, bristling. "Your hair—"

"—is lovely," Eleanor finished. "The gown looks well on you, Roanna. But you are late. I would have begun without you, but Brother Vincent is at Bordesley Abbey."

Sweeping past her, Eleanor took her place on the dais and waved Roanna to the small table near her. Roanna opened the large, bound journal of Kenilworth's justice, and dipped her quill, glancing up at the countess to let her know she was ready. Smiling, Eleanor arched a bemused brow at her charge, then turned to her chancellor, John Seward. "I think that now we may begin, Sir John."

The morning passed swiftly as Roanna recorded the tallages and fines and Eleanor's decisions on the disputes brought before her. She was gratified to find that there were few blotches on the parchments and that somehow she managed to keep up. Occasionally, during a lengthy dispute, she allowed her eyes to stray over the gathered company, looking for Giles; but apparently his duties lay elsewhere that morning. She found her thoughts drifting back to the hours of the past night, and she had to shake herself to attend what was happening in the great hall. Her gaze shifted, returning to the two men standing before the dais. Their worn, lined faces brought back a distant memory of a small village just beyond London. She smiled dreamily, refocusing her attention as she began to listen.

"—the barley be sold in good faith, m'lady," the taller of the two was saying. "'Twas not green, as she says."

"She took it, right enough," the other man insisted, "then says 'twas too green, after she took it."

"Enough," Eleanor commanded. She turned to Sir John. "Is the brewess here, to speak her part?"

"Nay, milady," the knight answered. "She has returned to Bosworth, but she has sworn to a written statement." He handed her the parchment in question.

Eleanor glanced over the letter, then passed it to Roanna to be placed in the records. Looking back at the two before her, she regarded them silently for a moment. "The brewess has been providing ale and mead to Kenilworth for many years. Never have I known her to falsify claims, as you have suggested here today. Therefore—"

"It is a lie."

Heads turned to Roanna, who was reading the parchment. She looked up, meeting Eleanor's surprised gaze. "It is a lie, milady," she repeated, more boldly. "The brewess states here that the barley was hard in the stalk and unsuitable for brewing. If it were so, it would be quite obviously green-tipped. No brewess would make such an error—and had she done so, indeed, the resulting ale would be unpalatable, sour beyond belief."

"Roanna—" Eleanor said sharply.

But Roanna was too taken with outrage over the brewess's blatant attempt to cheat the villeins to hear the warning in Eleanor's voice. "She would have to be blind to accept it. Obviously, the woman is lying."

The hall had fallen into a deathly quiet, as everyone looked toward the dais. Eleanor stared hard at Roanna, her face drained of color, and her eyes blue chips of ice. The silence held over the large hall until finally, in a low, barely controlled voice, Eleanor spoke, her eyes still locked on Roanna. "Sir John, you will take the maid's place and complete the day's notations. Mistress Roanna, you will await my pleasure in the library."

Roanna stood up, drawing herself straight as she faced Eleanor's furious glare. Then, as she stared into the enraged blue eyes, she realized what she had done. Turning, she stepped away from the table and crossed the hall through the company, which parted in a wave to let her pass. She kept her eyes straight ahead, her chin up, feeling the eyes upon her as she passed through the doors and into the ward.

Well, you've done it now, she thought ruefully as she crossed the ward to the library chamber in the east wall. What had she said, so very blithely to Giles, merely a day past?—that one could not be certain of one's principles unless they were tested, something like that. Well, Roanna Royston, she mused, no one could ever accuse you of doing anything in a small way.

Giles found her there a little while later, bent over a table reading a translation of Ptolemy. Shutting the door behind him, he threw his helm and scabbard on the end of the table. Still dust-covered from a morning's ride, he stood there for a moment, merely looking at her with an expression she couldn't define. "Sweet Mother, Roanna," he said at last, with an edge to his voice. "Can't I leave you alone for even one morning?"

"Are you suggesting that I need a keeper, Sir Giles?" she asked, turning a page.

"It's not a suggestion," he answered grimly. He leaned across the table and slammed the book shut, causing her to jump. "Roanna, for once, pay attention!" he roared. With his hands planted on either side of the book, he glared at her. "Do you have any idea what you have done?"

"The brewess lied," she answered simply.

"You contradicted Eleanor's word, in her own court of justice!" he yelled.

"She was wrong."

"Dammit, Roanna, you little fool, listen to me! Don't you realize that your life could be in danger?"

"Oh, Giles, really." She laughed nervously. "Over such a thing? She would not—"

"Wouldn't she? She's a Plantagenet; she can do any damn thing she wants—and no one, *no one* will question it! Eleanor does not show her rage often, but when she does, it is every bit as hateful, and as vengeful, as that of any Plantagenet who ever sat on the throne!"

"You told me to be honest with her!"

"Honest when questioned! Did she ask your advice?"

"Nay," she admitted.

"Come here," he said through clenched teeth as he came around the table and jerked her from her chair. He pulled her across the room, opening the door to the small bed-chamber Brother Vincent used when working late at night. "Stay in here. Do you understand me? Do not come out until I tell you—no matter what you hear!"

She stared at the door that slammed behind him. Shaken, she sat on the edge of the narrow bed, working her hands nervously. Drawing a steadying breath, she reached up and fingered the thick braid that hung over her shoulder. Then, realizing what she was doing, she held it up and looked at it. Frowning, she dropped it to her shoulder again. Bugger, what had happened to her convictions? She could not allow Giles to fight her battles.

She rose from the bed and took a step toward the door, reaching for the latch, then caught the sound of raised voices beyond the door. Angry voices, Giles's only slightly outmatched by Eleanor's. Backing up, she sat down hard on the bed. Lud, she had never heard people scream at each other like that. She swallowed heavily and stared at the door.

Finally, after what seemed like hours, the door opened, and she jumped. "Come with me," Giles said grimly.

"Where are we going?" she asked as he took her arm.

"To your chamber. You are to remain there until Eleanor can bear the sight of you again."

"But—how long will that be?" she asked breathlessly, trotting to keep up with his long strides.

"Probably until you are well into your dotage," he muttered.

14

She had ample time to think, to read, to study, but the darkness was nearly unbearable. Candles were her only light, except for moments when the door opened to admit the girl who brought her food and came to empty the chamberpot. She was allowed to leave the chamber after compline, when the other inhabitants of Kenilworth had retired to their beds. She was escorted on these sojourns by a silent guard who walked a few paces behind as she stretched her cramped muscles.

She was not totally without companionship. Brother Vincent returned to Kenilworth the day after her fall from grace. He came to her chamber each day, with books under his arm, and she continued her studies. It was from him that she learned that Giles had left Kenilworth.

He had left within hours after bringing her to her prison. A message had come from Lord Simon, recalling him to London. An offer by Louis of France, it seemed, to arbitrate the differences between the king of England and his barons had been accepted. The matter had been brought to a head following an attempt on Lord Simon's life by Prince Edward.

Four of London's wealthy citizens, with much to lose should Lord Simon have his way, had smuggled word to the prince that the earl of Leicester was to be found at Southwark. Fortunately for Simon, word reached him that the gates of London were being closed. When Edward reached the house with his followers, Simon was gone. The desperation of the situation thus highlighted forced both sides to agree to accept Louis of France as mediator, a last hope to avoid war.

"But Louis is a king," Roanna observed to the Franciscan over the dull, flickering light of the candle between them. "How impartial can he be? He is certain to decide for Henry, no matter how just the baronial cause."

"I would agree," Brother Vincent said reflectively, "if it were not for Earl Simon himself. He is a forceful advocate, as you would know if you heard him speak. He will plead his cause with the faith God gives him, and, I believe, find justice with Louis."

Roanna was less than convinced, but she let it pass, deferring to the wisdom and experience of the Franciscan. Besides, her mind was on other matters that struck much more closely to her heart. Giles had left without a word to her, not even so much as a note. Not that she could blame him. Lord only knew what difficulties she had created between him and Eleanor, and all because she hadn't known the difference between when to speak up and when to hold her tongue. But she had marked the lesson well, and learned by it. She would not apologize for what she had done, for she knew she was right; but never again would she act so impetuously. Indeed, the more important the cause, the greater the necessity of acting with forethought, she reasoned, particularly when dealing with someone of power. She had offended Eleanor's sense of power, and had lost. Wrong or right, she had lost—just as Simon could lose. Diplomacy was an art she fully intended to master.

She began to discuss history and politics with Brother Vincent, questioning the Franciscan eagerly until he threw up his hands and decried her inquisition, begging for a moment to breathe, eat, and comfort himself with a warm cup of wine.

It struck an amused chord within Roanna that, while she had become anathema to the countess of Leicester, her newfound talents apparently had not. Work was brought to her each morning—the painstaking copying of the household rolls. It was this that she bent to on a cold January morning; no blotches ruined her work as she carefully copied each line.

To Tomas, squire of the household, 8d., from the 8th. day of January, to the 20th. of said month, for wages.

To master Gascon, butler of the household, 8 ½ d., wages, from the 8th. day of January, to the 20th. of said month, for wages.

To the lord John Blakley, chancellor, for the repair of weapons, this 25th. day of January, 14s.6d.

To the hand of Niles, palfreyman, for the repair of saddles, this 25th. day of January, 2s.2d.

To Alan Trentworth, knight of the household, at Salisbury, for cloth for the wardrobe, this 25th. day of January, 52s.6d.

As she totaled the page, writing the figure at the bottom, the door opened. She looked up, blinking into the bright rush of sunlight, and managed to make out the form of a guard. "You are to come with me," he said curtly.

Bracing herself, she rose from her chair and calmly closed the journals, stacking them neatly. She stepped out into the sunlight, pausing for a moment to feel its welcome warmth, then smiled at the guard who stood waiting. "Oh, Tomas, do not look so dire. It is a beautiful morning."

She followed him through the ward to where he stopped before the door to Eleanor's chambers. Stiffening, she glanced at him, noting the grim look he wore. "Well," she murmured, "so it shall be." He leaned over and pushed open the door, and she stepped past him.

Eleanor stood by the window on the far side of the room, turning as Roanna entered. As the door closed behind her, Roanna noted, with some surprise, that they were alone. She stiffened her back, calmly facing the anger she saw in the countess's eyes.

"Well, mistress, have you had ample time to contemplate the error of your ways?"

"I have had ample time to consider many things, milady, most particularly whatever errors I have committed."

Eleanor jingled the keys at her waist absently as she studied Roanna for a long moment. "Giles pleaded your case well, Roanna. You may thank him for your well-being."

Roanna swallowed, forcing back the words that sprang to her lips. Such power, she mused. From birth to death, one's

life could be subject to the whim of another. She owed
Eleanor much, but not her life—and never, never her
freedom. "I am grateful to him, milady," she answered
calmly, veiling her expression.

"You should be. Now that it is settled, I have something
for you to do." She picked up a letter from her desk. "This
came this morning. I want you to read it, using the code you
developed with Giles."

Roanna's heart lurched, but she managed to maintain her
poise. A letter from Giles! So that was why Eleanor had
seen fit to forgive her; there was a letter to answer. "Aye,
milady," she murmured. Eleanor tossed it onto the table
where, Roanna noted, fresh vellums and sharpened quills
had been laid. The countess stepped away from the table,
gesturing for Roanna to sit.

She sat down, taking up the missive, her fingers trembling
as she opened it. Sitting back, she drew a deep breath and
began to read:

> By the Faith of God, and by His Word, Greetings:
> How dearly I despair of our separation. My life goes
> as well as I would expect, considering that we must be
> apart. It was painful to leave without a word to you,
> my dearest love, but as we both are aware, it was
> unavoidable. I trust that you received my note from
> Lady Eleanor.

Roanna stiffened, her head jerking up at Eleanor, who
stood looking out of the window. So, she thought, Giles had
left a note of farewell! Eleanor, in her spite, had kept it from
her! Swallowing her anger, she returned to the letter.

> My greatest joy, and the only matter that gives me the
> slightest pleasure beyond the presence of your loving
> face and smile, are the destriers I have begun to breed,
> in the hope of developing the race of mounts my
> father only dreamed about. I would remind you of the
> difficult mount he was forced to ride, never knowing
> when it would betray him. Alas, such is the case with
> highly-blooded animals. Though I am dealing with
> lines of the same blood, I hope to prove more success-
> ful than he.
> Regrettably, along our journey to Amiens, a mount
> I preferred to all others was felled by a hole in the

road near Catesby, breaking its leg. Praise God, the injury was not as first feared, and he will survive. However, the delay caused me to be late for the fair at Amiens, and the auction was held without me. Thus, I have failed you, Dearest Roanna, as our future will be delayed as well. Even the Mother Church seems to be against us, as I have yet to find the priest who will marry us, my birth ever proving an impediment to our happiness.

Do not lose hope, my beloved. Our faith and love will find a way.

In Loyalty,

Giles fitzWilliam,

Knight

God in heaven, she thought. As she laid the missive on the table, Eleanor turned, her face showing strain. "Well?"

"He writes that Lord Simon was injured on the way to Amiens, milady, but he assures me that it is not serious. However, they were unable to attend the conference, and their mission has failed. Louis has granted for the king. Furthermore, the Church has sided with Louis's decision."

Eleanor was grim-faced but recovered quickly, and immediately set Roanna to her answer. It took more than an hour for Roanna to write the message, then code it. However, in the final copy, she took the privilege of working some of her own lines into the letter, letting Giles know that she was well and that she had not, to her dismay, received the note he had left for her.

Following the arrival of that first message, Roanna was allowed a measure of freedom. She was given orders to remain close by, in the event that other letters arrived, as they did with regularity. She was amused to note Giles's words of caution to her, which she did not translate for Eleanor, if for no other reason than they were exemplified by a high-tempered cat, the symbol that they had, amid some laughter, agreed upon for the countess.

Spring brought dire news. Simon's castle at Northampton, one of the strongest fortresses in the kingdom, was attacked and taken by Edward. By now Roanna was able to translate directly from Giles's letters without stopping to laboriously work through the code, while omitting personal notes. Her own alarm grew as she read this latest news, pausing occasionally to glance at the countess, who had grown quite pale.

It occurred to Roanna, as she paused, that the young prince had learned well from his godfather, particularly regarding the element of speed and surprise. Edward had moved his forces more than thirty-five miles from Oxford to Northampton in little more than a day, appearing before the garrison without warning. While the fortress could not be taken easily, those within had no chance to prepare for siege. That first night, as everyone behind the walls stood watch over the prince's encampment, Edward played yet another surprising hand. The Cluniac monastery of St. Andrew stood at the wall of the fortress, near the north gate. Royalist sentiment had been fomenting within the monastery even before Edward's arrival, and the monks had begun tunneling beneath the fifteen-foot-thick walls. Morning found Edward's forces within the fortress itself. Eleanor and Simon's eldest son, Henry, who held Northampton with his cousin, Peter de Monfort, had surrendered the castle without further resistance.

The situation became worse. William of Valence, the most hated of the Lusignans, had returned to England at his uncle the king's joyous invitation. Exultant, Valence took it upon himself to lay waste to the lands about Northampton, reaching within miles of Simon's lands at Leicester. He razed manor houses, slaughtered innocents, and burned the villages in his path. Meanwhile, Edward moved south, finally capturing Tonbridge Castle, which belonged to Gilbert, earl of Gloucester. Within the castle was Alice of Angouleme, the earl's wife.

"Well," Eleanor sighed, "that, at least, may prove to our benefit, sealing Gilbert's loyalty at long last. Alice has been dallying with Edward for years, before her husband's very eyes. It is said that the little tart even looked Henry's way, although my brother is not the mold of his father. I have never known him to look beyond the queen, such are his tastes."

Roanna kept silent, though she could not help but wonder, if Eleanor was correct and Alice was unfaithful, how far her husband would bother to go to avenge her.

The question soon became irrelevant, as it was learned

that the countess of Gloucester had been released, by a
noble prince, to the arms of her grateful husband. Far more
importantly, word came from Giles that a great and deci-
sive battle had been fought at Lewes. Simon had been
victorious, thus abruptly altering the course of the war.

The news in Giles's letter was not kept from those at
Kenilworth. Indeed, it would have made little sense, as
word of the victory spread rapidly over England. Kenilworth became a festival of celebration as bonfires were lit,
ale flowed, and there was dancing in the makeshift streets of
the outer ward. But Roanna kept to herself, as she had over
the long months past. Her thoughts went beyond the
joyfully given news to more subtle considerations, and the
nuances in Giles's letters claimed her attention. Something
had happened; he had changed.

He had faithfully detailed the events of the battle, which
she had dutifully recounted to Eleanor. King Henry had
established his headquarters in the priory of St. Pancras
near the river Ouse, while Edward bided his time in a
nearby castle belonging to William deWarenne. The royal
party could afford to wait. It was only a matter of the tides,
which would bring the mercenaries raised by the queen.

Simon made one last attempt to sue for peace. Bishops
from London and Worcester carried an offering to the king,
declaring that the barons would pledge 50,000 marks if he
would reaffirm the provisions gained at Oxford. Prince
Edward rejected the offer out of hand. "Peace is forbidden
to them," he was reported to have said, "unless they find
themselves with ropes about their necks and they give
themselves over to us for hanging and quartering."

Simon had recovered from the injuries suffered in the fall
from his horse, but that fact had been kept well concealed
from his enemies. Openly riding about a chariot, he thus
continued to declare his incapacity to spies who would
report it to their masters. Meanwhile, he had another use
planned for the wagon, one that would long remain in the
memory of his enemies.

Giles's last letter touched briefly on the battle itself.
Roanna recounted the events to Eleanor, but her own
concern focused on what she read between the lines. The
missive carried barbs about the royalist forces, led by a king
who had never understood the complexities of war. But she
could sense the surprise and respect in his words as he

recounted how Prince Edward had swiftly moved to counter their threat with energy and cunning.

He detailed Simon's victory with pride, colorfully describing the white cross of the Crusaders that each knight wore on his back and shoulder to proclaim the rightness of their cause. Keeping her voice even as she read, she focused inwardly upon the bitterness she felt in his words while recounting Simon's decision that it would be unchivalrous to attack before dawn. She could sense Giles's feelings as he told of the long night spent in prayer, and the long lines that formed before the priests who would hear confessions.

She did find amusing, amid Eleanor's laughter, his account of the Royalists as they charged down upon Simon's chariot, only to find within, not the crippled leader of the barons, but four bound and trembling London merchants —the same four who had once betrayed Simon to Edward. The earl had returned Edward's spies to him.

But the final words he wrote sobered her, and she felt the regret in them as he told of the moments when Edward rode through the mayhem of Penvensly, its citizens frantically fleeing the clash of battle, to find his father sitting on the steps of the priory in utter defeat. She did not communicate his final words, glancing briefly at Eleanor before she closed with words of her own. "It is apparent, Roanna," he had written, "that in Edward there lies the energy and will to fight. Had Henry the wisdom to allow his son the command, I believe that victory would not have been ours this day."

Thus the baronial cause had been victorious. Henry, king of England, Richard, duke of Cornwall, and Edward, prince of England, had been taken prisoner by Simon de Monfort.

As Kenilworth erupted into a wild victory celebration, Roanna found solitude and peace. There was little need of her services now, as Eleanor was able to write openly to her husband. Weary of it all, Roanna withdrew, spending her time in the gardens against the west wall in the outer ward. She found release in the warm spring sun, the rich smell of newly turned earth, and the blessed exhaustion brought by physical labor. The work helped to keep her thoughts from dwelling on the disturbing voice in Giles's letters, which she reread in the quiet hours each night before sleep. She could only speculate on the meaning of his tone, without confirmation from its source. But she enjoyed working with the soil, learning from Kenilworth's gardeners, and the days passed slowly as she waited and watched for his return.

It came on a warm spring day in late April, as she bent to the base of a rose bush, tamping the soil firmly about its tender roots. "Dirt agrees with you, Roanna. I've never seen you look so content."

She froze at the sound of his voice, a rush of joy washing over her. Smiling, she continued her task. "I am content, Sir Knight," she said softly. "There is constant rebirth with the soil. Each spring it brings something new and wonderful."

He knelt next to her. "Here, like this. You are packing the soil too tightly. The roots must have room to grow."

She followed his lead, and when they had finished, they rose and stood looking at each other. He lifted his hand and brushed some dirt from her cheek. "I have never seen you look more beautiful," he said softly.

She reached out and touched his face. His blue eyes fixed with her expectant brown ones, bright with unshed tears, and then he gathered her into his arms. Their lips met and they kissed breathlessly, each drawing new life and renewed promises from the meeting.

Her arms wrapped about his neck, she searched his face, seeking some sign of what the past months had done to him. But before she could look too closely, he kissed her again, and yet again, until all thoughts fled before the prospect of being alone with him.

"Have you the same chamber as before?" he asked huskily, kissing the corners of her mouth.

Within the small room, as a candle burned on the table nearby, he made love to her. He had drawn her into the room, bolting the door before he came to where she stood expectantly by the bed. She turned to extinguish the candle, but he stayed her. "Nay," he whispered, capturing her outstretched hand and bending his head to kiss the up-turned palm. "I have waited through so many nights, thinking only of this—of you. There were nights filled with the moans of dying men, nights when I saw only darkness and the agony that light would bring. Through it all, I focused on the image of you, of your beautiful body."

Slowly, he drew her clothes away and unbound her hair, running his fingers slowly through its thick, silky mass.

"Oh, Giles," she whispered, tears gathering in her eyes. "Was it so terrible?"

"Shhh," he murmured, drawing his hands gently over her shoulders and breasts, lingering to touch her nipples with a reverence that brought a choked sob from her throat.

He loved her exquisitely, with a tenderness that decried what he had seen, the death and pain he had caused. His mouth claimed her breasts, and she yielded to him with a soft cry that revealed her joy and her passion for him. As his hands moved over her body and between the softness of her thighs, she opened to him, greeting his embraces unreservedly, whispering his name over and over, wanting him.

They came together in a mutual outpouring of love, healing the pain and anguish of the past months. Their ecstasy built until they cried out, calling each other's names, finding peace in that private place that belongs to lovers.

Returning to reality, they clung to each other, unwilling to relinquish the moment. A long, sweet time passed as they nestled in each other's arms. Then, wordlessly, she rose and left him. Returning to the bed, she handed him a goblet of wine, then curled up against the wall at the top of the bed. Adjusting the pillows at his back, he took a draught, then sat silently, staring into the ruby flickers glistening in his goblet.

"Were my letters clear?" she asked casually, drawing the blankets up about her. "I often wondered if I remembered the code correctly."

"They were fine," he answered absently.

She studied his profile, then dropped her gaze, idly tracing the rim of her goblet. "I know they were," she said softly, rejecting any further attempt at subtlety. "That is not what I want to know. But—I don't know how to ask you . . ." She looked up to find him watching her intently. She saw the pain lingering behind his questioning gaze, and suspected that he was unaware it showed. "You must be very proud of what you have done." She saw the glint of anger her words brought; encouraged, she pressed forward. "You were wrong about Simon after all—he has achieved a great victory."

His expression became grim and he returned his gaze to his goblet. "I do not wish to speak of it," he said quietly.

"But why not?" she persisted. "The Crown has been taken! Is that not what you have prayed for—Henry's and Edward's downfall?"

"Aye, we have won," he snorted, tilting his head back against the wall as his eyes wandered about the room, and he drew a calming breath. "Henry is king, but Simon is—will rule England." After a long moment, he glanced at her. "What else would you have me say?"

"What you are feeling," she said quietly.

"I do not know what you want of me!" he said angrily.

"We are alone here, Giles."

He rose from the bed, slipping into his chausses before crossing to the table by the door to refill his goblet. He stood there for a long moment, facing away from her, drinking from the goblet. Then he turned back and stared at her, his eyes filled with anguish. "He will fail," he whispered. "He is a great man. England needs him. His visions are beyond those of any who came before him—he cares about the common man. His cause is just, in a way man has never seen before . . . and he will fail." His eyes swept over the room. "Why—why was I born to see what could be, yet be so helpless to affect it? Why was I raised in the shadows of men who brought us so far, yet am condemned to be one who can only watch life pass by, influencing nothing? Why was I given this understanding with no power?

"Simon will fail! Oh God, Roanna, I see what will come, I know why he shall fail! Every man will desert him, and I know what he must do to stop it; yet I have not a word to say to him that he will listen to! I swear to you, I am not bitter because I was born as I was. I am grateful for the understanding I have, which can only belong to one who has lived as I have. I know what it means to be unclean, to be considered less than human, and it brought me an understanding of what it means to be human! But if I was cursed, it began at my father's side. From the marshal of England, I learned to lead men and experience the power it brings. From knowing him, I understand the potential for Simon's greatness. Yet, in my position I am helpless, watching him destroy his chances."

He turned to her, his eyes silently pleading for understanding. Her voice was gentle. "Tell me, exactly, what it is that will bring Simon to fail."

He sat on the edge of the bed, drawing one leg up under him. "His armies are sufficient to hold him for a time, but men already desert him, important men. He seems powerless, or unwilling, to stop it. Henry of Almaine came to him, unable to remain any longer under the pressure his father was bringing to bear upon him. He knelt before Simon, pleading with him to understand his position. He is the king's nephew, for God's sake! Simon should have understood—and used the loyalty Almaine had for him! I remember Almaine's words: 'I can no longer fight against my father, against my uncle. I must leave you, but I will never bear arms against you.' Simon could have held him—if not to fight at his side, then to pledge that loyalty whereby he would have withdrawn from the field. Instead, Simon found only anger, seeing only duplicity. 'I fear your lack of loyalty,' he said, 'more than I fear your arms.' Almaine is now in Edward's camp.

"He puts his trust in his sons," he continued painfully. "God's Faith, even my own grandfather did not do so with my father until he had proved his worth. He knew that even blood can only bear out by time and experience. Yet Simon places trust in Henry, Simon, Guy, and Amauri, excluding those more deserving. Only Richard, because of his youth, has not been given a position that should justly be given to greater men of more experience."

As his voice trailed off, she drew a deep breath, praying that she could find the right words to help him. "Perhaps, Giles, you are not meant to stop what is going to happen. You told me once that you were waiting for a sign to lead you to your destiny—a sign made by man. There was never a promise that you would like what you saw when it came. Simon must live his life from his own point of view. So must you—and you must not be afraid to read the signs. Look to your conscience, Giles, to your own inner voice, you'll know the truth."

"Roanna," he said, laughing, with sad affection, "you are, I fear, a hopeless romantic."

"Am I? A rather easy dismissal, I think."

They sat quietly. Many thoughts passed through her mind that she wanted to express to him. But she knew that he would not hear them; they would be meaningless, placating words he would not accept. She took the goblet from him, placing it on the table, and drew him to her, giving him the only comfort she could. Only time and his own discoveries would aid him. She prayed that someday, for his sake and for everything that he held dear, he would triumph over the legacy that tormented him, that held him from peace.

Part Three

Thou must be married to no man but me,
For I am he am born to tame you Kate.

—William Shakespeare
The Taming of the Shrew
Act II, Scene i

15

The wind whistled mournfully through the high rafters of
the great hall of Kenilworth. The massive fireplaces at
either end of the hall were kept burning day and night,
barely maintaining a semblance of warmth against the
frigid winter air. In the months that had passed since the
battle of Lewes, Kenilworth had become the hub of the
kingdom, a fact that had forced the countess to move
the household into the keep for meals. Dignitaries from
throughout England and the Continent sat at trestle tables,
which were set up by harried servants for each meal, only to
be immediately disassembled afterward. Conversations
heard within the hall had shifted from normal matters of
tillage and tallages to politics, laws, and matters of the
realm. Bishops conferred with barons. Knights, their tab-
ards emblazoned with colorful coats of arms, sported
badges on their sleeves of the greatest families of England.

Roanna sat below the salt among the priests, merchants,
squires, ladies of lower rank, and troubadours, the latter
having been drawn to come and entertain in hopes of
recognition and reward. Her eyes swept over the company,
but her thoughts were far away, in the unpretentious back
rooms of a tavern. They remembered with longing the
simple cloth of wool and linen dyed in colors of the earth,
worn by a people whose conversations struck to the heart of
a matter, whether it was banking, crops, or merchandise.
Those memories were in sharp contrast to the broken

phrases that reached her now, speaking of power, dalliance, and income. Perhaps, she mused, of all those present, the troubadours were the most in touch with life. They knew themselves to be actors, players whose successes or failures were determined by their wits and talents, competing against limited time when other bards would come along, more gifted in word and form, to take the lead role.

There was one exception, one who played the game even beyond the talents of the troubadours, one who could turn his lines with a true gift of the play. He had won her imagination, catching it to him in spite of her efforts to free it, her old worn resistance pulling relentlessly. Her eyes shifted to the dais, to the linen-covered dormant table and its three occupants. Odd, she mused idly; this was Kenilworth, seat of the earl of Leicester, but had he been in residence at this moment under more normal circumstances, he would not have been allowed to sit at his own dormant table in their company. Only those three could sit there, Plantagenets all. In the center, Richard of Cornwall, his rank as king of the Romans giving him the prominent position. To his right, his sister Eleanor, the daughter of a Plantagenet king. And to his left, the object of Roanna's musings, Edward, prince and heir to England.

Over the past months, she had felt the sun upon her face. She had been drawn, compelled by its heat, and the shadows had lifted. She had been shaken at first, rejecting the man as she clung to dear prejudices. Then, gradually, she had succumbed, stirred by hope, the golden-fringed aura of illusive, sought-after dreams. In his voice, in the words he spoke with deep conviction, she heard the promise of future.

She knew that others rejected his utterings as the complaints, the ravings of a captured prince. Which indeed he was. But with subtlety, he voiced feelings that echoed the cries of an oppressed and desperate people.

It wasn't reasonable—a rose could not germinate in sterile soil. But somehow, from somewhere, the spirit of this Plantagenet prince, raised in the isolation of the English Crown, had reached out to course though the blood of England's body, reaching her heart. Somehow, he understood as no prince had before him.

Roanna's eyes shifted to the shadows behind Edward's chair, to the knight who stood there in discussion with another. Her eyes softened, and her lips curved into a soft smile. She watched as Giles turned his head occasionally, distracted from his conversation, to observe the prince. Life's odd turns, she mused, catch us in ways we could not possibly conceive. To have an enemy, one most bitter, suddenly within our care and responsibility. . . . The gods, which Giles was so fond of invoking, had certainly proved their penchant for the perverse. To his shock and horror, Giles had been made Edward's keeper for the length of his imprisonment.

Roanna waved away the servant who would have refilled her goblet and rose from her place, moving along the wall toward the dormant table. She ignored the comments from various men as she passed, accustomed to the remarks her unbound hair inevitably brought. She had refused to cover it, continuing to wear it in the Saxon style as a statement, however small, of her independence and beliefs. To her relief and gratitude, Giles had allowed it. She was now openly recognized as his woman and, as such, only his word could have caused her to cover her head. She knew that pressure had been exerted upon him by those who disapproved, but to her he had said only in passing, and with a smile, "I trust, my love, that should you find yourself in the presence of the archbishop of Canterbury, you will save him anguish by wearing a kerchief."

She slipped up behind him, waiting until his companion had departed to tuck her hand in the crook of his arm. "You look weary, my love," she murmured. "Can you take a moment to walk with me?"

He smiled down at her as he laid a hand on hers. "Though I would wish nothing more, Lord Edward will be retiring in a moment. He has asked me for a game of chess."

She could have pointed out that the prince could easily find a match from many others in the hall, but she forebore. Giles had taken to spending more and more private hours with the prince of late, and their time together whetted her curiosity. "Then let me attend you," she offered. "It would not be thought odd, and I have had more experience in waiting upon men than any other here."

He studied her for a moment, and then his mouth curved into a grin. "Do you promise not to spill wine on him, or knee him in his private parts if he dares look at you? He is certain to do so."

"If I must," she answered, feigning disappointment. "If he behaves himself. In any other event, I cannot promise anything." With that she swept away, warming at the sound of his deep chuckle as she left him.

A little while later, she paused at the door to the chamber, balancing the tray of wine and goblets as the guard opened the door to admit her. Affecting a serious demeanor, she ignored the pair at the table before the hearth as she crossed to a low table to set down her burden. Edward glanced up as she set a goblet of hippocras next to him. His deep blue eyes lighted up and he forgot the game for a moment. Sitting back in his chair, he smiled, his eyes narrowed in apparent study.

"You are looking well, Mistress Royston," Edward said, grinning.

"Thank you, milord." She smiled. "It is kind of you to say so." The man was devastating, Roanna thought—tall, blond, handsome, with all the charm of youth combined with intelligence and power.

Edward brightened. "By Saint George, a thought just occurred to me! 'Twas I who brought you two together—at my banquet at the White Tower!" He turned a pleased grin on Giles, who was studying the game.

"You are wrong, Edward," Giles murmured. "'Twas a goat that did it."

Roanna threw Giles a nasty look and retreated to the corner, taking a chair behind them near the hearth.

"You will have to explain that, fitzWilliam," Edward said, laughing. "Dammit, man, forget your rook—aye, I know that is what you are considering—and talk to me! Or"—his voice lowered suggestively—"I shall inquire of the lady."

Leaning back, Giles grinned as he gave up the game. He launched into the story, recounting the events that had first led him to notice Roanna, to her considerable chagrin as she sat burning with embarrassment in the corner. Bloody buggers, she thought, listening to their laughter. But she kept silent, hoping that they would forget that she was there, as men often did when they were taken with the importance of their thoughts. There was much she wanted to know.

Later, when they were well into their third game, she rose

quietly to refill their goblets, and as she returned to her chair she began to hear what she had come to learn.

Edward moved his knight. "Give it up, Giles. My men are well protected," he drawled confidently.

"So it would seem," Giles murmured thoughtfully. "But the first two games have been divided equally. This last one could go either way. If you make an error, I shall have you."

"I will not make that mistake, Giles—too much depends upon it. The day shall be mine, do not doubt it."

"We shall see," Giles responded quietly.

Edward rose from his chair to stretch. "Make your play then, for all the good it will do you. I need a break," he said, moving to the window.

Giles made his move, then rose to join Edward at the window. The two men stood side by side, staring out into the courtyard below. They were silent for a long moment. It was Edward who spoke first, his voice oddly strained. "In all the time we have spent together, of the many things we've discussed, there is one subject I have never dared to ask you about."

"Dared?" Giles turned to regard the prince questioningly. "What would you not dare to discuss with me?"

Edward bent his head, appearing to study the stone casing of the window. "I would know of your time at Aldtern," he said quietly.

Giles's expression darkened, his jaw tensing as he threw a quick glance at the other man. "That time is for me alone," he countered grimly.

"Why?" Edward looked up, genuinely surprised. "Giles, you and I stand here, unique among men. Think upon it. By God's will I shall become, in my time, king of England. You are a knight of England, bearing the blood of the noblest of us; yet you have known a life I can only suspect. You know what it means to be a villein, to experience the desperation of the common man. Beyond that, you are my cousin, bound to my blood; hence we may speak of such things."

Roanna held her breath, her heart beating heavily as she watched, sensing the importance of the moment. Oh, Giles, she pleaded silently, for the love of God, do not let it pass!

Giles stared at the movement in the courtyard below him. His trained eye marked the positions of the guards on the wall of the inner ward and passed over the weaponry room. He noted the readiness of the pikes in their neat, triangular stacks, and the battered armor of an elderly soldier, past his prime, who crossed beneath the window. He drew a long breath. "Desperation of the common man, you said." His expression was grave. "The greatest element of life, of the human condition, is hope. It gives one the strength to bear anything. I remember finding it in the heat of a summer morning against my face, in the touch of a mare's soft muzzle, the warmth of her breath against my cheek, in the fact that I had a blanket to cover myself. And in dreams. Thoughts of my mother, though I had no memory of her face. The guarded hope that my master would die, that he would cease to be. Simple hopes, but any that would give me an excuse to live." He fell silent.

"Long nights of darkness," Edward said absently, as they both stared from the window. "Endless nights, when no one would come. Faces, expecting something from you that you could not comprehend. The threat of love withdrawn if you did not perform in some expected way." He sighed deeply, venturing a smile. "Giles, I do not pretend to understand what you felt, but I do know the terror of failing and being alone. Was it something like that?"

"Aye . . . something like that. Alone—but knowing that no one would come. That life would ever be that way."

"But someone did come."

"Aye, someone came. But through all those years I had no way of knowing that would happen. Moreover, for so many others, no one ever comes. For them, existence is scratched out, year after year, until the sun no longer warms and death becomes hope."

Edward leaned his shoulder against the corner of the embrasure, tucking his hands into the pockets of his tabard. "The peers of England, our esteemed barons, look upon their advantages as gifts of their birth." His lips twisted sardonically. "Their great wisdom is granted to them by God, Giles, or so they would have us believe. Tell me, have you ever truly known a wise man born of common birth?"

"Without question, milord. I have known many."

"If their thoughts and opinions were heard in a parliament, as Simon seeks to have it, would the result be to the credit of England, or would it lead to anarchy, as so many believe?"

"That, milord, would depend upon who was chosen to

represent them. I believe that wisdom is gifted to men by the whim of the gods. The beds they are brought to make little difference. Plantagenet beds could only wish always to have been so blessed."

Edward's head jerked about and his expression clouded. After a brief moment of anger, he suddenly grinned. "As my tutor was fond of saying, a man should not ask a question if he is not prepared to hear the answer." Shrugging, he then forced the conversation to lighter matters, the time passing easily until the bell rang for Matins, calling their attention to the early morning hour.

Turning from the darkened window, Edward laughed. "Obviously, Giles, I am not the witty fellow I thought myself to be."

Giles followed Edward's gaze to the far corner by the hearth. He shook his head with fond amusement at the sight of Roanna fast asleep in her chair. "Indeed, milord, we must be dry fellows. It is not like her to miss a word."

"She is lovely, Giles. You are a fortunate man."

"Aye, milord, she is that, and more—much more," Giles answered quietly.

"It is a shame to disturb such peaceful slumber. You may leave her here with me, if you wish."

Giles snorted. "You jest."

"You do not trust me, cousin?" Edward asked with feigned hurt. "I assure you that I would treat the lady with the utmost courtesy!"

"It is not the lady I would worry about," Giles countered with a grin, watching Roanna with a fond expression. "Within a day she would have you cowering at her feet, begging for mercy. Roanna has a way about her."

"You seem to have fared well enough," Edward remarked.

"Only on the outside. Inwardly I have been reduced to a simpering, jellied mass."

Edward chuckled, then regarded Giles speculatively before his gaze returned to the sleeping maid. He sighed wistfully. "I envy you, Giles fitzWilliam. For God's sake, man, guard her well."

"I shall, milord, I shall," Giles answered. He took up his cloak from the chair where he had thrown it, then went to Roanna, bending to awaken her with a kiss. "Come, sweetling, it is late," he murmured. Helping her up, he dropped the cloak about her shoulders and wrapped an arm around her waist.

Bidding Lord Edward a good night, they left the chamber. Giles paused as the door closed behind him to check the guards. The eyes of the two men were fixed on the sleepy maid, who had wrapped her arms about Giles's waist and was nuzzling her face into the soft velvet of his tabard. Their obvious amusement triggered Giles's irritation. Snapping out his orders, he swept her up into his arms and turned away, carrying her down the hallway and around the corner to his own quarters. Opening the door with his knee, he paused inside as Geoffrey rose from his pallet. His sleepy hazel eyes widened as he stared at his master and his sleeping burden.

Dammit, Giles thought grumpily, he couldn't very well carry her to her room. He couldn't walk through the hall and the knight's quarters at this hour! She'd have to stay with him. "Go bed with Ralph and Barnaby," he said gruffly, referring to his master-at-arms and his captain.

Geoffrey left the room quickly, struggling to hide a grin as he shut the door. Giles crossed the room and laid her on the bed. He reached down and removed her slippers, tossing them onto the floor, and pulled a robe over her and tucked it in about her. He stared down at her for a long moment, as she turned, mumbling contentedly as she settled more comfortably. "Sleep, Roanna," he murmured. "But when you awaken, there is a matter to be discussed— that of what is going to be done about you and me. And discuss it we will."

Roanna awoke slowly, at first aware of the soft feather mattress beneath her and the warm fur robe covering her. Yawning, she roused herself and rose up on her elbows to glance about, not knowing where she was. A low fire burned on the hearth across the room, and sitting in a chair next to it, his hand idly turning the goblet that sat on the small table next to him, was Giles. He had stripped down to his chanise and leggings, which were cross-gartered to his low boots. His long legs stretched out before him as he stared, lost in thought, into the fire. Lud, she realized with alarm, I am in his room—in his bed!

Sitting up, she swung her feet over the edge of the bed, encountering the cold boards of the floor, and she shivered, glancing about for her slippers. Finding them, she slipped them on and crossed the room to him, stifling a yawn as he looked up.

"It is not yet dawn. You should go back to sleep."

She pushed a wayward tendril away from her face, and took the chair on the other side of the hearth, tucking her legs up under her. "Go back to sleep? Giles, I do not even know what I am doing here. Have you been sitting there all night?"

"I slept for a while."

"Oh, Sweet Mother," she whispered, realization dawning. "I fell asleep in Lord Edward's chamber, didn't I?"

"You did," he said, smiling.

"Oh," she groaned. "What must he think of me?"

"He thought you were enchanting."

"But—why did you bring me here?"

"I could hardly carry you through the knights' quarters, sweetling."

"You could have awakened me!" she said, pouting. "Giles, it isn't proper—"

"Proper?" He laughed, a short, brittle sound. "You have an odd sense of propriety, Roanna. We have been lovers for six months, counting the time before it became a fact and was merely a show for Eleanor's convenience. It was a game then, but since then I have not thought it to be. Yet it is only when I come to you, in your chamber, that I am allowed to love you—"

"Giles, please—" she pleaded.

"Nay, dammit!" he exploded, rising from his chair. "We are going to speak of it, Roanna!" He placed his hands above him against the stone of the fireplace, pausing a long moment before he turned back to her, his emotions once again under control. "I have tried to understand your feelings, your need for the independence you insist upon. But I am tired of feeling like a thief, sneaking to the bed of my lover!"

"There has been no need to sneak, Giles," she said, attempting to control her own turbulent emotions. "I am openly acknowledged to be your woman. But I am a free woman; my love is given to you as a free woman. I will not move into this room with you, to become your—your—"

"My what, Roanna?" he interrupted sharply. "My mistress? My paramour? You are that now, my love. And worse is said, behind our backs. You know it—you once pointed it out to me, before it became a fact."

"It is no longer of importance," she answered quietly. "I know what my feelings are for you; nothing else matters."

"It matters to me!" he roared. "And it damn well should matter to you!"

She was silent, anguishing over the pain he was feeling, but knowing she could not say what he wanted to hear. She heard him sigh heavily, and looked up as he sat down again. Leaning his elbows on his knees, he ran his fingers through his thick chestnut hair in a frustrated gesture. When he looked up at her, his expression was strained. "Roanna," he said quietly, "I love you. There is no need for us to live like this." He paused, his eyes filled with determination. "Marry me."

She gazed fixedly at him. Hearing the words she had imagined over and over in her dreams, she despaired. Her heart seemed to stop in the constriction of her chest. Finally, she was able to smile, unaware of how sad a smile it was. "Nay, Giles," she said softly. "I cannot marry you." She drew a deep breath, seeing the pain that crossed his eyes. "I will stay here, at Kenilworth, until it is time for me to return to London. But the day will come when I must. I love you, with every part of me, but there is another place I belong. You know that as well as I do."

He picked up his goblet and drained it, then stared moodily into the empty pewter. "Love me? Roanna, it is the game you love," he said, his voice surly. "But then, you've done well at Kenilworth, haven't you? What you've learned here should serve you well. One thing about you, Roanna, you do know how to make the best of a situation."

She stiffened at his words, and stood up slowly, trying to ignore the searing pain they brought. "It is time I returned to my own chamber, Giles," she said as calmly as she could. "It will be dawn soon. You should get some rest if you can."

She left him, closing the door quietly behind her. She passed the guards outside Lord Edward's door, returning their looks of interest with a fierce glare, and descended the stairs to the hall. Servants moved about the predawn hours, lighting the torches, putting the dogs out, raking the rushes on the floor to release the herbs within, building the hearth fires. She passed them with her chin up, ignoring the sounds of the sleeping men who lay upon pallets in the alcoves. Slipping through the tower door leading to the knights' quarters, she crossed the small anteroom to the outer door beyond. The steps led down to a narrow alley, leading to the back of the stables, and there, in the shadows, she stopped, unable to go farther. She leaned against the wall, pressing her forehead to the cold stone, and allowed the tears to come in silent sobs.

16

In the quiet solitude of the garden, Giles could almost forget the matters plaguing him. The afternoon sun was warm against his shoulders, the surroundings peaceful; at the moment he could not even find fault with his company. Edward was allowed to walk each day in the garden or on the parapet of the keep, always with Giles as escort. Odd, Giles mused, that he could now actually enjoy the company of this man, whom only a short time ago he had so totally despised. They paused to watch the antics of a heron as it poised and then struck the water at the edge of the shimmering lake, bringing up a fish.

"You are quiet today," Edward observed as they began to walk again, following the path along the water. "Are we returning to those early days when you had hardly a word to say to me?"

"I have little to say at the moment, milord."

"Indeed, that is unfortunate," Edward said thoughtfully. "Your responsibility is to see to my welfare. I should hate to become bored. In that event, I should have no choice but to leave."

Giles laughed softly. "My responsibility, milord, is to see that you do not."

"Ahhh," Edward sighed. "Ever the jailer, never the friend. That saddens me, Giles, as I have enjoyed your company. But I will escape. You do know that, don't you?"

"You can try."

Giles knew where Edward's thoughts were leading. A begrudging respect had grown in him for the prince, a recognition of the younger man's shrewdness and brilliance, characteristics that had first startled him in a man he had thought to have the morals of his grandfather and the ineptitude of his father. "You are waiting for Mortimer and de Leyburn to free you, are you not?" Giles asked, smiling.

Edward's stride did not falter, but Giles, watching for the slightest nuance, noted the flicker of his eyes. "They are in the border countries," he said, dismissing them with a shrug of his wide shoulders.

"Ahhh, of course," Giles agreed. "You convinced Simon that they were needed to control the intractable Welsh. You were so concerned about the matter, in fact, that you agreed to remain as hostage, with Henry of Almaine. It had nothing to do with the fact that, as long as those two remained free, the royal cause would not be forgotten—nor would you be."

Edward glanced at Giles, a glimmer of guarded respect in his eyes. "You are imagining things, fitzWilliam. Simon has replaced my castellans with men of his own. My father has pleaded to my mother to cease preparations from the Continent, in fear for his hostage son. Moreover, he has become a puppet—Simon is now the ruler of England. What is it they have begun to call him—'Count Justiciar'?"

"And the papal legate, Cardinal Fulcodi, has declared that he will not rest until the king's full powers have been restored to him and the Provisions of Oxford are again banned," Giles countered.

"Simon has raised the largest army England has ever known," Edward argued, warming to the exchange, "levying men and funds throughout the country. Their cry has become 'Down with the alien!' and their cause to rid England, once and for all, of the foreign influence upon the throne."

"Ahhh, that would be a shame," Giles said wryly. "To see the Lusignans, along with the queen's uncles, expelled from England for all time. In particular, it would be hard to imagine how we would survive without William of Valence."

"Are you bitter because he was granted your father's lands at Pembroke?"

"Why should I be, if that were all of it? They were never

to be mine. But it does gall me when he attempts to lay claim to the title held by my father, and my grandfather, and my grandmother's father before him. I sometimes entertain myself with a fantasy—seeing that effeminate fop cornered in a tower at Pembroke Castle, and there before him the ghosts of Richard deClare, William Marshal, and my father, demanding the return of their title."

Edward burst out laughing. "By the Blood, fitzWilliam, I would like to see that myself! Lud, he would probably foul his chausses! Personally, I could never abide the man; I regret the blood we share." He chuckled again. "You need not fear on that account, Giles. Valence does not have the title, for all of his boistering. Moreover, I promise you, he shall never have it."

Giles glanced at the prince with surprise. He was about to offer his gratitude, but remained silent. He knew that Edward's decision had nothing to do with him; it was obvious that the decision had been made long before the present conversation. But he was stunned. Henry's loyalty to his relatives had always appeared unwavering, even as they threatened his throne. Was it possible that the son had a mind of his own? Everything he had seen in Edward over the past months inclined Giles heavily toward that opinion. A small, guarded flame began to burn within Giles; yet it also brought a vague, growing fear.

"I understand that you took my advice and purchased that mare from Eleanor," Edward remarked.

"Aye, she is a beauty. Her disposition will be of great advantage." A few weeks before, Giles had told Edward of his estates in Ireland, and of his dream of breeding destriers of new blood, mounts with the fire and courage needed for war but with a temperament that would enable the war-horses to be handled easily by their masters. It was an important dream, one Edward shared with enthusiasm. The prince's fascination with hounds and horses was well known, and Edward had barely heard of Giles's plans before he had dragged him to the stables to see a mare he had discovered. "Look at her!" Edward had exclaimed. "Look at her lines—and she is as gentle as a lamb." Giles had agreed immediately, recognizing the animal he had been in search of for years.

"Even as we speak, she is on her way to Erin," Giles said,

grinning. "Eleanor has begun to suspect that she made a bad bargain. She believed the mare to be too large-boned."

"Well, I am gratified that you took my advice on that matter, at least," Edward said with a knowing look. Seeing Giles's puzzlement, he shook his blond head. "I have observed Mistress Royston keeping her own company of late. But that should not last for long—not to judge from the speculative looks I see thrown in her direction."

"There are some matters I do not wish to discuss, milord," Giles said grimly.

"Ho! Storms do gather quickly when lightning strikes," Edward said.

"A bad comparison, milord. Storms gather before lightning strikes."

"Not always. I have heard it said that in some areas of temperate weather, lightning can strike without there being a cloud in the sky. Suddenly, whoosh!" He illustrated his words with a sweep of his hand.

"That's Roanna," Giles said, grimacing. "No warning. She just strikes."

"There are worse things than being in love with an exciting woman, Giles."

"Exciting?" Giles almost choked. "Temperamental, unreasonable, exasperating—and, aye." He paused. "Exciting, when she is not driving me out of my mind."

"As I said, there are worse things than being driven out of your mind by a woman. Marrying a child, for example, not knowing what the woman will be, although you are to spend the remainder of your lives together. I would like to be in love, Giles. I envy you your problems."

Giles frowned, glancing at Edward. It was, he realized, the second time that this man who would become king of England had said that he envied him. "She is determined—that she will not marry me," he said quietly. He braced himself, waiting for the laughter to follow.

"Why?" Edward asked quietly, his eyes fixed on the path.

Giles hid his surprise over Edward's reaction. Briefly, he told of Roanna's background, and her determination to return to the London docks. "She prefers that life to one with me," he said bitterly.

Edward's hands were clasped behind his back as he walked. His head, which was bent thoughtfully as he listened, rose on Giles's last words, his expression lightening. "It is simple! I shall order her to marry you!"

"You do not know Roanna," Giles said, smiling grimly. "She would not do it."

"She would if I commanded it!" Edward insisted, his eyes widening.

"Not Roanna. She values her freedom above all else. She might if her uncle ordered it, but even then I doubt it."

"She would obey her uncle, and not her prince?"

"You don't know Roscoe Dorking. Besides, I would not force her into a marriage; she means too much to me for that."

"Well, then, there is only one other solution. Court her, make it impossible for her to refuse!" Seeing Giles's doubt, he shrugged. "Of course, you could just give up." Falling silent, Edward fixed his attention on the summer morning, the deepening green shades of the trees they passed beneath, stifling a smile at the look of determination that had come over his cousin's face.

Roanna paused over the entry in the journal, tapping the end of the goose quill against her chin as she considered what to say next. The night was warm, and she had left the door open. She glanced through the doorway, momentarily forgetting her task as she gazed at the stars that hung above the wall of the inner ward. Drawn, she rose from her chair and went to the doorway, leaning against the frame as she looked up at the twinkling lights, wondering at their purpose. Beautiful, she thought, but why were they there? A question for her journal, and she mused upon the task that lay on the table behind her. A short time before she had begun to keep a record of her thoughts, at Brother Vincent's suggestion. It had been difficult at first, and she had spent a great deal of time merely staring at the empty pages. Slowly, she had begun, finally warming to the task, and had discovered a great comfort, an emotional purging that accompanied the writing of her ideas and observations.

The journal was healing, to a point, until she lay in bed at night, missing him. She tried to dismiss the pain, but he invaded her waking dreams. Oh, Giles, she thought desperately, why could you not leave things as they were? When he had asked her to marry him, she thought she would perish from pain, from the longing to say yes and gain that last piece that would have made her life complete. Complete for her, but not for him. She should have left Kenilworth before it came to this. She should have seen the moment coming in his growing restlessness, his dissatisfaction with their "arrangement," the anger that came into his eyes at the knowing comments or sly looks cast in their direction. Giles was a man of pride; she should have known it was coming.

Oh, God, how she loved him—far too much to marry him. Without her, he would find the woman suited to him, one wealthy and high-born who would bear him children in a marriage bed of honor. She knew it was time for her to leave—she had to leave. Was she so weak that she could not bear to depart? She could bear it, she would bear it, she was a survivor. She was!

Then her head turned, and she listened. A voice carried through the shadows of the ward, the sound of a lyre from somewhere above. She relaxed against the door frame as the troubadour sang a mournful lyric of unrequited love. She recognized the voice as that of a player recently come to Kenilworth, whose talents were far above the normal. She remembered mentioning him to Giles, and he had agreed, informing her that the man was a goliard and once a Franciscan, as had been his uncle. She listened, spellbound by the mellow, haunting voice. Then, slowly, the words of the song began to register and her eyes flared with disbelief. He sang of a beauteous young woman, a villein bound by her birth, mute of voice but strong of fire and determination. Her lover had sought her all his life, finding her at last, only to be rejected as unworthy, his heart broken.

Impossible! It couldn't be! Shaken, she stumbled back into her room and slammed the door. As she prepared for bed, she tried to make sense of what she had heard. He wouldn't! Would he? Nay, it was a coincidence, nothing more. It had to be!

She entered the great hall next morning to break her fast, having managed to put the disquieting episode of the previous night from her mind. Glancing about as she entered the hall, she was relieved to note that Giles was not in his place behind Edward—but she was puzzled by the amused smile the prince wore, and the disconcerting fact that he was watching her with obvious interest. As she went to her place, she stopped, dumbfounded. The table was strewn with flowers, even her place upon the bench. She groaned as a glance about confirmed that everyone in the hall had turned to observe her reaction. Even Eleanor was watching with an amused grin that was matched only by the prince. With as much dignity as she could muster, Roanna brushed aside the flowers, sitting in the space she had made. At that moment she wanted to murder Giles fitzWilliam.

The songs continued, and the flowers were there each morning. Roanna made a request to Eleanor that she be allowed to return to London; her request was denied, the countess merely commenting in passing that her services were needed. Perhaps, Eleanor had said, she could go in the fall, when the library was completed.

In addition to the songs and the flowers, gifts began to arrive—bolts of rich fabric; torcs, bracelets, girdles, and earbobs of gold and jewels; delicacies of sweetmeats that she would find upon the table in her room or during her hours with Brother Vincent. The Franciscan offered no comfort, availing himself eagerly of the foodstuffs with a rolling of his eyes and comments on the exceptional taste of her suitor.

To her added horror, amid all that was happening under the intent interest of nobility and servant alike as they awaited her ardent suitor's next move, she found that the old Roanna had returned to plague her. She tripped, spilling gravy on the bishop of Ely. In the countess's household roll she listed the earl of Nottingham, Lord Ladcrock, as Lord Largcock. Eleanor calmly pointed this out late one morning, noting that the description was entirely possible, judging from the size of the man, but hardly a suitable notation for her rolls. Kenilworth's animals seemed to have entered into a plot against her. She found herself in the midst of a dogfight that took three men and numerous buckets of water to disperse. A bird defecated on her shoulder, an occurrence brought to her attention by the duke of Cornwall as she served him ale.

The black cloud had returned. By the end of the second week she had had enough, and she went to find him. Odd, she thought later, that she had seen neither hide nor hair of him in more than two weeks, yet he had proved easy enough to find when she set her mind to it. He was in the stables, grooming his palfrey. "Giles, I cannot take any more!" she cried, planting her hands on her hips as she glowered at him.

"Shhh. You'll startle the horses," he cautioned, not pausing as he brushed the animal.

"I don't care about the bloody horses!" she cried. "Listen to me!"

Down the long row of stalls, the horses pulled against their tethers, stirring restlessly. Visions of a stampede crossed her mind. "Listen to me!" she hissed.

"I am here, Roanna. I'm listening," he said, patting the gelding comfortingly.

"I want you to stop it!" she hissed, stepping nearer to him. "I cannot bear it. My life has fallen apart, I've started dogfights!"

Giles paused as he turned his head to smile at her. "You realize, Roanna, that I am probably the only man living who would understand that remark."

"You did it!" she blurted out. "It is all your fault!"

"Roanna, when are you going to realize that you cannot live without me?" he asked, stroking the horse's back with the brush. "You had better give in and marry me, before you bring England down around your ears."

"Ohhh!" she flared, her eyes filling with tears. "I should do it! It would serve you right if I did marry you!" She turned and fled the stable.

He stared at the empty doorway for a long time, the brush poised in his hand. Serve him right? What did she mean by that? The palfrey turned and nuzzled his arm for attention, and he glanced back at the horse, absently stroking its muzzle. "Old boy, your master is a fool," he said quietly. His gaze returned to the emptiness she had left, and his brow furrowed in thought. "But even the greatest fools among us can learn," he added softly.

17

Giles's courtship ceased as abruptly as it had begun. Kenilworth's inhabitants were obvious in their disappointment; the courtship had become an item of relish as everyone had waited each morning for Giles's next move. Roanna, however, could feel only relief—until the days passed, and the emptiness began to grow.

She came into his company often, and each time they met her concern grew. He was unfailingly polite, even attentive, but there was a difference in him she could not define. The strangeness of it plagued her through long, restless nights, and she found herself growing irritable. The fact that she could not find a circumstance, or a person, upon whom to vent her feelings did not improve matters. Indeed, she knew she was being unreasonable. He had given her the distance she had asked for. She had known it would be difficult to treat him as a mere acquaintance, a friend, nothing more, yet she found herself wanting to scream at the most inopportune moments.

Then, at last, her attention was distracted from her own problems. Simon returned, and the news he brought plunged Kenilworth into a guarded state of alarm. The papal legate Cardinal Guy Fulcodi, sometimes known as The Fat, had attempted to send his bishops to England with papal sentences against the baronial cause. The prelates had been met at Dover, their satchels searched, and the bulls shredded and thrown into the sea. Upon learning of the treatment of his envoys, the legate reacted. At Hesdin, on October 21, as the bells of the cathedral tolled, he made pronouncement upon the Holy Bible. Taking the three-foot-long candle lit for the earl of Leicester, he dashed the flame to the tiles of the sanctuary floor. By bell, book, and candle, Simon de Monfort, the earl of Leicester, was excommunicated by the Mother Church.

Roanna listened to the conversation taking place in Eleanor's chamber, fascinated but puzzled as to why she was present. When she had been summoned, she had presumed that she was to keep a written record for the countess, only to find that Brother Vincent had been summoned for that task. She sat by the window listening as she tried to hide her awkwardness, certain that at any moment someone would notice her presence and demand her departure.

Waiting, her gaze shifted to Eleanor and, in turn, to Lord Simon and the de Monfort sons, Henry, Guy, Amauri, and Richard. Simon the Younger had remained in London. More importantly, Giles was here, standing close to her chair, a fact that filled her with particular feelings of disquiet.

"The people sing to you, Father," Richard was saying, "to 'Sir Simon the Righteous'! England acclaims the victory at Lewes, being finally rid of the royal relatives, and in spite of Rome, the bishops and priests support you as well, led by the Franciscans. Why, an unknown member of the Franciscans has even written a ballad for you! 'Now England breathes again,' the lyric says; 'It is one thing to rule, which is the duty of the king, another to destroy by resisting the law. . . . Read this, ye English; if victory had yielded to those who are now vanquished, the remembrance of the English would have become worthless!'"

Simon smiled at his youngest son's enthusiasm. "As flattering as that may be, there are far more important matters to be considered. The nobles are divided still. Those in the west, led by Edward's supporters, have come out openly against our government. Moreover, while it is true that the people support us, you must realize that it means little, beyond the satisfaction it gives me. They have little effect upon our government, though that is a condition

I wish to change. Only the barons' voices count in England, and too many of them remain silent. They await the outcome of what is happening, as has been so often the case."

Giles bent and murmured into Roanna's ear, "Are you listening carefully?"

She looked up at him with surprise. "Of course," she stammered, confused by the question.

"Good. I expect you to remember it."

She stared at him, bewildered, but he straightened and crossed to the hearth, where he refilled the empty tankard in Simon's hand. "It would seem to me that the barons have some cause to be dissatisfied," he said quietly.

Simon frowned as he glanced up at Giles. "What is bothering you, Giles?"

"Only this, milord: you make decisions with great courage, and none here question your vision . . ."

"But?" Simon pressed as Giles hesitated.

"You grant power to those not qualified and ignore others who are. The same offense you so often accused Henry of committing."

"Giles!" Eleanor admonished, shocked.

"Let him speak." Simon waved away her protest, but his look was guarded.

"For one, you have excluded Gloucester. While no one is more aware of the weaknesses of my cousin than I, he is bristling at being excluded. He was designated by the barons to rule with you. I should think that, if given a position that would appease his vanity, he would serve you well. Moreover—" He hesitated, bracing himself against the reaction his next comment would bring. "You have chosen to favor your own sons with positions that rightly should have gone to more experienced men."

Outcries followed, which Simon silenced with a shout. Then he turned back to Giles. "I have listened to you, Giles, and marked what you have said, but you must trust in me to make the correct decisions," he said heavily.

"You need the support of the barons, milord—"

"Enough, Giles. As I have said, you will support me, or no."

"You have my support, milord, as you well know," Giles answered grimly. "But I have spoken my mind." Putting down his tankard, he crossed the room to Roanna and, taking her arm, led her from the room. As they crossed the inner ward Roanna kept silent, though she was bursting with questions. It was Giles who spoke first as they reached the door to her chamber. "May I come in for a moment?" he asked, surprising her with his easy grin.

"I think you had better," she answered wryly. "For some reason that I cannot imagine, it appears that you have decided to involve me in this."

"Are you still keeping that journal you began?" he asked, waiting for a moment to shut the door until she had lighted a candle.

Her head jerked toward him in surprise. "How did you know about that?"

"Brother Vincent told me you were keeping one," he said, dropping into a chair. "Roanna, I want you to record what you heard today, as well as what I am going to tell you. Moreover, I want you to record your own thoughts and opinions on the information."

She was dumbfounded by the request. "But, why? I don't understand."

"I cannot explain now. Roanna, I know that we have had our differences, but I have hoped that we could remain friends. Would you do this for me, on faith alone?"

"Of course!" she exclaimed. "Oh, of course, Giles. I have never stopped . . . being your friend. If it is important to you, then I shall do it, on more than just faith. But—why would you want my opinions?"

He smiled, shaking his head. "Roanna, you underestimate yourself. Your background—that which you deride yourself for—is what is of value to me."

"I don't look down on my background!" she protested.

"Don't you?" One dark eyebrow arched, but then he shrugged. "Perhaps not. In any case, it is that viewpoint that I want, added to mine. I want a knowledge of all that has come before you, the understanding you have gained, your instincts, Roanna."

"I shall try," she said softly. She felt overwhelmed by his request, humbled but also thrilled, a feeling of excitement stirring within her at the challenge. "Oh, Giles, I shall do my best."

"I know you will. Now, sit down, and let us begin." He

stopped her as she went to sit at her table. "Nay, do not take notes just now. Your impressions are far more important than the exact words."

"But what if I forget something?" she asked, coming to sit beside him.

"We can correct that later; facts do not change. Now, tell me, do you understand what you heard this morning?"

Her brow furrowed thoughtfully. "Well . . . if what you said was correct . . . is Simon truly granting favors to those close to him?"

"Unfortunately, he is," Giles answered grimly. "Simon the Younger has been placed in command of the forces at Sussex and Surrey. Others of his inner circle have been given the commands of castles at Bamburgh, Nottingham, and Corfe. Henry de Monfort has been made governor of Dover. Moreover, when Edward was taken from Dover, before he was brought to Kenilworth, Henry was given custody of him—a fact that sorely rankled with our prince and, I fear, has added to the animosity he feels for Simon. This, at a time when Simon must deal with the anger of Rome, the forces in the west who remain loyal to the Crown, and the considerable efforts the queen is making in the royal behalf on the Continent."

"What has happened to him? Why has he changed?"

"He has not changed, Roanna. He is the same man he has always been, and his cause is just. But he is a man overwhelmed." His voice was weary as he rose to fill two goblets with watered wine. Handing her one, he returned to his chair. "It is not unreasonable for one in his position to draw men about him that he can trust—"

"Reasonable, if they are also capable," she finished for him. "If they are not, it merely shows a lack of faith."

His eyes shifted to her and he hid his smile behind his goblet as he drank. "Lack of faith in whom?"

"In the capabilities of others more deserving, of course." She shrugged. "I have heard of the plan he is finally attempting to bring about—Kenilworth is abuzz with it, though it seems impossible, despite the dream he has long had. A parliament with commoners as representatives— with a vote! Can he do such a thing?"

"He can—if he acts quickly."

"Why quickly? What is going to happen?"

"It is only my belief, Roanna," he said, sighing heavily,

"but I fear that he has not much time left—because of all the reasons I have mentioned, and because of the enemies he is making, the worst of whom is my dear cousin, Gloucester. He treats Gilbert as a minor problem, forgetting the power that intractable deClare holds. Moreover, he has forgotten how easily Gilbert's father changed his loyalties." Pausing, he stifled a sudden yawn, then rose and set his goblet on the table. "It is late. But I shall return tomorrow, if I may. I would like to see what you have written about this."

She nearly pushed him toward the door, so anxious was she to begin as her mind tumbled with thoughts she wanted to express. As the door closed behind him, she went to the table, drawing the candle close. Opening her journal, she wrote the date across the top of the page. Pausing, she forced down the excitement that was bubbling up in her, sensing the importance of her project.

Giles smiled with obvious pleasure as he scanned the page, pausing at certain lines; then he looked up at her with a quizzical smile. "'Lord Simon flees the hunter's horn'?"

She smiled sheepishly. "I just meant that—well, it seems that he often fails to follow the necessary path—that which would lead him to the destiny meant for him—as he turns away . . ." She flushed, suddenly uncomfortable at the way Giles was looking at her. "But I also gave good cause to his reasoning, acclaiming his purposes."

"Do not apologize, Roanna," Giles said softly, laying the journal in his lap. "Your words are true. But tell me, what is it that you think is holding him back? That, also, should be here. You are writing our history."

They were sitting beneath a large oak in the outer ward, a meeting place that granted a measure of privacy as the former occupants of the ward had long since departed for their homes in the surrounding hamlets and towns. Roanna leaned against the trunk of the tree, her eyes wandering over the bailey. "You once spoke of a bitterness he carried. I sense that in him now."

Giles was silent for a long moment, causing her to turn and look at him. "You are right, but he does not realize how it haunts him, after the passing of these many years. Moreover, I think he would be dismayed that it is so, if it could be proven to him. I have tried, but he will not see it, nor will Eleanor." He paused, taking chunks of bread and cheese from the basket they had brought with them, and he began to munch idly on the breakfast as he continued.

"Perhaps it was not just what Henry did, but how he did it. Following Edward's birth, the nobles gathered for the queen's churching. It was a great ceremony, all of England was rejoicing in the birth of an heir. Eleanor and Simon came to London to attend—and they were turned away from the church, humiliated before the barons. Stunned, Simon came before Henry at court, demanding to know why they had been treated thus. It was there, before all, that Henry accused Simon of seducing his sister, and Eleanor of adultery. He publicly denied any part in the marriage. This, after Eleanor had borne Simon two children, who, if the charges had stood, would have been declared bastards. This, when Simon had offered his sovereign nothing but loyalty. Simon might have been able to forgive Henry his duplicity toward himself, but never the injury he did to Eleanor. As for her—a Plantagenet does not forgive easily, and never forgets."

"Why would Henry do such a thing to his own sister?"

"Because Henry is weak," he answered grimly. "He listens too well to those who whisper in his ear. There have always been those jealous of Eleanor's power, the hold she had over her brothers, particularly over Henry. The woman is the best of them all, the brightest, the most discerning. If she had been born to the throne, England would not be suffering this now. But she was born a woman, and thus her power over the throne was looked upon as a threat."

"As was your father's," she said quietly.

He turned his head to look at her. "Aye," he said softly, "as was my father's."

"Who murdered him, Giles? Tell me."

"It will never be known." He shrugged. "My uncle Richard, wounded as he waged war against Henry, was allowed to bleed to death. His murderer was found and executed. But as for the others—they were never discovered. My father's murder could not even be proved. He was attending his sister Isabella's marriage to Richard of Cornwall. He was hearty, in great humor; but the following morning, Eleanor awoke . . . he was in her arms . . ."

"Poison?" she asked softly, horrified.

"I believe it to be so."

Roanna shuddered, imagining how Eleanor must have felt. She marveled at the strength of the woman, to be able to continue. "Oh, Giles," she breathed, voicing her thoughts. "How could Eleanor bear it?"

"That itself is a mystery," he said thoughtfully. "For me, she was only strength, even in the depths of her grief. But . . ."

She looked up at him questioningly. "What is it?"

"Eleanor has her own way of confronting grief," he answered dryly, his eyes taking on a distant look. "As I said, it was never proven who murdered my father—at least, it was never brought before the court. But I will tell you this." He paused. "Following my father's death, there seemed to be an odd rush of others who died—a strange epidemic of food poisonings, hunting accidents, and falls from high places. All the victims were men close to my father's archenemy, Peter desRoches. The last death was his."

"What are you saying?" she asked, wide-eyed.

"Nothing." He smiled grimly. "I am only recounting facts, Roanna; the interpretation must be yours."

"A Plantagenet's revenge?" she queried.

"I did not say that. But, as I have said to you, never, never underestimate Eleanor."

On March 8, 1265, beneath a brilliant sun uncommon for early spring, a great parliament was held in London. It was as if the very weather had shifted, granting its warmth in celebration of the event, its approval in accord with man's design. After seven turbulent months of rule, Simon de Monfort summoned the peers of the land, the bishops and two knights from each shire, to confer upon the laws of the land, and to grant even greater efforts benefiting the common man. So the word went out, calling the peers to what would become known as the Great Parliament. What met them, upon their arrival at Westminster, dumbfounded the greatest among them. There, to participate in the decision-making, were "good and loyal men" from each city and borough: plain men, merchants, and freemen to give a say in the laws that governed them.

Roanna was deeply moved. News reaching her of the parliament stirred something within her; she could not put quill to paper for many, many days, feeling utterly inadequate to the effort. She looked forward to Giles's return, eager to discuss with him the historic events, and the words she had finally committed to paper. When he did return, she was not prepared for his mood.

"Grain dealers, soap boilers, and clowns they called them," he said moodily. "They ridiculed their presence."

"Does it matter?" she asked quietly. "They were there. No one can take that from us."

"Nay," he said slowly, "no one can take that from us. The king presented a simple list, though there was no doubt that his words were Simon's. Henry and Edward are to continue to abide by the Great Charter and the Provisions of Oxford. But there was one thing gained—Edward has been delivered into his father's keeping. He may not leave England, nor support any who would come into England to free him, on pain of disinheritance. To that end, he is being sent to Hereford Castle, where he will be closely watched."

"Is that what bothers you so?" she asked. "That Edward is not to return here?"

His head jerked around to her and he frowned. "What are you talking about?"

She shrugged innocently. "It just seems to me that—you will miss him."

"Have you lost your mind!" he exclaimed angrily. "What is Edward to me? He has been my enemy, and will always be so!" With that, he strode away.

She shook her head and murmured softly, "Ah, Giles. How little you know of yourself." Then she turned to seek out her chamber, needing her journal and clarity of thought —the peace solitude would give her.

18

Two months passed before Roanna saw Giles again. He had ridden out from Kenilworth immediately following his return from the parliament. No one knew where he had gone, nor when he would return. However, she was not alarmed by his seclusion, nor hurt by his avoidance of her. She had begun to realize that he was facing a time of great decision and, if what she suspected was true, a time that could possibly destroy him.

She knew that she should leave Kenilworth, now, while he was gone. But she remained, unable to leave until she knew he was safe. She prayed during those days, alternating her prayers with fervent hopes that she would find the words to help him. She felt at once inadequate and fearful, afraid that when the moment came words would totally escape her, even as she knew that his answers had to be found within himself.

He appeared at her door one evening at vespers as dusk claimed the end of another day, wan and exhausted, though his smile denied it. She let him in and waved him to a chair as she poured him a goblet of wine, choosing a ewer of unwatered beverage. "Lord Simon has left for the western reaches," she said calmly, handing him the goblet. "Are you hungry? I have some cheese."

He shook his head, and drank. Her brows rose slightly as she watched him quaff the heady brew, but she did not comment. She sat next to him, waiting until he appeared to relax, stretching his long legs out before him, before she spoke, deliberately taking a frontal attack. "It is said that a new pope has been chosen at last—and moreover, that our friend Guy Fulcodi has been given the honor. It does not bode well for England. He has appointed one Ottobuoni Fiesco as legate to England, with orders to rid England of 'that pestilent man and all his offspring.' Moreover, the barons are defecting, angry that Simon will not grant them ransoms gained at the battle of Lewes. His decision to release the prisoners taken in an effort to create peace is losing him allies. I have been recording what I have learned, as you asked me, and . . ." She paused, wondering at the strange look he gave her.

"Roanna," he said quietly, "you have learned quickly, but then, I never doubted that you would. I am aware that Simon has left to 'squash' the menace rising in the western reaches. What is of far more importance, however, is that Gilbert is in the Forest of Dean, gathering a considerable army about him. John Giffard has joined him, along with Mortimer and de Leyburn and other knights loyal to Edward."

"How do you know this?"

"I was there," he said, drawing from his goblet.

She stiffened with alarm, looking at him intently. She forced her voice to remain calm. "What has brought you back to Kenilworth?"

He tossed her a weary look, but behind it she could read lingering anguish. "I came to warn him."

"Will you follow him?"

"As soon as I have rested."

Oh, Giles, she thought, how can I help you? "What of Edward?" she asked casually, rising to refill his goblet.

His head came up sharply. "What of him?"

"I just wondered how he fared. He is still at Hereford, is he not?"

"I am certain that he is well," he muttered, and drank from the goblet. "Henry de Monfort is with him."

"A death sentence," Roanna said wryly. "Edward must be dying of boredom."

To her relief, Giles laughed, the lines in his face easing. "That is unkind, Roanna. Henry is not boring, he's just—"

"Dull," she finished. "Giles, you must have some rest. A night, perhaps, before you leave."

He set the goblet down and rose. "Nay, I cannot." He pulled his cloak about his shoulders.

"One night," she said, furious with herself for reminding him of his responsibilities. "Surely it cannot make that much difference."

"I should have left the moment I learned that Simon was not here. But . . . I wanted to see you again." Leaning down, he brushed her cheek with a kiss. "Farewell, dear Roanna. Ever you are a source of comfort to me. I bid you well."

She stared at the door as it closed behind him, her heart torn by his last words. With a ragged breath she forced her feelings aside, focusing on the larger problem, the only one she could bear to think of. "Soon, Giles," she said to the empty room. "If you do not come to realize what is plaguing you, then I shall surely tell you, no matter what it may do to whatever lingering feelings you have for me." The words, bravely spoken, struck her painfully. She and Giles had so few ties left to bind them; could she speak the words that might sever those tenuous strands? She could only pray that she would find the courage.

Roanna heard the call of the tower guard as she crossed the ward toward the library. She froze, her head turning in the direction of the tower gate; then she hitched up her skirts and began to run, her heart lifting as the heavy inner portcullis was drawn up and a large troop of riders entered the inner ward. She slowed to a discreet walk as her eyes searched among the dismounting men, noting Simon's presence and those of his sons. And then she saw Giles. Oh, Sweet Mother, she thought, hoping that he had not seen her running toward them. He'll think me a hoyden—but then, no one ever accused me of being a lady.

She smoothed down her skirt and self-consciously patted her hair, hoping that she looked somewhat presentable. Then, drawing a deep breath, she started forward, only to stop dead in her tracks. Giles had turned to lift a young woman from her mount, one of the loveliest women Roanna had ever seen. As he set her on the ground, she turned her face up to him, laughing at something he said. Even from where she stood, Roanna could not mistake the languishing eyes the maid turned up to Giles, nor the warmth of the smile he returned as she pressed his arm against her side.

Geoffrey Wardell, holding the horses, looked up at that moment and caught sight of Roanna where she stood apart. His youthful face broke into a grin, which faded to puzzlement at her stricken expression. Turning to Giles, his eyes widened, then darted back to Roanna, filled with concern.

Roanna turned and fled. It took all of her control not to break into a run, thus making a complete spectacle of herself. But she could not stay the tears, and she stumbled, half-blinded, as pain gripped at her chest and she could hardly breathe. Fool! she thought. Why should it be so painful—was this not what she had expected, even wanted for him?

Halfway across the ward, someone grasped her arm and spun her around. "Roanna, where are you going?"

"Oh, you great lout, let me go!" Her foot shot out, connecting with his shin as her free hand came up and lopped him alongside his head.

"All right, Roanna. As ever, we'll play it your way," he grunted. With that, he hoisted her over his shoulder, where she landed with an oomph of expelled breath. As she gasped for air, aware of the laughter of the men behind them, she began pounding on his back, shrieking every unflattering name she could think of as he carried her across the ward. He kicked open the door to her chamber and threw her on the bed, stepping back to slam the door. She was off the bed in an instant, flinging herself at him. "You sodding bastard, let me go!"

He grabbed her, spinning her about. He wrapped his arms about her, holding her against him with a viselike grip as she kicked and struggled. "Go where, Roanna?" he said near her ear, ignoring her protests. "Where would you like to go? To Eleanor, to beg for protection?"

"She has gone to Odiham," she snarled, trying to wrench free.

"So she has," he said, chuckling. "That is near London, as I recall. Why did you not go with her? It is not far from Odiham to the Thames, and a certain tavern we both know. Why did you stay, Roanna?"

"Go to bloody hell!"

"I probably will, but not quite yet. There are some things I must finish here first, and this situation with you is one of them. You might as well stop struggling, sweetheart, I am not going to let you go until I have my say. Now, then, why can't you admit it? You stayed for me. You couldn't wait to see me again."

"Giles, I 'ate you!"

" 'ate?" He laughed. "Roanna, you're dropping your *h*'s again. Could it be something I said?"

"Dammit, let me go! I promise—I promise I'll behave myself—I can't breathe."

He released her. Leaning back against the door, he folded his arms as she stepped away and spun back on him, her eyes flaring with rage, which only seemed to add to his amusement. "Roanna, I do not expect you to behave yourself. In fact, I think I would be disappointed if you did. I'd settle for a screaming match if it meant we could deal with this."

"Why can't you leave this alone?" she cried, tears of anger and frustration pooling in her eyes.

"You don't want to leave this alone any more than I do," he said with infuriating calm.

"Why are you doing this to me? You have another now—leave me alone!"

He feigned puzzlement for a moment, then brightened with understanding. "Oh, you must mean Elizabeth. Aye, she's a beauty, is she not? Warm, gentle, tenderly reared. The essence of a lady."

She groaned, turning away from him. Gathering the last vestiges of her pride, she struggled to keep her voice even. "I am happy for you, Giles, truly. She is what you deserve —she will bring honor to you."

"Aye, she has. Though she is a lot like you in spirit. However, you are correct: she was born a lady and reared gently, given every advantage. And she is wealthy—she will bring much to her marriage bed. Not like what we have, Roanna, is it? A tavern wench and a stable boy . . ." He saw her body jerk slightly, as though struck, and he pressed on, his voice cutting. "Aye, she has reminded me of many important things about my family that I had forgotten, things I had taken for granted. Did you know that my great-grandmother was a princess, that she brought a broad fifth of Ireland to her marriage bed? Oh, that was a prize! That my great-grandfather was a lord marcher who conquered Ireland and became its overlord—not to mention the fact that he helped to bring Henry the Second to the throne?" He heard her groan as she lowered herself to a chair, her shoulders sagging with defeat as she stared at the floor. "Roanna, I can count king-makers throughout my family. They were said to be the most powerful family England has ever known, or is likely to know again. Shall I go on?"

She shook her head, too overwhelmed with misery to look at him.

"Well," he said firmly, taking the chair across from her, "I shall, in any case. There are some other things you should know. My great-grandmother's father, who was king of Leinster, was a traitor. His name is damned for all time among the people of Ireland. My mother was a whore. Oh, she had reason to be," he said as she looked up at him, her eyes startled. "Her father abused her in a way no woman should suffer until she fled from him, seeking love wherever she could find it. But none of this is important—none of it, not the position, the wealth, the shame. Let me tell you what I treasure.

"The women of my family were outcasts among women of their time." He smiled at the amazed look that came into her eyes. "Aye, they were that. They were strong, dominating, opinionated, and insufferable—to all but the men who loved them. My great-grandmother fought in a battle to free her people—"

"Like a man?" Roanna gasped. "Truly?"

"Like a man." He smiled. "She saved my great-grandfather's life that day. And then there is my grandmother, Isabel. She could swear like a soldier, and often did"—he laughed, remembering—"a talent she learned from her mother, who had been raised among men in a society much more free than ours. She ruled lands reaching from Ireland to Normandy with an iron hand. Her talents freed my grandfather to see to England's administration, even supplied him with the funds to see to the task. She too led forces against her enemies—not a very ladylike endeavor, was it? As for my aunts—the five Marshal daughters—

now, there was quite a covey! Ask Eleanor, they over-whelmed her. They married well, it is true, but it was their strengths that guided their husbands to greatness. I was raised amid the strength of these women, Roanna."

"But—" Lord, it was so confusing! "What has this to do with Elizabeth? Oh, Giles, why are you telling me all of this?"

"Which shall I answer first? Elizabeth? She is everything I said. I want you to meet her, and love her as I do." At the horrified disbelief that came into her eyes, he laughed softly. "She is Elizabeth Bigod, Roanna—my cousin, whom I have loved since she was a child. As for your other question, don't you understand, after all that I have told you? All my life I have respected strength in a woman. The woman I need is one who is certain of herself, one who will meet me, match for match. A woman who knows her own mind, who seeks her own growth, who cares fiercely for what is important to her, and to me, and will fight like a cat to defend it—and will tell me to go to bloody hell when I am wrong."

Elizabeth was his cousin? Her heart swelled with happiness; yet the rest of his declaration sent a quiver of fear through her. "It—it is impossible, Giles. I cannot be what you want."

He grinned. "Aristotle said that plausible impossibilities should be preferred to unconvincing possibilities."

"Oh, bugger, Giles, don't throw that at me now! How can you want this? Most men would put aside the woman you're talking about!"

"I am not most men. I can only be what I am. And the same is true of you."

She could not give him the answer he wanted to hear. She had fixed upon her reasonings, her feelings, for so long. She could not push them aside to accept the hope, the dreams that were so near, there for the taking. She had spent too much time and energy rejecting what she felt. Finally, her emotions spilled over. She could not yet reason why, but she could not push him away. "I—I love you, Giles. But I cannot marry you," she whispered.

"I have not asked you to marry me," he answered. He arched one dark eyebrow at the startled look she turned to him. "Nay, I will not ask you again. When we marry,

Roanna, it will be because you have asked for it. Only then will I know that you have accepted what I have told you."

She swallowed heavily. Words formed in her mind, phrases countering what he had said, but suddenly they seemed empty. She felt frightened, sad, desperate. "Make love to me, Giles," she said softly, pleading. "I need you."

"No." The firm response brought her head up, and she reddened with embarrassment. "I will not make love to you, Roanna, as much as I want you. When I made love to you before, I thought we had committed ourselves to each other. I was wrong. You have not committed yourself to me. I am a landed knight, Roanna, there can be no care-cloth for us. If I should give you a child it would be a bastard. I will not do that to you, or to our child."

"But—your father granted lands to you before his death. Could you not—"

"Christ, Roanna!" He rose from his chair, turning away from her for a moment before he spun back. "Do you know what it is like to be a bastard? My father was loving and generous, but he could never make up for my birth! I will not do that to my child!" He lowered his voice with effort. "Nay, Roanna. I love you, but I will not take you again until you swear yourself to me."

"Oh, Giles," she said softly, "how can you believe that I am the woman you are seeking? I would give years of my life to be so, but I am not."

He drew a frustrated breath, and crossed to the table. Taking up the journal, he turned and dropped it into her lap. "Read what is here, Roanna," he said quietly, his voice strained. "Read it. Why do you think I had you do it, if not that you could finally see what you are? Look into the depths of the one who put those words to the page. Was it written by an idle mind, one incapable of thought, lacking in strength? I, at least, can see the author as one I should like to know, one who would challenge my reasoning—one I could love, with all of my being." He paused, shaking his head slowly. "But then, perhaps we have both wasted our time."

He left the chamber, quietly closing the door behind him. She stared at the door for a long time, then dropped her gaze to her lap. Swallowing heavily, she opened the leather-covered wood cover, and stared at the lines on the first page, taking a deep breath as she read. "I, Roanna Royston, do commit these words to be true by my own reasoning . . ." Her own reasoning. Oh, God, she thought, who was Roanna Royston? What was reason? Could dreams . . . possibly be?

19

Silver strands crisscrossed the corner formed by the beam and the wall, intersecting threads in an intricate circular pattern. The small brown spider crossed yet again, patiently weaving her web. Oblivious to a larger world, she stepped across her previous designs, spinning her shimmering threads. Patiently crossing, she passed back to touch upon the first pattern before she expanded her horizon to new, daring points.

Below, cocooned in the warmth of wool and fur, with a candle lit to warm the darkness, Roanna watched, momentarily distracted from her dreams. Perhaps, she thought as she watched the spider, life was just that simple—plans made from some instinctive knowledge, followed without anguish; peace found in doing the best one possibly could, in not demanding the impossible.

She had lain awake most of the night, thinking upon the things Giles had said. She had countered each point with logic, formulating answers that contested with the hopes and dreams dwelling deep within her, until she confronted the dawn as confused as when she had retired.

She watched as a fly came too close, touching the edge of the web, and the spider poised, instantly ready. Buzzing, the fly struggled, then freed itself and flew off. After a moment, the spider resumed its patient task.

"It was there," Roanna whispered. "You almost had it. What you are waiting for—the purpose to all you are doing." Tears filled her eyes and she sat up, rejecting the self-pity that suddenly overwhelmed her. "Fuss and bother!" she whispered, crossing to the washstand to splash her face. Grabbing a cloth, she dried her face, then sat heavily in the chair near the desk. She leaned back with a sigh, as confounded as ever, and addressed the spider again.

"You don't give any thought to what will happen if that fly is never caught! You just go on, endlessly weaving, content with the design, having faith that it will be enough. But I know! You'll die! You'll wait and wait for that which will complete your life, and it may never come again!"

She glanced about the room. Another day, she thought. I could pretend that it is just like the one before—the sun will come up, and it will go down. Between prime and vespers I will go about my duties as I have done each day. But I won't be the same. Everything has changed.

He wants my commitment to him. He cannot know what he is asking. He wants me to reach beyond my dreams. I want him, but he is beyond who I thought I was. Why did I have to love him? Why has he become the center of everything for me? She glanced up at the beam above her. Why can't I be like you, dealing only with what I know?

Suddenly she laughed out loud, a bitter sound. Funny, she thought, all of this time I thought my resistance was for his benefit. But it was for me, my fears of being taken into a life I don't understand, of taking risks, finding myself among those who make me feel I am less than what I am. An irrevocable decision—where now I can walk away.

Then she saw him in her mind, the warmth of his smile, his humor and teasing, the glint in his eye as he laughed. Humor, she thought, that was the best of it. Perhaps, of all man's traits, that is the best. When one shares laughter with another, something exceptional happens. When it does not require explanation, when you are the only two who laugh, the bonding turns toward completion, and you find the one who looks upon life the same way that you do.

Could she reach beyond her dreams? Grab for life, Uncle Roscoe had said. Aye, and she could find herself among countless others who were miserable. But if she was one of the blessed ones—wasn't it worth the risk?

Oh, she was afraid. It was so much easier to remain in the confines of the familiar, to avoid the terror of reaching beyond them. To actually take a dream and make it reality?

How much easier it would be to find excuses for why one cannot. And she had done that, over and over, until Giles had begun to show her that she could be more than she ever thought she could be. She would not just be a wretch who could learn, letting others use her knowledge for their own, narrow purposes, but one who could learn to use her knowledge for herself, to grow.

So, Giles fitzWilliam, she mused with a wry smile, you say you want a woman with opinions of her own. Oh, I hope you meant that, for they come with the rest of me.

As the bell tolled for compline, Giles opened the door to his chamber. The room was cast in soft light from the fire burning low on the hearth. He smiled, pleasantly surprised to find a table before the hearth set with a light supper. He had not eaten since midmeal, but he did not think Geoffrey had been aware of it, as he had kept the squire busy throughout the day with other tasks. Tossing his cloak on a chair near the door, he crossed to the table and paused, his brows rising with amazement as he noted the delicacies waiting for him. The squire had outdone himself. Geoffrey's usual talents extended to bread, cheese, and whatever he could wangle from the cook. Tonight, instead, there were meat pasties, paindemain rolled in sugar, and plover roasted to a golden brown. "Geoffrey?" Giles said, glancing around, wondering where the squire had gotten to.

"He is not here, Giles. Shall I send for him?"

His head jerked in the direction of the bed. Roanna rose from the shadows of the bed curtains, and slipped down from the high mattress. He caught his breath as she walked slowly toward him, his eyes feasting on the delectable picture she made. Her glorious hair was loose, tumbling over her shoulders, its shining softness catching the flickering lights from the fire. Her soft, supple body was clad in a sheer bedgown of pale blue sarcenet that clung to her shapely form, outlining it for his observant, and hungry, gaze.

"Hungry, milord?" she asked softly, coming to stand before him.

"Ravenous," he answered huskily.

"Then sit down, and I will serve you."

Aching to touch her, he brought himself under control and sat at the table, his eyes never leaving her as she took the chair across from him and began to serve the meal. Taking a deep breath, he cleared his throat painfully. "Roanna, before this goes any further, we must talk. My mind has not changed."

"Ah, but mine has," she said softly, pouring wine into his goblet. "I want to marry you, Giles—if you will still have me."

It was a moment before he could speak. "I still want you," he answered easily, but she saw a muscle twitch in his jaw. "What changed your mind?"

"You. The things you said to me. The fact that I love you beyond life itself, that I cannot imagine a life without you. And knowing now that I must stop being afraid."

"What have you been afraid of, Roanna? Surely not me."

"Of course it was you—that you would grow to hate me for not being what you could have had in a wife. I bring nothing to our marriage but myself, Giles. I fear the day will come when that will not be enough. But now I am willing to take that chance."

"You are all that I want, Roanna," he said gently. "There is nothing else that I need. But if you still have doubts, why are you now willing to take a chance?"

Serving him a portion of paindemain, she shrugged. "Suffice it to say that your suit was well put. Moreover, I believe that you need me now, and the support I can give you."

He paused, his goblet halfway to his mouth. "Roanna," he asked guardedly, "what is going on in that lovely head of yours?"

Lovely head? She could have pointed out to him that he was being condescending, but she held her peace, choosing to take it as a compliment. She smiled sweetly. "Nothing you should worry about, luv. Merely plausible impossibilities."

Laughing, he put down his goblet and rose to step around the table and draw her into his arms. "Oh, Lord, I do love you, Roanna," he murmured. "Will you be my wife?"

"Aye, I will be your wife, Giles," she whispered.

He stepped back, cupping her face with his hands, and gazed down at her with love, his eyes searching hers for the answers he needed. Seeing the reflection of his own emotions, he bent his head and kissed her as her arms slid about his waist and she clung to him. The kiss deepened as her lips opened eagerly, forming to his. His hands slipped down to her waist and hips, pressing her to him. Murmuring soft words of love, he began a trail of light kisses across her face, touching upon the corners of her eyes, where tears had gathered, moving to the corners of her mouth and down her neck to her shoulders. She gasped softly when his hands reached her breasts and his thumbs began their play through the thin fabric. "If seduction was your plan, mistress," he whispered, "I was lost the moment I saw you slip from my bed." He unlaced the robe and, as it dropped to the floor, she heard him catch his breath sharply. He swept her up into his arms. "And it is to my bed you are going to return."

"Your supper will grow cold, milord," she said softly, her eyes dreamy.

"Not the supper I have in mind."

He carried her to the bed and lowered her onto the deep mattress. She watched with breathless anticipation as he drew his tabard over his head, flinging it aside. The chanise was quickly followed by boots and leggings. She felt her heart begin to pound as he drew off each garment, allowing her eyes to feast on the muscles of his arms and chest, the bronze of his skin in the firelight, the long legs, the narrow hips, and finally his engorged member with its promise. As he bent over, kissing her lightly, she wrapped her arms about him, sighing deeply as she tried to pull him to her.

"Patience, sweetling," he murmured, nibbling on her ear. His lips traveled to the nape of her neck, and she moaned. Then he moved to her breast, where he lingered, allowing his lips and tongue their leisurely play. His fingers found the taut tip of her other breast and she groaned, arching beneath him. She was dizzy with anticipation, her nerve endings alive with his touch, her hands moving over his body, stroking his muscled back and arms, slipping down to his hips.

Shifting, he began a slow, measured pace of kisses across the satiny skin of her stomach to her thighs. She cried out as his fingers and lips continued their quest, and the flames began to lick at her middle, spreading up over her body in a bittersweet tension that threatened to drive her mad with wanting. "Giles!" she gasped, as her hands pulled at him. Raising himself over her, he entered her with agonizing slowness, pulling back to tease her again, until she rose up to meet him. There, as they slowly built together, drawing and giving, Roanna found the dreams she had been so afraid to reach for. The simplicity, the peace of emotions, thoughts and hearts in perfect union. She soared apart and he joined with her, and for a brief instant she felt his soul touch hers.

As the grey light of dawn crossed the chamber, Roanna snuggled against him, sated and deliriously happy, her eyes closing in surrender. He was curved against her back, his long legs tucked behind hers, one arm laid gently against her breasts, filling her with security and peace. She sighed with contentment, then tensed with surprise as he laughed softly. "Is this not better, my love?" he murmured sleepily. "To sleep in each other's arms, knowing we'll be together in the morning?"

"Sleep, milord?" She stifled a yawn. "We've done little enough of that."

"True," he said, chuckling. "It will take a while to become accustomed to such a delightful body next to mine throughout the night. You touch me, and my mind turns to more rigorous, though pleasant, endeavors than sleeping."

She twisted about to look at him over her shoulder. "Truly? You have never slept with anyone throughout the night?"

"Truly." He smiled, squeezing her gently. "I've never before cared about a woman enough to want to wake up with her. Momentary distractions, sweetheart, nothing more."

"Not even Lisette?"

He paused and thought for a moment. "I imagined myself to be in love with her, and I wanted her. But I did not think beyond that. With you—I think of us living together, sharing moments, having children, growing old together. That is why I could not settle for having you as my mistress. The months when we were forced to pretend made me realize what it would be like if that was all I was to have of you. I wanted more for us."

She could not speak for a long moment. Taking his words into her heart, she nestled against him. "For a long, long time, I could not face the fact that I was falling in love with you. It frightened me. I had no right to love you, and I was certain I was going to be hurt if I allowed such a dream. I was determined not to destroy both of our lives, so I decided I would take as much as could be allowed, leaving us both our freedom."

His arms tightened about her. "Nonsense. Whatever feelings you tried to suppress before, you knew you were in love with me the day I first held you in my arms and we danced."

Her eyes flew open and she tried to twist about to look at him. "How did you know that?"

"You were obvious, Roanna, blatantly obvious." He grinned. "Flitting about, swishing your skirt, trying not to look at me. You flirted with every man there, except me."

"I did not!"

"You did. And I did not imagine that kiss you gave me. It spoke volumes. It certainly set me to thinking."

She turned her face into the pillow, groaning. "Giles, you are the most conceited man I know!" she said in a muffled voice.

"If I am wrong, why are you blushing?"

"It's dark in here, you can't know if I'm blushing!"

"Aren't you?" He reached up and touched her face. "Aye, you're blushing. Your face is hot." His hand slid beneath the covers. "God, you're blushing all the way down there."

He laughed as she began to squirm, holding her firmly as his lips dipped to the nape of her neck. "I am glad that Roscoe came when he did, Roanna," he murmured, caressing the tender lobe of her ear. "It was not yet time for us—and we might have lost what we have now. Besides, it certainly gave me something to think about, that long winter away from you." His hands and lips began plying her body, and she turned in his arms, her eyes shining with love. Soon, amid sighs and deep groans, the last vestiges of night faded away. Then they slept, falling into a contented sleep in each other's arms.

Delicious memories invaded her thoughts, remembrance of the past night returning even before she was awake. Roanna stretched like a contented cat, feeling every part of her body, luxuriating in its satisfaction. Her eyes, those deep, rich brown pools of delight, opened, and began to dance as she contemplated the mischief she planned for Giles. So, he had never awakened in the morning light with a woman in his bed? Her thoughts churned with possibilities as she considered ways of awakening him. Settling on her game, she turned slowly, biting her lower lip to keep from giggling, only to find the bed empty. Stunned, she sat up and glanced about. The room was as empty as her love nest. "Giles?" she called, confused, bitten with a deep ache of disappointment. Where had he gone? Lud, he had left her! She slid from the bed, gasping as the cold floor met her bare feet, and her temper flew out of control.

"Never had the pleasure of waking to a woman in his bed, eh?" she snarled to the empty room. Picking up his tabard, she stared at it for a moment, then flung it aside. "Ohhh, Roanna! I've dreamt of waking with you in my arms!" she mocked sarcastically as she flung aside discarded clothing with rage. She strode across to the washstand and stopped, staring at the dirty water in the bowl. "Couldn't even dump 'is own wash water!" she snapped. "Probably couldn't wait to get out of 'ere!" She slopped the water out the window, hoping that he was standing below it, then refilled the bowl from the pitcher on the table. "He's probably in the 'all, bragging about his conquest with Rodger or Geoffrey!" she gritted out, splashing her face. She came up sputtering and grabbed for a cloth, coughing. Slipping into the robe she had brought with her, she glared at the door. "Or are you with Simon, the past night the furthest thing from your mind? Men! Every blessed, sodding one of 'em is the same! Let's 'ave it, luv—then on to better things!" She picked up the pitcher and flung it across the room, and it shattered against the wall near the door.

Exactly at that moment the door opened, and Giles stood in the portal. His eyes fixed on the shattered pottery, then shifted to her. One eyebrow arched, and his lips twitched. "Good morning, sweetness."

"Don't good-morning me, you bloody bugger!" she cried, launching another missile in his direction. He ducked handily as the small earthen goblet swished through the doorway, crashing somewhere behind him.

"Out of sorts this morning, Roanna?" he quipped.

She stiffened, raising her chin. "Of course not. Nothing you could possibly do affects me in the least." Then her mouth dropped open as Giles stepped aside and two menservants entered carrying a copper tub, followed by others bearing buckets of steaming water. She cringed inwardly as they noted the shambles of the room, and their eyes shifted speculatively between Giles and herself. Oh, God, she thought miserably, I've done it again.

She plopped down heavily on the edge of the bed and watched numbly as the men filled the tub and left. Giles closed the door behind them and came to stand before her. "Would you like to fight, or take a bath? In all honesty, a fight might be interesting. I'm in the mood for a good tumble."

She looked up at him in misery. "Oh, Giles, I am sorry. I—I've embarrassed you again."

"Embarrassed me? With whom?"

"Don't patronize me. With the servants, of course. Who will it be next time—your family, your men? Can't you see now? This will not work for us! You'll have a termagant for a wife—I have the manners of a doxy—" She drew in her breath raggedly, trying not to cry. "How could you ever think of presenting me at court?"

He sat next to her, silent for a moment, and she winced at the patience in his voice when he finally spoke. "Roanna, when I was sixteen I went on a hunting trip with my father. We were gone for more than a week, just the two of us. We managed these trips quite often, and they left me with memories of him I cherish. But this particular time, he forgot to mention it to Eleanor or to my grandmother. When we returned to Chepstow, we found that King Henry had chosen the moment for a visit, with the full court in attendance." His mouth curved into a smile. "Perhaps, for my grandmother, that was the worst of it—she had been forced to entertain Henry, and she detested the man. For Eleanor, I think, the worst was having to admit that she had absolutely no idea where her husband had gone, nor did she know when he would return—a rather embarrassing admission to have to make to her brother, added to the fact that she was worried senseless about us.

"In any case, we returned during midmeal—unfortunate timing, as it turned out, for Eleanor and Isabel had an audience for their anger. My grandmother took me by the ear and plopped me down on a trestle table beneath the salt—a resounding lecture later followed. But I was let off easy. As my father turned to direct his conversation to his sovereign, he found a bowl of stew dumped in his lap. With that, Eleanor clicked her fingers and strode indignantly from the hall, leaving my father to pick meat and vegetables from his tunic with as much dignity as possible."

"She did that?" Roanna gasped. "Giles, you're making this up!"

"Nay, I am not. It happened, upon my life."

"Did he—did your father beat her?"

"Beat Eleanor?" He laughed. "He never laid a hand upon her except in love. I told you that I was raised by termagants. My father understood, as he explained to me later, that he had hurt her. She had worried, not knowing where we were, or if we were safe. He had been thoughtless and frightened her, not to mention humiliating her before the court. But it was never intentional. As for the stew, as I recall, he licked his fingers and declared it quite good."

"He didn't!" She burst out laughing.

"He did. Then he went to Eleanor and made up with her. I, on the other hand, was subjected to a lecture from my grandmother—I never worried her again. Though I seem to have caused worry to you, my love."

"I—I thought you had left me—that you didn't care," she said softly. "You said you wanted to wake up with me in your arms—but you were gone."

"I did wake up with you in my arms, sweetheart, and it was wonderful. I thought that I'd be back before you awoke."

She glanced at the tub and smiled sheepishly. "I would like a bath."

"Then in with you," he said, rising from the bed. Holding out a hand, he pulled her up. "Roanna, if you ever have something to say to me, then say it. There is nothing we may not talk about. Just give me the chance to have my say, before you decide that I'm a—bloody bugger." He grinned, bending to kiss the tip of her nose.

"I'll try to remember that," she conceded happily, spinning away from him. She faced the tub, then hesitated, glancing back at him.

He grinned at her. "Modesty, Roanna? I shall only peek once in a while, I promise."

Laughing, she dropped the robe and stepped into the steaming water, sighing as she sank into its warmth. "Oh, Giles, it is wonderful!" she exclaimed, splashing as she reached for the soap and the cloth on the stool that had been set next to the tub.

"Glad you are enjoying it," he answered from behind her. "But you'll have to hurry. We have important matters before us this morning."

"What?" she asked happily, scrubbing her arms.

"Finish, and I'll tell you."

At last she rose, took up the length of linen left for her, and stepped from the tub as she wrapped it about her. Drying herself, she looked up and gasped. Giles had changed into a magnificent tabard of deep green velvet shot with gold and leggings of a soft beige leather. "You look wonderful!" she exclaimed. "Where are you going?"

"Where would I be going this morning?" He grinned, and she thought he looked like a cat full of cream; his eyes were dreamy and filled with satisfaction.

"Where?" She began to feel unsettled.

"To our wedding, of course. I sent Geoffrey for the priest just after dawn. They should be here shortly."

"Our wedding?" she squeaked.

"Aye." He gestured toward the bed, where he had laid some garments. "I brought these for you from your chamber. I don't recall you wearing them before."

Her eyes shifted to the bed. There was a bliaut of sky-blue silk, a fine linen chemise, a girdle of golden links, a narrow, delicate fillet banded with golden roses, and a coif of sheer blue sarcenet. He should recognize them, she thought wryly, since they were some of the gifts he had showered on her during his "courting." Her body felt numb, and she turned to stare at him. "I can't," she said in an anguished voice. "Not yet, not so soon!" Oh, Lord, it was happening too fast!

"But you will," he said firmly. "I told you, Roanna, there can be no care-cloth for us. Even now you may be carrying my child; today you will become my wife. Now dress, they are waiting."

He helped her dress, lacing the back of the silk as she tried to comprehend the fact that it was actually happening. She trembled as she stood before the small silvered mirror over his shaving stand, willing her hands not to tremble as she fixed the fillet over the veil. He came to stand behind her and their eyes met in the mirror; then she closed her eyes, trying not to cry. He took her shoulders, turning her about. Reaching into the pocket of his tabard, he withdrew something. Taking her hand, he pressed it into her palm.

"I give these to you now, my love; they would not be understood by the others," he said softly. "With them, I pledge my honor to you."

She opened her fingers and stared at the three gold coins in her hand. Tears trickled from her eyes as she recalled the words he had whispered in her ear, so long ago, as they stood before a small church: ". . . It is not commonly done—he must love her very much."

She raised her tear-filled eyes to his, understanding the pledge he was making to her. Smiling tremulously, she wrapped the coins reverently in her kerchief and tucked them into her pocket. As he led her from the chamber she ventured a glance at him, a look that he answered with a satisfied smile. She was too overwhelmed to speak. He seemed so sure of himself, so certain of what he wanted. For this moment she was part of that, and she prayed that it would always be so. She leaned toward him, drawing strength from the feel of his hand beneath her arm, as he led her across the hall and out into the ward, to the chapel.

When they entered the cool darkness of the small stone chapel, she glanced about, stunned by how many had chosen to attend. How had he done all of this, and so quickly? Rodger Farnham winked as they passed by, and Geoffrey was grinning broadly as he exchanged approving glances with Giles's men. A quirk of amusement struck her as she passed Lady Margot, whose face was stern with disapproval though she would not absent herself from the marriage of Eleanor's stepson. Near the altar, Lord Simon smiled at her with approval, and by his side stood Lady Elizabeth, her fair eyes bright with friendly curiosity. As their eyes met, Roanna flushed, remembering what she had thought of the young maid.

Friendly faces swam before her and she answered their smiles distractedly, then found herself kneeling before the priest. Words floated, their meanings vague; then, like a whirling storm that suddenly cleared, everything focused. She was marrying Giles. He knelt at her side, his hand clasped about hers in the folds of her gown, his head lifted to the priest's words. Fascinated, she watched his upturned profile as he answered the priest, his voice strong and certain. In a moment she would be his wife—unless, when the priest turned to her, she answered nay. Just that swiftly, she could end it. In that moment she could have control—

as she would never have again in her life. She drew a deep breath, closing her eyes as the possibility tossed crazily, compellingly, through her mind. Now, or never again.

The priest was waiting. She opened her eyes and stared at him. Aye—or nay. One simple word that would irrevocably change her life. She felt a wave of fright, the terror of the unknown. To grab the dragon by the tail, to feel its fire, not knowing if it would give life or destroy.

From somewhere deep within her the answer came, softly. The priest had to ask her to repeat it, which she managed in a stronger voice. "I take thee, Giles, as my husband." She felt him squeeze her hand gently, and looked up to find him watching her, a smile on his wondrously handsome face, and she felt the warm rush of the dragon's breath, touching her in a kiss.

20

The man's short legs carried his winded body up the rise. He paused, drawing in gulps of air, then slid down the sloping walls of the gully toward the campfires burning below. Barely glancing at those huddled in the fog-shrouded encampment, their own interest in the passerby little more than a flicker of momentary curiosity, he sought out a fire at the far end of the gully near a small copse of birch.

"Sweet Mother Mary," he muttered under his labored breath, "I'm too old for this." Dropping down into a heap by the fire, he held out his plump hands to the meager flame, rubbing them together in an effort to restore feeling to his bluing fingers.

"Well?" said a voice from beneath a heavy woolen hood that cloaked a form across the small campfire. "What did you find out?"

"Nothing you had not already heard for yourself." He glanced about. "Amazing, the information that can be garnered—hereabouts."

"From whores, you mean." She laughed quietly. "Dear Brother Vincent, to what have I brought you? To lie among the fallen?"

"'Judge not according to appearance,'" he quoted with an unaccustomed smirk. "We have been accepted, and to a great measure, protected. Would I so condemn?"

"Nay, you would not, my kindly Franciscan," she said softly, glancing about. "But you would do well to keep your

257

tonsure covered beneath that serf's cap. They would be swift to judge, and would not look kindly upon finding one of your ilk in their midst."

"And you, Lady Roanna—would they look kindly upon you?" he asked in a low voice.

"Oh, dear brother," she said, "I am a lady by title only, as granted by my husband. The grace of my speech you did refine, the manners I learned from my time at Kenilworth. I am not concerned about women who follow an army, or even the thieves who prey upon the fringes of camp, but"—her voice lowered as she glanced in the direction of the ridge—"what lies just beyond." Returning her attention to the Franciscan, she leaned forward. "It is certain, then? Lord Simon is near?"

"Nay, merely rumors, nothing is certain. Some swear that he is in England, others that he is in Wales. But it is said that there is a war council being held."

"We must find out what is happening! There is so little time!"

Understanding the young woman's thoughts, the Franciscan spoke gently. "Do you think that he is with him?"

"Where else would he be?" she answered, not realizing how much bitterness was in her voice.

He knew that there was little that he could do to offer comfort, nothing he could say to soften the pain she was feeling. "You should try to get some rest, Roanna. Tomorrow—"

"Tomorrow?" She laughed softly, sadly. "Soon Giles and I shall be at war with each other—though he will probably never know it." She paused, sighing deeply. "Good night, dear brother, and sleep well. You are correct that we need rest—dawn will come soon enough."

Discouraging further conversation, she lay down, drawing a blanket over her. After a moment she heard the Franciscan settling beneath his bedding. But sleep resolutely eluded her as she lay staring at the foggy night. Her tortured thoughts played over and over the events that had led her here, to lie in a narrow gully among the camp followers of Edward Plantagenet's army.

Oh, Giles, she thought, what happened to those beautiful, exquisite days we shared, so brief but full of joy? They had passed as if in a dream, and like a dream perhaps they were not truly real. In those days following their marriage, she had been filled with him, touching, giving, loving him so completely and being so totally loved. The laughter, the warmth . . . why did he send her away?

She turned her head toward the sleeping form across the campfire, and smiled sadly at the sound of his exhausted snores. She rose quietly, wrapping herself in her cloak, and leaned against the trunk of a birch as her eyes wandered over the flickering campfires. Lady Roanna fitzWilliam. The thought brought a wry smile. Wife of Sir Giles, and whore in the camp of Edward Plantagenet.

Her thoughts drifted, longingly, back to those sweet hours in the middle of the night, that last time she had awoken in Giles's arms. The memory of his mouth kissing her awake, his hands playing lightly over her body until she responded sleepily with soft, pleading moans. The sound of his soft, deep laughter when he knew she was awake—interrupted suddenly by the pounding on the chamber door. Giles had muttered profanity as he swung his feet to the floor, pulling on his chausses, and admitted the agitated form of Rodger Farnham to their bedchamber. Poor Rodger, so recently returned from Wales, only to find himself amid a war. The war had begun that morning.

Damn you, Simon de Monfort! She bit her lip against the resentment, the rushing feeling of hatred that went through her. But she knew that this bitterness was not for the man, but for the fates that had turned her life upside down and now threatened the one she cared about most in this life.

If only the countess had been there! Eleanor could have spoken reason to Giles—convinced him that a woman could give strength to a man's cause! But Eleanor was at Odiham Castle in the south. . . .

Roanna drew a steadying breath, leaning her head back against the tree and gazing up at the drifting fog that swirled among the branches above her. Who are you trying to fool? she thought. You did it yourself. Perhaps he did send you away because he sought to protect you—that is what he insisted, after all. Or, perhaps it was that he could no longer bear to listen to the wretch you had become. You spoke your mind, opening it to him, and he now hates you for making him see what he would someday have to face.

Oh, why could Rodger not have delayed, giving them one last moment? But the news he brought was the end of an irretrievable time, and the beginning of . . . Edward had finally escaped his captivity, Rodger reported. The earl of Surrey and William of Valence had landed in England, and with them forces to support the Plantagenet heir. Simon was in Wales, attempting to subdue those who would have attempted to release the prince, unaware that it was now a wasted effort. The countess had left Odiham swiftly, with the decisiveness that could only be envied by her brothers. With only a shepherd to guide her across the narrow mountain paths, she had made her way across England to Dover to secure the eastern ports against an invasion supported by France.

". . . the message must reach her, Rodger, and swiftly. If you leave immediately . . ." Roanna barely heard the conversation. She could only think of the fact that, upon Simon's departure, Giles had been charged to defend Kenilworth. She knew that he would fulfill that pledge upon his life. And she saw, when they were again alone, the turmoil that stormed within him. Compelled, despite an inner voice that cried out for caution, she turned to him.

"What are you going to do?"

"Do?" He looked at her quizzically. "I have been charged to defend Kenilworth."

"Kenilworth is rock and mortar."

"It is the passage to the west." He looked at her strangely for a moment, then crossed to a table to pour himself a goblet of wine. He glanced at her and smiled, but the smile did not reach his eyes. "Go on, my love, your silence is fascinating. The very fact of it warns me to caution."

Again she heard the warning voice, but once again she ignored it. "I cannot be silent and watch you destroy yourself. You are wrong in what you are doing."

Had pain crossed his eyes? Now, thinking back, she could not be certain. She could only remember the sudden coldness that entered them. Leaning against the wall near the hearth, he had smiled grimly. "Go on. I cannot wait to hear this, Roanna. After all, we both know this has been a long time in coming. Say it."

Indeed, it had been a long time in coming. She drew a breath, and plunged forward. "You believe in what has been given to the common man. I've seen it in you in countless ways; I saw the excitement in your face when you returned from the Great Parliament. You love Simon, I can understand that. 'Twas he who shaped the dream we both share.

But there is another, one who will make it a reality, not just a dream. For you, if not for England, I have prayed that Simon and Edward would find peace and work together for what could be. But they did not, and thus they have forced you to make a choice. You love Simon, but that love will not be enough if you see all that you believe in destroyed! Giles, you are Edward's man, not Simon's."

He stared at her, his face contorting with disbelief. "By the bloody, suffering gods," he swore. "Roanna, of all the inane things I've heard you say . . . I'd laugh if it didn't make me so damn crazy!"

"Why? Because I speak for that wasteful libertine? Giles, I have much to learn, but I am street-smart. On those docks I've served and listened—to lords, priests, merchants, sailors, and the dregs of humanity—and I've learned. When men are young, they puff with pride and react as their emotions dictate. While age should grant wisdom, too often youthful braggarts become elderly bores. But there are those who emerge with wisdom, and a blessed few who become leaders. Something touches their lives to change them, to transform a disguised, inner strength. Edward was so touched, in large measure by Simon, and the boy, the libertine, became a man."

She drew a breath, trembling. He was silent, but she could not tell by his expression how her words had affected him. "Giles, what happened to you when your father found you in that stable? You could have lived your life irrevocably embittered. But you responded to the love he offered you. You grew to the man you are today—can you credit Edward with less?"

He glared at her. "If you knew anything about my father, you would know that the blood flowing through me is that of loyalty. Yet you, my loving wife, see me as a man who could dishonor that to which I have pledged myself."

"Oh, Giles," she said with gentle sadness, feeling his anguish. "It is your position that is damned, not your motives. You could never be disloyal. Your father died, leaving you to Eleanor's care—and to Simon's. Yet I wonder what your father would be doing if he were alive today? He would have continued to manage the king, I would imagine, and thus would support Edward, guide him.

"Uncle Roscoe once said to me that you are a Marshal,

the only Marshal left to England. I believe that your position, of all those who have come before you, is the hardest. You did not choose the side that claims your loyalties; it was decided for you, right or wrong. And it is you who will have to live with the results—unless you claim your destiny."

"My destiny?" He laughed emptily, and drank from his goblet. "I am nothing in this scheme, Roanna."

She rose and crossed the few feet between them, gripping his arm. "Nothing? Oh, Giles, he said it himself! He pleaded with you for understanding! Edward reached out to you, the stableboy become a knight! You are unique! Only you, of all of them, can tell him what he needs to know! And you are bound to him, Giles, by blood and marriage; thus none can deny your place beside him!"

He glanced down at the hand resting on his arm and then his gaze rose to meet hers. His voice was light, and she could not read what lingered in those blue eyes that were fixed with her own. "I thought you were asleep when we talked."

"I was, for the last of it, but not until I heard what I wanted to hear." She did not realize, at first, what he was doing as he reached up and pushed her hand slowly from his arm.

"I told you that I would always listen to what you had to say, and I have given you that courtesy." He reached up and touched her cheek, regret crossing his expression, softening his anger. "I have loved you well," he said absently. Then he seemed to gather himself, and his eyes hardened. "Go back to bed, Roanna—now," he added firmly as she began to protest. "Now, without another word."

He aroused her before dawn. While she dressed, she heard the words she most dreaded; he was sending her to London for safety. Brother Vincent was to accompany her, with an escort. But it was not until she was seated on the wagon that would carry her from Kenilworth that she faced what was happening. With her escort gathered about her beneath the dawning shadows of the gate tower, she looked down at Giles as he fixed a blanket about her knees. His hand came to rest upon her thigh and their eyes locked. So much had not been said, in all of the words spoken. Her eyes lingered with his in a look of love intermingled with pain.

"I will find you in London," he said quietly. "I have no doubt that Roscoe will keep you safe."

"That he will, milord," she answered, anguished. Then her voice softened with meaning, filled with thoughts she could not say. "God keep you, my love."

Oh, Lord, their parting seemed so long ago! She loved him, oh, how she loved him; yet he had sent her away. She looked now about the encampment, the memories of those moments passing through her, and she felt herself harden. This was now, she thought. The past was gone, and the future would define itself. Of the escort Giles had sent to protect her, only the Franciscan was left; Edward's outriders had seen to that. She would never forget the disbelieving laughter of Sir Bryce as the posted guard had rushed into their night's encampment that night, his eyes wide with horror as he stammered out words of a Plantagenet army. But the knight's laughter was quickly stifled as war-horses plunged into the clearing, accompanied by battle cries declaring for the throne.

It was the Franciscan who saved her, yanking her to her feet and pulling her with him into the trees. Her mind was numb as they ran, shock blocking the reality of branches tearing at her face and clothes, of the sound of men's screams behind them. That reality returned later, much later; the sounds would remain with her for a lifetime. Suddenly the cleric had stopped, thrusting her before him into a thicket of undergrowth. She watched with vague wonder as he untied the cords about a bundle he had worn strapped to his back since they left Kenilworth. Since the morning of their departure he had not been without it; their escort had teased him about its mysterious contents, accusing him of absconding with the treasures from Kenilworth's chapel.

She stared vacantly at the treasures as he thrust them into her hands. "Put them on, milady, quickly!" he urged as, to her added shock, he began to divest himself of his cassock. She blinked as the little Franciscan, revealing the clothing beneath his cassock, was suddenly transformed into a villein, and looked down at the garments she held. Then she finally moved, changing as quickly as she could, without regard to modesty. "How did you know?" she asked breathlessly.

"I didn't, but I suspected it." He tossed her a strip of

linen to bind her hair, and she blinked, feeling an odd, uncomfortable feeling of déjà vu. "Lord Edward would not escape only to flee England with his tail between his legs. Moreover, his escape was too well planned for it to be a quirk of chance."

"Edward?" Wrapping her hair, she paused and gaped at the Franciscan. "Those were Edward's men?"

"I'd bet my cassock on it." He snorted, staring at the item in question. "Though it is not worth much at the moment." With that, he tossed it into the bushes.

"But—" She glanced after the disappearing robe. "How will this help? If we are caught, these disguises will not save us. A serf is as easily raped as a lady—and you are less protected as you are now."

"That is true, Roanna," he said grimly as he took up her discarded garments and sent them in the direction of the cassock. "But what would their reaction be, after they raped you, when they discovered who you are? Would you want them to be able to use you against Giles? Wars have been lost by hostages, and your husband holds the gate to the west."

Giles's words came back to her, and she shuddered, realizing the truth of the cleric's calmly given statement. "It cannot be Edward's army," she protested lamely. "He escaped only two days ago. . . ." Her voice trailed off; she knew, with certainty, that Edward Plantagenet was fully capable of rising like a phoenix from the ashes. "So you planned this," she said softly.

"I always carry a change of clothes when I travel," he said. "A habit acquired in my youth—when many elements of our populace did not look kindly upon grasping, greedy members of the Church. This time, however, I thought it prudent to bring a costume for you as well."

Neither spoke of the near-impossibility of reaching London on foot with Edward's men all about them. In silent agreement they set out, both resolved to accept whatever would come.

"Sweet Mother of God!" the Franciscan swore under his breath. Roanna's own shock prevented her from being startled at the unaccustomed profanity from the cleric, as she too stared, dumbfounded. Wandering throughout the night, expecting to be captured at any moment, they had come up a ridge just as dawn broke to find that they had, quite innocently, stumbled into a waiting army. From their vantage point among a copse of trees on the ridge, they stared, transfixed by the sheer size of it. Above the largest tent, in the center of the camp, flew a large, square banner bearing the three leopards of Edward Plantagenet. Roanna's stomach churned and her chest tightened into a fearful knot. So many, she thought, slightly dizzy, so many.

"Think they need a pastor?" Brother Vincent asked wryly.

She jerked her head about, blinking at the cleric. Then, realizing the impossibility of the situation, she burst out laughing. "Lud, luv, the pope 'imself couldn't absolve the sins they be about to commit!" She planted one hand on her hip and swayed a few steps forward, pausing to look back at him. "But there be one place we'll be right safe enough," she said, grinning. "Though it'll probably set ye to a lifetime on yer knees confessin'."

A hair-pulling match and a swift teeth-cracking blow to the jaw of her opponent—a talent she'd learned long ago from an admiring young sailor off a ship from the East—established them quickly in the disreputable fringes of the camp. It took her longer to soothe the appalled Franciscan. Finally, as they settled in and made camp beneath the birch copse in the spot vacated by her opponent, she managed to convince him of the necessity of her behavior. Among the thieves, prostitutes, and brigands that followed an army, newcomers were looked upon as prey, unless they could supplant a resident; thus, Roanna had picked out a leader among the camp followers, and had quickly dispatched her to the fringes.

"A tavern is no different," she assured him, to his disbelieving look as he checked the moldy blankets, left by the previous owner, for vermin. "Barmaids find positions by their will, not by right. Besides, the men encourage it—they love a good catfight—as you saw for yourself."

He shot her an astonished glance. "Your uncle allows this?" he asked angrily, forcing himself to lower his voice as an afterthought.

Understanding his shock and disapproval as she never could have a year before, she shrugged, taking the blanket from him. "Here, pass it over the fire. Singe it, and it will be clean enough. Brother—had you spent time on the docks, you would know that there are few places where one can be secure. A position as a barmaid grants a girl the protection of the owner—if he is at all reputable—as well as a bed, and food. The alternative is the docks themselves; thus a maid must fight for one of the few positions available. It may not seem right, but I, for one, do not see an alternative."

"And when they can no longer win the fight?" he muttered angrily.

"Someone else has a brief time off the docks."

"Don't you care what happens to them?"

"Of course I do—some, at least. But then, they don't live much beyond that anyway. If cold or hunger does not kill them, rotting sickness does. Be angry with me if it helps you, but there is absolutely nothing you can do about it."

The camp begrudgingly accepted the new additions. To Brother Vincent's chagrin he was passed off, with a sparkle in Roanna's eyes, as her "brother." True enough, he reasoned, except for the disturbing fact that he was also presented as the most deft cutpurse the docks of London had ever produced. His stomach had almost flipped into his mouth—while simultaneously he had been forced to offer what, he hoped, amounted to a cruel, cunning smile—when she had added that he had personally sent more than twenty men to their maker. He sent a prayer upward, his mouth frozen into the smile, as he hoped that his maker would accept that he had tried to send at least that many to Him, in spirit if not in deed.

At moments—God forgive him—he almost wished he possessed the dubious abilities Roanna credited him with, as he anguished over how he could possibly protect her from the consequences of her own declaration of trade. The thought that she might . . . but he could not consider it. She wouldn't . . .

She laughed softly at his question, so painfully asked, aware of what it cost him. "I lived at the Flying Sail for almost seventeen years. I will admit that Uncle Roscoe protected me to a great extent, but nothing he could have done would have served as my own wits served me. Trust me. I shall be the most productive whore that has ever followed an army"—she smiled as she saw him wince—"but I swear to you, no man shall touch me. Illusions, brother, illusions. They will see what they expect to see."

For all of her bravado, Roanna surprised even herself. Odd, she thought in a passing moment, one does not realize one's talents until they are suddenly forced to emerge from some elusive place within. She swiftly became established, and was recognized, with hostile and begrudging respect, as the best, most sought-after whore in camp. This happened in less than a week, yet no man had laid a hand on her. She managed it through elusiveness, a coy attitude, knowing looks and smiles, and allowing those who frequented the fringes of the camp to play against each other, as not one was prepared to admit that he had not experienced her exquisite delights amid the shadows of the copse of birch. Thus, the ultimate defense proved to be the vanity and smugness of man, a lesson Roanna had learned well, and used.

Brother Vincent played his part and—to his chagrin and pride—played it to a fare-the-well. He became a rather adept Franciscan pimp, assuaging his conscience with the knowledge that it was a play, nothing more, while trying to ignore the fact that he was having a rather glorious time, defining and refining his abilities as the London cutpurse-murderer who smoothly "arranged" Roanna's next clients. He tried not to think about the hours he would spend in penance for lying.

Unlike Brother Vincent, who was immersed in his role, Roanna knew that their charade must be short-lived. It was only a matter of time before they were found out, and only she knew how swift retribution would be. Unlike God, their newly found peers would not be merciful. But what troubled Roanna's thoughts far more than the events of their narrow, restricted world was what was happening beyond. She knew that Edward had not escaped to join a ready army merely to stand waiting.

The day after their arrival, her alarm had heightened when Edward suddenly left, taking half his army. It was three days before he returned. It was obvious by the exhausted condition of his men that they had traveled a far distance, and from the fact that some were wounded, that they had seen battle. Then, to her horror, thirteen banners were placed in the ground before Edward's pavilion; captured banners of barons who had supported Simon de Monfort.

Determined, Roanna pushed herself away from the shelter of the copse, and strolled in the direction of the lingering campfires. She had been wrong to allow the gentle brother to spy for information in her place. Giles was out there, somewhere, and she was in a position, as the Franciscan would never be, to determine what his fate would be.

The wavering campfires revealed shapes and forms she recognized; bits of conversations reached her ears as she sauntered through the camp. Part of her was chilled, recoiling from the sordidness of man that she observed in the groping forms in the shadows, the sounds that reached her. Yet she recognized this debasement with a clarity that now shocked her. She had known it all of her life; yet now it touched her strangely, recognition mixed with revulsion. She felt as one caught between two worlds, recognizing both yet unable to touch either. Suddenly, she found herself smiling. She knew, then, that neither world was to be rejected; both simply were—a fact of existence.

She watched the movement about her, the soldiers lolling about, waiting their moment with those willing to service them. She laughed softly, attracting a quizzical glance from a grizzled man-at-arms who stood nearby. Her cold, clear look quelled whatever momentary interest stirred in him, and he looked quickly away. The two worlds of her existence had focused and she knew what must be done. She felt prepared to deal with it, as perhaps no other could. Her gaze shifted to the large tent in the center of the camp, the square banner with the three leopards flying from its peak to declare that the prince was in residence. Only there would the answers be found. She would become Edward Plantagenet's whore—and it would take a lady to accomplish the task.

21

Giles stood on Kenilworth's battlements, staring across the water to the embankments beyond in total disbelief. "Christ! The bloody fool!" he swore violently. Whirling, he strode along the parapet, shouting for his horse to be brought. He rode out across the causeway with a small party of knights, reaching the encampment amid the confusion of unpacking and the raising of tents. Arriving at its center, he dismounted and strode toward the man he was seeking, his anger barely controlled.

Simon the Younger looked up from the meal that had been hastily prepared by his squire. He blinked at the fury in Giles's expression. "Have you eaten, Sir Giles? This plover is rather—"

"I did not come here to eat!" Giles snapped irritably. "Dammit, man, what are you about? The walls of Kenilworth are just beyond you!"

"My men are fatigued, I will not subject them to the overcrowded conditions they would encounter within." He waved off Giles's protest. "Leave it, man, there is nothing to fear. In a few days, when we have had time to rest, we will move west to meet with my father, squeezing the Royalists between us. Ah, you look doubtful. You are a fool, fitz-William. Edward does not even know where we are."

Giles's brain seemed to burn; for several moments he was

269

bereft of speech before such blatant stupidity. He could only stare, realizing that there was nothing he could say that would convince the young noble of his folly. His gaze lifted, wandering over the encampment, and his stomach tightened. "At least disperse the destriers," he said with more calm than he felt. "You have tethered the war-horses together. Without them—"

"Let be, fitzWilliam!" the young man exclaimed. "You were charged by my father to hold Kenilworth, not to question me or my decisions! I am in command of the barons—and the destriers," he added with a nasty smirk. "Retire behind the walls, Giles, and let be."

Giles spun on his heel, gesturing for his men to follow. He swung into the saddle, his eyes sweeping over the forming camp with disgust.

"You've done all you can, Giles," said Rodger at his side. "As it says in the Holy Book, 'fools rush in—'"

Giles leveled a silencing glare at his friend, then turned his mount and rode for the walls he was pledged to defend, leaving behind him half the baronial forces of England lazily making camp amid open meadows, just beyond the impregnable walls of Kenilworth.

It seemed that he had barely laid his head upon the pillow before the door to his chamber flew open. Half-listening to the captain's disjointed words as his squires pulled him into his armor, he quickly turned his thoughts to what had to be done. He snapped orders, crossing the wards while checking their defenses, which he had planned with such painstaking care over the past weeks, and finally reached the battlement.

If hell were real, he faced it now. To be impotent, to realize what might have been, and to know it was too late. He heard the screams, watched the butchery reflected in the moonlit lake as the world he had known crumbled before him. Those on the wall watched, as transfixed as he. He sensed them glancing at him, waiting for his command, and he set his jaw rigidly as he struggled not to answer. He knew his resources, what he could offer, and he would hold the wall at all cost. Beyond that he could do nothing—but watch.

"Edward?" Rodger asked, coming to stand at his side, his own expression fixed with a distorted fascination.

"Who else?" Giles answered calmly.

"Christ, how did he get here so quickly?"

Giles snorted, his face grim. "The only way he could—if he had been told that the barons were coming here. There are those who would trade their soul for a quid."

After a moment's silence, Rodger shook his head, and said softly, "This spy should find particular favor. Imagine Edward's surprise to discover our young Simon encamped beyond the walls."

"Indeed," Giles agreed icily. "I can only pray for the day when I shall cross the path of the one who caused this."

Just after dawn, as the bells tolled lauds, Giles left Kenilworth with his men, twenty knights and sixty-seven men-at-arms. The great castle was no longer his charge. He had given that responsibility into the hands of Simon's son, who had, the previous night, swum the lake to save himself. Exhausted, he lay sleeping in the south tower as Giles rode out with his men across the causeway, beyond the carnage left by Edward's forces, to the rolling hills beyond.

Edward was gone. He had left as swiftly as he had come. Grimly, Giles sensed what he was about. The Prince would turn his forces from the devastated northern line of resistance to what remained of the opposition—Simon de Monfort's faction somewhere in the south. Giles's last effort would be to warn Simon of what had happened and to aid him as he could. His first problem was to figure out where Simon was. The earl could not know what had happened. Thus it could be assumed that he was making every effort to reach his son. Giles had to reach him before Edward did. They rode to exhaustion, and pressed forward to outrun the prince's army, pausing only briefly to spare their mounts.

They found him as he was attempting to cross the Severn at Kempsley. Giles was ushered into his presence immediately, and he had to brace himself to keep from falling from exhaustion. Ordering him to sit, Simon dismissed those attending him and forced a goblet of wine into the younger man's hand.

"Tell me what has happened," Simon demanded grimly, staring down at the fatigued knight. "You would not have left Kenilworth without good cause." The look of unguarded anguish Giles turned to him made the earl wince.

"Edward has defeated them," Giles answered, drawing a

deep breath. "Most of the baronial leaders have been taken, including Oxford. Thirteen banners were captured, as well as all of the destriers."

"But how—" Simon blurted with disbelief. "Edward was at Worcester yesterday! You expect me to believe that he traveled more than forty miles in less than twenty-four hours—and took Kenilworth in one night! Impossible!"

"As I recall, you traveled that far once, and nearly as swiftly," Giles answered wearily. "As to how they managed to take it in one night, Kenilworth has not fallen yet. They—our forces were not within Kenilworth's walls." He regretted the pain he must cause this man he loved, but he would not garnish the truth. He respected Simon too much to lie to him. "Simon chose to encamp beyond, in the meadow. He did not believe Edward to be so near."

Simon had risen as Giles spoke. The face he now turned to him was tight with anguish, but he was in control. "How could Edward know? Only a few of us knew where I had ordered the other half of our forces to gather."

"That is a question that has been plaguing me," Giles answered, rising from his chair. "Once Kenilworth was fortified, no one was allowed to leave . . ." He paused, looking confused. Then he turned an uncomfortable look on Simon. "No one, that is, except Roanna and Brother Vincent. Eleanor had written, requesting that the Franciscan return to Odiham in her absence—I thought it best that Roanna return to London with him. I—"

"You need not explain, Giles," Simon said with a sigh. "I am glad that she is well out of it. Certainly, I do not suspect either of them. As for the rest of your news . . . you look about to drop, and I need—some time alone. Your quarters should be ready. Rest, and we shall talk later."

Geoffrey was waiting outside the earl's tent to show Giles where they had been billeted. The squire was prepared for the grim look his master wore, but he was puzzled by the distracted gaze that lingered as they walked toward the hastily erected tent. He jumped as Giles spoke suddenly.

"Geoffrey, I want a man sent to London immediately. I wish to be advised of Lady Roanna's safe arrival." As the young man hurried off, Giles paused before the tent, his eyes again becoming distant. "Roanna," he murmured, a disturbing, gnawing doubt plucking at him. She was so convinced that she was right about Edward. To what length would she go for her beliefs? Unwilling to dwell further upon his doubts, he denied them with a sigh and ducked through the flap of the tent, only to stop short, his face falling into unmasked astonishment.

"God's Blood! Landon!"

The tall knight sat tilted back in a camp chair with his booted feet propped on the camp table, holding a tankard of ale on his stomach. His face was weathered from years spent in the sun, causing crinkles at the corners of the pale blue eyes that scintillated with amusement. His hair, once sandy-blond, was now liberally sprinkled with grey, and the once lean form, while still hard, had broadened. "I hope your expertise on the battlefield has improved, Giles," he drawled, raising the tankard slightly. "Your taste in ale hasn't—it's still piss-poor."

"You sorry bastard, where did you come from?" Giles grinned with pleasure. "Get your feet off my desk."

"Get me some more of this rotgut, Farnham," Landon said easily, handing the empty tankard to Rodger, who stood nearby, grinning.

"If you find it so distasteful, don't drink it," Giles countered, leaning his hip on the edge of the table. "Besides, from the look of you, you should cut back anyway. You're getting fat, Landon."

"I can still take you on, you young dog. There isn't one damn thing I taught you that you've remembered."

"Name one," Giles answered smoothly. "I'll be glad to take you on, any time you name."

"Oh?" The older knight laughed. "Pretty confident, aren't you? As I recall, you were the only page I ever trained who could never remember not to fart at the table."

"That was Robert de Laney."

"So it was."

"So, d'Leon, what are you doing here? I trust that I still have lands in Ireland." He took the tankard Rodger offered.

"Aye, lad, we both do, though mine were always safe enough. Kinnell, on the other hand . . . Christ, Giles, what did you do to get Henry's dander up? It took me four months to beat the bastards off."

"He thinks I'm a traitor." Giles shrugged, drawing from his tankard.

"Well, you come by it honestly. He accused your father of it four times."

"But he never dared to touch what belonged to my father," Giles said evenly.

"Good point. But then, your father was more powerful than Henry was—which was the first lesson I thought I taught you: never engage when you cannot win."

"I haven't lost—yet," he observed dryly. "Moreover, I did not engage this battle, Landon; it was chosen for me."

"Really," the knight grunted, drawing from his tankard.

"Food!" Rodger interjected suddenly, beaming at the squires who had entered with mazers of roast woodcock, loaves of manchet, and a large wedge of goat cheese. "You can talk; I'm going to eat," he added, dropping into the remaining chair as he proceeded to attack the meal.

Seeing that his own chair was not going to be vacated, Giles pulled up a stool and broke off a hunk of cheese before Rodger could devour it all. "You have explained what happened, but not why you are here."

The knight's eyes softened for a moment and the corners of his mouth drew into a hint of a smile. "Why wouldn't I come, Giles?"

They exchanged a look of understanding, a moment reaching back through the years to a small, frightened boy and the squire who had befriended him. "How did you know where to find me?" Giles asked.

"I knew that you would either be here or at Kenilworth."

"Kenilworth is lost," Giles said grimly. He related the moments leading up to their appearance in Simon's camp. "The fool will never be able to hold it. Eleanor might, but she is in the east and, I fear, there is no way she will be allowed to return."

"How is she?" Landon asked softly, his voice touched with unaccustomed warmth.

"The same." Giles smiled. "Ever the same. Nay, that is not quite true; more bitter, perhaps."

"That came with Will's death, and even revenge did not unshackle it. I am not surprised, with all that has happened, that it has grown. She should have been queen in her own right. If she had been, we would not be sitting here now, facing a war."

"You have no faith in Simon?" Giles asked, slicing off a hunk of manchet.

"Simon is not our sovereign, Giles. He may attempt to

rule as one, he may even have the talent to rule, but he is not a Plantagenet. Do you remember Stephen Langton?"

"Of course I do. Archbishop of Canterbury, and the author of the Magna Carta—Lord, Landon, even if I do not recall the man, I know of the legend."

"He shared great visions with your grandfather. As they penned the Great Charter, his mind fevered beyond it. Perhaps a touch of madness is part of true vision, and greatness cannot come without it—at least, it seems to be so. Langton used to speak of a time when men would elect their leaders, all men, not just a few. Your grandfather declared that it would be anarchy. The answer is beyond me—though I have thought upon it often in the years past."

"I recall. Remember, my father spent his early years of knighthood with Langton. We talked often of those times," Giles said, reflecting. "Anarchy? Perhaps, but it seems to me that we could do worse, and we have. To accept whatever is given from the marriage bed has proven rather chancy. However, corruption of a system of elected rule concerns me far more than poor decisions by the masses. I wonder if we would not be thrown into a continual, secret state of war by those who would seek power? Our given rulers may often be lacking, but I fear most what I do not see."

"Be that as it may, my friend, the question is, at least for the moment, not in dispute. We still must deal with the product of that royal marriage bed, and it is that bed Simon seeks to ignore. Yet, we have not the structure, nor the understanding, to ignore it. The blood the Plantagenets give, and they do offer their blood to us, is something we can understand."

"Simon has offered new hope, new vision for England," Giles argued.

"Aye, the Great Parliament. The common man speaking to form his own laws. He has given that to us, Giles, and it shall be remembered forever, perhaps someday to be built upon. But that alone must be his destiny." Seeing the shadow that crossed Giles's face, he smiled sadly. "Giles, your father could have taken the throne with little effort. Once, when he was struggling yet again to deal with a maddened king, I asked him why he did not. He looked at me and smiled. 'Landon,' he said, 'I am not a king, but a king-maker. A far more difficult position in which to be, as the vision must be preserved.'

"I did not understand what he meant until after he died. His loss was never filled. But I know, now, that a king is only as strong as those who support him, those who create the vision. Even if he is merely a figurehead, it is a vital role, Giles. Man must have something to look up to on this earthy plane, heaven being beyond him for another time. Not God on earth, but a man, someone his subjects can curse, blame, revere—and love. Simon will make us feel common. Oh, he will give us a measure of freedom, but if he continues to rule, in the end we will hate him for it because he is just like us."

Deep silence fell over the tent. Rodger's brow was furrowed; Geoffrey stood silent in the shadows. Giles's eyes were unfocused as he gave into his own thoughts, and Landon watched him with a slight smile. Where had the years gone? he wondered. The boy, the squire, the man withdrawing into the private realm of his own thoughts. He cleared his throat, breaking the silence. "I understand you've married."

Giles turned his head to regard the knight with an amused smile. "Sorry you could not be there. She swept me off my feet."

"It was rather abrupt," Landon agreed. "What happened, did you have to make an honest woman of her?"

Rodger began coughing.

Giles's eyes glinted darkly. "That is none of your damned business, d'Leon," he said smoothly.

"It's been my business since the first wench you bedded at fifteen," Landon countered with a grin. "I recall that she set her brothers on you—wanting marriage—though she had not seen her maidenhead since she leapt into the hay with one of my brother squires a full five years before. Would have caused a rather nasty episode if I hadn't paid her off—over your satisfied, cocky grin—and from my own pocket, you ungrateful pup."

"Do you want the coin now?" Giles said with a laugh.

"Nay, just tell me about your lady."

"She's—she's a termagant." Giles smiled, unaware of the warmth that leapt to his eyes. "She is the most impossible, unreasonable woman I've ever met. She reminds me of grandmere. And she's beautiful, the most beautiful woman I've ever seen."

"Where is she? I'd like to meet this paragon."

"She—" Giles hesitated, rejecting the thought that flitted through his mind. "She is in London." Turning the subject aside, he was unaware of Landon's interest, the slight raising of a greying brow, as Giles's hesitation was caught, to be examined again.

The paragon was shrieking a stream of oaths as she clawed wildly at the arms that gripped her. Managing to set her teeth into the arm of her captor, she landed the heel of her boot just below his kneecap and found her freedom as he released her with a grunt of pain. The uproarious laughter of his fellow guards stopped abruptly with her sudden release, and hands groped for her as she managed the last few feet and flung herself into the tent.

In hot pursuit, the guards caught her just inside the large canvas pavilion. "Let me go, you bloody bastards!" she shrieked, flailing her arms in an attempt to free herself, her fist meeting successfully with the nose of one of the guards.

"What is the meaning of this!" a voice roared.

"Beg pardon, milord," one of the guards grunted as he managed to catch a kicking leg. "She got by us."

"She got by you," the voice repeated cuttingly. "How many of you? Let her go."

"Milord—" the other guard protested, holding a bloody nose. "She's just a whore—probably has a knife on her—"

"I said, let her go. The wench has obviously gone to a great deal of trouble to see me. As for my safety, Gloucester here will be glad to protect my person, should the need arise. Won't you, Gilbert? Think you can handle it?"

"I believe so, Your Grace," the other said dryly. "However, it may be prudent to search her."

"Perhaps," Edward Plantagenet agreed, smiling affably. "Is it necessary to search you, wench? Do you have a knife concealed about you—one, perhaps meant for my belly?"

"If I did, your men would now be missing a few parts," she snarled, her voice muffled against the shoulder of one of the men holding her.

Edward laughed as the guards let her go, still watching her warily. His amusement ceased abruptly, however, as she stepped away from them and her coif remained clutched in the hands of one of the men. Her hair tumbled about her shoulders in all of its glory.

"Corp an Chriost!" Edward gasped. "Roanna! Where in blazes did you come from?"

"I've been right here, Your Grace, the past week."

"Here?" His face paled, for her garb left little doubt as to what part of his camp had sheltered her. His gaze shifted to the gaping guards. "Leave us!" he snapped. As they departed, with obvious reluctance, he sat down heavily on the edge of his war-table and stared at her. "Are you telling me, Roanna, that you have been in the—ah, fringes of my camp this week past?"

"Aye, milord. Brother Vincent is here, too."

Edward's eyes widened. Before he could respond, Gloucester cleared his throat uncomfortably. "Obviously you know this—person—milord. Would you care to enlighten me?"

Edward glanced at the other man, his eyes narrowing in a moment's study, then glinting with amusement. "How thoughtless of me. Of course, you must be introduced. After all, the lady is your cousin."

Gloucester sputtered, glancing back and forth between Edward's grin and Roanna's own astonishment. His complexion warmed within shades of his carrot-hued hair, and his broad shoulders stiffened. "I fail to appreciate the jest, Your Grace," he growled.

"Your lack of humor is not the issue, Gilbert." Edward grinned, then he affected great seriousness. "Gilbert de-Clare, my earl of Gloucester, may I present Lady Roanna fitzWilliam, recent bride to our favored cousin."

Two pairs of eyes turned to him with shock, Gloucester's with disbelief, Roanna's with wonder at how he could know that she had married Giles so recently. Gloucester recovered first and he glared at Roanna with contempt. "Giles married a—"

"—a lovely young woman," Edward finished for him, his eyes hardening, a fact that the earl missed. Rising from the edge of the table, Edward held out his hand to Roanna. "Come, milady, sit down. You must have supper with me." He ignored the sound of Gilbert's intake of breath and continued to smile at Roanna as he addressed the disapproving earl. "Gilbert, on your way out, advise my cook that there shall be a guest for supper."

"Your Grace—we have little time—"

"There is always time to sup with a beautiful woman," Edward responded easily.

Hearing finality in the prince's tone, Gloucester left the tent, muttering under his breath.

"Now, tell me why you are here," Edward said when they were alone.

"We were on our way to London when we were waylaid by your men," she explained. "My escort was killed, and Brother Vincent and I barely escaped with our lives. We stumbled into your camp and took refuge among the camp followers."

"Just like that."

"Just like that—milord."

"Good God, how did you manage it? Tell me, I am fascinated."

His hearty laughter drew bemused looks from the squires who entered the tent a little later, bearing supper. To their disbelieving eyes, he was sitting across the table from a comely harlot who was apparently entertaining the prince with nothing more than conversation. "Brother Vincent the procurer," he said, still chuckling and wiping away tears. "Sweet Mother. You kept this up for six days? How did he manage to, ah, arrange your—appointments—without ever actually bringing one of them to you?"

"He made lists."

"Lists?"

"Aye. He'd put their names on a list, telling them that he would inform them when their name came to the top. Obviously, we could not have kept up the game much longer." She paused as the food was set before them. Her eyes widened at the display, her mouth instantly watering at the aroma. "Lud, I've not eaten such fare since I left Kenilworth. We've scrambled for what we could. Do you think that I could . . . that is—"

"Where is he?" Edward said, smiling.

"Somewhere out there. We had quite a row when he knew I was going to come here."

"John," Edward said, gesturing to one of the squires. "Somewhere, out in the shadows, is a short, portly man who is watching this tent like a hawk. See that he is properly fed. And John," Edward added as the squire turned to do his bidding. "Be respectful. The man is a Franciscan." He smiled at John's shocked expression, and then gestured dismissively to the other squire. "You may leave also, Miles."

The two squires exchanged amused looks as they left, closing the tent flap behind them.

"I believe that they misread your intention, Your Grace," Roanna said, fixing her eyes on the tightly closed tent entrance, then shifting them back to Edward, who was dishing her a portion of pickled lampreys. "Or did they?"

"Is that a question or a request, Roanna?" he asked quietly.

"A question, milord. I am in love with my husband."

"I never doubted that, my dear. But 'tis a pity," he sighed. "Moreover, at the moment I deeply regret that I am so fond of Giles. Pheasant?" he offered. "It is particularly good, the cook stuffs them with grapes."

"I should be serving you, milord."

"Nonsense, it pleases me to offer this meal to you. You should have come to me before, Roanna. In spite of your entertaining stories, it does not please me to think of you there. You will enjoy this Gascon wine."

"How could I come to you before? You left the day I arrived," she countered, her voice growing tight as she approached the reason she had come. "Then you returned —with those thirteen banners that are placed before your tent."

He set the ewer of wine on the table and glanced at her as he began to cut his pheasant. "Undoubtedly you are aware that Giles's banner is not among them. We did not take Kenilworth, Roanna, and as far as I know, Giles is still there."

She felt momentarily light-headed with relief and it was a moment before she could speak again. "Please," she pleaded softly. "Tell me about it."

She listened intently as he spoke, biting her lip a few times to keep from interrupting with questions. The most pressing one, that which kept pounding through her mind as he recounted the battle, was how he had known? Who had carried word to him, so swiftly, that Simon the Younger and the baronial forces were to be found at Kenilworth?

Then an idea came to her, even as caution whispered its warning. Easy, Roanna, she thought. Go easy.

"Thank God that Giles is safe," she murmured as he finished.

"No concern for the others, Roanna?" he asked, arching a tawny brow.

"You were correct, this wine is delicious. Not particularly, milord. If I had had my way, Giles would be here with me, not with them."

"Sir Giles the procurer?" he chuckled, imagining the prospect.

"Nay, milord," she answered evenly. "Sir Giles, knight to Edward Plantagenet."

He stared at her for a moment, his eyes boring into hers. Then he smiled wryly. "It is most wise to choose the winning side. But then, I never credited you with stupidity, Roanna."

"It has yet to be proved that you will win, milord."

"Ah, I see. Faith and loyalty to the Crown."

"Not to the Crown, Your Grace. To Edward Plantagenet."

He fingered the stem of his goblet, his eyes narrowing as he studied her. "Mistress, either you are as you claim and exceptionally loyal, or you are a great liar. It has not been my experience to find loyalty in de Monfort's allies."

"There is only one among de Monfort's camp to whom I owe allegiance, milord—my husband. Moreover, there is no baron in England, the earl of Leicester included, that I care a whit about. I am of the London docks, and but for what I give to my husband, therein lies my heart."

"You were given much at Kenilworth. Have you no feeling for those there, not even gratitude?"

"Gratitude?" She laughed bitterly. "For what? To be looked down upon? A favored horse is better treated."

"Eleanor befriended you."

"She used me for her own purposes. I was valuable only as a pawn, serving as a link to her husband's forces through coded messages passed to Giles. When I dared to speak my mind to her, she locked me in a windowless room for weeks on end. Oh, aye, I owe her much." Noting the lack of surprise in Edward's expression, Roanna caught her breath and reached for her tankard, as if to soothe her emotions, while actually seeking to cover the realization that her suspicions were true. He knew all of what had happened. Whoever was spying for him had done so for a long time. So much for wondering how he knew of her marriage to Giles.

She lingered over her wine in order to collect her thoughts. Truth sprinkled liberally with lies, she thought, it was the only way. In spite of her feelings toward Edward, she had to know who had been informing on them. The very thought of a spy living among them, telling of their every movement, endangering the lives of those she cared about, caused her stomach to churn. Sighing, she set the goblet on the table. Affecting a serious look, one touched with sorrow and concern, she raised her eyes to his.

"I am not adept at words, milord, but I—I believe you to be the man we have been waiting for since the Conqueror. A real king for England. A man of England. Giles feels the same, though he does not know it yet. That is the heart of it. We had a bloody fine row before I left, discussing the matter. That was the reason I was sent away."

"Such honesty deserves the same, milady," Edward answered, smiling gently. "I know that he is struggling with himself. His dilemma does not pass me by. He is the one man within my enemy's camp whom I could forgive for his transgressions. But that forgiveness can only be a personal one. Though I may love him, treason cannot be forgiven. Those who have committed offenses against the Crown must, without exception, suffer the results."

She drew a steadying breath, and closed her eyes against his words, feeling a moment of death brush her. Everything else of importance fled, leaving her empty and bereft of all feeling. "Even—even Eleanor?" she asked, to divert his attention. "She is your aunt, one who loved you well—until all of this."

"Even Eleanor," he answered grimly. "Aye, she did love me well. I understand how she feels, and I cannot disagree with her feelings toward my father. I would not forgive him, had he done to me what he committed against her."

"Then why—"

"Because it is treason," he said sharply. "Henry Plantagenet is king of England. The barons who now raise arms against him once gave him their oaths of fealty. Those oaths are what we live by, Roanna. They are the strength of this nation, its unity. That unity must be preserved." His voice became gentle as he saw the anguish in her eyes. "One makes choices, Roanna. Eleanor has been given the chance to make one now, and will live by the results of that decision. I wrote her at Chatham, giving her the opportunity to return, and repent. It is up to her."

Roanna's eyes dropped to the goblet she held between her hands, and she struggled to mask her nervousness, the sudden, erratic beating of her heart. Odd, she thought distractedly, to know now, when she no longer cared. Edward's words had vanquished everything but thoughts of Giles. Yet now, with Edward's last words, she knew for certain the identity of the spy.

22

"Nay, Giles, Edward does not fight for his father's throne, but his own. Henry is done."

Simon de Monfort smiled sadly at the rigidity in the younger man's face as they sat facing each other in the commander's tent. "Oh, Henry's banner flies above this camp, and within his tent he plays king. But in truth, he has not been king of England since the battle of Lewes. Edward fights with anger, to punish me and the barons who fight with me, for what has been done to his father—and even for what was done to his mother. The queen broods in London, reminding him, until he will never forgive us for what happened to her when she attempted to flee the Tower. But more than anything, he is a man who fights with a sense of his own destiny, which makes him a dangerous opponent."

Staring at a distant point, Giles turned his gaze to Simon. "Why do you persist in this? You must turn to London, go away from here. He is waiting for you."

Simon shook his head. "I will not abandon my son, nor the forces remaining with him."

"It is suicide."

"Perhaps." The older man shrugged. "But I must make the attempt."

Giles left the earl soon after. Confused, needing to be alone, he avoided his tent and made his way to a small knoll overlooking the vale of Evesham. Landon found him there, leaning against the trunk of an ancient oak whose weight of years Giles felt to be barely heavier than his own. The older knight came to stand beside him in silent companionship.

"He could send to Edward to parley," Giles said at last, his voice filled with pain as he continued to stare out at the distant, shadowed landscape.

"There will be no truce."

"They are damn fools, the both of them! Together they could—"

"—destroy each other," Landon interrupted calmly. "The master gives knowledge, but the student must, by nature, become superior to what he has learned. It is the last lesson."

"Then it is inevitable."

"When the teacher will not relinquish his position. Hindsight is a most uncomfortable viewpoint, one which both Simon and Edward must be considering tonight. There were so many moments in their lives when they could have altered the outcome. Now it is too late."

A long silence fell between them. Finally Landon spoke again. "What will you do?"

"Do?" Giles laughed shortly. "What I am pledged to do. There is no choice."

"There are always choices." Landon glanced sideways at Giles's profile. "You said to me that your greatest fear was of that which you could not see. In that event, your greatest fear must be apathy—not the apathy of one who does nothing, but the greater danger, the apathy of one who claims a duty he does not believe in, yet acts upon it in fear of the alternative."

"I—I cannot go against Simon," Giles said through clenched teeth. "I am pledged to Eleanor—"

"Eleanor is wrong!" Landon snapped angrily. "Your pledge was founded in blind, misguided love, not loyalty!" He ignored the angry jerk of the younger man's head. "Loyalty can only be given based on a principle, not an emotion. Giles, emotion has ruled Eleanor's head for years, ever since the morning she awoke to understand truly the depth of her brother's depravity. I was there, Giles, and in the years that followed. Christ, man, she could have done so much! The barons were in shock; to a man they were appalled, shaken by what had happened to your father. A word, Giles, one word, and they would have rallied to her! She had the ability and the power to use the love and reverence that was held for your father, to make his death mean something! But what did she do? She set up a purge of meaningless revenge. Perhaps the worst sin of all is how she handled Henry. No one, not even your father, could bend him as she could then. Yet she abandoned that opportunity, because first she wanted revenge, and then she wanted de Monfort."

"She spent thirteen years alone!" Giles protested.

"Aye, alone and grieving. Her only nourishment was the revenge she took, fed by self-pity. And now there will be a war, and many men will die tomorrow. She could have stopped it, Giles, years ago. With Henry, the brother and king whom she could bend like a reed to her will; the barons, who would have rallied to her upon a word; or Edward, who so adored her that she could have shaped events to help him lead us, without the battle that now faces us—or even the ones that have gone before."

"You would make her the devil incarnate," Giles said sulkily.

"So it would seem," he said sadly. "It may seem odd, but I love her, too. Who cannot feel so who has known her? But we were speaking of choices. You have yours before you now, Giles, and it must be made from your heart, your inner voice, not your head. Do not hold yourself to any man—or woman—because of something born of habit that has formed into a misguided idea of honor."

"Those who went before me were men of loyalty. Can I strive to be less?"

"Loyalty is not inherited, Giles. You must find it within yourself. You can only be loyal to that which you truly believe in."

Upon arrangement, Giles arrived at the appointed hour and was admitted to the magnificent pavilion located in the center of the camp. He paused just within the entrance, suddenly wondering why he had felt it so necessary to come. Pushing his doubts aside, he genuflected, murmuring his respects. "Your Grace, I am grateful that you allowed this audience."

"You may be seated," the king of England responded

affably, gesturing to the chair to his right. Still lean, his glorious mane of blond hair now heavy with grey, he fixed his Plantagenet blue eyes, so like Eleanor's, on the younger man. His expression became vaguely confused, and he frowned as Giles sat down. "You resemble your father," he said, somewhat distantly.

"So it has been said, Your Grace."

"Are you like him in manner as well?"

"In some ways, milord."

"Of course you would be," Henry said. "You are his son—his only true son." He nodded to his attendants, who stepped forward to pour them wine. "A pity that you were not legitimate. As it is, I cannot grant you much."

"I do not ask anything of you, milord."

"If that is so, you are unique, Sir Giles," the king said with a laugh. "You will understand my doubt. God, you look like him." Henry took a long draught from his tankard, then wiped the corners of his mouth with a kerchief. "You have a good man in d'Leon; he handily repelled my attempts against you. I understand he is here. I should have him hung for his resistance."

"So you should, milord, had I been proven to be a spy—and as would I, had you bested him."

"Well said!" Henry laughed. "Now, tell me the truth, fitzWilliam; are you for me, or no?"

"I have not decided, Your Grace," Giles answered evenly.

Henry started, taken aback. "Saint George, you are blunt! I could have your head for such impertinence!"

"Not by the law, milord. I have not given my oath to any man, nor have those who serve me."

Henry's gaze fixed upon him keenly for a moment; then he grinned. "God's Breath, you are like him! He would lay his neck under my boot, and laugh at me as he did it! Aye, your father was unique among men, Giles. I loved him dearly. Never again have I had a friend like him."

Is that why you had him murdered? Giles wondered.

"Ah, the times we spent together," Henry sighed. "How I miss him." He looked over the tray at his side and selected a sweetmeat. "There is so much to tell. I remember once . . ."

Giles stumbled out of the pavilion. He reached the grove on the perimeter of the camp and braced himself against the trunk of a tree, willing himself not to be sick. Losing the battle, he bent against the trunk and lost the contents of his stomach, retching again and again until he could retch no more. He straightened and dragged his hand over his mouth, tasting the bitterness that was left. His soul was sickened, tainted with what he had heard. All of his life, his father had followed that pathetic form of a man. . . .

A legacy, an almost irrevocable, binding legacy. For a moment he hated his father, someone he had respected, revered, loved so totally. Landon had been right about one thing; there was nothing that existed beyond one's own vision of reality. Beyond it, nothing could be believed, or trusted.

The moon drifted from behind the clouds, lending an eerie quality to the shadows of the trees, conjuring the thought of specters and ghosts wafting silently through the fog-shrouded night. The party of men was silent; the only sounds rising from it were an occasional snort of a horse's breath as it softly protested the tension sensed from the men, the muted clank of armor against leather, and the dull thud of hooves striking against the hard-packed ground.

The rush of water could be heard beyond the trees that lay just ahead, where ran the river Avon. The crossing would be irrevocable, and that knowledge was uppermost in the minds of those in the party as they approached the shadows before them. The light and warmth of campfires lay behind, but they pressed forward silently.

Giles carried the heavy weight of responsibility for his followers, who were bound to him by a loyalty he had only begun to accept. Their trust amazed him, and touched him with guilt. They had drawn their lots, knight, squire, and man-at-arms, accepting Giles's decision with an ease that left him restless. Never before had he truly felt the weight of obligation to others. Oh, it was power that he had recognized in others. That or their lack of it. But, he realized now, he had always expected his men to give to him what he had agonized over giving to another.

They entered the trees and he felt himself relaxing, his fear for their safety disappearing in the knowledge that they had managed to depart undetected. He turned in his saddle to give orders releasing the men from silence, but then the words caught in his throat. The bright moonlight that cut through the drifting fog illuminated Landon's face as the knight stared at a point beyond him, his eyes wide with disbelief. Jerking about in his saddle, Giles drew his breath in sharply, even as he raised his hand to halt the column.

Landon drew his mount even with Giles's. "I will hold them here," he said evenly.

Giles slid from the saddle, tossing the reins to the knight, and walked slowly forward toward the shadows. He stopped before the figure waiting beneath the trees at the edge of the forest. "How did you know?" he asked softly.

"I knew the moment you left camp," Simon answered.

"I thought we had done it rather well," Giles said with a rueful smile.

"You did. I would not have known but that I expected it. Do not concern yourself, Giles. No one knows but me, and those I set to watch you."

"Yet you allowed me to leave."

Simon reached out and laid his hand upon the younger man's shoulder. "I did not come to condemn you, but to say farewell. I ask only one thing of you . . ."

"You have but to ask."

"I know, and thus I will request only what you can freely give. Send word to Eleanor—your message will get through to her, where mine will not. Tell her that I love her, that she was last in my thoughts."

Giles swallowed against the pain that rushed through him. "Nothing has been decided, milord."

"Oh, Giles." Simon laughed softly. "Do not seek to humor me, not you, not now. As ever, between us let there be only truth. I came to tell you not to grieve for me. I do not wish it to end like this—there is so much more that I want to do; a moment more . . . But I do not discount my accomplishments. I have done more than most, and realized many dear dreams, and in that I am blessed. You will not understand until you reach my age, Giles, but peace is found in knowing that one's life has been full, and that one has been loved, truly loved."

"You have but to ask me to stay," Giles said in a strained voice.

"Why would I? Oh, Giles, was I not once your age? Do not insult me by implying that I do not remember what it is to dream, to know that sense of purpose that leads you forth. Do not go from here with guilt, nor with regret, but with the knowledge that I am proud of you, that you will give what I no longer can."

"Simon . . ." Giles choked out.

Simon pulled the younger man to him, clasping him in a quick embrace. "Go you to your fate, Giles fitzWilliam," he said thickly, holding him at arm's length. "Giles, son of William, do not forget me."

He was gone, disappearing into the darkness. Giles stared after him for a long moment, until he heard a rustle beside him. Looking up, he met Landon's gaze. Wordlessly, the older knight bent down and handed him the reins of his mount. Giles swung into the saddle and turned the destrier's head toward the Avon, riding into the dawning sun, leaving behind him only shadows.

"Declare yourself and state your business!" the sergeant repeated, the sharp impatience in his voice causing his men to tighten their circle threateningly about the group of riders. Giles's destrier shifted nervously, recalling his attention from the stand of baronial banners that waved in the light August breeze. Angered by the sight of the captured coats of arms, Giles quickly turned to the soldier.

"My business is with Lord Edward; my coat of arms is well known to you," he snapped. "You will stand aside and let us pass or, by God, I'll run you through where you stand!"

"Your business is with me, Sir Giles, and your banner declares you for de Monfort. Dismount and surrender your weapons, or my men will cut you down!"

In a flash of metal, the tip of Giles's sword was at the man's beefy neck. "So, you do recognize the lion of my arms," he said softly. "Then you must know its teeth to be those of a Marshal. The king's nephew does not conduct business with a soldier. Step aside, man, or you will die where you stand."

Doubt crossed the sergeant's expression as beads of sweat began to form on his brow. "Let them pass," he growled, as his dark eyes flashed with hatred.

Spurring his mount forward, Giles glanced at Rodger, frowning at his friend's grin. "What is so damned funny?"

"You," Rodger said, chuckling. "All of your life you have rejected being the king's nephew."

"My acknowledgment quite possibly just saved our lives, Rodger," Giles observed grimly. "Would you have preferred to see our coats of arms among those?" he added, jerking his head toward the captured banners as they passed.

"Of course not. But I can't help but wonder if you will use the same tactics with Edward. We may still see our banners there."

They drew up before the royal tent and dismounted, handing their reins to the soldiers who hurried forward. Rodger laid a hand on Giles's arm. "I once told you that my fortune is aligned with yours, Giles," he said, all trace of humor gone. "If your banner is struck this day, mine will gladly follow, as there will be nothing left for any of us."

Giles nodded solemnly, touched by his friend's words, then turned to announce himself to the guard. In a few moments the guard returned to say that the prince would see him—alone. Removing his helm, Giles handed it to Geoffrey and grinned at his friends. "Try not to get into trouble out here—no dicing or women."

"I'll try." Rodger shrugged. "At least about the dicing."

Ducking his head, he stepped into the coolness of the large tent. Edward was standing by a large oak war-table, scanning a sheet of vellum when he entered. Bending to the table, the prince took up a quill, scratched his signature across the bottom, then handed the page to a waiting knight. As the man left, Edward looked at Giles for the first time. Then, to Giles's surprise, he ordered the others in the tent to leave.

When they were alone, Edward propped his hip on the table and took up the quill, turning it in his fingers as he stared at it thoughtfully. "You have come to me armed, Giles. Is it to be war between us?"

"No sane man would travel unarmed in these times, milord," Giles answered evenly. "As for what will happen between us, that will be for you to decide. If you would know of my intention, ask me directly and I will answer in truth."

Edward snorted. "Giles, I am ever surrounded by tongues that weave and evade their true purpose. I had forgotten how blatantly honest you can be—but a diplomat you are not."

"I do not believe that diplomacy should be used by the inexperienced. In the mouth of one who does not understand its true purpose, it is nothing more than smoothly spoken lies."

"And that it is, more often than not." Edward grinned and then sobered as he regarded Giles keenly. "Can I trust you, Giles fitzWilliam?" he asked.

"You can, milord. However, as you once said, you should not ask a question unless you are prepared to hear the answer."

"And if I were to ask a question, one you did not want to answer—how would you respond?"

"I simply would not do so."

"If I ordered you to?"

"I would not do so."

Edward paused thoughtfully. "Sit down, Giles. You need not stand." He gestured to the chair in front of the war-table. As Giles took the seat, he pushed a goblet of wine over to him, then filled another for himself. "You were in Kenilworth when I attacked, weren't you?"

"I was."

"Simon the Younger escaped. Is he safe?"

"He is."

"Many others escaped that night. How many?"

"I will not tell you that, milord."

A tawny brow arched at the answer, but Edward merely snorted in humor. "You came here from Simon. Nay, do not deny it, I know that you did. Furthermore, I know that he has crossed the Severn. Where is he, Giles?"

"I cannot answer that question either, milord."

"Cannot?"

"Will not."

"I see." Edward paused, drinking from his goblet. "Why are you here? Certainly not to spy on me—you know that I would never allow you to leave here alive. Have you brought a message to me from Simon?"

"Nay, Lord Edward. I have come to give you my fealty."

Edward's blond head jerked up and his eyes widened. "Now, *that* surprises me." His handsome mouth drew into a grin. "Tell me, dear cousin; whatever has brought this about? Whyever would you give your oath to one you loathe?"

"I do not loathe you anymore, Edward. Quite the contrary, I have come to believe that you are the man for England."

The prince chuckled. "So, you admit it. You did loathe me once."

"Unquestionably. You were of the mold of your grandfather, John—or so I believed. I was wrong."

"Nay, you were not." Edward sighed. "But now, tell me. Why have you left Simon?"

"I will not discuss Simon with you, Your Grace. He is a part of my past that is locked away. It is for me to deal with those memories, only me."

"Oh, but it is not, cousin. Definitely not. You come to me from my enemy, declaring that you will give me your oath. What assurances do I have of your faith?"

"You have my word."

"Ahhh, your word," Edward countered smoothly. "And what of the oath you gave to de Monfort?"

Giles drew a breath, the memory of his parting from Simon still painful. "The only man to whom I have ever bent my knee was my father. To Simon, I gave love, never my oath. I am a free man, milord, my fealty is unbound."

Edward considered this answer for a moment. "Giles, your father was marshal of England, thus he was keeper of the Code. I trust that he taught you well in the verse of chivalry?"

"He did. I would not betray my oath, upon death."

"Yet you will not answer my questions regarding the baronial cause. Will you do so, once you have given your oath to me?"

"Nay, milord."

"How can you justify this?"

Giles drew a steadying breath and regarded Edward evenly. "Milord, I am a culmination of all that I have ever been, and known. Simon de Monfort is a large part of what I am. Even the strength I have drawn upon to come here has come, in large measure, from him. I will never betray that part of me. I believe in Simon; I no longer believe in his methods. I tried, many times, to convince him to make peace with you, as I believe that through you solutions will be found to finish what he began. It was this, the cause, that has become primary for me."

Giles rose from his chair, carrying his goblet as he strode a few paces away, forming his thoughts. Turning back, he glanced at Edward and shrugged with a smile that bespoke his sadness. "Simon de Monfort is responsible for recognizing the needs and rights of the common man. I am part of that, the cause he sought to promote. Indelibly etched in me is the feeling of desperation, the hopelessness, the pain men feel—the majority of men—not just those born to wealth and position.

"I tried to deny it. Fate took me away from it, and for a long time I tried to pretend that that part of my life had never been. But things have happened in the past year that made me remember, that brought all of those feelings back. The loneliness . . ." He stared into his goblet, remembering. "Not the loneliness of a man without companionship, but that of a man without a god. The terror of a man who lives without hope. In the past year I have remembered, and I have felt shame that I had forgotten.

"The cause brought me here, Edward. The cause that was begun by Simon and the barons who follow him. I will not betray them to you, though it is my belief that you will bring about what Simon began."

Edward remained silent for several moments. Then he placed his goblet on the table and stood. "We are both committed to this purpose, Giles. I believe that England's strength is to be found in its people, whose wants have been too long denied for the benefit of a few. Kneel before me, Sir Giles fitzWilliam, so that I may accept your oath."

Giles set his goblet on the table, then he sank to one knee before the prince. Edward took Giles's proffered hands, clasping them between his own as Giles spoke, his voice strong and even. "I pledge to you my arms, my vassals, and the resources of my lands, which I hold to you in faith. I accept you, Edward Plantagenet, prince of England, as my liege lord, holding to you my faith in all matters of the realm. Before God."

"I accept your pledge, Sir Giles fitzWilliam, knight to England." Bending, he gave Giles the kiss of peace, then pulled him to his feet and turned to take up the goblets. "Let us drink, Sir Giles, to bind the bargain." When they had drunk deeply, Edward lowered his goblet and grinned.

"Welcome home, Giles. The throne has been too long without the company of a Marshal."

"Pack it all up again," Giles ordered curtly as he stepped into the tent. "We're leaving."

"Leaving?" Geoffrey paused in the act of setting out Giles's personal articles, and exchanged a dismayed look with Rodger and Landon. "Has Lord Edward ordered us to leave?"

"Everyone will be leaving." Giles grimaced, slamming a trunk lid shut as he passed.

Rodger blanched. "You told him of Simon?"

"Of course I did not tell him!" Giles roared.

"Then how did he—"

"Apparently he has other sources of information," Giles answered sarcastically. "Geoffrey, pour me some wine."

"We do not have any, Sir Giles."

"Then get some!"

As the young man scurried from the tent, Giles slumped into a chair, moodily ignoring his friends' speculative looks. "He knows that Simon will try to reach his son and what is left of the baronial forces." He picked up a tunic off the table and flung it into an open wardrobe chest as the muscles in his cheek twitched in frustrated anger. "Oh, he kept talking, watching my expression as he weighed the possibilities—London or Evesham. Then a message came, one that brightened his day considerably. He deliberately dropped it on the table within my seeing. There were only three words on the page—'Evesham to Kenilworth.'"

"Christ!" Rodger swore.

"When do we move out?" Landon asked.

"The order has not been given yet," Giles answered wearily. "A war council was called. As Gloucester and Mortimer were to be there, and considering the strained relations between us, Edward thought it best that I retire. However, he will send for me when it is concluded—to hear my opinion of what is decided," he added with a grimace.

"Can you do it, Giles?" Landon asked quietly. "Can you raise arms against Simon?"

Giles glanced up at him, silent for a long moment as his eyes grew cold. "It is a little late to wonder about that, wouldn't you say?"

Geoffrey returned with the wine, bread, and cheese he

had managed to wangle out of Edward's cook. As they ate, Giles found a moment to study the faces of his friends. The disquieting thought struck him that they were avoiding looking at him. "You might as well have out with it," he grumbled, leaning back in his chair. "Things could hardly get worse." Seeing the discomfort his statement brought, he glanced at his squire, who suddenly became quite busy repacking a warchest. Then his gaze passed speculatively to the others. "Landon?" His eyes grew hard as he stared at the knight. Landon finally shrugged.

"While you were with Edward, we did a little investigating of our own," the older knight said tiredly. "What we discovered was a bit of a surprise, not at all what we expected . . ." Giles's brows rose slightly as the knight's voice trailed off uncomfortably, and he waited, wondering what could cause such reluctance in one who was normally so outspoken. "It seems that—until this very morning —your lady wife was a guest in this camp."

It took a moment before Landon's words registered. "Roanna, here?" Giles gasped, dumbfounded.

"So it would seem. Actually, we would not have known but for dumb luck and a slip of the tongue by one of Edward's captains. When I pursued the matter he became close-mouthed; nothing I said could pry another word from him."

"I tried as well, with others," Rodger added. "Evidently, they have been ordered not to speak of her visit."

"The only thing we know, Giles, is that she was Edward's guest for the past three days. She left with an escort this morning."

Giles felt himself grow cold inside. He welcomed the chill, drawing it into him, needing it to dull the pain that ripped through him.

"Edward never mentioned her being here?" Rodger asked, his voice ragged, seeing the torment in Giles's expression.

"Not a word," Giles answered grimly. "But then, he wouldn't, would he? Not when her visit was so obviously one of secrecy." Suddenly he laughed, bitterly. "It is fortunate that the man I sent to London, to see to her safe arrival, has not caught up with us." He did not add that he had sent the man because of his suspicions about Roanna, suspicions he had hoped would be proven wrong. Instead, they were now confirmed. Part of him seemed to die with the knowledge, leaving a hollow, bitter core in its place. "Imagine how upset I would have been to discover that she had not arrived with Brother Vincent and her escort—the one I sent her with, that is." He added somewhat distantly, "I rather imagine I would have hurried off, concerned with her welfare. It would seem that my lady is well able to care of herself."

"Giles, do not jump to conclusions," Landon cautioned. "We do not know why she was here." Despite his words, his voice was thick with doubt.

Giles merely smiled, though it did not touch the coldness in his eyes, and his voice was bitter. "Don't we? It is obvious to all of us why she was here. But do not worry, this changes nothing. Why should it? Roanna has merely followed her convictions, as she always has done." His voice hardened. "But then, so have I. I could hardly find fault with her for doing the same." Except to me, he thought.

In the strained silence that followed, Edward's man appeared, requesting that Giles attend the prince. Giles found him pacing the outer chamber of the large pavilion, his hands clasped behind his back, deep in thought.

"The plan is actually quite simple, Giles," Edward began as they bent over a map on the war-table. "Our forces will be divided into three parts. Two of the wings will be under the commands of deClare and Mortimer. The third will be mine, and I wish you to attend me, at my left. Gloucester will take his forces down the west side of the Avon to prevent de Monfort's retreat. Mortimer is to cross to the east to prevent an escape to London. We will drive against him, directly to Evesham."

As Giles listened, a distant, unwanted memory played over in his mind—a moment beneath a grove of trees with a picnic supper, and Roanna. "It seems to me," he could hear her saying once again, "that you cannot truly know what your principles are until they are tested." How little had he known then how dearly that knowledge would cost them!

He realized that Edward was waiting for his opinion. "I cannot find fault with your plans, milord," he said, stepping back from the table. "But then, I am hardly the man to give an opinion on this venture. I have given you my fealty, milord, and I will not break it, upon my life. However, I must tell you that while I will protect your side, I will not wield arms against Simon unless your person is directly threatened."

"You would protect me from de Monfort?" Edward asked, watching Giles's face for the answer.

"Aye, milord, I have said so." Just before I give up my own life, he added silently.

"So be it," Edward grunted. "Then you shall be in the van with me. I give you leave to go, Sir Giles. We leave at first light."

As Edward stared after him, his lips pursed pensively, a voice came from behind him.

"Can you trust him?" Gloucester stepped from the bedchamber of the pavilion, where he had been listening to the exchange.

"Would I have him at my left if I did not believe so?" Edward answered, glancing at deClare with a flicker of impatience.

"You did not tell him about his wife," the earl observed.

"What purpose would that have served?"

Gloucester, staring at the door through which Giles had departed, missed the look of distaste that had passed over Lord Edward's face at his own question. "It could have brought his loyalty to a test."

"Don't be a fool, deClare," Edward answered with disgust, turning to the maps on his war-table. "I will not test a man's loyalty to me through his affections for his wife." It occurred to him that his grandfather, John, would have done just that. "Lady Roanna is safely on her way to London, and Brother Vincent is on his way to the coast to join my dear aunt. Should I tell fitzWilliam that his wife was a camp follower in my army, brought to those circumstances by the actions of my men? I need that man now; I will not compound the doubts that must already be pulling at him. He will learn of it soon enough—but it will be later, when it will no longer affect the outcome of tomorrow's events."

"Then you do not trust him!" Gloucester said, smiling with satisfaction.

Edward stared at the earl for a moment. A tawny brow

arched slightly as the cool blue eyes regarding the earl grew colder. "I do not trust anyone, my lord earl. Not anyone."

Well before dawn, Edward Plantagenet's army was moving toward the vale of Evesham. It traveled with amazing swiftness through the wooded country, in spite of the long column of armored knights, the measured foot of men-at-arms, the tortured squeaking of the heavy wheels of the lumbering baggage train, and the choking dust that arose among horses and wagons to slow the progress. Throughout the day the army moved forward, pausing only for brief rests, and then pushed on into the night.

Giles, riding near the head of the column, thought about Roanna and the changes in his life since that morning when he had first seen her from the ramparts at Durham House. So much found, so much lost. He had given his oath to Edward and he would not fail it, but, oh, what a price.

She had believed in Edward long before he had come to recognize what she had begged him to see. He tried to think upon that, to think clearly about her, to put aside the feeling of betrayal, and the paroxysm of pain it brought. He could still hardly believe that she was the spy—he did not want to believe it, even now. But he could not allow his feelings for her to blind him to the facts. Roanna had known of his plans, of the fact that Simon the Younger was moving his forces toward Kenilworth, and of the approximate location of Simon's forces. He smiled grimly, realizing that he had made that last betrayal possible. But then, she had protested going, he argued silently. Perhaps she had not formulated her plans until he had sent her away. But it made no difference. She could not even wait, to allow me to make my own decision, he thought. Always, it had to be what *she* needed. Ever he was to bend, even to this. But this time she had found the one thing he could not forgive her for. Perhaps love was not blind, as it was said to be, but it certainly made fools out of men.

"It will be light in a few hours. Are you prepared?"

Giles identified Edward's voice in the darkness as the rider drew up alongside, and answered grimly, "As much as any man is for battle."

"Ahhh. Is not the blood rushing, the fear mingling with anticipation?"

"Not for this battle, milord," Giles answered dryly. He could feel Edward watching him in the shadowed moonlight, and added quietly, "You need not fear that I will betray you, Edward. I will fight beside you in this battle, for I have sworn to do so."

"I do not doubt it, Giles," Edward answered solemnly. "Dear cousin, I feel your sorrow. I would that it could be different. You know that it cannot."

"That is why I am here. But there is something else that you should know, and I would have you know it now. Once done, once it is over, if I survive . . ." He paused, measuring his words. "You should know that Gilbert of Gloucester is my enemy. As much as William of Valence. I will resist both of them."

"Valence is clear to me—but I do not understand your feelings toward deClare. It would seem that he has done no more than you."

Giles's jaw tightened against the sharp reminder Edward's words brought. "I am here because I believe in you and what you will effect, milord. Gloucester is here because he wants to be on the winning side. Causes mean nothing to him."

"You could apply the same stricture to many here. Yet, of all of those with me, it is only Gloucester you single out. Why?"

"Because he, of all of them, has less cause to be weak and vacillating."

Edward was silent for a moment. "And, he is a Marshal. Is that not where the torment lies, Giles?"

"He is heir to it all!" Giles hissed, his fury building.

"Giles, you expect too much," Edward countered. "Aye, deClare is heir to it all—the titles, the lands, the wealth, the position as one of the leading barons in England. You should feel pity for him, not hatred."

"Pity?" Giles drew in his breath, glancing at the man beside him with amazement. "Edward, if you were not my prince I would call you mad."

"And if you were not so caught up in your own dilemma, you would know I am right. It is too often the fault of a strong man not to understand weaknesses in others. It breeds intolerance."

"I am not a strong man, nor can I have tolerance for Gilbert," Giles growled.

"Ah, but you are, and you must. Your position has given you your strengths, Giles, and, I fear, a sense of false modesty—for which *I* have no tolerance. Have done with it, Giles, and face who you are, or you are of no use to me. As for Gilbert, he deserves your pity, not your hatred. He was born to it all; yet, as was true of his father, he is not worthy of a portion of it, but for his ability as a soldier. What would you suggest? That he give it all over and cry, 'Let another claim it, I am not worthy'? He is not evil or calculating, Giles. More's the pity, perhaps, for that, at least, would give him guile, a talent I could use.

"I know no more than you why one is born to tread the path the fates offer. I have had more reason to ponder that question than any other." His soft sigh was heard in the darkness. "I look at my father, and recall my grandfather, and shake my head in wonder that God could determine to make them kings. I look at you, and our mutual cousins, and wonder why it is that you have each been given your places when a more satisfactory arrangement seems obvious." Giles tensed in amazement that Edward would speak so familiarly, even to criticizing his own father, whom he knew Edward loved deeply.

"Our sovereign," Edward continued, "my father, would look upon fate as the will of God. My grandfather, that infamous lord, John Plantagenet, would have dismissed that deity, and thought upon fate as something he alone could control, by his own will. My great-uncle Richard, called the Lion-Hearted, would, if he thought upon it at all, wonder about evil spirits sent to torment him, and would probably have looked for a witch to blame. And so it has been."

"And you, Edward?" Giles asked, glancing at the prince. "What would you say?"

"I give destiny to the fate of birth," Edward answered easily. "God has his hand in it, and touches each of us. He gives each a chance to succeed or fail, but it is to us that our fate is given."

"You should have been born a villein," Giles snorted grimly. "Face that life, and attempt to succeed."

"Ahhh, but there I have you, Giles," Edward responded. "Your father took you from that life, and had you not been born the son of a great earl, your life would certainly have been far different. However, there is no doubt in my mind that you would have pushed beyond the limits of your condition. If there is not one way for a capable man, there is another. Oh, you would not have become a knight, but I have no doubt that, at the very least, you would have become the best damned groomsman one could find."

"Very comforting, milord," Giles muttered.

"Edward—when we are alone," the other corrected.

Giles glanced at him, suddenly irritated. "You really do not understand as much as you think you do. You cannot know of bright, capable men, who live out their lives in the desolation of hopelessness. Those who are born with such disadvantages, wasting whatever talents they might have. Can you honestly believe that one can overcome all? Edward," he added bitingly, "you are a fool, if you truly believe that."

"Nay, Giles, I am not a fool, for a fool cannot learn. And I have done that," Edward said easily, unruffled by Giles's outburst. "You know of my beginnings. Simon helped me to see what he revealed to you as well. I will admit to you now what I have never told another man—in my youth I was lost, my excesses spent in searching for a purpose beyond what was offered with such ease from my birth. I lived the life I was expected to live, but I did not realize how empty it was until Simon. He struck a chord in me that brought fulfillment. But you have missed my point. I accept that one is bound, most greatly, by circumstances of birth. But I believe that one will discover and achieve the limits of one's life. As for the matter of wasted talents, it must, necessarily, be so. I cannot see that particular offense to humanity ever being changed. To give every man the opportunity for greatness? The world is not big enough, Giles. Only the few may succeed. Some who are born to it will fail. Others, struggling to it, will succeed. And we know that this truth extends beyond our puffed-up nobles, don't we?" He grinned on the last words, then became serious once more. "Simon's Great Parliament was only the beginning, Giles. I shall extend it further and give it a life of its own. Aside from the barons, knights and burgesses alike must have the power to represent their own cities and boroughs. Moreover, if each man, common or noble, is to realize his full potential, he must be protected by written statute to guarantee those rights, not merely by common law that we presently adhere to."

Giles listened, transfixed. Edward's words left him bereft of speech. In that moment, while he still feared to hope, he knew in his soul that he had chosen to follow the right man. Finally, he found his voice. "It will never be allowed," he said softly.

"Not allowed by whom?" Edward laughed. "Do not ever attempt to compare me to those who have gone before, Giles. No one will stay me from what I want—in this matter, or anything else. No one."

A thought came to Giles, and with it a guarded feeling of hope. "If this is true, Edward, and I know you believe what you say, what of Simon? Surely there is a common ground to be found there. Your beliefs, your desires are the same."

"I would give much if that were so," Edward said, sighing heavily. "It was Simon who first gave me these thoughts, the stirrings of my inner mind. I will hold him close, forever, for that. But there can be but one ruler of England, and that is Henry Plantagenet. He is our sovereign, and on the morrow shall be again, in fact as well as in name."

They fell silent after that, the moment of closeness lost with Edward's final words. The prince urged his mount forward, to see to other duties, leaving Giles to dwell upon what had been said.

Blood does tell, Giles mused. For all of his denials, it compels. But he could not fault Edward; would he not do the same, had all been taken from his father? Love drives deep. Moreover, Giles realized, even as he resisted the knowledge, Edward was right. He had given his oath because he knew that Edward would bring about a rebirth, a hope to the common man that no other could bring. And with this hope, above all, there could only be one ruler in England. Only one king.

23

The sky lightened to a murky grey. Shadows lengthened, becoming grotesque forms as the sun rose behind them, illuminating the crest of Green Hill and the city in the valley below. The rising sun shone on the banners that stood boldly in the ground before the lines of men, declaring that the waiting forces were for de Monfort.

"Will he believe it?" Rodger asked quietly, waiting next to Giles.

"Of course not. Simon knows the banners were captured —and who has placed them there. Edward means them now only as a rebuke," Giles said grimly, his eyes fixed on the walls of the town. "But he might have, had we not warned him of what happened at Kenilworth."

Rodger glanced at his friend, imagining the turmoil that must be churning through Giles at this moment. "You have given him that, at least."

"Aye, I have given him that," Giles muttered, turning his mount's head as he rode toward the lines, away from the waiting city.

As he rode, he thought of those within the walls. Why had Simon paused here? he wondered with anguish. His forces must be exhausted. It would be the only reason that would keep him from pressing toward Kenilworth, where relief could be found.

He took his place near Edward, pulling up his mount at a slight distance. He saw Edward glance in his direction, and nodded. Aye, my prince, he thought grimly, when the time comes I shall draw near, but not yet. Not quite yet.

The horse moved restlessly beneath him, and his hand went to the hilt of his sword. He fingered the cold bronze idly, recalling when his father had given him the weapon, on the day of his knighthood. It had belonged to his great-grandfather, Richard deClare, and had remained for years in Landon's safekeeping. Overwhelmed with emotion, he remembered the words he had said to his father as he took the sword, vowing to use it only in honor. He could not but wonder if, by day's end, that vow would be broken.

The destrier sidestepped nervously, bringing him out of his reverie. He pulled at the reins and offered soothing words to the animal. What had gotten into him? He was the best Giles had, and he had never known him to be so skittish.

A sound in the valley below drew his eyes to the city. His body tensed as he saw the gates opening, and a mounted column appeared. His eyes shifted, searching the column until they found Simon, and he felt his heart grip painfully in his chest. Forcing himself to look further, he found another rider of interest, and his gaze shifted to Edward. He wondered if the prince had found him also. His mouth drew into a grim smile as he realized what Simon had done. King Henry's tabard was unmarked; there was nothing to identify him. The king of England might easily be mortally wounded by those knights who sought to free him.

Then, through the still morning, as the approaching column halted, Simon's words carried to the waiting forces: "By the arms of Saint James, they come on well! It was from me they learned it!"

Giles swallowed heavily. He felt a stirring pride in the earl's words, and the honor he brought to himself. He knew that Simon would prefer to perish rather than surrender in humiliation. He shifted his glance to Edward, whose eyes were fixed stonily upon Simon and Henry.

Then, to the shock and horror of the opposing armies, it seemed that God himself intervened. As cries rose on the battlefield, a darkened cloud began to swirl across the sky, appearing in a force of wind that blew against men and horses in a blasting fury. It enveloped them, blowing dry and hot against shouts of fear from the startled forces. The men could not see their companions next to them, even as their captains shouted them forward. The battle was engaged amid the tempest, the sounds of commands barely heard above the punishing wind, the strike of steel against steel, and the cries of men as blood was drawn.

The great cloud started to dissipate in stirring wisps, allowing brief glimpses of the battlefield. Giles struggled to reach Edward's side, pushing his destrier forcibly through a thick line of men. The prince was engaged in heavy combat, and Giles countered a side attack with a parry and thrust that, in the push, nearly did not find its target. As a new wave of men fell upon them, Giles spurred his mount to meet the threat. From his throat, rising from some distant memory that was almost instinct, a deep cry came, an ancient Irish battle cry. Such war cries having been all but forgotten, the attacking forces about him froze for an instant, turning in shock to the inhuman sound. It proved enough. In the pause, he reached Edward's side, and his sword sliced once, then yet again, vanquishing threats that would have claimed Edward Plantagenet's life. He moved on, unhesitating, as Edward's blade came up to join his, pushing the opposing army farther and farther back.

They came in waves, one upon the other—faces recognized and put aside. He felt numb regret as his blade found its mark, plunging and withdrawing. Edward, always Edward, he thought, as he protected his side. His mount stumbled over the fallen, its hooves slipping in the gore and regaining their grip in time for Giles to bring his arms and shoulders up for a strike. Then came the one moment in the battle when he faltered. Movement at his left brought him about, as a knight broke through and nearly reached Edward. Giles brought his sword up when suddenly his eyes, shadowed beneath the nosepiece of his helm, met those of John de Vescy. Shifting, he brought his blade down across the other man's sword, knocking it aside with a reverberation that sounded in his brain. An endless moment passed as their eyes locked; then, with a slight nod, de Vescy turned his mount and disappeared into the fray.

The dark mist cleared suddenly as Giles pulled his blade from a knight who came in from the side and would have taken him. His sword crossed his mount in an arch, parrying its mark in a deep thrust that cut the knight from his horse, then taking a man-at-arms who came in from below. Giles spurred his horse just as Edward leapt forward, his bloodied sword idle at his side. Overtaking him, Giles pulled up to view what Edward had maneuvered to see. His eyes widened with horror. There, below him, was Simon. The scene etched itself in his mind, as five knights closed in about the earl, their swords raised for the kill. Simon saw what was happening; his voice cried out above the tumult, "It is time for me to die! God's grace!"

Giles was immobile for that moment, Simon's cry striking him with horror. His body leaned forward, his heels bent their spurs to the flanks of his destrier; but even as he tensed for battle, he knew, with desperation, that he could not reach the earl before it was too late. In that instant, all the years flashed before him, glimpses of laughter and sharing, giving to him so much of what he was. Riveted, he watched as despair ripped through him, lacerating him with pain. Suddenly, the sound tore from him, the guttural inhuman sound crying over the battlefield.

"Siiii—monn!"

Unaware that Edward had drawn to his side before he cried out, he did not see the hand that lifted above him, clasping the hilt of a heavy sword, nor the downward sweep, the swift blow to the back of his head. He was only aware of a deep enveloping pain that met the anguish tearing at his mind, and then a sudden, still blackness.

Part Four

Fear not, sweet wench, they shall not touch thee, Kate,
I'll buckler thee against a million.

—William Shakespeare,
The Taming of the Shrew
Act III, Scene ii

24

Roanna finished peeling the turnips and tossed the last one into the pot. The root bounced off the edge of the kettle, ricocheted off the table, and rolled across the floor and out through the open door. "Bugger," she muttered, crossing to the door. Finding it just beyond the jamb, she bent down to retrieve the elusive turnip. Pausing, half-bent, her hand on the root, she stared eye to beady eye with a large billy goat, which had spied the tasty morsel rolling into its territory.

"Scat!" she snapped.

The goat backed up with a start and scurried away to the safety of the far side of the small courtyard.

"What did ye do to that poor animal?" Roscoe asked, his eyes following the frightened animal as he appeared through the gate to her left with a heavy sack of flour on his shoulder.

"He'd better not mess with me."

"No one 'ad better mess with ye," Roscoe mumbled as he passed her, and ducked through the doorway into the kitchen.

"What?"

"Nothin', luv." He dumped the heavy sack into the flour bin. "Ye've 'ad poor old George since ye were a babe. Why would ye want to go and scare 'im like that?"

She threw him a glare in answer and crossed to where the tavern aprons were hung. "Ah, lass, just where d'ye think ye be goin'?"

"To serve, of course, where else would I be going?"

"Yer Aunt Matilda can 'andle it. Ye'll be stayin' 'ere in the kitchen."

"When was that decided?" she flared.

"When ye dumped the tankard on the sheriff of Merton."

"The old fool," she grumbled. "He deserved it! Spouting off that England was well rid of the de Monfort pestilence!"

"That be not the point, Roanna, and ye know it. Ye cannot go dumpin' good ale on the customers." He paused, shrugging his massive shoulders. "Asides, if ye'd waited a bit, others would 'ave taken care of it. 'Twas not a popular sentiment the sheriff voiced, and ye knew it."

"I wanted to do it."

As he opened his mouth to respond, Roscoe's nose twitched, and he turned to the bubbling pot over the fire. Bending over it, he frowned. "What be this?"

"Stew."

"It don't smell like stew."

"Well, it's stew!"

Taking a ladle down from the wall, he dipped it into the suspect brew and raised it to his lips. Frowning, he studied the flavor for a moment; then his face became immobile, his muscles going rigid as his eyes widened. His mouth opened, but no sound came out for an interminable moment, and then he released a long, winded rush of air. Lunging for the bucket on the counter by the door, he took it in his huge hands and sucked in water. Lowering it at last, he turned tearing eyes to her. "Too much ginger," he wheezed.

"Oh?" she asked, turning a puzzled glance toward the pot. "Are you sure?"

"I'm sure," he coughed.

"Hmmm." She glanced into the pot.

He sighed, wiping the water off his hands with a towel. "Roanna," he said, then paused, glancing warily at her as she dumped flour onto the table, creating a cloud, and threw bread dough onto the flour. "Luv, for my sake. For the sake of the Flyin' Sail. For George's sake. Per'aps I could go see 'im—"

"Nay!" she snapped, attacking the dough. "I told you before—he knows where I am!"

"We don't know that."

"Of course he knows! Where else would I be?"

"Roanna—"

"Don't start again, Uncle Roscoe! We've been over all this! It is obvious that he was perfectly happy in London with the court, and now he has left England, returning to his precious Wales without so much as a by-your-leave. I'll not go begging, and neither will you!"

Roscoe nearly gave up at that, but as he watched her pound the bread to saddle-leather, he became determined. Crossing the room, he picked her up, ignoring her protesting squeak, and plopped her down amid the flour. Drawing himself up, he crossed his arms over his chest and glared at her. "Roanna, when ye returned, ye kept yerself locked in yer room fer weeks. We waited. Then ye left yer room, gracin' us wi' yer presence to mope—between great, 'eavin' sighs. I let that pass. Then ye started to work again. I've lost customers. I've paid condolences in food and rooms to those ye've offended. I've let it pass. But it cannot go on. Talk to me, Roanna, now. All of it. Or I swear I'll send ye, bag and baggage, back to yer 'usband."

Sniffing, she drew an arm, covered with flour, across her eyes.

"No tears, Roanna," he said sternly. "No more of it. None of what ye've done matters in the least, but fer the fact that yer unhappy. If we're to find a solution fer it, ye must tell me what has 'appened."

Sliding off the table, she took up a towel and slowly wiped the flour from her arms and face. Resigned, she slumped into a chair as he took the one across from her. Slowly, painfully, she recounted the events that had led up to her departure from Kenilworth.

"I was a shrew—a harridan—I handled it so badly, Uncle Roscoe, I know that now. He hates me, it is over for us! I'm certain of it. He . . ." She sniffed, taking a kerchief from her pocket to blow her nose. "He didn't even answer the letter I sent him when I returned to London."

"Even if what ye say is true, lass, I cannot believe that 'e would leave ye fer that. There must be more . . ."

"Oh, there was more. After all, I won, didn't I? He went to Edward. And he fought against Simon. Simon died, Uncle! Everything is gone! When I think of the last words between us—and what has happened since. How Simon died, how his body was dismembered and scattered." She swallowed painfully. "That Henry de Monfort was slain —so many he knew, had been close to . . ."

Roscoe smiled sadly, reaching his hand out to cover hers where it lay on the table. "Then 'e also would know that Edward granted Simon an 'ero's burial at Evesham Abbey. That 'e wept over 'enry's body, rememberin' how they 'ad played together as children. All of England knows it, so Giles must."

He winced, seeing the pain-hardened eyes she turned to him. "And what of Eleanor?" she asked, her voice taut. "How did he feel when she had to flee to the Continent with her remaining children, and can never return? Eleanor was the only mother he ever knew, Uncle Roscoe. And I pushed him to it!" Slowly, her eyes cleared and she drew herself up, her expression becoming resolved. "If you were to force me to go to him now, he would either reject me out of hand, or he would merely tolerate me, bound to me in duty as my husband. I could not bear either. But you are right. There is no excuse for my behavior. When I married him, one way or another I did not expect it to last."

Roscoe frowned, confused. "Don't ye love 'im, lass?"

"Love him!" She laughed shortly, deep pain in the sound. "Love him? With all of my heart and soul, though it was never enough. Because I love him, I should have left him long ago. We were never right for each other. There was never a time that I would not have lost him, had I tried to hold him."

"Then why did ye marry 'im?"

"Because—there was a time, a brief moment, when I was foolish enough to dream. You know . . ." She paused, reflecting. "I don't regret a moment of it, Uncle Roscoe, not one minute spent with him. Perhaps—I didn't handle it so badly, after all. If he had not gone to Edward, he would have destroyed himself. But, with that decision, he released his past—and I was part of that past. The fact that he has not come for me is proof of it."

Roscoe stared vacantly at the table, unable to counter what she had said. All of the arguments that passed through his mind merely fed a deep, growing anger toward fitz-William, and he damned the man for his weakness. Giles had been out of London, but not to Wales, though Roscoe could not tell his niece that now. He had gone to France —to Eleanor de Monfort. He had returned to court four weeks ago. And he had made no effort, before or since, to claim his wife. Roscoe's brown eyes shifted to her, and he hid his anger and grief.

"What of the child?" he asked softly.

Her hand went instinctively to her swelling middle. "It is mine," she answered softly. "He will never know of it." Seeing the doubt that crossed Roscoe's face, she reached out and grasped his hand. "Don't you understand? I have this of him—no one can take it from me." He did not look convinced. She sighed and pressed on, determined to make him understand. "Listen to me, and believe this. I—I've been angry the past weeks, and I've taken it out on everyone. For that I am sorry. Perhaps a part of me still hoped that he would come, and grieved when I knew he wouldn't. But that is over now. You've helped me to that. Do you remember, long ago, when you told me to grab for life, not to let it pass me by? I've done that! The time at Kenilworth gave me a chance to grow, to learn things I never dreamed possible. It also gave me the time I had with him—I will never forget a moment of it. I've had more in a year than most have in a lifetime. And I've just begun! Now I have this child—his child—the most precious gift he could have given to me."

He gazed fixedly at her for a long moment, searching for the truth. Then he smiled. "So be it, then. Ye 'ave yer 'arbor 'ere, luv, as I promised ye. Can ye be content wi' it?"

"Aye," she said, smiling. There was peace in her face for the first time since she had returned. "I will never forget him, nor stop longing for him. But truly, Uncle, I know that I have reached beyond my dreams, and found them. I am content."

Roanna leaned her elbows on the bar, resting her chin on her hand as she laughed over a comment from one of the customers. In the past weeks she had been almost happy. She had meant what she'd said to Roscoe—she was as content as she could possibly expect to be. Her memories, her ghosts, were hers alone, and it was for her alone to reconcile them. She was ashamed of the way she had behaved following her return to the Flying Sail; but she was generous with herself, knowing that she had been entitled to a few weeks as a termagant. Now it was over.

As for her memories of Giles . . . memories of a morning

turning all too quickly to the light of day, then caught in a shadow, drawing into spiritless night . . . her heart caught poignantly when she thought about him. A glimpse of a pair of blue eyes could make her heart pound recklessly, until she found that the face did not match. A set of broad shoulders, a familiar turn of a hand, sun-lines crinkled in the corners of an eye, other more subtle reminders, caused her breath to catch. But she knew she could bear it. She knew that eventually her memories would be locked within her, and no one could then remind her of him but a voice within herself.

Soon she would have the child, she reminded herself. And she would have her love to focus on it. Until then, she could fake the smile, her laughter could mask the pain, and she could ease another's loneliness with a moment's attention and a little, easily given warmth. Each day helped, and time healed her. Each moment was a little easier than the last.

Stepping from behind the bar, she moved among the crowded tables, pausing to visit with regulars. Ordering a barmaid to clear the remnants of a meal, she looked up as the door opened, a smile set on her lips to greet the new arrival. Her smile faded as the doorway filled with armed knights. The men paused, then moved into the room as the tavern fell silent, and everyone's interest turned guardedly to the soldiers. In moments Roscoe appeared from a back room, his sudden presence affirming his miraculous touch with the goings-on of his inn, the silence from without having drawn him.

As the knights spread out along the walls near the door, one came forward, his weathered face easing into a wary smile as he approached the owner of the Flying Sail. "From the description I was given, I presume that you are Roscoe Dorking," he said easily, saluting the other man.

"I am."

"Roanna, Lady fitzWilliam, is your niece?"

Roscoe frowned and stared at the knight, ignoring the mumblings that rose throughout the tavern, and the surprised glances that were turned toward Roanna where she stood, transfixed. "She is," he answered at last, the sound a growl coming from deep within his chest.

"She is to come with us."

"On whose order?" Roscoe's eyes narrowed.

"By the order of Edward Plantagenet," the captain answered unflinchingly.

Roscoe continued to stare at the man. Then, from where Roanna stood, she could have sworn that she saw his mouth twitch in a smile. He wouldn't! she thought, panicking.

"She's over there." He gestured with a jerk of his thumb in her direction. "But ye better brace yerself—she won't go easy."

Her eyes shifted from the stupidly grinning face of her uncle to the captain, who turned toward her with surprise, and then to the expressions of the customers about her. Some were staring at her with amazement, obviously stunned by the realization that they had been waited upon by a "lady"; others, who knew her, were waiting with expectant, amused grins. No aid from any quarter.

"Bloody hell, I will," she breathed, backing away.

"Lady Roanna?" the captain asked, stepping toward her.

"Go bleedin' rot!" she cried, backing farther away until she came up against a table. "I won't go! Tell friggin' Edward he can bloody—"

"Roanna!" Roscoe bellowed.

The captain's confused look turned quickly to one of determination. "Lady Roanna—" The man flinched as a pewter mug barely missed his left ear, ale splattering his tunic.

As she grabbed another missile, Roscoe crossed the room in a few long strides. "That's it, lass." She was swept into the air and landed with an oomph on his shoulder. "Where do ye want 'er?" the huge tavern-owner asked, turning to the befuddled knight.

"There's—there's a horse out there." The man gestured lamely.

"Ye'd better tie 'er to it," Roscoe remarked, striding across the room as Roanna pelted his back with her fists, screaming profanities that caused mixed chortles and coughs as they passed. As he passed through the doorway, Roscoe grabbed a cloak from a peg near the door, and beckoned to the remaining knights. "Come on, lads."

Stepping into the dusky evening, he plopped her onto the back of a mare. "Fer once in yer life," he sighed, "be'ave yerself, Roanna."

"Behave myself?" she cried, as he held her to the saddle.

"Ye've been summoned by Lord Edward! 'Tis a command, ye 'ave no choice!" Sighing heavily, he clasped her hands on the high pommel of the saddle. His voice was pleading. "If ye 'ave no care fer yerself, or fer me, think of yer poor aunt, turned from 'er 'ome and 'er livin', and . . ." He sighed raggedly, "She's gettin' on in years, Roanna. What'll become of us if ye do not obey a royal command?"

She blinked, her mouth slackening with horror. Then her eyes narrowed, and her lips drew into a reluctant smile. "You old fool."

He shrugged, smiling. "Could be."

She glanced at the captain, who was mounted next to her, waiting. "All right. I'll go. But if something dire happens to me, it will be on your head, Roscoe Dorking!"

Roscoe watched as the party rode away, and he noted the brave set to Roanna's back. He chuckled softly, then turned to mount the steps back into his inn.

As they rode along the wharf and through the streets of London, Roanna glanced at her stern-faced escort, wondering if she could learn anything from them about their mission. Why had Edward sent for her? Why an armed escort? It did not bode well for her, that was certain. But what had she done to deserve such treatment?

A sudden thought sent chills down her back and she shivered despite her heavy cloak. Her journals! Could it be? Could someone have found them and read them? But they couldn't have, she reasoned as her palms became clammy. She had written in one just the past night. She kept them locked in a chest at the end of her bed, and none had been missing, nor had the lock been tampered with. Besides, she had not written anything too terrible, just her own accounts and reasonings, such as her opinion of Edward's early days. Surely he would not hold that against her. And her opinion of King Henry, his indulgences, his ineptitude, the fact that his weakness had led to the war in England, and the fact that she felt him to be indirectly responsible for the deaths of the Marshal men. Words, if they fell into the wrong hands, that would brand her as a traitor—along with all who were close to her. Most certainly Uncle Roscoe and Aunt Matilda—and above all, Giles.

Giles. Her breath caught and she bit her lower lip as she thought of what such a disgrace would do to him. He could never return to England again, ever. And the babe, to have a mother branded as a traitor— Then another possibility struck her, even more horrifying, leaving her weak and shaking. The babe! Oh, Sweet Mother, why had she not thought of it before? Edward knew of the child! Through the laws of primogeniture, the child belonged to Giles! Moreover, if a son, this child could inherit! They were in it together—both of them—for surely, if Edward knew of the child, then Giles knew also. He wanted his son, and they meant to take it from her! She turned to the man who was riding beside her. "Captain? Where are you taking me?"

The soldier turned to her, startled. Even in the failing light he could see how pale she had become. "Milady, are you ill?" he asked with concern.

"Just answer my question," she snapped. "Surely you can at least tell me of our destination."

"We are for Winchester." His confusion deepened as color began to return to her face and it became set with determination.

So, she thought, they were not bound for the Tower. At least, not for the moment. But she had no doubt that they would lock her away until the babe was born and then discard her like so much baggage. The realization tore at her painfully. How could Giles do it? Could he hate her so much, forgetting even their happy, loving moments together? Somehow she would escape them!

Then a wave of despair washed over her. Who was she fooling? Giles's grandmother, Isabel, had been incarcerated in the Tower by Henry the Second, for almost a year. The wealthiest heiress in England, she had been locked away until Henry had pledged her to William Marshal—just to keep control of her wealth and titles. The thought weakened Roanna, and she had to grip the pommel of the saddle to steady herself. If Isabel deClare, with all of her wealth and resources, had not been able to escape from the Tower, how could she, Roanna Royston fitzWilliam, possibly do so?

By the time they reached Winchester, Roanna was in a fine fit of rage. No one, not Giles, nor even Lord Edward himself, would take her child from her, ever! She kept her cloak wrapped tightly about her as she was led through the long halls of Winchester, her spirit and determination rising with each step, forming into resolve as they halted before a pair of tall oak doors. Taking a deep breath, she stepped by the guard and entered the large room.

She paused inside the door, startled to find the room

almost empty. She had expected that Edward would be surrounded by his bachelor companions, whom he was rarely without, and members of the court. Instead, he was quite alone in the massive chamber, sitting at a desk before the far window, his blond head bent over a missive as the quill he held moved along the vellum with purposeful strokes. She stood awkwardly, uncertain how to proceed, as the door closed quietly behind her. This wasn't what she had expected, this serious, engrossed prince, and her thoughts tossed with confusion.

"Milord?" she stammered, clearing her throat.

"A moment, Lady Roanna," Edward answered, continuing to write.

As she waited, tapping a slippered foot idly, her eyes wandered about; slowly she became intrigued by the beauty of the room: the high, vaulted ceiling, the tapestries that hung along the walls, the rich rugs that warmed the planks of the floor. A small, particularly delicate statue of a woman caught her eye, and she stepped over to the pedestal and reached out, smoothing her fingers over the cool stone of the graceful form.

"She is Aphrodite," a deep voice said from behind her, causing her to jump. "She is the Greek goddess of love." Edward reached out to lift the statue, placing it in her hands. "Beautiful, isn't it?"

She tensed, fearing that she would drop it, but the cool feel of the stone was soothing. "Aye," she whispered, somewhat awestruck by the graceful form she held in her hands. "Is it marble?"

"Aye, and done by a master. Alabaster, being softer and easier to carve, is normally used for such a small piece. The marble alone makes it unique. It is my favorite work."

"The Greek goddess of love?" Roanna mused softly in wonder, then looked up at Edward, her eyes sparkling with mischief. "Has a cleric seen this? They cannot approve."

"You are right, most do not." Edward chuckled. "But a few can look beyond their dogma and appreciate her beauty. But it matters not. I like her, that is what is important, Roanna." He took the statue and returned it to the pedestal. Taking her arm, he led her to some chairs near the fire. "Would you care for some refreshment?"

His solicitous offer stirred her anger and fear and she sat stiffly in a chair. "Nay, I do not need refreshment, milord, only answers. Why have you placed me under arrest? What have I done?" Instinctively, she gathered her cloak more tightly about her as she spoke.

"Are you chilled?" he asked with concern, noting her gesture.

"Nay, milord, just curious as to your answer."

He smiled at her, shaking his head. "Roanna, you are not under arrest, I assure you. Your escort was for your protection. 'Tis my concern for you that has brought you here, nothing more."

"You need not be concerned for me, milord," she answered quickly.

"Ah, but I disagree. You are the wife of my cousin, therefore you are my cousin as well. We Plantagenets are great believers in family." He smiled, then sighed. "Giles is not the same man he was, Roanna. While we have never discussed it, I know that he has been deeply hurt. What happened between you?"

Roanna shifted uncomfortably. She was completely taken aback by the conversation—this was not what she had expected. Groping for a response, she squirmed again, unaware that her cloak had fallen open. When she looked up, she found Edward staring at her middle, his handsome brow etched in a deep frown. As he raised his gaze to hers, he arched one tawny brow in disapproval.

"Well, this would explain your bout of chills. You have not told him, have you?"

"It does not matter," she answered curtly, her dread growing at the expression in his eyes.

"Does not matter?" he said calmly, but she stiffened at the hardness that entered his voice. "His child does not matter?" He ran his fingers through his hair and regarded her with disbelief. "This is worse than I thought. What did happen between you? Nay, it does not matter now," he said, dismissing his own question with a wave of his hand. "Well then, mistress, this is how it shall be. I brought you here seeking to play Cupid, believe it or not. But that reason is now moot, though you will remain and this will be resolved."

"What can be resolved?" she cried, her fear making her bold. "He does not want me, he has not even remained in England! I cannot see what you think this will accomplish!"

"Not in England?" He frowned. "Of course he is, he

returned a month ago. Moreover, neither of you will leave Winchester until you settle your differences. I do not know what has gone between you, and frankly, I care not. You are with child, and that child is his legal heir—and that most certainly does concern me, along with its fealty for the lands in Wales and Ireland. I fully intend for you to remain here, if I have to be the babe's godfather. Do you understand what I am saying?"

"Oh, without doubt, milord," she flared. "The Plantagenet lion, before all."

"Three leopards, Roanna," he corrected with a sudden grin. "I am my own man." But despite his sudden humor, she did not miss the determined gleam in his eye. "Aye, the child shall be for me."

"And if I do not agree? The child is mine—to give or to take from you, by whatever means."

"Would you go that far, Roanna?"

"Aye, milord, without hesitation; I would give up my life if I thought the babe would be taken from me."

"Taken from you?" He blinked with surprise. "Do you believe I would do that?"

"Wouldn't you? Wouldn't Giles? Why else have I been brought here?"

"I told you why I brought you here," he said, sighing. "I did not even know of the babe. However, if you do not believe me, it cannot be helped. You will remain here, Roanna. You will see him, and resolve these differences, do you understand?"

"Please," she whispered in anguish. "I cannot."

"You will," he insisted. Rising from his chair, he crossed the room, opening the door to give orders to someone without. Minutes later, they were joined by another lady, somewhat older than Roanna. "This is Lady Lodema," he said, turning to her as Roanna rose from her chair. "She will be your companion while you are with us—and will keep you well."

Roanna studied the woman briefly, shifting her glance to Edward's. Her eyes grew cold as she realized the prince's meaning.

"I wish for you to enjoy your stay here, Roanna," he said evenly. "There is no need for you to be unhappy—you can only bring that upon yourself. But you will meet with Giles and make every endeavor to make peace with him."

Roanna followed Lady Lodema from the royal chamber, down the long corridor to the rooms set aside for her use. She was oblivious to the sumptuous decor of her quarters, her nerves raw as she thought upon what Edward had said and realized that she would be forced to meet with Giles.

She glanced idly at the other woman as she was settled in, and became determined not to like her. A companion? A jailer, more like! She certainly fit the role: a wide-hipped, large-boned woman with a face like a horse, accentuated by a stern visage. Oh, lud, she thought, sinking into a chair as the woman delivered orders to the servants, you've found yourself in a fine fix now. It seemed that she was about to have a bath. Did the horse-woman think that, being from the docks, she was automatically dirty? Roanna roused herself, years of training from those docks coming to her aid. Dirty, was she? Well, Lady Lodema, brace yourself.

25

What fops, she thought, watching a young nobleman bend
gracefully over a lady's hand. She was pretty, Roanna
mused, but she used too much skin whitener. Roanna bet
he'd have her beneath the covers before dusk, judging by
the giggle his caress brought. Shifting her gaze, she studied
another couple who passed by her in the garden, and her
mouth twisted in wry amusement. Those two will be
quickly coupling in the bushes if they don't leave. Lud, she
thought, the only differences from what she saw on the
docks were the clothes, the titles added to the names, and,
perhaps, a few affected manners. Now, those two are in
love, she decided, watching a young woman blush as the
knight next to her bent to whisper in her ear. She is as
innocent as spring, and he adores her. No, it is no different
from the docks of London; only the surroundings add
flavor—not spice, just a different flavor. In fact, she felt pity
for these people and the roles they were forced to play. How
much better to be yourself.

She drew her gaze from the players, preferring the view of
the garden to the imperfection of man. It was beautiful, so
very beautiful, the fragrance of the blooms filling her
senses. This is the advantage that position and wealth bring,
she marveled. She did not care about the trappings of
wealth but about the time and freedom to explore a deeper
sense—the form and feel of a work of art, the sound of an

324

experienced player stroking the strings of a lyre, the exquisite beauty of a manicured garden and the deep fragrance of a single, cultivated rose.

Her eyes drifted dreamily, glistening in the late afternoon sunlight. She could live here forever, her senses drifting. The sun felt warm against her shoulders, and her thoughts wandered idly. Smiling softly, she leaned back against the tree that formed the back of the solitary bench she had claimed for herself. She allowed her mind to wander, feeling the brief, precious peace of mind that one so rarely has, knowing she would remember this moment with longing.

Unable to contain a soft laugh of contentment, she clasped her hands across her gently swelling stomach. Then her eyes widened with surprise as she felt movement within herself for the first time. She waited, hoping that she had not imagined it, and then she felt it again. Swallowing heavily she pressed her hand to her stomach and closed her eyes against the intense love that she shared with her child. And she laughed softly, filled with joy, as she felt the soft flutter against her hand as the baby moved deep within her.

Smiling, she opened her eyes and stared at the shadowed branches above her. Then she lowered her eyes and glanced about, wanting to share the experience, pitying those who could not know what she was feeling.

Then, disbelieving, she saw him. He stood on a pathway below her, two other men at his side whose heads were bent in conversation. His face was rigid as he stared at her belly. She sat up quickly and their eyes locked, holding for an interminable moment. Slowly, he left his companions and walked up the grassy slope toward her.

He didn't say anything for a long moment as he paused before her, his gaze dropping to her middle before returning to her face. "Why?" he asked quietly.

She felt confused at the pain in his voice and pushed down the irritation the word brought, remembering what they had shared. "Why, Giles? It is too simple a question; there are a hundred answers."

His eyes grew cold. "Then answer just one. When were you going to tell me of my child?"

She winced at the anger in his voice. "It is my child, Giles."

"Yours?" He laughed shortly, his eyes stony. "Alone?"

"Mine," she said calmly. "You have what you need, Giles, and so do I. Let us be content with that, I pray you."

"Madam, do not plead with me. We will not speak of it now." He gave a short, brittle laugh. "God's Blood, it will take me some time to accept this. But care well for my child, Roanna, for we shall certainly speak of it later." He turned and left the knoll, striding away to rejoin his companions. She watched him go, her heart crying out to him, even as she steeled herself against the look he had given her. Never, Giles, she whispered, I will not give this to you, I cannot!

She returned quickly to her chamber, vowing not to leave it again until Edward had come to see the futility of this madness and allowed her to leave. Lady Lodema was there, sitting by the fire with her ever-present needlework. She looked up as Roanna entered, her expression clouding with concern as she noted the younger woman's agitation. "What has happened? You look as if you have seen a demon!"

Roanna laughed shortly. "Not a demon, Lodema, but one I fear far more." She dropped into the other chair set near the hearth, and leaned toward the flames to warm her suddenly chilled hands.

"What has happened?"

Roanna wondered how much she could tell this woman. She had learned a difficult lesson in the two days she had been at Winchester, and it had left her feeling ashamed. Aunt Matilda had always taught her not to judge by appearances; yet she had been guilty of that error upon meeting her companion. It had only taken a few hours in Lady Lodema's company for Roanna to realize that the woman's untoward appearance masked a gentleness of spirit and a generosity that reached out to envelop her. Widowed these past four years, she had come into Edward's service following the death of her only child, a daughter, who had died while attempting to give her German husband a child. Endowed with a small inheritance, Lady Lodema had been able to avoid spending her remaining years in a convent, and had come to Edward, calling upon favors the prince owed to her late husband. For the first time in her life, Roanna felt that she had found a woman friend.

"I saw him," Roanna said quietly, staring into the fire.

"Giles?" Lodema asked, frowning. "Did you speak with him?"

"Oh—" She expelled a breath. "He spoke to me. He is furious, of course. He—he wants the child."

"Of course he does," Lodema snorted, leaning back in her chair as she picked up her embroidery. "What are you going to do?"

"Fight him!" Roanna said fiercely, her eyes fixed on a flaring tongue of flame.

"And just how do you propose to do that?"

"I—I don't know, but I'll think of something."

"I think, child, it is time that you began to face the facts of the matter," Lodema said firmly as her hands worked the needle without a pause. "Try to approach it as unemotionally as you can. Firstly, do you love him?"

Roanna drew a deep breath. "Aye. I—I do. But—"

"No buts," Lodema said curtly. "We can always find excuses if we look for them, but rarely a valid reason. You must look only upon facts, if you are to find a solution. Next, what are your choices? Not what you wish, but what is."

Roanna slumped in her chair, tilting back her head and staring at a point in the shadowed ceiling. She could try to escape, she thought, but they would find her. She could kill herself, as she had threatened to Edward—but that was only a threat; she could never do it. Moreover, she would never do it to her child. So much bluster, she thought. "I have no choices," she said bleakly. "If he wants the child, he will take it."

"Aye, he could do that," Lodema agreed. "But you do have a choice, as I see it. You could stay with the child."

"Go back to him? He—he does not want me!"

"Has he ever told you so?"

"Not in so many words," Roanna admitted. "But I know it is true!"

"So you have told me. He hates you, you say; you are anathema to him, a constant reminder of the pain in his life. Perhaps it is so, I cannot say. But what strikes me is that he has never actually told you so. It seems to me, Roanna, that you have nothing to lose by discussing it with him."

"You do not know Giles," Roanna said grimly. "He will try to be noble. He'll attempt to convince me that he wants me, even if it is not true."

Lodema snorted. "What would you want with such a weak man? Perhaps it would be better just to—"

"He is not weak!" she protested. "Giles is anything but that!"

"Nay? A strong man does not vacillate and twist the truth."

"That is not what I said! He—he would try to be kind, that is all."

"But you just said that he does not want you, so why should he attempt to be kind? Dear me, Roanna, you have left me most confused. You must discuss it with him, it is the only way. Perhaps, out of all this tangle, a small amount of reason can be found."

They fell silent, and Roanna stared broodingly into the fire, her mind tossing between reason and turmoil. They took supper, discussing lighter matters, and finally as the bell rang for vespers, Roanna readied for bed, no closer to a solution than she had been when she entered the chamber. As she slipped her bedgown over her head and Lodema gathered up her things to leave, there was a sharp rap at the door. The two women exchanged a surprised glance, and Lodema crossed to the door.

"Don't answer it!" Roanna gasped.

"Don't be ridiculous," Lodema said over her shoulder. Opening the door, she regarded the man standing there, his face rigid with frustration and anger. Her mouth twitched slightly with a vague smile. "You must be Sir Giles," she said calmly.

"I am here to see my wife," he answered curtly.

"Of course you are." Her nose wrinkled as she caught the strong aroma of ale. "I trust that you will bring no harm to her."

"Don't be absurd!" he snapped. "Is she here?"

"She is," she murmured, stepping by him. Pausing, she laid a hand on his arm. "She is your wife, Sir Giles, but I am her guardian—by order of Lord Edward. My room is next to this one. Keep that in mind."

He stepped into the room, shutting the door firmly behind him. Leaning against the door, his gaze passed over her where she stood by the bed, clad in the thin linen bedgown. "Put on a robe," he said thickly. Not waiting for a reply, he crossed to the hearth and poured himself a goblet of wine.

"Giles, why have you come here?" she asked, joining him by the fire when she had robed herself.

He turned his head and regarded her with a frown. "Why? A rather inane question, madam. It is obvious that we have an important matter to discuss."

"Can't it wait until tomorrow?"

"Why should it? I am your husband, it is hardly unfitting that I should be here. I have a right to your bedchamber, Roanna, or have you forgotten that—along with everything else?" His gaze dropped meaningfully to her middle.

"You know that is not what I meant."

"Nay? What did you mean?" he asked sharply.

"Only that this is not comfortable for either of us. We could set a more appropriate place and time for a discussion—"

"Perhaps I plan to do more than just talk." Hearing her sharp intake of breath, he smiled grimly. "Frightened by the prospect, Roanna? Why? I am your husband. I do not recall relinquishing my rights as such. Besides, why should you be afraid? You used to want me to touch you."

"Giles . . ." she began pleadingly. "Please, Giles, I cannot come back to you now."

"What makes you think that I want you back?" he asked coldly.

She drew a slow, painful breath. "Then why are you here?"

His eyes dropped to her middle. "I thought that was obvious."

"Oh, Giles, please," she gasped. "You would not—take the child!"

"Without question, Roanna. The child is mine."

"You can't!" she cried softly. "You cannot take him from me! I could not bear it."

One dark brow arched as his mouth twisted into a cold smile. "You should have thought of that before."

She stumbled to a chair and slumped into it. "I'll—I'll kill myself!"

"No, you won't. You love life too much, Roanna."

"Do you hate me so much?" she asked, unable to look at him.

"Don't!" he said sharply. "Do not put the blame for this on me!" He stared at her bent head for a moment, then sighed in disgust. "You've always made your own choices, Roanna. What you want, what you believe in. This time, madam, we will do it my way. You will remain here until the babe is born. Then—you may go where you wish. I will see that you are cared for. You will not want for anything. I owe you that much." He ignored the soft sound of a sob that tore from her, and left without a backward glance.

Edward's eyes passed idly over the room, and he grimaced with distaste. Winchester was well appointed, but the Tower was the only home that spoke to something within him. Each stone and section of mortar, but for the old Roman wall, had been placed there by one of his line. The majestic and imposing fortress built by the Conqueror was now known as the White Tower, ever since the day his father had been taken by a sudden whim to whitewash the entire thing. Edward smiled at the memory. His father. He was certain that England would remember him as a bumbling, erratic man of narrow vision. Only time would confirm the contributions he had made, though Edward suspected that they would never be given their proper due. Henry the Builder, a man who envisioned great beauty, who gave England magnificent edifices of architecture that would last for centuries. England would care even less that he was a man capable of giving great, abiding love to his family. No, none of that would be remembered.

But, oh, what Henry had built. The additions to the Tower itself, as well as Westminster and Windsor. The wharf—Edward suppressed a chuckle, remembering his father's rages as attempt after attempt crumbled into the Thames. Through pure determination and tenacity on the part of its builders, it finally held. Someday, Edward promised himself, he would add to what his father had begun—but with a decided difference. What he would build would last and be remembered with reverence, because he understood what his father had never grasped: that a ruler holds his position by the will of the people, by respect earned with true strength. Those who sought to govern by sheer force inevitably failed. His grandfather, John, was the best evidence of that, he thought, shaking his blond head slightly. True strength came to one who listened to the people, understanding their moods and needs, then used those needs to bring about a desired result. One who instilled trust in others, but never entrusted true power to another. He shifted his gaze to one man at the table, and he frowned. Such belief had a price: true friendship could never be claimed, for to do so would be to give that power into the hands of another.

The object of his attention looked up at that moment and arched a dark eyebrow at the glower on Edward's face. "Is something amiss, milord?"

"Nay, Giles, nothing." Edward's frown was replaced by a smile. "Except, perhaps, for this jellied eel. It is soured."

Giles raised his hand and signaled for the prince's squires to remove the dish. Glancing back at Edward, his look became guarded. "Milord, you do understand the reasons for my request?"

"I understand why you wish to return to Wales, though I am not pleased. But then, I shall not become difficult, Sir Giles. This is, after all, a supper of farewell, and I will not dampen it."

Giles smiled, and Edward had to prevent himself from laughing at the openly relieved look that crossed his favorite's face. His favorite. Others would take his place, as he had taken the place of those before him, but—damn! The sense of loss struck him acutely. Edward had an uncanny sense for those who were truly faithful, and he knew that Giles would be hard to replace, perhaps impossible. True friendships, those that held back nothing, that gave honestly and without guile, were dear. . . .

A burst of laughter drew his attention, and he smiled at a quip from Sir Landon—he would miss that one, too, though he could not count him as a friend. Hours spent with the man over dice and a chess table had warmed him—and Landon knew more bawdy stories than Edward had known existed, and Edward's own early years had hardly been isolated from the rawer side of life. Aye, he trusted him, too, even though he knew that Landon did not particularly like him. Nay, perhaps because he knew it, just as he knew the reason. Landon d'Leon was faithful to only one man: the son of Will Marshal. Edward drew a deep breath to suppress a sigh. To have and be able to keep such loyalty . . .

His eyes passed quickly over the others in the room, who

carried little importance to him. But each was there for
Giles; they were those who knew and loved him best, there
to say farewell. There are so few, he mused, for one so very
important. The things we've talked about, the things I've
learned from him. The knowledge I've gained about those I
needed to know about—from the thoughts and philoso-
phies of those who once guided him. My father is a dolt, he
thought. He could have learned directly from those men,
even from the Good Knight, the wisest and most courageous knight of his age. But Henry had been too foolish to
hear, to listen. And now, Giles, your farewell banquet is so
frightfully spare, he thought. Those who would have been
here are gone; all who would have paid homage to you are
gone. He glanced at the doorway, his thoughts returning to
the present. Where is the chit? I ordered her to be here.

She entered the room, as if drawn by the silent order.
Unsure, she paused, glancing about, and Edward, who was
the only one who had noticed her entrance, saw the look of
panic that flashed across her face. That's it, he thought,
watching the poised expression of calm that replaced it, be
easy, be careful. . . .

Roanna stiffened, and she carried herself to the table with
as much aplomb as she could manage. She was furious with
Edward for demanding her appearance. What did he hope
to prove by it? If he sought her complete and utter humiliation, it was certainly won, but she'd be damned if she'd
show it! Reaching the table, she dropped a deep curtsy to
the prince. Rising, she tightened her mouth as he gestured
for her to take the seat next to Giles. Fury touched her eyes,
an expression seen only by Edward, who met it with silent
amusement. She hardly noticed as someone moved to make
a place for her, and she settled herself next to her husband.

She fixed her eyes on the table, burningly aware of the
obvious swelling of her stomach beneath the blue brocade
silk of her bliaut. She would have worn a cloak if Lodema
had not snatched it from her, clucking her tongue and
declaring how ridiculous it would look. Finally, with an
effort, she forced her eyes up to Giles's. "Milord," she
acknowledged, wincing at the coldness of the vibrant blue
gaze that settled on her.

"Milady," he murmured, then turned his face away from
her to others at the table.

Damn, she thought, swallowing. Couldn't he even pretend? But then, why should he, especially before his friends? She was nothing to him now. Turning away, she looked up and met Edward's interested gaze. "Be of good cheer, milady," he murmured, reaching across the narrow table to pour wine for her, as her husband had not. "I expect you to brave it out."

She swallowed against the dry lump in her throat. Brave it out? Why was Edward doing this to her? Forcing her gaze up, she glanced about the intimate gathering. There were knights and retainers of Giles's, some who had become close to him in the months of battle—and their ladies. Then, halfway along the table, her gaze widened with shock. Hateful memories struck her with almost physical force, and for a dizzying moment she thought she might be ill. Her eyes locked with those of Lady Margot, and she tore her eyes away as those memories nearly overwhelmed her.

As the next quarter of an hour passed, Roanna struggled with herself, confounded by her own promise to herself to be silent, not to speak to him. She was deeply shaken, her perusal of the room having left her shocked and filled with anguish. She owed him nothing; his rejection of her and his promise to take their child had released her from any feelings of obligation. So reason dictated, while her emotions became more and more turbulent. She glanced at Edward, and her mouth tightened into a line. He knew, oh, he certainly knew; yet he had said nothing. They were sitting here, laughing and toasting mundane matters, discussing life as if they had not a care, while a spy sat among them. A traitor to all but Edward, one who had betrayed so many dear to each of them. One who had taken choice from them.

How could it have happened? Surely Giles could not bear to sup with one who had so cruelly betrayed Simon. He couldn't know— Oh, Lord, he had never gotten her letter! The one she had sent upon returning to London, warning him! All this time she'd thought he had simply chosen not to answer her. He must have left Kenilworth before it arrived. Lud, it was probably still sitting there!

Glancing at Giles from the corner of her eye, she made a decision. Regardless of what had passed between them, she owed him this. If not for the protection of their child, a consideration that was paramount, then for what they had once shared. As long as the spy remained unrevealed, those she cared about were in jeopardy. And she still did care about Giles, she did care.

Lifting her voice, she turned to Edward. "Milord, you must be most satisfied with the outcome of Evesham." Edward's hand paused in the act of lifting his tankard, his eyes widening with amazement at her statement. She heard Giles's intake of breath. "Indeed," she persisted in the silence, "the outcome would have been quite different, had it not been for word brought to you of Earl Simon's whereabouts, and that of his sons. You owe much to the one who brought you that information—"

The coldness that came into Edward's eyes might have quelled her, had she cared a whit about what he might do; but, to her shock, it was Giles who stayed further comment. He grasped her arm painfully and twisted her toward him, his eyes burning, and her next words caught in her throat. "Enough!" he snarled furiously. "Dare you boast of it now, when you caused so many to be lost? Be silent, if you value the child you carry!"

Vaguely, she felt sharp spears of pain run up her arm from his grip, but her eyes focused on the anger in his own and her brain slowly assimilated the meaning of what he was saying. Mother of God, she realized, he thinks that I was the one! She jerked away suddenly, the unexpected movement enabling her to wrench from his grip, and she leapt up, backing away from the table. Her gaze flew to Edward, who was watching intently, and then darted down the table and back to Giles, who had risen from his chair. "Don't touch me, you bloody bastard!" she hissed as he stepped toward her. "Giles fitzWilliam, you can rot in 'ell!" And then she turned and fled the room.

Lodema looked up with surprise as she burst into the room. Laying down her needlework, she watched with alarm as Roanna threw open the doors of the wardrobe and began tossing garments on the bed.

"What are you doing?"

"I'm packing!" Roanna snapped, struggling to pull a heavy trunk from the corner. Giving up, she snatched a mantle from the wardrobe, spread it out, and began throwing selected garments upon it.

"You cannot leave," Lodema began in a reasonable tone. "Lord Edward has—"

"I don't give a bloody damn what Lord Edward wants!" Roanna snarled. "I am leaving, and I dare any rotting son of a bitch to stop me!"

"Tell me what happened," Lodema said calmly.

"What happened?" Roanna paused in her haphazard packing to stare at the woman as if she had lost her senses to even ask such a question. "He thinks I betrayed him! That addle-brained nitwit thinks that I am the spy who informed Edward of Simon's whereabouts!"

Lodema lost her composure for a moment and gaped at Roanna. "Whatever made him think that?"

"I don't know!" Roanna cried, waving her hands about in frustration. "I—I tried to tell him the truth, to warn him, but I had barely brought it up before he turned on me! Damn him, how could he think that it was me?"

Lodema turned the question over rapidly, her mind filtering all of the things Roanna had confided in her. "It may not be unreasonable for him to have thought so, Roanna. After all, you were there, in Edward's camp—"

Roanna, struggling to tie the cloak into a bundle, paused to glare at her. "Oh, I was there. And from that I am assumed to be guilty? What of trust, the supposed love we once shared?"

"There would seem to be heavy evidence against you, Roanna. Perhaps you should consider what he must be thinking. The pain he must be feeling, believing that you were indeed the one—"

"I will not listen anymore!" Roanna cried, pulling her bundle from the bed. "I am leaving!"

"You will never be allowed to leave," Lodema pleaded, rising from her chair.

"Watch me."

Lodema's eyes widened as Roanna crossed toward the windows, and she realized that the young woman meant to cross through the gardens. She watched with horror as Roanna opened the shutters and sat on the windowsill, swinging her feet to the other side. Her thoughts filled with a terrifying vision of guards striking out at a suspicious shadow before questions were asked. Turning, she fled from the room, moving with an agility she would have not thought her age would allow.

Roanna dropped the six feet to the ground and landed with a jar, feeling the shock reverberate through her pregnant body. She steadied herself for a long moment, her hand pressed to her middle, until she gradually was able to draw a comfortable breath, knowing that the child was safe. Lud, she thought, what a priss she had become. Women tilled fields next to their husbands and bore healthy babes. Titles brought to one the suggestion of fragility—no wonder noble women had so many problems bringing a babe to term. Straightening, she picked up the bundle she had dropped before she jumped, and her eyes searched the darkness for some evidence of movement. Moving into the darkness, she determined that she would be free. Free, from everything she now resolutely left behind her.

26

Roanna peered out across the shadowy, moonlit landscape from where she was hidden beneath the sheltering umbrella of a large, gnarled oak. Above her in the tree, an owl whooed. Her heart leapt in her chest, then settled into an erratic pounding. Taking a deep, calming breath, she glanced up into the tree, glaring. "That's the trouble with the country," she murmured with a grimace, "too bloody quiet."

Inching out from her sanctuary, she crept forward through the heavy silence of Winchester's immense gardens, toward the black shadows that lay about the wall, clutching her bundle. She paused, scanning the clearing before her, regretting that there was not so much as a bush between her and the wall itself. Her eyes traveled down the wall to where she could just make out a small, wooden gardener's gate.

'Tis passing strange, she thought, the information one's mind will store, remembering it when desperation calls it up. The day before, she had heard several ladies of Edward's court tittering about a certain young noblewoman and her commoner lover. 'Twas said that each evening at dusk they met in a garden, and he did not leave until dawn. It had to be here, Roanna reasoned, since the lady's chambers were in the same wing as her own. And this had to be the gate where she let him in—it was the only one that would not lead them by a guard tower. She hoped desperately that they had not locked it.

Bracing herself, she moved from the shadows and ran across the small clearing, throwing herself into the protective shadow against the wall. Breathing deeply, she trembled, relieved that no guards had called out. Inching along the wall, she paused as she came abreast of the gate. Swallowing, she reached for the latch, praying that it would open. Suddenly the gate swung wide. Too startled to cry out, she jerked her hand back and gaped with terror at the form standing in the portal. A large knight stood there, the moonlight casting a ghostly light over his jazerant-work hauberk and the smooth metal of his helm, whose nosepiece cast the face into a blackness that seemed to defy the presence of a face.

"You!" a voice exclaimed, echoing from the depths of the helm.

She stumbled back as a scream garbled up into her throat, coming forth in a strangled, choked cry. The knight stepped forward and seized her arm, yanking her toward him. She caught her breath and opened her mouth to scream, just as a large hand clamped over her mouth. "God's Breath," the spectral face swore in a whisper, "be silent!"

Stunned, she was pulled through the gate and led to a small waiting party of mounted men. The hand about her mouth was pulled away and she sucked in air, but her cry came out in an oomph as she was swept from the ground and thrown on to a saddle. "You must ride astride," the deep voice growled as the knight leapt onto a large destrier next to her. "Keep up with us."

The fact that she had managed to find her voice was lost as her mount was slapped sharply on the hindquarters. It took all her concentration not to fall off. She felt vaguely amazed that it seemed easy to remain astride the swiftly moving horse, its rocking gait surprisingly smooth. Her only comparison was the picnic with Giles, when her mount had insisted upon trotting, in spite of her constant sawing on the reins. However, she did not even want to contemplate what would happen when they slowed their pace, as eventually they must. They did slow somewhat after a time, to a rolling canter, and she held onto the high pommel of the saddle for dear life.

Who were these men, and why had she been abducted? Perhaps they thought to hold her for ransom. They were in for a mighty shock when they discovered that Giles would not pay as much as a quid for her. But then he might, she thought ruefully, for his child.

She lost track of time, and her body became numb; she could no longer feel her bottom at all. But she knew, with dread, that she would certainly feel it when they stopped. Which they did, finally, just as the greying sky began to lighten along the horizon to a pink hint of sunrise. Her abductor, who had stayed close to her side throughout their ride, called to his men to stop. Hearing his order, she panicked. "Nay!" she cried, all too well aware of what would happen if the horse slowed. It was too late. As the others began to pull up, her mount followed the actions of its own kind and its rolling gait slowed to a trot. Her bottom left the saddle, returning once in a slamming jolt, and then she left it again, her hands flying from the wide pommel as she met the emptiness of unwanted freedom.

Braced for hard-packed earth, she felt a strong arm about her middle as she slammed against a man's body. Her feet swung, touching only air, and she realized that the knight had caught her as she arched away from her horse.

"Are you all right?" he growled, holding her tightly as the destrier shifted nervously beneath them.

"Nay, I'm not all right, you sodding, insufferable bastard!"

"You're fine," he said, chuckling deeply, relief in his voice as he bent and set her upon the ground.

Before she could react, he was on the ground beside her. "We'll make camp here," he said to the others, his hand darting out to grab her arm as she turned to run. "There, beyond the trees."

"Who are you?" she cried, struggling against his grip as he led her into the trees. "I don't know what you want, but I assure you that you have the wrong person!"

"From what I just heard, I think not," the knight remarked. "I was told that you swear like a man."

"I can use a knife like one, too!" she hissed, twisting to reach for the knife on his belt.

"I am sure that you can," he said with a chuckle, pulling her about. "But not on me."

Beyond the trees the landscape broke into a large, wide meadow. The men quickly set to making a temporary camp at its edge as the knight removed his mantle and handed it to her. "Keep warm while we see to the horses. Then I'll make a fire."

Begrudgingly, she pulled the cloak about her, feeling the dampness of the air now that they had stopped. She glanced about, wondering if she could make an escape, but she knew that she could never outrun them on foot. And she had no idea where she was. Sulking, she watched as the knight built the promised fire. As the wood began to crackle and flames leapt up, she was drawn to its warmth in spite of her unwillingness to be near him. She stood rigidly, stretching out her hands to the warming flames, refusing to look at him.

"You need not stand."

That's what you think, she thought with a grimace. "I prefer to."

Bending to the saddles nearby, he took out a wrapped bundle and handed it to her. "'Tis only a bit of jerky and some biscuits, milady, but it will give you nourishment."

She was surprised by the kindness in his voice. Lud, she thought, did he think that a kind gesture could atone for what he was doing? "I do not want anything from you—except that you let me go!"

He sighed. "Lady Roanna, I regret that you were treated so rudely, but there was little time for amenities. If you had remained in your chamber, I could have explained. As it was, when I found you there in the garden, where any might hear, there was nothing for it but to leave as quickly as possible."

She turned her head and gaped at him with confusion. "I do not understand."

"Introductions are in order, if necessarily a bit belated. Milady, I am Landon d'Leon, a loyal friend to Giles fitzWilliam, and thus a friend to you."

D'Leon? Sweet Mother, she had heard of him—he was Giles's oldest friend; the man had practically raised him! D'Leon here, in England? He had abducted her? As she stared at him, he removed his helm, dropping it by the saddles, and ran his fingers through his hair. "You!" she gasped. "You were at the banquet!"

"I was. I regret that there was no time for a proper introduction."

"I—do not understand," she stammered. "Why have you done this?"

"Because of your unfortunate topic of conversation. You were not cautious, Roanna, in bringing up the subject of Edward's spy in open company. I fear that your life is in danger, and it is for that reason that Giles bid me to spirit you away from Winchester and out of England. We are for Wales, and we must be beyond the king's writ before Edward's men can find us."

It was a moment before she could find her voice. "Giles? He asked you to do this?"

"He did. He would be here himself, but that his presence would be missed far more quickly than mine."

She regarded the knight with stunned amazement. Giles did not believe that she was the spy! He wanted to protect her, thus he must still have some feelings left. . . . Then her first feelings of joy were replaced by a dull ache. Of course he would do this, she reasoned dully. He would do it to protect his child, from Edward, from the whole of England. And she had forced him to it by acting rashly, forcing the issue. Well, he might not be interested in her protection, but for the sake of their child, her child, she was grateful. Taking a deep breath, she reached out and took the offered jerky and a biscuit. "My thanks, Sir Landon. I will eat. I find myself rather hungry."

He considered with puzzlement at the gamut of emotions that had passed over her lovely young face, the joy he had seen for an instant, and the deep sorrow that quickly replaced it. Time enough for questions later, he reasoned; it seemed not the moment for even the one most pressing on his mind. "When you have eaten, try to sleep, milady. We will be leaving in a few hours. Perhaps we may talk of this more while we ride."

Perhaps, she thought dully, gnawing at the hard biscuit as she thought of another day in the saddle. Lord, she was so tired; the aches of her body claimed her thoughts. She wanted nourishment, then sleep. One day, one moment, taken at a time.

She awoke and held herself still, afraid to move as her muscles and joints protested. Finally, steeling herself, she turned to the sound that had awakened her, and offered a small smile to Landon as he knelt near the fire. He rose and crossed to her. "Feeling better?" he asked with a warm grin.

"Somewhat," she lied, returning his smile. Then she glanced about the empty camp, puzzled. "Where are the others?"

"I have sent them out to mark the approach of anyone who might be looking for us. You have a few moments before they return—to see to your needs. . . ." he added awkwardly, nodding toward the trees behind them.

She stifled a smile, amused and touched by his discomfort. As she made her way to the privacy of the trees, she wondered if she would ever grow accustomed to the deference paid her as "Lady" Roanna. But then, perhaps it had less to do with the title, and more with an attitude. Not all "noblemen" treated her with respect; a bruised bum could attest to that after an evening in Edward's hall. But there were gentle men among the nobility, as there were among her own kind. Even as they had fled Winchester, Sir Landon had not been unkind. And now, his easy, gracious treatment of her had put her at ease in an awkward, frightening situation. Had he been crude, she would have felt little comfort.

Then, oddly, it struck her—what Giles had tried for so long to tell her. Innate kindness, caring about others, a passion for justice, were the values that truly made one noble. Moreover, manners were not just affectations; they allowed one to express those feelings, to put others at ease. Bugger, she thought, I could have been a "lady" all the time, and I just didn't know it!

Suddenly, she burst out laughing. Lord Almighty, here she was, squatting behind a bush in the middle of nowhere, kidnapped by a virtual stranger, and fleeing for her life from the most powerful man in England, next to the king himself. Her husband did not want her, she was being taken to a place that was completely foreign to her—and she was squatting here musing on the merits of being a "lady."

"Roanna, ye sot," she said out loud, "ye've gone clean off the deep end, luv—yer bloody daft."

As she made her way back through the trees, she began to plan. They would have days and days ahead of them before they reached Wales, and she fully planned to use the time—to ask Landon about all of the things she did not know about Giles, and about his life before she knew him. Perhaps, just perhaps, the information would serve her well. After all, somehow Giles knew now that she was not responsible for Simon's betrayal. That knowledge was a beginning. Aye, it definitely presented "plausible impossibilities."

She was humming when she reached the edge of the meadow. As she stepped into the clearing, her eyes swept over the golden stretch of grasses and she drew a deep breath of happiness. She reveled in it, realizing that it was the first time she had felt so hopeful in a long, long time. She returned to the makeshift camp, eager to share her good mood with Sir Landon. Her smile faded as she glanced about; then it turned to a puzzled frown. The camp was empty. Where . . . ? Then she stopped short. Her hands flew to her mouth as she cried out. He lay collapsed near the campfire, his body twisted in an unnatural pose. Even from where she stood she could see the blood spreading on the back of his tabard.

Instinctively, she started toward him, then stopped abruptly and began to back away, her eyes darting about. Oh God, she thought, there was only one person who could have done this—one reason . . .

"You can run, Roanna, but you won't make it."

She spun about as he stepped from the trees. Backing away, her eyes flew about wildly seeking a means of escape, even as she recognized the truth of his words. Her heart pounded and she struggled against a wave of terror that left her light-headed, but she steeled herself, fighting for calm. Slowly, she turned and faced him.

27

"Rodger. What have you done?" She forced herself not to look at the body by the fire, knowing that if she did, she would break.

"That's obvious. I am protecting myself."

"There are others," she said, attempting to look confident. "They will return soon—"

"Nay, there is no fear of that," he said, smiling unpleasantly. "Giles should have sent others. It was too easy, actually—they trusted me. Fortunately for me, especially with that one—" He jerked his head toward the fire. "I would never have gotten near to him otherwise. . . ." His voice trailed off as he glanced at Landon, then his gaze shifted back. "It is just the two of us now, Roanna."

"What are you going to do?" she asked coldly, with more courage than she felt. She was trembling, but she'd be damned if she would let him see her cower.

"Silence you, of course. You know that I must. But I do regret it, Roanna. I am actually quite fond of you."

"You do not care about anyone but yourself," she said tightly. "And you should think of yourself now, Rodger. You can't survive this. If you kill Giles's babe—as you have his best friend—he will not rest until he has avenged them. If you leave now—"

"Don't bother, Roanna. Your mount is saddled and ready."

She stared at him. "Where are you taking me? What purpose—"

"What purpose?" he interrupted. "When the others are found, it will be thought that a band of felons attacked them, and carried you off. . . . I shall, of course, be in London to grieve over the loss when I am told of it. I am there now, in fact, as will be sworn by witnesses."

"Rodger, you are mad!" she exclaimed.

"Probably. But soon that will not matter to you."

Taking a step toward her, he grasped her arm and pulled her in among the trees to the waiting horses. Her heart sank as she saw that he had eliminated any means of escape. Her horse was already tied to his, effectively preventing her from trying to get away while he mounted. Wordlessly, they left the grove and rode across the wide meadow to the fringe of heavy forest beyond.

They rode deep into the forest, following a narrow track that wound through the heavy underbrush, and eventually stopped as they broke into a clearing. She glanced about, her horror growing as she realized the extent of Rodger's efforts. There was evidence of a camp that had not been used for some time. But a fire had recently been burnt, and the remnants of a meal taken by many men was scattered about. The ground was covered with the hoofprints of horses. She couldn't help but marvel at his planning.

"You did all of this, in just the night past?" she asked.

"It was easy. He made it quite convenient for me, choosing this direction. And he saved me the trouble of taking you from Winchester. I couldn't have planned it better myself," he said, tying the reins of her mount to a low branch of a tree before he dismounted. "I was fostered on estates near here. I know the country well, including this place."

Before he could approach to lift her down, she slipped from the saddle, repelled by the thought of his touch. "This is to be the brigand's camp, where I shall be found, is it not?" He smiled with satisfaction, and she caught the shift of his eyes toward a ledge running down to a deep ravine below. Swallowing heavily, she stared at him hard. "And that is to be my resting place. Should anyone find me, your freebooters will be blamed." Seeing the coldness of his look, a new thought chilled her. "Brigands would not simply throw me into the ravine, would they, Rodger?"

"Regrettably not."

"I must give evidence that I was—well used. Is that not so?" she asked breathlessly, realizing what he intended to do to her.

"It must be. Though I must admit that I do not find the prospect distasteful," he said silkily, walking toward her.

"Should I be flattered?" she sneered, backing away from him. Stall, Roanna, she thought frantically; any moment won was another moment of life. "You owe me something, Rodger."

He stopped, a flicker of interest crossing his face. "Oh? What would that be?"

"Answers," she said simply. "Before I die, I want to know why. Why did you betray Giles?"

"Why?" He shrugged. "Why not? I have nothing against Giles, I merely saw an opportunity."

"An opportunity?" she gasped. "Oh, Rodger, you are not mad, you're vile! Have you no honor, no sense of loyalty—"

"Loyalty?" he snorted. "To whom? Giles? I was born of the nobility, in the marriage bed, but a third son. Thus I was turned out with nothing. Giles was born a bastard. He knew no life but that of a villein; yet he was given wealth, lands, position. For years I've had to serve him, caring for *his* lands, obeying *his* orders. But that is over now. Edward trusts me. Once Giles is gone, along with that whelp you carry, the lands will be mine! Edward owes it to me. Now, I have answered your question, so you will satisfy one of mine. How did you know that it was me?" He stared at her, waiting for her answer. When she continued merely to look at him with undisguised contempt, he reddened with anger. "Answer me, you bitch! How did you know?"

She smiled, knowing that the answer would torment him long after she felt whatever he could do to her. "Go to bloody 'ell, Rodger Farnham."

"He will, Roanna," a deep voice said. "But first he will plead for it."

They both spun toward the voice. Giles stood at the edge of the clearing, his sword clasped easily in his hand, his eyes burning with a deadly fire as they fixed upon Rodger, whose face had gone decidedly pale. Other men moved silently out from among the trees, surrounding the glade. Among them, to Roanna's astonishment and joy, was Landon, his shoulder heavily bandaged, his face wan from the loss of blood, but his eyes burning with the same intense hatred as Giles's.

"How—" Rodger gasped, stepping back as he quickly drew his sword.

"How does not matter, Rodger. I am here." Giles smiled tightly. "And I have been here long enough to hear what I needed to know." He stepped into the clearing. "You are going to die, Rodger." Seeing the frantic look that Rodger cast about him, he smiled grimly. "Do not worry about them. This is between you and me."

Knowing that Giles's words would be honored by the others, Rodger smiled slowly. He began to circle, his sword raised. "So be it, fitzWilliam. Just you and me."

He lunged first, bringing his sword down in a two-handed arc that was met by Giles's blade. Its reverberating sound was accompanied by a rush of starlings that lifted from the trees above them. Giles brought his weapon up in a sweep to meet another stroke, then countered with a thrust that nearly met Rodger's shoulder. Turning the blade aside, Rodger sidestepped and came in to Giles's side, laughing as he felt the tip of his blade slice through flesh. Giles grunted, jumping back. As he moved, he felt the tip of Rodger's blade catch in the jazerant-work of his hauberk and he used the fraction of a second to parry, bringing his blade down into the flesh of the other's upper arm.

They continued thus, striking and countering again and yet again, the heavy steel ringing and clamoring, until they felt their muscles begin to burn from fatigue. They were well matched. Years of practice with each other had given each man a knowledge of the other's skill and faults. Each watched the other for a mistake, a moment of advantage. It came in a pass when their eyes met, in the need to study an opponent's will. Rodger saw his hell burning in Giles's eyes, and he faltered, knowing a chill of fear that brought a fatal instant of doubt. It was enough; Giles's blade sank between the rings of his hauberk, deep into the warm flesh between his ribs.

Rodger's sword slipped from his fingers as he stared at Giles, an instant of regret flickering in his eyes as a ghost of a smile lifted the corners of his mouth. His hands grasped the blade as he sank to his knees. "It would seem that the day is yours—" he rasped, and swallowed against the burning pain. "Again—yours. But I did come close."

"Only in your dreams," Giles said harshly. He jerked the blade free, opening the fatal wound. With a moan, Rodger collapsed, and was still.

Heavy silence fell over those who watched, as Giles stood looking down at the body. "Do not grieve for him, Giles," Landon murmured, coming to stand by him.

"We were friends—once," Giles answered without emotion, his face a mask.

"I think that one's capacity for friendship was left in childhood."

"Along with my innocence," Giles rejoined. Turning, the bloodied sword still in his hand, he left the grove.

Landon watched his sudden departure with surprise, then glanced at Roanna, who stood across the clearing, her face drained of color. Their eyes met and Landon flushed, his anger swiftly rolling into a storm at Giles's thoughtlessness. She lowered her eyes, but not before he saw the pain and helplessness that glimmered there. The storm broke and he spun on his heels to follow Giles. But suddenly, he wavered, a wave of light-headedness rushing over him; then he stumbled. With a soft cry, Roanna ran to his side.

She tried to support him as she turned her head to the men, who remained standing about the corpse, gazing after their master, as astonished as she was over Giles's rude behavior. "Someone help him!" she said angrily.

Two men rushed forward to take the failing knight, who was now close to passing out, and helped him from the grove. The remaining men exchanged puzzled glances, wondering what they should do. Giles had not ordered them to follow, yet what were they to do about Lady Roanna? Finally, Geoffrey stepped forward, his hazel eyes filled with compassion for Roanna's embarrassment. Never for a moment in his young life had he doubted Giles's judgment, nor felt shame for his master, but he painfully did so now.

"Milady," he said gently, "I would be honored if you would ride pillion with me. I think it would prove more comfortable than riding astride." He reddened slightly with his last words, as his eyes touched on her gently swelling belly.

"That will not be necessary, Geoffrey—she shall ride with me." All eyes turned with surprise toward Giles as he entered the glade. His hair was damp; his surcoat and armor were gone, as was his sword, and he had stripped down to his chanise. His only weapon was a knife tucked into his belt. Roanna stared with wonder as he took her hands in his, raising them one at a time to his lips. "Roanna, forgive me," he said, his eyes moving tenderly over her face before they met hers, deepening with concern. "You have much to forgive me for—"

"We presumed that you had left, Sir Giles," Geoffrey said disapprovingly. Still upset, he was not quite prepared to accept that his lapse of faith had been misguided.

"Only for the moment, Geoffrey," Giles said, smiling grimly as he glanced at his squire. Then his gaze returned to Roanna, pleading for her understanding.

Looking deep into his eyes, she studied him for a moment, then suddenly understood his need. "Geoffrey, your master's armor is by the stream below. It will need cleaning." Quietly, the men moved to pick up Rodger's lifeless form and Geoffrey left to see to Giles's armor. Soon they were alone.

He slipped his arms about her. "How did you become so wise?" he said smiling.

"By loving you," she said smiling back.

"It—was more than just a need to rid myself of his blood. I could not come to you with it on me." Sorrow filled his eyes, and deep regret. "I have hurt you so much—he could have killed you."

She reached up and placed a finger against his lips. "Do not," she said softly, and then her voice broke. "Oh, Giles, how it must have hurt you, to believe that I had betrayed you—betrayed Simon. I have suffered no more than you."

"When one loves—there should be trust," he said heavily.

"Pah! A platitude," she scoffed. "Giles, what happened to us was not some petty thing. Thinking me to be guilty of such a betrayal, your anger was well justified. I see clearly now that fate played against us cruelly; certainly I was in the wrong place at the wrong time."

"But you were guiltless, so why did you keep yourself from me?"

"I didn't! I waited, for so long. You never came. I thought—that you did not want me. And that was true enough, wasn't it?"

"What reason did you give to it?" When she did not

answer, fixing her gaze on the middle of his chest, he placed a finger under her chin and raised her face to his. "Roanna?"

"I—I thought it was because you were angry with me—because of what I said to you before I left Kenilworth. That I drove you away—and then Simon died. . . . Once you were within Edward's court, with a new position, I knew—thought—that I was no longer the wife you needed—or wanted." Seeing the anger that came into his expression, she rushed on. "Don't look at me like that, Giles fitz-William! When you did not come, I had to give some reason to it! My own self-doubt found the answer. But I know better now." Her eyes, searching his deeply, became determined. "I know that what I did was not wrong, and that I can make you happy." She smiled. "I am *definitely* the woman for you."

His eyes widened at the mischief that leapt to her eyes, and he grinned suddenly, relief filling his expression. He swept her to him and his mouth came down upon hers, his kiss speaking of his feelings, as her emotions rushed to answer his appeal. Giles broke away first, his voice betraying a tremor that she also felt. Her knees were barely supporting her. "Oh, God, Roanna, I want you. But not here, not in this place." He lifted her into his arms, and, with a light kiss of promise, carried her from the glade.

The fire crackled and snapped as Geoffrey threw another dry log upon it, pausing a moment to watch as it claimed the wood hungrily with a leap of flames. He returned to his blanket and sat down, taking up the hauberk and cloth once again, and resumed polishing the heavy chain links. His head came up as he heard Landon grunt, and he watched for a moment to see if he was needed, but the knight only shifted his weight in an attempt to make himself more comfortable. Noting that the new bandages showed no signs of fresh bleeding, Geoffrey returned his attention to his polishing.

Landon moved against the saddle and blankets propped at his back, and a hot spear of pain shot through his shoulder. He gritted his teeth, not daring to utter a sound or Roanna would be all over him again like fleas on a hound. The large knight smiled at the thought. Actually, it was rather nice to be fussed over. Then he frowned. But not that much. Besides, there were other things for her to think about now than a grizzled old knight who would, in spite of her ministrations, live. If it had not been for Geoffrey and the healing arts he had learned from his mother, he probably would have bled to death.

His eyes shifted to Roanna where she sat a few feet away, wrapped contentedly in her husband's arms. Now, there's a sight, he thought contentedly, his mind drifting. Will Marshal, my old friend, he mused, the boy's going to be all right. And the lass?—you would have liked her. Nay, you would have more than liked her. She's a real woman, just like you had. Just then Roanna's gaze shifted from the fire to him, and he braced himself with a moment's alarm as her eyes narrowed speculatively, fixing on his bandages.

"Well, now," he said quickly, clearing his throat. "What with all the unnecessary fuss that has been made over me, we've barely had time to talk. You two may be content to sit there and goggle at each other, but I need some answers. I'm not complaining, you understand, but, Giles, how is it that you managed to appear when you did?"

"Aye!" Roanna exclaimed, pulling away from Giles so that she could turn and look at him. "He's right, we've been so busy the past hour that there's been little time to think upon it, but I have some questions as well."

Everyone's eyes shifted to Giles. Glancing around, he noted that the other men, who were lolling about the small camp, also had fallen silent and were waiting to hear what he would say. "You may thank Lady Lodema and Edward for your rescue," he answered, grinning at Roanna and Landon as their eyes widened with surprise. "Roanna, after your outburst at supper, when you fled the room with your, ah, sweetly offered words of departure, I began to think upon it." He grinned, squeezing her hand. "I may be slow, my love, but I'm not a complete nitwit. I recalled your words, your reaction, and it began to dawn on me that you are never more angry than when you deal with injustice. Your rage spoke volumes. I knew then that you were not the one—and that, since you were not, you must have been trying to warn me. Moreover, I knew that you were in great danger, for the spy must also have guessed that you knew, and I feared Edward's reaction on as well. Thus I sent

Landon to you." He paused, shaking his head. "Lord"—he shuddered—"if that had been all—I would not have been here in time.

"When you fled Winchester, Lodema went directly to Edward. She knew that only he had the power to intercede with his guards, and she was fearful of what might happen when you tried to escape. Edward sent the guards to find you. When they reported that you were gone, he came to me, and told me who the spy was."

"He told you?" Roanna asked, amazed.

"He checked on Rodger's whereabouts immediately, and finding that he too had disappeared, he came to me."

"Then you knew that it was Rodger, even before you left Winchester," Landon said quietly.

"I did not want to believe it." His gaze shifted to Roanna and his eyes grew cold. "Until I found Landon, and saw what Rodger had planned for you." He snorted. "Poor Rodger. He thought that so much would come to him. But he underestimated Edward." He paused, shrugging. "That is a common error, I fear. Perhaps, after all, it is because we have grown accustomed to ineptitude in our Plantagenet rulers. This one will be different, so very different. . . ."

Realizing that his thoughts were drifting, he sighed. "In any event, there is little doubt now as to why Rodger was so eager to accompany me to Edward's camp, instead of returning to Wales—and I smoothed the road for him."

"Don't blame yourself, Giles," Roanna said urgently. "Look to Edward. He allowed that coward to live among you—he even allowed you to think that I was the one, all this time!"

"Edward is not above using spies, Roanna; they are part and parcel of any good army. But a traitor is something else. Oh, Edward willingly used the information Rodger brought to him. But the first time Rodger opened his sniveling mouth, any loyalty Edward might have felt for him was gone. The irony is that Edward has only suffered him of late because of me, and our friendship, to save me the pain of knowing the truth. The moment I left for Wales, Edward planned to send him away—far away." He shook his head and smiled sadly at Roanna. "So many misunderstandings —Edward and I had never discussed Evesham, not once. My love, until your outburst, he had no idea that I had thought you to be the person who had betrayed Simon."

She stared at him with amazement. Then Edward had told the truth, that day when she had been brought to Winchester. He truly had no idea why she and Giles were estranged; his concern had been real.

"Well, it is over," Landon grumbled, shaking his head. "If you had not blundered and asked the ill-timed question, Roanna, we might have embraced the bastard to us forever, never knowing."

"Nonsense," she scoffed. "My question was deliberate. I knew, when I saw Rodger sitting there, that Giles did not know." Her eyes softened as she looked up at her husband. "Even though things were—somewhat awkward between us—I could not allow you to go on thinking him to be a trusted friend. That's why I tried to send you a message, warning you, when I returned to London."

"You sent me a message?"

"Aye," she said, sighing. "I had no way of knowing that you had already left Kenilworth. I imagine it is still there, waiting for you."

"Perhaps . . ." he murmured.

She turned her head to look at him, wondering why he looked so pensive. "What is it?"

"Probably nothing." He shrugged.

"Tell me."

"Just—something that Margot said to me, in passing." He glanced at her briefly, noting the angry flare to her eyes. "She merely said that she had something . . . that I might want. . . ." he finished awkwardly. Landon snorted.

"Really," Roanna said tightly, one eyebrow arched. "And just what did you think she meant?"

"Well . . ." He grinned at her, and shrugged. "I hadn't pursued it."

"Would she have been at Kenilworth when the missive came?" Landon asked quickly into the heavy pause.

"Aye," Giles answered seriously, ignoring the way Roanna was glaring at him. "Eleanor did not want her to share her exile."

"She probably couldn't bear suffering the lady's disposition, along with everything else," Roanna remarked with a smirk.

Giles seemed not to hear her comment as he turned and looked at her strangely. "Wait—you said you sent a missive. You knew even then?"

"Of course I knew—I knew before Evesham," she said impatiently. "That's what I'm trying to tell you."

"Before—" Landon frowned. "Impossible. How could you know? Rodger was with us."

She glanced at Giles and then Landon, seeing the doubt in their expressions. "If you had received the message, you would have known. Rodger Farnham's duplicity did not begin with Evesham. He had been reporting to Edward since before the battle at Kenilworth—perhaps long before. How did you think that Edward knew where the baronial forces were?"

The silence was deafening, broken only by the crackling and hissing of the campfire. Finally Giles spoke, his voice grim. "You are certain of this? That it was Rodger—even then?"

"Absolutely. I knew who the spy was when I dined with Edward, three days before I left his camp. Edward told me." She laughed at their dumbfounded expressions. "He told me that Eleanor was at Chatham."

Giles stared at her for a moment, frowning with incomprehension. Then suddenly understanding dawned and he burst out laughing.

"Would someone mind letting me in on this?" Landon grumbled.

Giles winked at Roanna and kissed the tip of her nose. Then he turned to Landon and grinned. "Long ago, Roanna and I devised a code for sending information between us. Actually, it was Eleanor's idea, but the code was ours. There were only three people, only three, who knew the code: Roanna, me, and later, Eleanor herself."

"In the code," Roanna picked up, "whenever a location was named, we used the nearest town or city to the north beginning with the same letter, if it be at least twenty miles distant, but no more than thirty, in which case—"

"Sounds bloody complicated to me," Landon grumbled.

"Not if you understand it." Giles grinned. "But that's not the point. Eleanor was not in Chatham, but Chilham, to the south." He waited, grinning, until comprehension began to dawn in Landon's face.

". . . And besides the three of you, only someone who had seen the missives would know what had been written."

"Rodger carried the last message to Eleanor—but to her courier stationed in Chatham, not to Eleanor herself. Messages were always routed this way, to confirm what was written in the event that they were read, and to allow as few people as possible to know of Simon's actual whereabouts."

"A wise precaution for Eleanor's sake, as proven out with Rodger," Landon grunted.

"Indeed. Sometimes I used to tease Eleanor about her intricate planning and excessive precautions. I was wrong. Thankfully, Rodger had no way of knowing that Eleanor was not in Chatham."

"I rather imagine that Rodger was somewhat disgruntled not to meet Eleanor herself at the end of his journey, but only a mere courier," Landon remarked.

"Probably, but he could hardly complain of it to me. Besides, the information in the message would satisfy him."

"It satisfied us all," Roanna said softly. "Thank God that you had the presence of mind to code it, Giles. I would have been tempted not to, considering that it was carried by someone we thought we could trust."

At the import of her words, a heavy silence fell once again. This time it was broken by Landon. "Well, there is one thing for it. The mistaken information Rodger passed to Edward gave Eleanor time to escape."

"Aye," Giles said softly, "there is that."

The thoughts of each turned then to the same consideration: that somehow Simon should have known that the man who betrayed him had unwittingly served to save the lives of his wife, daughter, and remaining sons. Edward had sent men to Chatham to seize her. If she had not been warned by her own spy, stationed there, she might not have had time to escape to the Continent.

"By the Blood of Saint George," Landon muttered suddenly. "Listen to us! This old body needs its rest, and as for the others . . ." His voice rose, barking orders. "Everyone had best be to their blankets, as we've a hard ride before us at first light!" Turning back to Giles and Roanna, his voice lowered and he grinned. "As for you two—why you choose to keep me company when you've been apart these many months, I cannot fathom. Times certainly have changed since I was a young buck. Now, if I were you, Giles, I'd have the lass off to myself, and would have done so long before this. There's a spot over there"—he gestured behind him with his thumb—"at the far side of the meadow, that looks quite promising."

Roanna flushed at Landon's bluntness. The soft laughter of her husband brought her gaze up to him, and her eyes widened at his wolfish grin. He rose and held out a hand to her. "Roanna?"

"You can both go rot!" she snapped, thoroughly embarrassed, as she jumped up and backed away from him. Landon's laughter rang in her ears as she was suddenly swept up into her husband's arms. "Put me down!" she shrieked, hearing the laughter of the other men.

"Never, sweetling," Giles murmured as he carried her away from the campfire. "By God's Truth, I'll never let you go again."

She softened, suddenly aware only of his arms, the tenderness in his voice, and the promise it held as he carried her away from the camp. "Oh, Giles," she said breathlessly. "Do you promise?"

"On my soul." He stopped in the middle of the meadow, the camp behind them, and set her on the ground. He wrapped one arm around her as he reached up and brushed her hair back from her face, gazing at her lovingly in the moonlight. "My love, we've been through so much. Can we forget all that has happened and begin again?"

"Nay, Giles, not that," she answered softly. "I do not want to begin again, but to build on what we've had."

"Even the bad times?"

"Especially the bad times! We have survived what has happened, and we still care for each other. That was my greatest fear, Giles—that we could not suffer the hard times and survive. Now I can look to the future, and not be afraid of my dreams."

He bent and kissed her tenderly, then smiled. "Golden dreams, a little tarnished but with the ability to endure forever."

She broke away from him, intense happiness rushing through her at his love and understanding. She was so blessed to have found this man, one who understood her so completely, and loved her just as she was. She backed away, then stopped, holding out a hand to him. He took her hand, pulling her slowly toward him. Suddenly, his arm went about her and he swept her up, laughing. With a promising gleam in his eyes, he carried her toward the trees.

Epilogue

Why, there's a wench! Come on, and kiss me, Kate.

—William Shakespeare,
The Taming of the Shrew
Act V, Scene ii

Wales
August, 1276

Lady Roanna gazed out the window, her thoughts dwelling on the work waiting for her, even as she idly watched the goings-on in the courtyard below. Carts moved ponderously past, carrying produce to the kitchens of the manor. A small group of men engaged in conversation; children played; women crossed the bailey in their errands. Sighing, she began to turn away when her attention was suddenly caught and she leaned forward.

A young maid had emerged from the shadows of a wall chamber, her arms filled with a nondescript bundle. She had paused, encountering a large puddle, and neatly turned aside to pass around it. But Roanna saw what the lass did not, and she watched with interest. A large hound lay sleeping in the warmth of the afternoon sun. From the left, a half-grown pup came scampering, chasing in leaps and starts some unseen bug. The unsuspecting lass continued, her face raised to the warmth of the summer sun, a look of contentment on her lovely face.

They came together like constellations converging into an exploding mass. The pup jumped in a ferocious attack upon its prey, landing squarely upon the sleeping hound. The dog leaped up, snarling, just as the young woman stepped into its domain. She cried out, tossing her bundle into the air as the dogs plunged into combat. Dust, dirt, and fur flew into a cloud. The maid's cry stopped the men in mid-conversation, and they came running. As everyone turned toward the din, one cart rammed into another cart, causing the driver of the first to tumble from his seat, while the second struggled frantically with his reins. Dogs ran toward the fray; horses and assorted livestock about the bailey neighed, bleated, and shrieked in their pens; and pandemonium reigned below.

Amid the outward confusion, the door opened and Giles entered the room. He paused as Roanna turned to him with a grin. "What has happened?" he asked, responding to her look of delight.

"Nothing at all, my love," she answered. "It is merely comforting to know that life does go on."

"Hmmm," he grunted, afraid to ask what she meant by that. "Have you finished the estimates for the tallages?"

She picked up a thin ledger from the table and handed it to him. "I decreased some of them, Giles. There is the case of one villein who fell, injuring his back, and—"

"Spare me," he said quickly, lifting a hand to stay her. "Roanna, you will see us into ruin." But the affectionate smile he gave her belied his words. "I will go over them," he promised. "There are those who would play false—"

"Who?" she asked indignantly.

"Never mind, I'll see to it."

"Don't patronize me, Giles," she warned.

"I wouldn't dream of it." He propped a hip on the corner of the table. "There is another matter. I had a letter from London today." Seeing the dismay that crossed her face, he braced himself and went on. "Roanna, there are far worse things than having one's son called to court."

"He is too young," she said tightly, suddenly very busy at her desk.

"Richard is fourteen, my love," he said with quiet understanding. Then he drew a breath, and said firmly, "You must let him go, Roanna."

"I will never understand the customs of the nobility!" she said curtly, refusing to look at him. "To send one's flesh and blood to live with others—it is insensible!"

He stifled a weary sigh, regarding this woman he loved

more than his life, though, dear God, how she tried him. "Would you have *me* train him to be a knight?" he asked. The muscle in his jaw tensed as her head jerked up and she regarded him with anger. "I understand how you feel, Roanna. You love him. So do I. But if I should try to train him myself, he would only come to hate me."

"That is ridiculous!"

"Nay, it is not. The training he will go through is painful. It challenges a man's soul. Not everyone can survive it; many fall along the way. Would you have me cause my own son such pain? Or would you deny him knighthood? Roanna, Edward has asked for Richard. Our son will be guided and knighted by the king himself. Would you deny him that opportunity?" He waited, not wanting to force the issue, as he must if she could not agree.

"When will he go?" she asked softly.

"In the fall," he answered, softening at the tearful sound of her voice. He wanted to reach out to her, but he held back, knowing that comfort now would be misplaced. It would only weaken her defenses. He'd come to her later, tonight when he could do some good, he thought, warming to the prospect. His mood lightened, and he rose to leave, pausing with an afterthought. "By the way, has something happened to Isabel?"

"Why?" Roanna asked, looking up with concern.

"She drifts about with an inane expression on her face, and when I speak to her she smiles vapidly and answers my requests with a patently patient, 'Of course, dear father.' Is she ill?"

"Nay, Giles, she is fifteen," Roanna answered as she sorted the papers on her desk.

"Is that supposed to mean something?"

Roanna glanced up at her husband with affection. "She's in love, Giles."

His eyes widened, his chest tightening painfully. "Who is he?" He coughed. Then he cleared his throat.

"You need not worry, my love," she said calmly. "It will pass. Painfully—but it will pass."

"Who is he!" he flared. "Tell me!"

"Not on my life. Giles, you must trust me on this. I will not have you bearing down on her like an outraged father. What is happening to your eldest daughter is perfectly natural. Just love her—a talent in which you are unsurpassed. Do not alienate her; soon she will need your comfort more than ever."

He stared at her blankly; then suddenly he began to laugh. "Oh, God, Roanna," he chuckled, "we are a fine pair. If Richard and Isabel survive our good intentions, the other three should do well by what we learn."

"Perhaps," she said, grinning back. "But somehow I think that Eve, William, and Joanna will survive us quite on their own. To their credit."

He chuckled in agreement, then grinned broadly as a new thought struck him. "Roanna, did I ever thank you for not insisting that our children be named for your family? Roscoe fitzWilliam . . ." he mused, shuddering.

"Aye, you did—often," she answered, bending to her work.

"Good," he grunted. "I just wanted to be certain." But again, as he started to leave for other business, he thought of his daughter. He turned back, his eyes narrowing as he studied her. "Roanna—did you have a first love, before me? Tell me, I really want to know."

She stiffened, the question taking her by surprise. Quickly regaining her composure, she looked up at him and smiled. "Before you? My love, how could there be? My life began with you."

He grinned and left the room, closing the door behind him with a click of satisfaction.

Smiling, loving him, she set down her quill and leaned back in her chair. Oh, Lord, she mused, how bloody good the years have been. Rising from her chair, she crossed to the shelves and took down several books, carrying them back to the desk. Laying them out, she looked at them for a moment. Then she took the first, pulling it toward her, and reverently opened the cover. She spread her hands across the first page and the words written there: "I, Isabel Marshal, do note these words . . ."

So many lives, Roanna thought, her eyes scanning the page. They lifted to the other journals that lay on her desk. Isabel and William Marshal. Richard and Eve deClare. Each journal was filled with lives reaching back over a hundred years. They had come to her, she who was raised in a tavern on the Thames. Her eyes sparkled with sudden mischief. Plausible impossibilities.

Her eyes drifted to a small volume of *Tristan and Isolde,* and she opened it to observe on the inside cover the breathtaking sketch of a unicorn bearing a knight and his lady. Under it was an inscription in Will Marshal's bold hand: "From your heart, my love, I have seen truth." Her eyes misted. She never wanted to know the meaning of the precious little volume, sensing that it was deeply personal to Eleanor and Will. So much of significance was laid into her hands.

She was filled with a sense of purpose. She had never spoken of it to Giles, yet she knew he understood. Her memory turned back to the morning when he had entered this chamber, carrying a large bundle wrapped in heavy linen. She had looked up, her expression brightening at his presence. But this time he had given no greeting. He had laid the package on the table before her, and left, closing the door silently behind him. Slowly she opened it, peeling back the linen to reveal what was within. Journals. Accountings written by women in his family. The last volume touched her the most deeply, and it was a long time before she could read what was written, longer still before she recovered from the words. She had taken the book to him, and they had read it together, their tears falling unashamedly.

The journal was Eleanor's. The last page was addressed to Roanna, whereupon she charged her to keep the journals that had been, years before, given by Will into her keeping.

They wept as they read of her endless days of solitude in the Dominican convent of Montargis, as she lived on a pension from her dower lands, granted by Henry before his death, of five hundred pounds a year.

In a convent room, abandoned by the life she had known, she had spent the last painful months of her life. Eleanor Plantagenet, who had once fired the king of England to justice, who had loved her first husband with an unyielding passion, and after years of grief over his loss, had chosen another who would lead England to rise for the common man, with her strength of will guiding him forward. Oh, if she had only lived to see what those days had brought—the justice, the reforms that had come to England under Edward through what Simon and she had begun. But she had died—alone, attended only by her daughter and youngest son, in the small confines of a distant convent, her last thoughts for England, and all that had gone. . . .

The journals had been sent into Roanna's keeping by a dying Plantagenet, by the woman who had taught her to reach above herself. Eleanor had given her that. Oh, Roanna had suffered that Plantagenet rage, but she had also known the depth of her kindness and had learned from her courage.

Her eyes passed over the journals, the legacy given: Eve, Isabel, Eleanor—to her. She had long ceased to doubt, accepting that what was given in trust must be taken on faith, and the only reasonable choice was to do it well. And she would. Reverently, she restacked the journals in a corner of her desk. Pulling a large bound book to her, she opened the cover and turned to the first blank page, her own recountings.

Dreams are only as one perceives them, she mused. We can love or hate, be bitter or gladdened, depending on how the mind views the life given. Mine has been blessed. Her visions drifted, wavered, expanded. . . . She smiled, and dipped her quill, setting it to the page:

> We find in life that which we envision. It will be for some to reach beyond what seems, at first view, quite unattainable. . . .

Highly Acclaimed
Historical Romances From Berkley

BESTSELLING TALES OF ROMANCE

___ 0-515-08977-X **The Rope Dancer** $3.95
by Roberta Gellis

The magical story of a spirited young woman and the minstrel who awakens her to the sweet agonies of new-found love amidst the pomp and pageantry of twelfth-century England.

___ 0-441-06860-X **Blue Heaven, Black Night** $3.95
by Shannon Drake

A passionate tale of the bastard daughter of Henry II and his fierce and loyal knight—set in England's most glorious age.

___ 0-515-08932-X **Crown of Glory** $3.95
by Rosemary Jarman

The saga of beautiful Elizabeth Woodville, who captures the heart of Edward IV, King of England, during the bright days of chivalry.

___ 0-425-09079-5 **A Triumph of Roses** $3.95
by Mary Pershall

Betrothed to the powerful Earl of Pembroke against her wishes, the raven-haired princess of the roses is caught in a struggle where surrender means love.